W9-ACX-797

THE NOUVEAU ROMAN:
FICTION, THEORY AND POLITICS

The Nouveau Roman

Fiction, Theory and Politics

Celia Britton
Carnegie Professor of French
University of Aberdeen

St. Martin's Press

First published in Great Britain 1992 by
THE MACMILLAN PRESS LTD
Houndmills, Basingstoke, Hampshire RG21 2XS
and London
Companies and representatives
throughout the world

A catalogue record for this book is available
from the British Library.

ISBN 0-333-56813-3

Printed in Great Britain by
Antony Rowe Ltd
Chippenham, Wiltshire

First published in the United States of America 1992 by
Scholarly and Reference Division,
ST. MARTIN'S PRESS, INC.,
175 Fifth Avenue,
New York, N.Y. 10010

ISBN 0-312-08093-X

Library of Congress Cataloging-in-Publication Data
The nouveau roman : fiction, theory, and politics / Celia Britton.
p.   cm.
Includes bibliographical references and index.
ISBN 0-312-08093-X
1. French fiction—20th century—History and citicism—Theory,
etc.   2. Experimental fiction—France—History and criticism.
3. Politics and literature—France.   I. Title.
PQ671.B74   1992
843'.91409—dc20   92-6158
                                                              CIP

Contents

Acknowledgements

Some of the material in Chapters 3 and 4 of this book originally appeared in an article in *Paragraph* (Volume 12, 1989), and I am grateful to Oxford University Press for their permission to reproduce it. I would like to thank Christian Bourgois of 10/18 for allowing me to use material from the two volumes of *Nouveau Roman: hier, aujourd'hui*, the published proceedings of a conference held at the Centre Culturel International de Cerisy-la-Salle, edited by Jean Ricardou and Françoise van Rossum-Guyon; and, similarly, the University of Illinois Press for allowing me to quote from Lois Oppenheim's *Three Decades of the French New Novel*. I would also like to express my gratitude to Rhiannon Goldthorpe for her comments on Chapter 1.

Introduction

The writers belonging to the Nouveau Roman group are of course primarily novelists. Some of them have also written plays and directed films, which I shall not be considering here. In addition, however, they have produced a substantial amount of *theoretical* writing. In fact one of their most distinctive features as a group is their involvement in literary theory and criticism; from the 1950s onwards, the novels themselves have been accompanied by constant discussion of general issues such as the evolution of fiction as a genre, realism and the political significance of literature. This has taken the form of books, articles, conference papers, interviews and so on. Much of it has appeared, at least in the first instance, in a journalistic form – indeed the label 'Nouveau Roman' was to some extent a creation of the media. Other articles or interviews were published in more specialised literary journals – *Les Temps modernes* or *Tel Quel* as distinct from *L'Express* or *Le Monde*. But all of them were from the outset part of a collective debate: the nouveaux romanciers were responding to critical comment on their novels, and their own articles invited, and got, active responses from other critics. This theory, in other words, was developed through a process of interaction and lively argument.

What distinguishes the nouveaux romanciers from other literary theorists is, in the first place, the simple fact that they are practising novelists. This will be the starting point for the approach to their theory that I shall adopt here. In other words, how does the way in which a *novelist* relates to theoretical issues differ from that of a 'pure' theorist? What kinds of use does a novelist make of literary theory? What kinds of personal investment are made in the construction of theory *per se*? And how does that affect the particular theoretical positions that are developed?

This does not mean simply using the nouveaux romanciers' theories as a kind of key with which to 'explain' their fiction – an attitude which is often adopted, particularly in the academic context within which the Nouveau Roman is most usually read. Nor, conversely, does it mean using the fact that they are novelists as a way of simply dimissing the theories: the equally widespread idea that they are 'really' much better at just writing novels and ought

1

to stick to that. But it does mean that the theory cannot be taken entirely on its own terms; it cannot, I would argue, be understood fully in isolation from the fictional texts of the Nouveau Roman. Rather, it is a question of reading fiction and theory *together*, as a single body of texts evolving in interaction with each other. The activity of writing novels is itself a source of theoretical insights into the general nature of fiction, insights which are perhaps not available to academic critics. But this is not to say that the theory develops solely on the basis of the fictional practice.

It is also important to look at the more general intellectual context within which the nouveaux romanciers' work is situated: to look, in other words, at where their theory *comes from*. They have been influenced by a number of the literary and intellectual movements of the post-war period, and subsequent chapters of this book will trace the different stages of that process. But they were not 'influenced' in the sense of passively absorbing someone else's ideas; it was far more a question of selectively appropriating, re-working and adding to existing theoretical concepts in order to serve their own purposes. One of the major functions that theory performs for them is that of defining and legitimising the Nouveau Roman as a group – staking out a place for them in the literary landscape.

As this suggests, their theoretical writing has, broadly speaking, a double role. There is in the first place the 'internal' relation between their theory and their fiction, and, secondly, the 'external' relation between their theory and other people's theory – the wider context of the literary and intellectual avant-garde. Both of these have in common the fact that theory is constructed and used *strategically*: it is less a disinterested pursuit of abstract truths than a recognition of what will be most productive for the fiction, and what will most effectively consolidate their position as a group in competition with other literary movements.

In its 'internal' relation with fictional practice, the role of theory is often difficult to define with any precision. It is rarely, if ever, a case of straightforward application of theory to practice; they do not rely on their theoretical concepts to tell them what kind of fiction to write, and the basic motivation for writing novels in the first place does not come out of theoretical discussions. This is particularly true of writers such as Nathalie Sarraute and Claude Simon, who both started publishing long before the Nouveau Roman as such was invented. As this implies, the disjunction between theory and fiction is also to some extent a disjunction between individual and collective projects: the theory operates on a more collective level than the fiction ever can. (The tensions that result from this are discussed in Chapter 6.) And, precisely because of the individual differences between them the writers of the Nouveau Roman conceive of the relation between theory and fictional practice in different ways. Jean Ricardou comes closest to the idea of writing fiction *according* to a pre-established theoretical position; but he, unlike the others, is definitely a theorist first and a novelist second: while his critical and theoretical work is widely regarded, even by those who disagree with it, as of central importance, his novels are hardly ever read. Sarraute is at the opposite end of the scale, in that the process of writing fiction is for her an entirely spontaneous and intimately personal one. Simon's fiction has gone through markedly different stages, with a period in the 1970s where he seemed to be more directly influenced by, in particular, Ricardou's ideas than previously or subsequently. For Robbe-Grillet, theory stimulates fictional production 'perversely', by giving the writer something to react *against*: the value of a theoretical account, by him or by a critic, of one of his novels is, he says, that it makes him want to do something completely different next time (see Chapter 6). For Butor, finally, the relation is less perversely dialectical, in that the process of writing a novel itself gradually clarifies a number of problems that can then be theoretically formulated (see Chapter 4).

Despite these marked differences, however, the idea that fiction and theory interact in a two-way process – the fiction advances the theory and vice versa – was generally accepted by most nouveaux romanciers most of the time. Connected to it is another dominant emphasis on the *conscious* nature of writing fiction. This involves rejecting the notion of inspiration in favour of a more rational, lucid approach (as discussed in Chapter 4). Such a conception of writing – whether or not it accurately reflects their actual practice – in itself tends to narrow the gap between theory and fiction: producing fiction is not a blindly intuitive activity but itself almost a kind of theoretical work. This idea is already present in Robbe-Grillet's *Pour un nouveau roman*, particularly in 'A quoi servent les théories'. But it plays an increasingly important role later on, as even the titles of their books suggest: from Robbe-Grillet's *Pour un nouveau roman* in 1963 to Ricardou's *Pour une théorie du nouveau roman* in 1971. Ricardou in particular moves towards the idea that the text, if read correctly, contains its own theory (1971, 48). Thus the boundaries between fiction and theory at times becomes increasingly blurred:

it is above all through writing fiction, Robbe-Grillet comments, that the writer's 'research' progresses (see Chapter 3). The tactical advantage of this merging of the two levels is that it can serve to downgrade the importance *either* of fiction or of theory: for Ricardou it means that fiction is merely theory in disguise, while for Robbe-Grillet it (sometimes) means that theory is superfluous because the important ideas are in the novels anyway.

The 'external' function of theory is however at least equally and arguably more important. That is, the Nouveau Roman's construction and use of theory does not develop according to an autonomous, self-contained logic of its own; from the moment of its inception, the Nouveau Roman was caught up in a series of vigorous and often acrimonious debates. The early novels of Sarraute, Simon and, in particular, Robbe-Grillet were attacked by the conservative literary establishment who, as Sarraute puts it in *L'Ere du soupçon*, '[proclament] sur le ton qui sied aux vérités premières que le roman, que je sache, est et restera toujours, avant tout, "une histoire où l'on voit agir et vivre des personnages", qu'un romancier n'est digne de ce nom que s'il est capable de "croire" à ses personnages, ce qui lui permet de les rendre "vivants" et de leur donner une "épaisseur romanesque"' (69). At the same time they were criticised by the Communist and Sartrean left for their lack of political commitment, and, later on, found themselves outflanked in their abandonment of traditional realism by the younger generation of *Tel Quel* writers who accused them of not being sufficiently radical. Unlike theorists who are not also practising writers – and, indeed, writers of particularly controversial novels – they were thus never in a position to work out their theory of the novel in scholarly isolation from the literary scene. Their theoretical work is not a carefully consistent, precise and logical construction elaborated in the light of a single overall principle; it is largely the result of tactical skirmishes with hostile critics combined with the desire to clarify, in rather piecemeal fashion, their ideas for themselves as well as for their readers. The Nouveau Roman's theory, in other words, emerges in response to a series of different pressures, possibilities and contradictions. Had it developed under more peaceful conditions, it might have been both more original and more coherent, but these failings are outweighed, it seems to me, by another kind of significance which arises precisely from the Nouveau Roman's insertion into a situation of very active debate. It is in this sense that I have characterised their use of theory as 'strategic': theories are not elements of pure knowledge, but tools and, often, weapons. As Robbe-Grillet puts it, his theoretical works are 'des ouvrages de combat'.

The arena in which these debates occurred was primarily the literary avant-garde, but some of the issues involved went beyond purely literary terms of reference. Structuralism, for instance, extended through linguistics and the social sciences, so that literary criticism itself was forced to confront more general theoretical problems. But perhaps the most salient feature of the French literary avant-garde throughout this period – i.e., from the 1950s to the 1970s – was its highly *politicised* nature. Writers and critics were involved, emotionally and sometimes actively, in political struggles such as de-Stalinisation in the Soviet Union, the Algerian war and the events of May 1968. Conversely the publication of Sartre's *Qu'est-ce que la littérature?* in 1948 set the agenda for a discussion of literature in political terms that continued – although with major shifts of emphasis – for almost the next thirty years. The central questions were: how can literature best participate in political struggle? What is the relation between literature and the dominant ideology? How does the evolution of the novel as a genre reflect social evolution? Sartre was followed by Barthes, Althusser, and Kristeva – and each of these significantly different figures (who themselves individually went through significantly different theoretical phases) redefined an essentially political problematic for the novel with which the Nouveau Roman had to engage.

Thus the political dimension of literary theory is a dominant consideration throughout this book. But alongside it, and often to some degree related to it, are other questions: for instance, the status of realist representation, the relative importance of structure and different ways of conceptualising it, the position and role of the reader, and the individual writer's relationship to the language he or she is using. All of these, and others, are at some point taken up by the nouveaux romanciers, and none is originally initiated by them. Their theories were to a large extent inspired by the dominant issues of the moment. Above all, perhaps, they are indebted to Roland Barthes. *Le degré zéro de l'écriture* is, as I argue in Chapter 1, a crucial theoretical text for the group as a whole, and Robbe-Grillet in particular; and Barthes's subsequent structuralist work was also helpful to them (see Chapter 2). Equally, they adopted the notion of texual production as elaborated by *Tel Quel* (see Chapter 3). But they used these generally current concepts in particular and distinctive ways, enriching them with their individual practical experience of writing fiction. Thus the description which Simon gives of the Lévi-Straussian 'bricolage', for instance, is invested with a personal and workman-like dimension lacking in the original formulation (Simon, 1972). Similarly, Butor's conception of structure is charged with very different *moral*, as well as practical, implications from that of Lévi-Strauss – or indeed that of Robbe-Grillet (Chapter 2).

For tactical reasons also, their adherence to other people's theories was usually not without reservation. The ambivalence they show towards structuralism and towards *Tel Quel* results, as will be seen, from a mixture of intellectual and pragmatic reasons, and it plays an important part in the shaping of their own theoretical positions. Conversely, their *rejection* of opposing theories was often less total than it at first appeared. This is especially true in the case of Sartre; in Chapter 1, I argue that their vociferous opposition to him *coexists* with a large number of shared assumptions on a less explicit level. Later on, the apparent rejection of any kind of theory at all turns out upon closer examination to be much less of a dramatic break with the past than it seems (Chapter 6). Their attacks on opposing theories are thus sometimes overstated, and oversimplified, in relation to the concrete differences between them. As this suggests, the fact of opposition itself performs a positively useful function: they *need* to have enemies – not just for the publicity this brings them but also, more seriously, because in providing something to define themselves *against*, opposition enables them to clarify and develop their own positions more fully.

The presence of theoretical opponents also serves a more specific purpose in *uniting* the members of the Nouveau Roman. The collective identity of the group could be more strongly affirmed when faced with a common enemy. This is an important issue, because the unity of the group has always been rather precarious. So far in this introduction, I have referred to 'the Nouveau Roman' as if it were an unproblematic entity, but this was never really the case; the differences between individual members, both in terms of the kind of fiction that they wrote and in their views on theoretical questions, have always been almost as prominent as their areas of agreement. For at least the first twenty years of their collective existence, they saw themselves as a group and were concerned to define a common project for the future development of the novel. Therefore, one of the major strategic functions of their theory has been to provide them with a distinctive collective identity. But this ultimately proved self-defeating (see Chapter 6); the very process of clarifying supposedly common aims often led only to a more precise awareness of the disagreements between them. The harder they tried to weld themselves together into a coherent unit, the more cracks kept appearing.

As a result, although the Nouveau Roman is one of the most self-conscious collective entities on the French literary scene, membership of it is not always easy to ascertain. What had initially been a journalistic label applied from the outside to a number of novelists whose work was all perceived as in some way unconventional, was then internalised by the novelists themselves; and so the identity of the Nouveau Roman became not only a question of objective similarities in the fiction of Robbe-Grillet, Sarraute, Simon, etc., but also a question of who was invited to which conferences and whether or not they agreed to come. Marguerite Duras, for instance, who in the early stages had been seen as a nouveau romancier, was the first to drop out: by the time she refused her invitation to attend the conference on the Nouveau Roman at Cerisy in 1971, she had already been making it clear for some time that she did not wish to be associated with them. Michel Butor's position also quite quickly became rather marginal; while on the other hand figures such as Claude Ollier and, above all, Jean Ricardou joined the group only rather later.

Thus, although my purposes in this book require me to refer to 'the Nouveau Roman', the individual writers that I shall be discussing do not constitute an exhaustive list of its membership. The most obvious omission is Robert Pinget (referred to briefly in Chapter 6), whom I have excluded on the grounds that he is almost entirely unconcerned with theory and played no part in the development of the Nouveau Roman's theoretical work – and the same would be true of Claude Mauriac. Claude Ollier deserves greater attention than I have given him, but since he never played a very prominent role in the Nouveau Roman (he was also associated with *Tel Quel*) I have not considered his work in any detail. Conversely, I have devoted more time to Butor than his ambivalent position in the group might seem to warrant; but he was extremely important in the early period of the Nouveau Roman's development, and his theoretical concerns are so closely allied to theirs that it would have been difficult to leave him out. Thus the five writers that this book is centrally concerned with – Robbe-Grillet, Sarraute, Simon, Butor and Ricardou – have been selected on the grounds that they are the key figures in this particular problematic: the relation between the fiction, theory and politics of the Nouveau Roman.

One area in which all the writers associated with the Nouveau Roman are in complete agreement is the status of the traditional realist novel. Indeed, it was the rejection of this kind of writing that founded the group in the first place. The classical nineteenth century French novel, incarnated above all by Balzac, is seen as having put in place a particular model for fiction that has outlived its usefulness and is now positively damaging. The twentieth-century imitators of Balzac, in other words, are perpetuating a false picture of the reality they aim to represent; but the strength of the model is still such that it inhibits attempts to break free of it and explore more innovatory kinds of text. For Robbe-Grillet, it imposes a falsely transparent and reassuring order on social and personal experience:

> Le récit, tel que le conçoivent nos critiques académiques – et bien de lecteurs à leur suite – représente un ordre. Cet ordre, que l'on peut en effet qualifier de naturel, est lié à tout un système, rationaliste et organisateur, dont l'épanouissement correspond à la prise du pouvoir par la classe bourgeoise. En cette première moitié du XIXe siècle, qui vit l'apogée – avec *La Comédie humaine* – d'une forme narrative dont on comprend qu'elle demeure pour beaucoup comme un paradis perdu du roman, quelques certitudes importantes avaient cours: la confiance en particulier dans une logique des choses juste et universelle. (1963c, 36–7)

For Sarraute, the problem with traditional realism is centred rather on the 'trust' which the reader is obliged to place in the realist character, and which, she argues, is no longer viable in this 'age of suspicion':

> La vie à laquelle, en fin de compte, tout en art se ramène . . . a abandonné des formes autrefois si pleines de promesses, et s'est transportée ailleurs. Dans son mouvement incessant qui la fait se déplacer toujours vers cette ligne mobile où parvient à un moment donné la recherche et où porte tout le poids de l'effort, elle a brisé les cadres du vieux roman . . . Quant au caractère, [le lecteur] sait bien qu'il n'est pas autre chose que l'étiquette grossière dont lui-même se sert, sans trop y croire, pour la commodité pratique, pour régler, en très gros, ses conduites. Et il se méfie des actions brutales et spectaculaires qui façonnent

à grandes claques sonores les caractères; et aussi de l'intrigue qui, s'enroulant autour du personnage comme une bandelette, lui donne, en même temps qu'une apparence de cohésion et de vie, la rigidité des momies. (1956, 77–9)

Butor, Simon and Ricardou have made similar comments on these and other aspects of traditional realism. They are, however, much less united on the question of what should be put in its place, and these differences will form much of the subject matter of my subsequent chapters.

The form that this book takes is very loosely chronological. It follows through the various different stages in the evolution of the Nouveau Roman's theoretical writings in conjunction with the changes in the novels, and with larger-scale developments in literary and political theory in France from the 1950s through to the 1980s – at which point, I argue in my final chapter, the Nouveau Roman as such comes to an end. The first chapter deals with the polemic against Sartre and the notion of the political commitment of the writer, setting this against a continuing, more positive, Sartrean influence both in the fiction of Sarraute and Butor and in Robbe-Grillet's *Pour un nouveau roman*. Chapter 2 discusses the Nouveau Roman's rather ambiguous engagement with structuralism: the very selective use of some structuralist notions, and the substantially different ways in which these are put to use by Butor on the one hand, and Ricardou on the other. It includes an analysis of two novels by Robbe-Grillet as hypothetically 'structuralist novels'.

Chapter 3 marks a return to a more explicitly political discourse on literature, showing how, from the mid-1960s to the early 1970s, the structuralist Marxism of Althusser was developed into a more narrowly defined theory of 'textual production' in the pages of the journal *Tel Quel*. For these theorists – principally Julia Kristeva, Philippe Sollers and Jean-Louis Baudry – bourgeois ideology was to be subverted and eventually overturned by an attack on its representational use of language, especially in literature. This project was in turn taken over, strategically pruned of some of its complications, by the Nouveau Roman under the leadership of Ricardou. Chapter 4 covers the same period of time and looks at a different aspect of the concept of textual production: what it implies in respect to the actual *process* of writing and the individual writer's relation to his or her text. The anti-individualist and rational basis of textual production is contrasted with Romantic conceptions of creativity and expressiveness. Chapter 5 examines the concept of intertextuality which was constructed, mainly by Kristeva, again in the late 1960s and 1970s, but juxtaposes it with fictional texts by Sarraute, Simon and Butor which largely pre-date its formulation. Finally, Chapter 6 gives an account of the process whereby in the 1980s the Nouveau Roman apparently abandoned many of its earlier positions, reacting in particular against the dominance of Ricardou's theoretical views in the 1970s, and replacing these with a new – but also more traditional – emphasis on the freedom of the individual writer and a more directly personal mode of writing.

I have been concerned throughout to sustain the connections between theory and fiction, and the book as a whole is thus a mixture of commentary on the nouveaux romanciers' theoretical positions, as expressed in conference papers, articles, etc., and critical interpretations of their fiction in the light of these. Rather than keep to a rigid schema of juxtaposing the two at every point, however, I have found it more productive to focus at times on both, but at times purely on theoretical discourse or, alternatively, on fiction. Thus the first two chapters cover theory and fiction; but in Chapters 3 and 4, the theoretical questions do not have any direct repercussions on individual novels. In Chapter 4, this is because the discussion concerns ways of conceptualising the *activity* of producing texts rather than the resulting end-products. In Chapter 3, however, it is because the attempt to specify the precise way in which anti-representational texts subvert the dominant ideology ultimately proves impossible: and this is why it has no real effect on the level of fictional practice. Chapter 5, conversely, is mainly devoted to an analysis of three fictional texts. These are placed in relation to Kristeva's concept of intertextuality, but not to any theoretical positions of the nouveaux romanciers themselves – precisely because they do not incorporate intertextuality into their own theory to any significant extent. My argument here, put crudely, is that they should have: in other words that the intertextuality which is so active in their fiction could, if theorised, have offered a way out of the problems posed at the end of Chapter 3.

The balance between theory and fiction thus works out differently in different chapters. Similarly, discussion of 'pure' theoretical questions is interspersed with a more anecdotal level of events such as conferences, personal interactions and media reportage. But this very heterogeneity is an essential part of the phenomenon of the Nouveau Roman; while their importance must rest ultimately on the novels that they have written, it is the scope and intensity of the *connections* made between the novels and the intellectual and social context they were working in that has concerned me here.

1

The Reaction against Sartre

RELATIONS BETWEEN SARTRE AND THE NOUVEAU ROMAN

The Nouveau Roman's opposition to traditional realism was accompanied by an equally fundamental antagonism to the more modern notion of politically committed literature. The key text here is Sartre's *Qu'est-ce que la littérature?*, and in particular the first section, 'Qu'est-ce qu'écrire?', which develops the basic argument of 'engagement': unlike the poet, the prose writer *uses* language to *communicate* a certain view of the world, and is *responsible* for the moral and political significance of this representation; this constitutes a mode of *action,* which Sartre names 'l'action par dévoilement' (30). The Nouveau Roman's opposition to this is based on the idea that writing is not a means to an end but an end in itself, an area of free exploration that cannot be constrained by any predetermined meaning.[1]

Committed literature fulfilled a similar function to the Balzacian novel in providing an opponent that the Nouveau Roman could define themselves against. In fact their hostility towards it was far more vehement than their opposition to Balzac. This was partly just because Sartre could, and did, fight back – at least Balzac never attacked the Nouveau Roman. But it was also, ironically, because the nouveaux romanciers held broadly similar political views to the proponents of committed literature. Most of them saw themselves as part of the large group of left-wing intellectuals which existed outside the Communist Party; they participated in political activities; Robbe-Grillet, Sarraute, Simon and Butor were among the one hundred and twenty-one intellectuals who signed the 'Manifeste des insoumis' protesting against the Algerian war, for instance.[2] As Robbe-Grillet puts it, they have 'des opinions politiques généralement classées à gauche' (1963a, 446), and 'Sur des problemes tels que la guerre, ou la conscience sociale, nous avons des réponses prêtes ... C'est là notre vie de citoyens, qui

12

commence au moment où nous déposons un bulletin de vote dans l'urne électorale et qui peut se poursuivre dans les luttes politiques où beaucoup d'entre nous sont engagés' (447). The dominant figure in this milieu in the 1950s and early '60s was undoubtedly Sartre (he organised the 'Manifeste des insoumis'), and it was impossible for the nouveaux romanciers not to take account of his views on literature's role in political struggle – the notion, in other words, of the 'engagement' or commitment of the writer, which at the time was still vigorously supported as a modern progressive view of literature. Opposing Sartre thus ran the risk of undermining the nouveaux romanciers' political credibility; and this in turn meant that they had actively to clarify and defend their own position on the relation between literature and politics.

But the situation was complicated by the fact that they had also started their literary careers against the background of the debate being conducted both in the Soviet Union and in Western Europe over *socialist realism*. Sartre's position is actually very different from this, but, perhaps inevitably, the two issues tended to be merged together. The issue of socialist realism is therefore important as part of the context which shaped the nouveaux romanciers' attitude to Sartre. Its basic tenet is that the writer must place his work at the service of the Party; he must produce a representation of social forces that is realistic – i.e., convincing – but not politically neutral: in Zhdanov's words: 'At the same time as we select Soviet man's finest feelings and qualities and reveal his future to him, we must show our people what they must not be like and castigate the survivals from yesterday that are hindering the Soviet people's progress' (1950, 49, quoted in Caute, 326–7). The so-called 'Zhdanov theses' had been expounded in the Soviet Union in 1932, and formally endorsed by the French Communist Party (the PCF) in 1934; Louis Aragon wrote his *Pour un réalisme socialiste* in 1935. It was only after the war, however, that socialist realism came to the forefront (the theses were not translated into French until 1948, for instance), and was extensively and acrimoniously debated within the French left as a whole. The PCF's adherence to it was one of the factors leading to a large number of the younger intellectuals (including Marguerite Duras) leaving it; finally the Party itself, in its fifteenth Congress in 1959, officially recognised that it had been an error.

The nouveaux romanciers were always unanimously opposed to the Zhdanov theses. It is Robbe-Grillet, however, who articulates their position in the most detail. His article 'Sur quelques notions périmées', published in *L'Express* in 1957 (and reprinted in *Pour un nouveau roman*) contains a section on 'l'engagement' which, although it argues briefly against Sartre's version of commitment, is mainly devoted to an attack on socialist realism as practised both in the Soviet Union and by the writers of the PCF. The reason that 'ce schéma idyllique: l'Art et la Révolution avançant la main dans la main' (40) is not realisable, he argues, is that social revolution and revolutionary art (i.e., innovative, experimental art) are actually antagonistic to one another. The Revolution has to subordinate everything to the one overriding aim of the liberation of the proletariat, whereas the artist, even if he is fully committed, *qua* citizen, to the aims of the revolution, cannot allow his work as an artist to be subordinated to *any* external aim or directive (42). Art is not an *instrument* to be pressed into the service of the cause; the proof of this is that the works which have been produced under these conditions are simply so bad that they do more harm than good, both to art and to the revolution: 'La totale indigence artistique des œuvres qui s'en réclament le plus n'est certes pas l'effet d'un hasard: c'est la notion même d'une œuvre créée *pour* l'expression d'un contenu social, politique, économique, moral, etc., qui constitue le mensonge' (43). In 1963 Robbe-Grillet spoke as one of the French delegates to an international conference at Leningrad which had been organised by the Union of Soviet Writers.[3] Despite the apparent thaw in cultural relations which such a gesture suggested, he was still horrified and angered at the Soviet and Eastern European writers' views – in particular their descriptions of western avant-garde art as decadent and formalist.[4]

In both the above papers, Robbe-Grillet is arguing a serious case against a real and still powerful opponent. But he had no subsequent confrontations with Soviet writers, and in France by the beginning of the 1960s the battle against socialist realism had been definitively won. Why, then, do he and other nouveaux romanciers go on attacking it, well into the 1970s? Perhaps because, once it has been politically discredited, it acquires a new function as a means of establishing the Nouveau Roman's own political relevance through an alignment with the anti-Stalinist left. If this is the case, it also goes some way towards explaining why they consistently associate socialist realism with *Sartre*'s rather different conception of 'engagement' – since Sartre continued to exert an important influence on the literary-intellectual milieu in France throughout the '60s and so could still play the role of a credible enemy.

It is of course true that Sartrean 'engagement' and socialist realism have in common the basic presupposition that the novel should give a realist representation of the world, and this the Nouveau Roman increasingly rejects. But their critique of Sartre concentrates exclusively on the opening section of *Qu'est-ce que la littérature?* which contains the famous, and indeed rather crude, definition of prose as an *instrumental* use of language, and ignores his subsequent refinements and redefinitions of this position.[5] Also, they ignore the profound reciprocal hostility that existed between him and the writers in the PCF: given that Thorez's exhortation to socialist realism in 1947 involved a denunciation of 'the pessimism without solution and the retrograde obscurantism of the existentialist "philosophers"',[6] and given Sartre's vehement criticism of the PCF writers in *Qu'est-ce que la littérature?*,[7] there is something rather disingenuous about the Nouveau Roman's habit of mentioning them both in the same breath: as in Robbe-Grillet's formulation, for instance, that 'le réalisme socialiste ou l'engagement sartrien sont difficilement conciliables avec l'exercice problématique de la littérature' (1963 c, 8), or – as late as 1971 – Simon's vigorous attack on those who recommend that art should serve a cause, characterised as 'ces "utilitaristes" (car c'était déjà le nom que se donnaient, au XIXe, en Russie, les précurseurs des théories jdanoviennes ou de la "littérature engagée"' (1972, 83).

One reason for this is, as I have suggested above, that Sartre took over the role of 'enemy' which could no longer be attributed to socialist realism once the PCF had abandoned it. On another level, however, the Nouveau Roman's opposition to Sartre is motivated simply by his antagonism towards them. His view of the Nouveau Roman was on the whole negative, and grew more so in the course of the 1960s through a series of rather polemical journalistic interchanges. This is an important factor in understanding the *ambivalence* of their position, which I shall discuss in more detail later. In other words, because their hostility towards Sartre arose from fairly specific (and often personal) arguments about the Nouveau Roman, it was able to coexist with implicitly more positive attitudes to his philosophical ideas in general.

The first direct contact between Nouveau Roman theory and Sartrean ideas on literature comes in Robbe-Grillet's article 'Sur quelques notions périmées' in the section entitled 'L'engagement', where he attacks the 'roman à thèse' in its most recently revived forms: socialist realism in the Eastern bloc; and 'engagement' in the west – as practised by the PCF writers on the one hand, and Sartre on the other. In fact, however, most of the section is devoted to an attack on socialist realism, and Robbe-Grillet explicitly distinguishes between this and Sartre's position. All he actually says about Sartre here is: 'Sartre, qui avait vu le danger de cette littérature moralisatrice, avait prêché pour une littérature *morale*, qui prétendait seulement éveiller des consciences politiques en posant les problèmes de notre société, mais qui aurait échappé à l'esprit de propagande en rétablissant le lecteur dans sa liberté' (46). But this position too is refuted on the same grounds as socialist realism; in other words, simply in the light of his premise that only non-signifying literature *is* literature. He continues: 'L'expérience a montré que c'était là encore une utopie: dès qu'apparaît le souci de signifier quelque chose (quelque chose d'extérieur à l'art) la littérature commence à reculer, à disparaître' (ibid).

Sartre's first comments on Robbe-Grillet are made three years later, in an interview with Madeleine Chapsal (1960). By this time, his notion of 'engagement' is being reshaped by the newer stress on the *totality* elaborated in his 'Question de méthode', first published in 1957. On the basis of this criterion he expresses unreserved admiration for Michel Butor, seeing him as 'quelqu'un qui a l'ambition et toutes les chances de devenir un grand écrivain, le premier depuis 1945' (216–17). Conversely, he dismisses both Robbe-Grillet and Sarraute for their inability to encompass 'le tout' in their writing. Thus, Robbe-Grillet's attempt to liberate readers from a bourgeois vision of reality by stripping objects of all significance is bound to fail because 'l'objet total qui figure dans un roman, c'est un objet *humain* et qui n'est rien sans ses significations humaines' (215); the end result is merely 'une schématisation de laboratoire' (216). In the case of Sarraute, in whose work 'la totalité brille par son absence', the corresponding abstraction is from social rather than perceptual reality; she thinks she has reached the basic minimal elements of interpersonal relations in general, but in fact 'elle ne fait que montrer les effets abstraits et infinitésimaux d'un milieu social très défini' (213). And in depicting this restricted social group she has not elucidated the *relations* between individual and milieu, so that 'nous restons sur le plan indifférencié et illusoire de l'immédiateté' (214). This emphasis on the importance of theorising the relation between individual and class via all its mediating agencies (such as the family) is formulated in 'Question de méthode' and characterises Sartre's work from the 1950s onwards; it is this that he recognises in Butor's novels, saying of *Degrés*: 'Jamais on n'a fait tentative plus habile et plus profonde pour saisir la personne à travers les relations de famille, de métier qui l'ont produite, qui la conditionnent et qu'elle transforme' (217).

The contrast in attitudes to Butor on the one hand and Robbe-Grillet and Sarraute on the other illustrates the diversity of the texts grouped together under the heading Nouveau Roman. Nevertheless, the opposition between Sartre and an entity known as the Nouveau Roman (although Butor took virtually no part in the debate) was already becoming a familiar and increasingly entrenched polemic. The next major meeting between them was at the Leningrad writers' conference of 1963; Robbe-Grillet and Sarraute, along with Bernard Pingaud (replacing Butor who was ill), constituted the French delegation selected by a French committee; thus presenting the Nouveau Roman as the dominant force in contemporary French literature, and ensuring a confrontation at the conference between the Nouveau Roman and a modernised, post-Zhdanov form of socialist realism. Significantly, Sartre and Simone de Beauvoir were invited separately by the Soviet Writers' Union. On this occasion, however, there was no direct confrontation between Sartre and the nouveaux romanciers; Robbe-Grillet's speech, as mentioned above, was extremely aggressive towards the Soviet writers; Sarraute – despite or because of her Russian émigré background – was far more conciliatory to them and in fact showed a greater understanding of the difference in the situation and problems facing Soviet and Western writers. She was also less intransigeant in her rejection of engagement: 'Il y a eu et il y a des œuvres dites engagées qui sont des œuvres d'art authentiques' (1964, 73). Sartre's summing up of the whole conference is notably far more critical of some of the Soviet writers – because of their refusal to enter into discussion on any of the issues raised – than of the French delegation. He makes a politely hesitant criticism of Sarraute's idealism,[8] mentions Robbe-Grillet once to agree with him on the assumptions behind attacks on the Nouveau Roman (82), and otherwise avoids discussing it at all.[9] Back in France, however, the following year, he renews his negative comments in an interview with Yves Buin in *Clarté*, the Communist Student Union journal.[10] This time, also, he includes Simon in his attack, remarking dismissively: 'Il écrit sur le temps, sur la mémoire. Au fond, que montre-t-il de plus que Proust?' (42).

Of much greater impact, however, was an interview he gave

about the same time in *Le Monde* (1964a). The initial reason for the
interview was that his autobiography, *Les Mots*, had just come out;
but his replies to Jacqueline Piatier's questions go far beyond this
text and amount to a complete re-evaluation of literature as such.
The main theme is his disillusionment with the power and value
of literature in the face of material poverty, especially in the Third
World. The writer's problem, he says, is not metaphysical suffering,
which is a luxury, but simply 'Que signifie la littérature dans un
monde qui a faim?' His own earlier literary production was vitiated
by a lack of awareness of this reality: 'J'ai changé depuis. J'ai fait
un lent apprentissage du réel. J'ai vu des enfants mourir de faim'
– and he concludes, in a sentence which quickly became notorious:
'En face d'un enfant qui meurt, *La Nausée* ne fait pas le poids'. The
widespread outrage which greeted these remarks in which Sartre
was seen as denying any *autonomous* value to art in general, was
compounded by his insistence that the *only* valid position for a
writer to adopt was to write for the oppressed majority of the
world's population, to 'se ranger au côté du plus grand nombre, des
deux milliards d'affamés . . .   Faute de quoi il est au service d'une
classe privilégiée et exploiteur comme elle'. Thus he condemns Gide
for writing for a privileged leisured class, and Samuel Beckett for
his metaphysical pessimism, but his most trenchant criticisms are
reserved for Robbe-Grillet:

> La faim du monde, la menace atomique, l'aliénation de l'homme,
> je m'étonne qu'elles ne teintent pas toute notre littérature.
> Croyez-vous que je puisse lire Robbe-Grillet dans un pays
> sous-développé? Il ne se sent pas mutilé. Je le tiens pour un
> bon écrivain, mais il s'adresse à la bourgeoisie confortable. Je
> voudrais qu'il se rende compte que la Guinée existe. En Guinée
> je pourrais lire Kafka. Je retrouve en lui mon malaise.

Here, in other words, the relatively sophisticated insistence on art
as totalisation has been replaced by an outright rejection of all art
that does not explicitly ally itself with the victims of world-wide
exploitation. Whereas the 'totality' could be seen as an *aesthetic*, as
well as a philosophical, value in its own right, this new position
is exclusively *moral*, and subordinates art to external directives.
More specifically, it also marks a shift in the scope of his criticism
of the Nouveau Roman; from previously being merely politically
irrelevant, it is now seen as actively reactionary. This view is

partially restated in another interview Sartre gave the same year to *Playboy*, which was published in the May 1965 number. Here the 'stocky, walleyed 59-year-old ex-professor' (as *Playboy* introduced him to its readers) claims that:

> There are no great writers in France today. The practitioners of the "New Novel" are talented, and viewed as experiments in form, their books are interesting. But they bring us absolutely nothing except a justification of our technocratic, politically sterile French social order. Literature should be the work of clear-eyed men who take into account the totality of mankind. Literature has got to realize that it exists in a world where children die of hunger. (75)

The interview in *Le Monde* provoked a number of vehement responses. *L'Express* published, under the heading 'Deux écrivains répondent à Jean-Paul Sartre', articles by Simon and Yves Berger whose piece, entitled 'Nous ne sommes pas des traîtres', is a fairly traditional justification of the imaginative power of literature as compensation for the deficiencies of reality. Simon's response is a more specific defence of the Nouveau Roman. He starts by making points similar to those in *Pour un nouveau roman*: writing is essentially unpredictable, and so the writer cannot be held responsible for the political implications of his text. Therefore also, art has nothing to do with morality (a point he illustrates with the rather odd choice of Picasso's *Guernica*) and moralists such as Sartre cannot understand art. The rest of the article is a mixture of cogent critique and savage personal abuse. He points out, for instance, that if actual readership is to be the criterion of political value, then Sartre is just as bourgeois as Robbe-Grillet, that there is something unpleasantly self-righteous about Sartre's castigation of his own former errors, and something distinctly patronising about the assumption, made in the abstract, that the oppressed are not capable of or interested in intellectual debate. It is also quite reasonable to suggest that novels like *La Jalousie* and *Dans le labyrinthe*, with their 'refus des interprétations toutes faites, l'exigence rigoureuse d'écarter les significations confortables et rassurantes' do embody a 'malaise' close to that which Sartre finds in Kafka.

But his statement that Sartre the moralist reduces art to 'une simple fonction économique' *because* he is incapable of appreciating artistic value simply trivialises the issue.[11] And the further insinuation that this is secretly motivated by Sartre's envy of 'real' writers – 'Il est si commode à tel qui a conscience de son échec et de ses manques de se dire qu'il s'est "sacrifié" à une noble cause et d'injurier en même temps ceux que, confusément, il envie' – is both unjustified and gratuitously offensive. The rather spiteful tone that creeps into his critique distinguishes it from otherwise similar attacks on Sartre by Robbe-Grillet. But it has to be remembered that Simon's anti-Communism is far more virulent than that of for instance Robbe-Grillet or Butor. He echoes *Pour un nouveau roman*'s view of the antagonism between art and social revolution, and ends his article with the familiar tactic of identifying Sartre with the Soviet intelligentsia; but this is here taken to new extremes of vehemence as the latter are characterised as frightened animals who kill anything that they cannot recognise: 'Dans les ténèbres de l'ignorance et de la peur, on tue'. At the same time, however, Simon's total lack of sympathy with Sartre's position is slightly at odds with his own *fiction* which, far more than that of his fellow nouveaux romanciers, displays a constant awareness, based in personal experience, of the importance of material hardship and oppression, and a corresponding scepticism about the value of philosophical debate and, indeed, literature. On the basis of a reading of *La Route des Flandres* or *Le Palace*, one might have expected Simon to be more receptive to the fundamental question posed by the *Le Monde* interview: 'Que signifie la littérature dans un monde qui a faim?' This disjunction is perhaps indicative of the kind of ambiguity mentioned above, which I will discuss in more detail later.

The *Le Monde* interview had a further repercussion: the public debate entitled 'Que peut la littérature?' organised by *Clarté* in December of 1964 was held mainly in order to explore further the issues that Sartre had raised.[12] Sartre was supported here by Simone de Beauvoir and Jorge Semprun; Yves Berger was asked to speak for the other side, presumably because of his article in *L'Express*, as were Jean-Pierre Faye and Jean Ricardou. Semprun and Faye both make valuable attempts to move the debate out of the impasse of Nouveau Roman-versus-engagement; Semprun by clarifying the difference between Sartrean engagement and socialist realism and arguing that the rejection of art as a means to an end need not imply Robbe-Grillet's conception of art as creation 'pour rien'; and Faye by claiming (a little optimistically) that 'par-delà l'opposition anachronique entre "littérature engagée" et "nouveau roman", quelque chose se dessine à nos yeux par lequel cette opposition cesse d'être pertinente' (69), in other words a conception of 'engagement' in the transformation of the meanings that mediate reality for us (72). But the central axis remains the direct clash between Sartre and Ricardou. Although he is of a different generation from the other nouveaux romanciers, Ricardou appears as the main proponent of the values of the Nouveau Roman; and his arguments do in fact run along very similar lines to those of previous commentaries by Robbe-Grillet and Simon.

Thus he picks up Barthes's 'écrivain/écrivant' distinction,[13] which Simon had used in *L'Express*, and uses it to contest the prose/poetry opposition in *Qu'est-ce que la littérature?*; he brings out the parallelism between Sartre's example of the evocative *poetic* force of the name 'Florence', and Proust's exploration of the resonances of place names in his *novel*, and goes on to cite similar examples of word-play and phonetic associations in the novels of Simon, Robbe-Grillet, Roussel and Joyce – to conclude that these are just as typical of prose fiction as of poetry. His next point, more or less restating arguments of Robbe-Grillet and Simon, is that 'le sujet du livre c'est, en quelque manière, *sa propre composition* – il n'y a aucun sujet préalable, aucune hiérarchie prédéterminée des sujets' (56), and that 'cet *acte d'écrire* fait surgir un nouveau monde dont la structure est celle même du langage' (57).

Finally, he turns to an explicit consideration of Sartre's interview in *Le Monde*: firstly to claim that Kafka is just as 'literary' as Robbe-Grillet, secondly to say that it is pointless to try to compare a novel with the death of a child, and thirdly to side-step the whole problem by advancing the rather hazardous proposition that art *is* man: 'Car l'art, c'est l'homme même, c'est la qualité *différentielle* par laquelle un certain mammifère supérieur devient *homme*' (59). This too may have been inspired by Simon's remark in *L'Express* that a world without art would be like a humanely run concentration camp 'où croupiraient non plus des hommes mais des bêtes'; but his own development of it leads him to conclusions that are, to say the least, dubious for the left-wing Marxist that he later claims to be: for instance that literature *should* be inaccessible to the exploited because its inaccessibility makes them realise that they are underdeveloped and should do something about it (60); and – his conclusion – that if 'la littérature en tant qu'art' is not a continual presence in the world, 'alors, je vous le dis, les pays sous-développés, la politique, vivre ou mourir, quelle importance?'

(61).[14] Sartre's reply to this, not surprisingly, accuses Ricardou of essentialism and of promoting an alienated relation between reader and text: if the work is an end in itself, then the reader is of necessity merely a means to that end, and loses his freedom; the freedom proposed by the reflexive or aleatory text – in which the reader can for instance choose his own ending – is a deceptive illusion (113). He returns to the attack on the Nouveau Roman the following year, claiming that 'écrivain' versus 'écrivant' is a false distinction because a writer should be both,[15] and in extracts from a conference paper on the avant-garde, published in *le Nouvel Observateur*, in which he argues that writers (such as Robbe-Grillet, among others) who merely explore the possibilities of language are not a 'real' avant-garde.

In outlining the sequence of direct interchanges between Sartre and the Nouveau Roman over the first half of the 1960s I have tried to bring out the main theoretical issues at stake, but also to show how these became gradually clouded by, and bogged down in, a rather narrow, sterile and often acrimonious polemic. But this level of relations is not the whole story; in fact, as I have already suggested, the polemic obscures a more diffuse interpenetration of ideas which, although it sometimes results in contradiction, is in many ways more interesting. The rest of this chapter will examine instances of this, firstly in relation to one of the major early theoretical texts of the Nouveau Roman, and then to the fiction of Sarraute and Butor.

ALAIN ROBBE-GRILLET: *POUR UN NOUVEAU ROMAN* AND *QU'EST-CE QUE LA LITTÉRATURE?*

The text of *Pour un nouveau roman* brings together a collection of articles previously published in *L'Express* and *La Nouvelle Revue Française* between 1955 and 1963. As such, it does not provide a single unambiguous statement of Robbe-Grillet's position on the direction the novel should be taking, and a perceptible evolution in his views can be traced through the various different articles. Within this general framework, he criticises Sartre on two different grounds: as well as the concept of 'engagement', there is a more substantial and specific analysis of the representation of objects in *La Nausée*. In both cases, however, the argument overtly made against Sartre itself contains strong traces of a Sartrean influence.

The break with previous literary theory is far from absolute, and the continuing pressure of the existentialist-marxist paradigm makes itself felt as an undertow throughout.

Thus the most interesting point about the critique of *La Nausée* is that it is undertaken to a large extent from a point of view sympathetic to existentialism; it accuses Sartre of not being consistent with his own ideas – by implication, of not being existentialist *enough*. It occurs in 'Nature, humanisme, tragédie', one of the longer pieces in *Pour un nouveau roman* and one which came to be considered as a kind of manifesto. In it he argues that humanism rests on a fallacious 'pan-anthropomorphism', or assumption of complicity between man and nature. Tragedy is a further and more desperate stage of this complicity; it arises out of a perception of man's real separation from the world but then transforms this into a metaphysical *relationship* of non-communication.[16] Existentialism, and in particular the notion of the absurd, is interpreted as the most recent, and in a sense most desperate, version of tragedy: as a last-ditch attempt to recuperate meaning through making the absence of meaning 'mean' the absurd. It thus surreptitiously reintroduces a *transcendental* dimension to literature: 'l'absurde, qui est théoriquement la signification nulle, mais qui en fait mène aussitôt, par une récuperation métaphysique bien connue, à une nouvelle transcendance' (181). This kind of pseudo-meaninglessness, which in reality *recuperates* man's relationship with the world, is denounced throughout *Pour un nouveau roman*, but in particular through his critique of Camus's *L'Etranger*. He couples *La Nausée* with *L'Etranger*, as 'Deux grandes œuvres . . . [qui] nous ont offert deux nouvelles formes de la complicité fatale: l'absurde et la nausée' (70). He does, however, present Sartrean existentialism as a whole in a more positive light than Camus's conception of the absurd, and makes it clear that he considers *La Nausée* to be an important step forward in the modern novel.[17]

There is also – although Robbe-Grillet does not mention it – at least an initial similarity in his own and *La Nausée*'s representation of objects. For both authors, the truth of objects lies first of all in the fact that they are not under man's control; Robbe-Grillet's comment that one must reveal the world 'dans la mesure où il refuse de se plier à nos habitudes d'appréhension et à notre ordre' (23) and his description of objects as 'comme se moquant de leur propre sens, ce sens qui cherche en vain à les réduire au rôle d'ustensiles précaires' (23) apply very accurately to *La Nausée*. But Robbe-Grillet's argument is that nausea, like the absurd, institutes *another kind* of anthropo-morphic complicity with objects: Roquentin's relations with objects are 'viscérales', concentrating on the more 'intimate' senses of touch and smell, and on colours rather than visual forms or contours; objects are shown to have 'personalities' and to be 'alive'; rather than observing them Roquentin identifies with them, saying for instance: 'Tous les objets qui m'entouraient étaient faits de la même matière que moi, d'une espèce de souffrance moche'; and: '*J'étais* la racine du marronnier' (quoted in *Pour un nouveau roman*, 76). Moreover, since anyone who refuses to see the world in this way is characterised by Sartre as a 'salaud', the 'souffrance moche' takes on the quality of a tragic necessity; Robbe-Grillet comments: 'Nous sommes, cette fois encore, dans un univers entièrement *tragifié* . . . rachat (ici: accession à la conscience) par l'impossibilité même de réaliser un véritable accord, c'est-à-dire récuperation finale de toutes les distances, de tous les échecs, de toutes les solitudes, de toutes les contradictions' (75).

It is, however, noticeable that Robbe-Grillet's criticisms of the novel are themselves couched in very Sartrean language. Thus Roquentin's rejection of 'le regard' is countered by using Sartre's own terms against him: 'La subjectivité relative de mon regard me sert précisément à définir ma situation dans le monde. J'évite simplement de concourir, moi-même, à faire de cette situation une servitude' (82).[18] Equally, the tragic necessity of suffering is rejected in the name of freedom (76). Sartre, in other words, has not been consistent with his own beliefs, and *La Nausée* illustrates the difficulty of extricating oneself from the presuppositions of the very positions one is attacking: 'Tout se passe donc comme si Sartre – qui ne peut pourtant pas être accusé d'essentialisme – avait, dans ce livre du moins, porté à leur plus haut degré les idées de *nature* et de *tragédie*. Une fois de plus, lutter contre ces idées n'a fait d'abord que leur conférer des forces nouvelles' (76). Thus the critique of *La Nausée* is far from a total rejection of Sartre's philosophical ideas; in effect, Robbe-Grillet is saying that he has not, in this novel, taken them far enough.

This perhaps makes it less surprising than it would otherwise have been to find that throughout 'Nature, humanisme, tragédie' anthro-pomorphic complicity is denounced very precisely as (although Robbe-Grillet does not use the term) a form of *bad faith* in the Sartrean sense – in other words, the refusal to accept one's existential freedom. Robbe-Grillet argues that the underlying assumption of humanism is that nature imposes a form of predestination on us, an essentialist model to which we willingly submit (64). In accepting and indeed cultivating the tragic relation we are refusing our freedom to change reality and our orientation to the future: 'Chemin vers un au-delà métaphysique, cette pseudo-nécessité est en même temps la porte fermée à tout avenir réaliste. La tragédie, si elle nous console aujourd'hui, interdit tout conquête plus solide pour demain . . . Il n'est plus question de rechercher quelque remède à notre malheur, du moment qu'elle vise à nous le faire aimer' (68).

I have quoted at some length from this section of *Pour un nouveau roman* in order to give an idea of the pervasively Sartrean atmosphere in which the whole book is bathed – despite the major disagreements between him and Robbe-Grillet.

Robbe-Grillet's rejection of 'engagement' has been outlined above. But the gap between him and Sartre is not as large, or as straightforward, as my previous description might suggest; for one thing, the section 'L'engagement' itself gives the impression that Robbe-Grillet has nothing *in particular* against 'engagement' (as distinct from socialist realism): it is merely one of the many kinds of literature which aim to communicate an 'external' meaning. The text of *Pour un nouveau roman* as a whole, moreover, often describes the writer's activity in terms which, although they exclude the possibility of 'engagement', are curiously similar to Sartre's general definitions of the *project* as a central concept of existentialist theory. That is, there is the same combination of the lucid conscious choice and the idea that the real nature of the project and its original motivations are only apparent retrospectively – it reveals itself through action (as discussed in the final section of this chapter). Thus Robbe-Grillet rejects the nineteenth-century idea of literary genius – 'sorte de monstre inconscient, irresponsable et fatal' (11) – in favour of a conscious, lucid 'réflexion continuelle' on the problems of writing as the 'moteur' for creativity. At the same time, however, the work always exceeds the writer's intentions; his search is not entirely conscious, and 'tout n'est pas clair à l'instant de la décision' (13). Therefore the writer's motive for writing a particular book is to find out why he wanted to write it (ibid). As Inès remarks in Sartre's *Huis Clos*: 'Seules les actions décident de ce qu'on a voulu'.

Moreover as Robbe-Grillet develops this idea it comes to sound increasingly like the action of 'dévoilement' that in *Qu'est-ce que la littérature?* constitutes the essence of 'engagement'. Sartre sees the efficacity of the writer's action in making readers conscious of issues in their own lives that they had previously been only dimly aware of,[19] an emphasis that Robbe-Grillet echoes when he writes: 'Car la fonction de l'art n'est jamais d'illustrer une vérité – ou même une interrogation – connue à l'avance, mais de mettre au monde des interrogations (et aussi peut-être, à terme, des réponses) qui ne se connaissent pas encore elles-mêmes' (14).

Pour un nouveau roman thus never quite discards the general terms in which the problem of 'engagement' is conceived, although it is concerned to give them a different content. The enduring relevance of the problematic is implied in the conclusion to the 1961 article 'Nouveau roman, homme nouveau', which defines the writer's project (and the choice of this eminently Sartrean term seems quite deliberate) as a 'projet de forme' and claims that: 'C'est peut-être, en fin de compte, ce contenu douteux d'un obscur projet de forme qui servira le mieux la cause de la liberté. Mais à quelle échéance?' (153). In other words, conscious experimentation with literary form is *in itself* a kind of political 'engagement'.

This is an idea which gradually comes to dominate Robbe-Grillet's thinking on the novel; and the question of how and why it does so is an important factor in the understanding of his relationship with Sartre. It is important, in other words, to analyse precisely how his views change in the course of *Pour un nouveau roman* – that is, through the articles originally written between 1955 and 1963. The central emphasis throughout is the idea that the novel cannot serve as a vehicle for the expression of 'external' meanings, whether these are moral, metaphysical or political: but, conversely, what it can and indeed should do changes quite fundamentally.

Initially meaning as such is rejected in favour of a purely descriptive, material 'presence' of things; in 1956 he writes: 'l'adjectif optique, descriptif, celui qui se contente de mesurer, de situer, de limiter, de définir, montre probablement le chemin difficile d'un nouvel art romanesque' (27). A year later, however, he concludes 'Sur quelques notions périmées' with a section on 'La forme et le contenu' in which literary form has become the dominant value, and in which meaning is not to be excluded but to be seen as a product of the *form* of the text (49). In other words, the distinction is not now between *meaning* and *description*, but between *pre-existing* meanings and the *new* meanings that the text itself *generates*: 'L'art . . ne s'appuie sur aucune vérité qui existerait avant lui; et l'on peut dire qu'il n'exprime rien que lui-même. Il crée lui-même son propre équilibre et pour lui-même son propre sens' (51).

One of the most striking features of this section of 'Sur quelques notions périmées' is the extent to which it borrows from another text, first published four years earlier: namely, Barthes's *Le degré zéro de l'écriture*. If new forms produce new meanings, it is equally true that reactionary forms reinforce reactionary meanings; and to make this point Robbe-Grillet leans heavily on Barthes's claim that literary form carries an ideological weight of its own, and his consequent critique of both traditional narrative and socialist realism. Thus in the first place nineteenth-century realism can meaningfully be defined as 'bourgeois'. 'La forme et le contenu' reiterates Barthes's view of it as the imposition of an artificial, intelligible, reassuring order onto reality; and, as in *Le degré zéro*, identifies the main agents of this as the *passé simple* and the use of the third person. Barthes's formulation that 'Le passé simple est donc finalement l'expression d'un ordre, et par conséquent d'une euphorie. Grâce à lui, la réalité n'est ni mystérieuse, ni absurde; elle est claire, presque familière' (26) is echoed in this passage of 'La forme et le contenu':

> Tous les élements techniques du récit – emploi systématique du passé simple et de la troisième personne, adoption sans condition du déroulement chronologique . . . tout visait à imposer l'image d'un univers stable, cohérent, continu, univoque, entièrement déchiffrable. Comme l'intelligibilité du monde n'était même pas mise en question, raconter ne posait pas de problème. L'écriture romanesque pouvait être innocente. (37)

This in turn means that socialist realism, far from being the politically revolutionary art that its proponents claimed, actually inhibits the process of social change because it reinforces the formal stereotypes of narrative order. Robbe-Grillet can thus turn the tables on his political opponents; and the attack he mounts in 'La forme et le contenu' is equally indebted to *Le degré zéro de l'écriture*. Barthes had accused socialist realism of counteracting its own revolutionary aims by clinging to the outdated bourgeois formal conventions of realism: 'le dogme même du réalisme socialiste oblige fatalement à une écriture conventionnelle . . . l'écriture communiste . . . bien loin de rompre avec une forme, somme toute typiquement bourgeoise – du moins dans le passé – , continue d'assumer sans réserve les soucis formels de l'art d'écrire petit-bourgeois' (51). Robbe-Grillet, in very similar terms, writes: 'Une chose devrait troubler les partisans du réalisme socialiste, c'est la parfaite ressemblance de leurs arguments,

de leurs valeurs, avec ceux des critiques bourgeois les plus endurcis'
(47). He rejects the idea that form can be separated from content,
and warns the socialist realists that 'c'est aussi dans leur forme
que réside leur sens, leur "signification profonde", c'est-à-dire leur
contenu' (49).

But the relevance of *Le degré zéro de l'écriture* extends much
further than these particular borrowings. The text as a whole is,
I would argue, of crucial importance in the development of the
Nouveau Roman's theoretical positions, although they do not often
refer to it. In particular, the relationship between *Qu'est-ce que la
littérature?* and *Pour un nouveau roman* on the question of 'engagement' cannot be fully understood without taking it into account.
The connections are not explicit; *Le degré zéro* does not mention
Qu'est-ce que la littérature?, and *Pour un nouveau roman* does not
mention *Le degré zéro*.[20] Nevertheless, the latter occupies a transitional position between Sartre and Robbe-Grillet, in so far as
Barthes's concept of *'écriture'* transforms Sartre's 'engagement' into
something which legitimises the novelist's concern with problems
of form and language *as a type of socio-political action*; and this
then opens the way for Robbe-Grillet to refute Sartre's own accu-
sations that the Nouveau Roman is politically irrelevant and/or
reactionary, while at the same time preserving its freedom from
externally imposed directives as to its political 'message'. Indeed
Barthes himself saw no contradiction between his definition of
'engagement' and the writing of the Nouveau Roman; when in
an interview in 1964 he is asked why, with his view of writing
as commitment, he approves of 'uncommitted' writers such as
Robbe-Grillet and Butor, he replies: 'ces écrivains eux-mêmes vous
ont répondu souvent qu'ils ne se considéraient nullement comme
étrangers ou indifférents à leur temps, à l'histoire des hommes
parmi lesquelles ils vivent. Entre l'histoire et l'œuvre, il y a de
nombreux relais, à commencer précisément par l'écriture' (32).[21]

The interrelationship between the three texts is thus worth studying in some detail. The leverage which *Le degré zéro de l'écriture*
offers *Pour un nouveau roman* is made all the greater by the fact
that *Le degré zéro* is in many ways heavily influenced by Sartre.[22]
The title of its first chapter, 'Qu'est-ce que l'écriture?' is a deliberate
recall of *Qu'est-ce que la littérature?* (and *its* first chapter, 'Qu'est-ce
qu'écrire?'), and the essay as a whole takes the same view as
the latter on several fundamental issues. Both Sartre and Barthes
explain the historical evolution of the novel in terms of the changing

relationship of the writer, as an increasingly marginalised member of the bourgeoisie, to the dominant ideology (although they do not always agree on what this relationship is for a given historical period); the way in which the novel evolves is determined by the individual writer's choice of an 'écriture', for Barthes, or of a particular readership, for Sartre, made from within the constraints of the historical situation. Thus Barthes's 'écriture' is defined as the writer's act of commitment – 'le choix général d'un ton, d'un éthos, si l'on veut, et c'est ici précisément que l'écrivain s'individualise clairement parce que c'est ici qu'il s'engage' (14) – to a social and historical position: 'l'écriture est un acte de solidarité historique' (14).

But the originality of *Le degré zéro de l'écriture* lies in the radical change which Barthes makes to the concept of the writer's commitment: that is, he defines its object not as a particular world view to be expressed in the text, but as an 'engagement' of the literary form itself.[23] The act of commitment constituted by 'écriture', in other words, stems from the realisation that literary *language* is as much an ideological reality as the views expressed by it; thus 'l'écriture est une fonction: elle est le rapport entre la création et la société, elle est le langage littéraire transformé par sa destination sociale, elle est la forme saisie dans son intention humaine et liée ainsi aux grandes crises de l'Histoire' (14). This insight was to prove seminal for literary theory as a whole in the 1960s and '70s (and will be discussed in that context in Chapter 3).

Robbe-Grillet picks it up as early as 1957. He concludes his section on 'L'engagement' with the following redefinition of the term:

> Redonnons donc à la notion d'engagement le seul sens qu'elle peut avoir pour nous. Au lieu d'être de nature politique, l'engagement c'est, pour l'écrivain, la pleine conscience des problèmes actuels de son propre langage, la conviction de leur extrême importance, la volonté de les résoudre de l'intérieur. C'est là, pour lui, la seule chance de demeurer un artiste et, sans doute aussi, par voie de conséquence obscure et lointaine, de servir un jour à quelque chose – peut-être même à la révolution. (47)

In thus retaining from Sartre the idea of the writer's commitment but reformulating its object as work on the problems of his language, Robbe-Grillet is making a similar move to that of Barthes. The political nature of 'écriture', however, is for him still far more tenuous: little more than a pious hope that it might work out like that one day.

But his position finally moves on one stage further. The chapters of *Pour un nouveau roman* entitled 'Nouveau roman, homme nouveau' and 'Temps et description' were originally written in 1961 and 1963 respectively; and in these and the introduction to the reprinted collection, Robbe-Grillet makes it clear that the new meanings generated by the text are no longer to be seen as purely reflexive (as they were in 1957: 'l'on peut dire qu'il n'exprime rien que lui-même' (51)), but as *socially relevant* and as contributing to a transformation of society. He states unequivocally that 'les œuvres nouvelles n'ont de raison d'être que si elles apportent à leur tour au monde de nouvelles significations, encore inconnues des auteurs eux-mêmes, des significations qui existeront seulement plus tard, grâce à ces œuvres, *et sur lesquelles la société établira de nouvelles valeurs*' (156, my italics). The curious thing about this is that, rather than sticking to Barthes's argument, Robbe-Grillet seems to be as it were overshooting *Le degré zéro de l'écriture* and ending up back in the same kind of *instrumental* view of literature as he criticises so fiercely in his attack on *Qu'est-ce que la littérature?* For instance, in the introduction to *Pour un nouveau roman*, he defines the nouveaux romanciers as 'tous ceux qui sont décidés à inventer le roman, c'est-à-dire à inventer l'homme' (9), and as those who know that lack of formal innovation is dangerous because 'en nous fermant les yeux sur notre situation réelle dans le monde présent, elle nous empêche en fin de compte de construire le monde et l'homme de demain' (10) – a rhetorical flourish that would not be out of place in the Zhdanov theses, let alone in *Qu'est-ce que la littérature?*

The overall evolution of Robbe-Grillet's views can perhaps best be summed up as a change in the significance which he attaches to, precisely, significance. The initial rejection of any kind of significance, the limiting of prose fiction to 'pure' neutral visual description of objects, gradually turns into a rejection of *pre-existing* meanings in favour of the text as a self-generating structure whose forms produce *new* meanings; in the final stage these new meanings are also seen as relevant to the world outside the text.

Equally, however, Sartre's definition of committed literature also evolves somewhat in the course of *Qu'est-ce que la littérature?* The interesting point about these two trajectories is the significant extent to which they *converge*. The beginning of *Qu'est-ce que la littérature?* defines fictional prose as an instrument which the committed writer

uses in order to communicate a politically responsible view of the
world to his readers; and the beginning of *Pour un nouveau roman*
defines the new novel as, firstly, constructing a representation of
reality in its simple material presence, excluding all interpretation
or value-judgement (all 'signification'); and secondly, as an end in
itself rather than a 'moyen au service d'une cause qui le dépasserait'
(42). At this point these positions are mutually exclusive; but then
they both begin to move. The direction taken by Robbe-Grillet
has been outlined above. Sartre, on the other hand, develops his
argument through a growing emphasis on the appeal to the reader's
freedom.[24] As a result, he comes to see the novel not as a means
of influencing the reader to believe certain things – because that
would be to deny the reader's freedom – but as a 'fin': 'Ainsi
le livre n'est pas, comme l'outil, un moyen en vue d'une fin
quelconque: il se propose comme fin à la liberté du lecteur' (60).
This in turn leads him to place increasing stress on the *autonomy*
of art: 'L'œuvre d'art est gratuite parce qu'elle est fin absolue et
qu'elle se propose au spectateur comme un impératif catégorique'
(282).

Thus by the end of both *Qu'est-ce que la littérature?* and *Pour un
nouveau roman* it is, ironically, possible to produce a composite
definition of the aims of the novel to which both Sartre and Robbe-
Grillet could subscribe: the novel should be a free and autonomous
process of discovery, offering its readers new meanings which will
help them to change their own situations.[25]

NATHALIE SARRAUTE AND *L'ETRE ET LE NÉANT*

Sartre's impact on the Nouveau Roman was not, however, confined
to the formulations of their theoretical work. His presence can also
be traced in some of their fiction, with the difference that here the
relevant references are not *Qu'est-ce que la littérature?* but the more
general philosophical works. The connections between the texts are
thus much less strained; now that it is no longer a question of
competing literary theories, but rather of fictional manifestations
of Sartrean conceptions of subjectivity, praxis, and so on – which
have in themselves nothing to do with literature – the novels need
not be forced into the kind of intellectual fudging that can be found
in *Pour un nouveau roman*. In fact the contradictions that occur here
are not in the novels but in Sartre's discourse about them. Thus his

interview with Madeleine Chapsal in 1960 is, as I have said, critical
of Sarraute's novels for their bourgeois world view – for lacking any
grasp of the mediations between individual experience and social
determination that he had himself started to analyse in 'Question de
méthode'. But this contrasts strongly with a much earlier, and much
more positive, evaluation of her fiction which appears as his preface
to her *Portrait d'un inconnu* (1948), and which discusses the novel
implicitly in the terms of his own earlier work in *L'Etre et le néant*
(1943) on inauthenticity and bad faith. Thus what will be dismissed
in 1960 as the typical paranoia of the leisured classes (Chapsal, 214)
is here taken seriously as the existential fear of authentic contact
with others, the fear underlying bad faith: 'Les livres de Nathalie
Sarraute sont remplis de ces terreurs: on parle, quelque chose va
éclater, illuminer soudain le fond glauque d'une âme et chacun
sentira les bourbes mouvantes de la sienne' (12–13).

Portrait d'un inconnu is, in other words, here presented as an
existentialist novel – he concludes: 'Pour moi je pense qu'en laissant
deviner une authenticité insaisissable . . . en s'attachant à peindre
le monde rassurant et désolé de l'inauthentique, elle a mis au point
une technique qui permet d'atteindre, par-delà le psychologique,
la réalité humaine, dans son existence même' (14). Moreover, the
description he gives is very convincing. Whether or not Sarraute was
consciously 'influenced' by Sartre, her writing clearly lends itself to
a Sartrean analysis – and in ways that go beyond the comments that
he himself makes on it. For instance, the novels can also be read as
containing brilliant illustrations of another concept central to the
early phase of Sartre's thought: 'being-for-others'. In Part 3 of *L'Etre
et le néant* Sartre explores the implications of this idea – namely, that
my self-consciousness is inextricably bound up with my awareness
of others *as consciousnesses*, and therefore also with the awareness
that I exist as an *object* of the other's consciousness – an object in a
world that is subjectively organised around the other, as opposed to
'my' world which is organised around myself as subject. Therefore,
relations between consciousnesses are fundamentally antagonistic:
each tries to reduce the other to an object in order to maintain his or
her status as subject. Intersubjectivity is based on conflict – although
this conflict may be masked by a number of manœuvres: as Sartre
says, 'Telle est l'origine de mes rapports concrets avec autrui; ils
sont commandés tout entiers par mes attitudes vis-à-vis de l'objet
que je suis pour autrui' (430).

The reader of any of Sarraute's novels is immediately plunged into a psychological milieu of conflict and rivalry; all interpersonal relations, almost without exception, are power struggles, as one character attempts to dominate or manipulate the other. More specifically, these struggles are played out in conversations in which each speaker subtly but ruthlessly tries to reduce the other to the object constituted by the image that the speaker has of him or her. If I can make you accept that you *are* the way I *see* you, then I nullify any power you might have to do the same to me. Moreover, my ability to do this does not depend on any particular individual qualities I may possess: in both its motives and its weapons, the struggle is so universal that most of the time, especially in the later novels, its outcome is unpredictable and always reversible. This accounts for much of the drama of the novels, and it is of course exactly parallel to the situation in Sartre's *Huis Clos*, in which each character is simultaneously victim and torturer of the other two. But in Sarraute's first two novels, *Portrait d'un inconnu* and *Martereau*, which are more exclusively focused on a single central figure, one of this narrator's distinguishing features is that he loses most of his intersubjective battles. In other words, he exists above all as an object for the consciousness of others. I propose, therefore, to give a brief account of some of the ways in which *Martereau* may be seen as a staging of being-for-others.

Its unnamed narrator sees himself as inert, undefended, a vacant space to be overrun by other people: in a striking image (oddly reminiscent of one of Sartre's favourite settings: 'Je suis dans un jardin public . . . ' 1943, 311) he becomes a *park*:

> Ils entrent sans vergogne, s'installent partout, se vautrent, jettent leurs détritus, déballent leurs provisions; il n'y a rien à respecter, pas de pelouses interdites, on peut aller et venir partout, amener ses enfants, ses chiens, l'entrée est libre, je suis un jardin public livré à la foule le dimanche, le bois un jour férié. Pas de pancartes. Aucun gardien. Rien avec quoi on doive compter. (24–5)

In being-for-others, then, my subjectivity is 'stolen' from me by the Other's consciousness; I exist only as the image that he has of me. The predominance of this theme in Sarraute's texts explains the obsessive need the characters have to know (or guess) what this image is. Martereau himself acts – at the beginning and end of the novel – as the dominant subject, with the narrator desperately trying to resist 'mon image [. . .] qu'il plaque aussitôt, férocement, sur moi . . sous laquelle il m'étouffe . . . je gigote pour me dégager, mais il me tient, je cède, il a raison, je me sens cela, je suis cela' (241). Resistance, however, co-exists with a kind of sick fascination – 'l'image que je vois en lui me fascine, je me penche . . . notre image à tous ici: malsains, frivoles, désœuvrés, gâtés' (ibid.) – that Martereau exerts not only on the narrator; the narrator's uncle, too, is fascinated to the extent that he *allows* his behaviour, almost consciously, to be dictated by Martereau: 'fasciné qu'il était probablement, comme cela arrive aux gens nerveux, par cette image de lui-même qu'il voyait en Martereau, exécutant docilement les mouvement que dirigeait en Martereau une baguette invisible' (220–1).

In the first pages of *Martereau* this attitude is developed further, as one of the strategies adopted by the victim; rather than fight against becoming an object, he tries to avoid the conflict by assuming his 'objectness' as it were voluntarily, turning himself into the *perfect* object, carefully removing any trace of subjective activity – that is, judgement on the other – from his presentation of himself. The novel begins: 'Rien en moi qui puisse la mettre sur ses gardes, éveiller tant soit peu sa méfiance. Pas un signe en moi, pas le plus léger frémissement . . . Je me tiens dans la position voulue . . . ' (7) – and in the next paragraph he comments on his 'étrange passivité, cette docilité que je ne suis encore jamais parvenu à bien m'expliquer'. This attitude is similar to what Sartre terms *seduction*, in which I become a fascinating object in order to captivate the other's subjectivity *as* subjectivity: 'Dans la séduction, je ne tente nullement de découvrir à autrui ma subjectivité; je ne pourrais le faire, d'ailleurs, qu'en *regardant* l'autre; mais par ce regard je ferais disparaître la subjectivité d'autrui et c'est elle que je veux m'assimiler. Séduire, c'est assumer entièrement et comme une risque à courir mon objectivité pour autrui, . . . c'est courir le danger *d'être-vu* pour faire un nouveau départ et m'approprier l'autre dans et par mon objectivité' (439). Seen in this light, the narrator is perhaps less a straightforward victim and more manipulative than he claims.

Martereau's dominance, posited at the beginning of the novel and rather ambiguously reinstated at the end, is however severely undermined in the middle sections of the text. There is a lengthy passage in which the narrator imagines Martereau's realisation that, rather than doing the uncle a good turn as one friend to another, he has merely been used by the uncle who despises him. Here two other important aspects of being-for-others are demonstrated: the distinction between the other as an abstract possibility and as a concrete individual, and the relation between being-for-others and reflexive self-consciousness. That is, Sartre explains that certain demonstrable mental states such as *shame* presuppose the existence of other consciousnesses, and that this intuition is the basis of *self*-consciousness. It follows that being-for-others does not depend upon the empirical presence of another person; the Other-as-subject is 'cette présence originelle [qui] est transcendante' (337); and 'l'être-pour-autrui est un fait constant de ma réalité humaine et je le saisis avec sa nécessité de fait dans la moindre pensée que je forme sur moi-même' (339).

The sequence of Martereau's reactions starts with the quintessentially shameful realisation that he has been placed in the rôle of 'straw man': 'la foudre s'abat: un homme de paille: c'est cela' (191) – which he experiences as a paralysing objectification: 'Il reste cloué sur place, pétrifié, calciné: un homme de paille' (ibid.). The 'Other' who has done this to him is at first seen as a purely general, abstract and anonymous 'they': 'Ils sont forts. Ils sont très forts. Ils ne font rien qu'à bon escient. On peut se fier à eux . . . Un homme de paille . . . ils ont découvert cela depuis longtemps [. . .] ils lui ont donné un nom, ils ont étudié toutes ses propriétés [. . .] tout est connu, reconnu, classé: un homme de paille – c'est cela. Et je suis cela, moi, moi! Son homme de paille' (191–2).

But this is immediately followed by a new and separate realisation which identifies the Other-as-subject with the concrete individual – the narrator's uncle: 'Un nouvel éclair, le tonnere, la foudre tombe, il brûle: son homme de paille . . . pour lui aussi . . . *c'est cela que je suis pour lui*' (ibid., my italics). Finally, the third – and most painful – stage consists in Martereau's *own* assumption of his identity as 'straw man' so that it becomes part of his reflexive self-consciousness, and he sees himself as he believes the uncle saw him: 'Nouvel éclair. Atroce brûlure . . . Bien sûr . . . il avait raison [. . .] Martereau entend son propre rire obséquieux, pâmé, mouillé, quand l'autre lui a tapé sur l'épaule' (192); and the episode ends with Martereau's vision of himself as pure object, a mechanical toy activated by the other: 'et l'autre était là qui l'observait, actionnait les manettes, les leviers de commande: il connaissait ces machines à la perfection et celle-ci fonctionnait que c'en était un plaisir' (193).

It would seem, in other words, that the relation between Sarraute's fiction and the earlier phase of Sartre's thought – that represented by *L'Etre et le néant* – is much closer and more productive than his subsequent comments on her would lead one to expect.

MICHEL BUTOR AND *QUESTION DE MÉTHODE*

Butor is undeniably the most Sartrean of the writers associated with the Nouveau Roman. In fact, it may be argued that it is precisely his closeness to Sartre that eventually disqualifies him as a nouveau romancier. But, despite his own emphasis on the difference between his novels and those of Robbe-Grillet, he shares so many of the central concerns of the Nouveau Roman in the 1950s and '60s that any discussion of the movement in this period would be impossible without taking him into account. I have therefore included him in this discussion on these grounds; and for the further reason that the intellectual climate of the Nouveau Roman in general is very alien to Sartre, with the result that critics working within it have tended to underestimate the extent to which Butor's novels are situated within a Sartrean problematic – especially since they relate to the later and more Marxist work, which is less familiar than *L'Etre et le néant* to literary scholars – and it therefore seems worth making the case in some detail.

Butor's own theoretical comments on the writing of fiction, while they do not actually refer to Sartre, are consistently similar to the views expressed in *Qu'est-ce que la littérature?* – when he says, for instance, in reply to a question from Madeleine Chapsal: 'Pour moi il n'y a pas moyen de séparer l'esthétique et la philosophie de l'existence. Toute œuvre d'art doit avoir un certain dessein, un pouvoir, répondre à des situations réelles. Les œuvres d'art sont des solutions à un certain nombre de difficultés' (Chapsal, 61); and, while he rejects the idea that fiction has any power as political propaganda,[26] he also emphasises the writer's moral obligation to become conscious of his work as an instrument of liberation[27] and to address the reader's freedom by constructing the novel as a question: the writer writes in order to 'donner un sens à son existence' (op. cit., 20), but 'Ce sens, il ne peut evidemment le donner tout seul; ce sens c'est la réponse même que trouve peu à peu parmi les hommes cette question qu'est un roman' (ibid.)

Conversely Sartre himself, as we have seen, distinguishes Butor from the rest of the group and approves of his novels completely. His remarks on Butor in 1960 are largely restricted to *Degrés*, published that year, and they centre on its representation of the 'mediations' whereby the individual character is related to the social totality. But the parallels between Sartre's ideas and Butor's fiction extend back further than *Degrés*. Both *L'Emploi du temps* and *La Modification* are based on a very Sartrean view of subjectivity. In 1957 Sartre published in *Les Temps modernes* the article 'Question de méthode', which reappeared three years later as the first part of *Critique de la raison dialectique*. I intend to show how Butor's two best-known novels can be read in the light of the main ideas of 'Question de méthode' – those, in other words, which characterise Sartre's work of the 1950s and '60s, rather than the earlier period of *L'Etre et le néant*.

First, however, it is necessary to give a brief exposition of these ideas. Sartre's starting point is a critique of contemporary Marxist thought which, he says, has betrayed the original Marxist dialectic. Truth can exist only as a *totalisation*, that is, as a moment in a dialectical process: a continual detotalisation and retotalisation, subsuming new contradictions and moving to and fro between the object of analysis and its social-historical environment. Contemporary Marxism, however, is unable to analyse the *specific* factors relating each individual to social reality: it is not enough to say that the poet Paul Valéry is a petty bourgeois because not every petty bourgeois is Paul Valéry. Between the individual and his/her class is a series of *mediations* which must also be identified – above all, the influence of the family, but also the particular choice of profession, and so on. Orthodox Marxism lacks the means to do this, and until it acquires them must be supplemented by the 'auxiliary disciplines' of psychoanalysis and existentialism.[28]

The analysis must work on the multiple dimensions of the significations of human reality: 'chaque signification se transforme, ne cesse de se transformer, et sa transformation se répercute sur toutes les autres. Ce que la totalisation doit découvrir alors, c'est l'*unité* pluridimensionnelle de l'acte' (69). Equally, because of this interrelation, it is not enough to study the object analytically: totalisation, as the term suggests, is also a *synthesis*: 'Les significations superposées sont isolées et dénombrées par l'analyse. Le mouvement qui les a rejointes *dans la vie* est, au contraire, synthétique . . . on perdra de vue la réalité humaine si l'on n'envisage pas les significations comme des objets synthétiques, pluridimensionnels, indissolubles . . . L'erreur est ici de réduire la signification vécue à l'énoncé simple et linéaire qu'en donne le langage' (73).

The above quotation implies that the 'synthetic' approach is closer to the lived experience of the individual being studied. The totalisation, in other words, must also reconstruct the 'subjective moment' of the dialectic of human action. Sartre's other main criticism of orthodox Marxism is that its overly generalising approach results in a mechanistic and deterministic view of the human individual; because the 'mediations' are missing, the individual can only be theorised as the passive product of the socio-economic forces acting on him. But a truly dialectical totalisation of the individual's point of insertion into the social must consider him also as an *agent*, acting as well as acted on. That is, in Sartre's terms, it must take into account the *project*. Man always exists in a situation in which he is constrained by objective conditions, but he also acts on and against these and thus 'depasses' them, arriving at a new equally objective situation which is (partially) the result of his action. The project is thus both a negation of the present given and a positive movement towards some as yet unrealised future reality[29] – which is of course also objectively determined by the subject's 'field of possibilities'. It can never be a complete break with the original situation – the term 'dépassement' implies a dialectic which simultaneously *transforms* and *preserves* the original conditions: 'Fuite et bond en avant, refus et réalisation tout ensemble, le projet retient et dévoile la réalité dépassée, refusée par le mouvement même qui la dépasse' (64). This is particularly relevant when the 'given' to be depassed by the project is the individual's childhood; the child revolts blindly against the social conditioning imposed by the family, but 'Dépasser tout cela, c'est aussi le conserver: nous penserons *avec* ces déviations originelles, nous agirons *avec* ces gestes appris et que nous voulons refuser' (68–9). Since these are retained as well as refused, the past is not only 'depassed' but also 'depassing': the past subsists *as our future* in the sense that the childhood roles still motivate the adult project. Thus for Sartre, 'character' is the combined result of the social conditioning and the project which depasses it while still being inflected by it.

The project is therefore not a completely free, transparent or conscious act. We are not usually fully conscious of our motives or fully able to predict the outcome of our actions; and in the objective result (or 'objectivation') of our action in the world, 'les contradictions originelles qui s'y reflètent témoignent de notre *aliénation'* (69). In fact Sartre's starting point for the section 'Le Projet' situates it in relation to alienation and argues that even if action is alienated it is still *human* action and not wholly determined by objective conditions. Moroever, the project itself in its movement towards the future can *reveal* its own underlying contradictions: 'En nous projetant vers notre possible pour échapper aux contradictions de notre existence, nous les dévoilons et elles se révèlent dans notre action même . . . Ainsi, l'on peut dire à la fois que nous dépassons sans cesse notre classe et que, par ce dépassement même, notre réalité de classe se manifeste' (69). Finally, the project is what defines man as human: 'Pour nous, l'homme se caractérise avant tout par le dépassement d'une situation, par ce qu'il parvient à faire de ce qu'on a fait de lui, même s'il ne se reconnaît jamais dans son objectivation' (63).

The individual's relation to the social is thus a combination of the determinations of the objective situation and the subjective project, and the totalisation must be able to account for both, and for their interaction. Sartre's 'progressive-regressive method' attempts to formalise this double approach. Briefly, the regressive phase is an analytical study of objective factors, and the progressive phase is a synthetic reconstruction of the subjective project. The regressive movement analyses a number of different levels of objective reality and cross-refers between them but keeps them separate: in the case of Flaubert, whom Sartre takes as an example here, it explores his novels, his childhood, existing contradictions in the contemporary petty bourgeoisie, etc., and reveals 'une hiérarchie de significations hétérogènes . . . Chacune éclaire l'autre mais leur irréductibilité crée une discontinuité véritable entre elles' (93). The different levels, in other words, cannot simply be collapsed into one another. The only valid way of synthesising them is by reconstituting the dialectical movement of Flaubert's *project*; and this is where the progressive method comes into play: 'il s'agit de retrouver le mouvement d'enrichissement totalisateur qui engendre chaque moment à partir du moment antérieur, l'élan qui part des obscurités vécues pour parvenir à l'objectivation finale' (93). The progressive-regressive method thus also invokes two different temporalities: the regressive looks *back* at a sequence of facts, while the progressive adopts, at each successive moment of the sequence, the position of the project looking *forward* to the future.[30]

Reading *L'Emploi du temps* and *La Modification* from this perspective, the concepts of alienation and the project immediately become relevant. In both novels the hero is initially characterised above all by his alienation. For Jacques Revel, it is exacerbated by exile; the alienation which Bleston, as an extreme case of all large industrial cities, imposes on all its inhabitants, is intensified in his case by his ignorance of both the city and the English language. He is thrown into an unfamiliar situation in which he feels lost; but, significantly, as his familiarity with it increases, the feelings of blindness and suffocation – 'cet obscurcissement de moi-même' (10) – through which his alienation is experienced do not lessen but actually get worse. For Léon Delmont, it is more clearly linked to his long-term position in society: his job and his lifeless relationships with his wife and children force him into a role (efficient businessman, good Catholic, faithful husband) which, he feels, frustrates and betrays his 'real' self.

The starting point of both novels is the same: the hero's *prise de conscience* of his alienation, which motivates the project of overcoming it. In both cases also the narrative consists entirely in the working through of the project: the writing of Revel's diary, and Delmont's plan – eventually aborted – to leave his wife. The theoretical relation between alienation and project is thus central to the novels. Sartre's stress on their continuing interdetermination is illustrated by the very limited and confused consciousness *with* which the heroes grope towards greater clarity: 'cette conscience qui est malade et encrassée mais qui subsiste et qui cherche maintenant son chemin vers la guérison et le jour' (1956, 112), as Revel describes it. He is tunnelling away in the dark; the project of the diary is 'ce souterrain que je creuse vers mon réveil' (118). The agency of the unconscious is prominent in both novels in the form of dreams, *actes manqués* and so on; and Butor would certainly concur with Sartre's recommendation of the psychoanalytic method as an 'auxiliary discipline'.

There is also a more specifically Sartrean sense in which the project to overcome alienation is *itself* initially conceived in alienated terms, but then the impetus of the project uncovers the contradictions on which it based, with the result that the project is transformed. This is particularly clear in *La Modification*. Delmont's plan to break free of the alienation of his Parisian life is based on an alienated fantasy of Rome: his 'myth of Rome' is a cultural stereotype (the joyful pagan sensuousness of the Roman Empire) produced by the *same* social structures that condition his existence in Paris. Equally, it is based on his belief that he is a completely free agent, undetermined in any way by his socio-cultural environment; he thinks that because he consciously rejects Catholicism, for instance, he thereby escapes all the ideological effects of the Catholic tradition, whereas in reality, as his lover Cécile tells him, he is 'pourri de christianisme jusqu'aux moelles, malgré toutes [ses] protestations' (1957, 168). By the same token, he believes that by a simple act of will he can cut himself free of his past and start a new existence with a new identity.

But once embarked on this project, the contradictions that fissure it inevitably make themselves felt; hence the recurrent image of the 'cracks' that he at first tries to resist – 'Alliez-vous laisser s'augmenter cette mince lézarde qui risquait de . . . faire tomber en poussière tout cet édifice de salut' (109) – but that eventually become 'cette faille de plus en plus large et profonde . . . cette faille où s'engloutissent peu à peu toutes les constructions que vous aviez faites' (281). What this 'detotalisation' involves is the beginnings of a more authentic experience of the individual's subjective relations with his past and with social reality: a recognition of the continuing force of the 'passé dépassant' and hence the impossibility of a clean break with the past, and a new awareness of the social and historical determinations which in part constitute him as an individual. He attains, in other words, a fuller understanding of the individual's point of insertion into the social – exactly what Sartre is trying to do in 'Question de méthode'. It will be achieved through a re-examination of the myth of Rome in its function as mediation between himself and history: 'ce qu'il vous faudrait examiner maintenant à loisir et de sangfroid, c'est l'assise et le volume réel de ce mythe que Rome est pour vous . . . les voisinages de cette face sous laquelle cet immense objet se présente à vous, essayant de le faire tourner sous votre regard à l'intérieur de l'espace historique, afin d'améliorer votre connaissance des liaisons qu'il a avec les conduites et décisions de vous-même et de ceux qui vous entourent' (238).

This involves above all the realisation that the myth of Rome is also a myth of himself: that his belief in his own autonomy is underpinned by a less conscious conception of the relation between individual and social world as a purely formal homology. That is, the myth of Rome is ultimately revealed as a previously unconscious fantasy about *unity*, both in the world and in the *self*: the belief in a 'centred', unified and hence free self is predicated on a nostalgia for the imperial organisation of the world around a central city, for the time 'où le monde avait un centre' (277). Now, however, 'le souvenir de l'Empire est maintenant une figure insuffisante pour désigner l'avenir de ce monde, devenu pour chacun de nous beaucoup plus vaste et tout autrement distribué' (277). Therefore he cannot heal the split in himself merely by rearranging the circumstances of his personal life, because 'cette *fissure béante en ma personne* . . . donne sur une caverne qui est sa raison, présente à l'intérieur de moi depuis longtemps, et que je ne puis prétendre boucher, parce qu'elle est en communication avec une immense *fissure historique*' (274, my italics).

As a result his original intention to leave his wife for Cécile is 'modified' into a decision to write a book in an attempt to clarify his experience and communicate it to other people. But it is not a case of the narrative first pursuing one project, then abruptly switching to another. Rather, the contradiction is there right from the start; every move that Delmont makes in the belief that it is bringing him closer to Cécile is in fact bringing him closer to the realisation that the project is based on bad faith, and hence to 'l'abandon de votre projet sous sa forme initiale qui vous paraissait si claire et si solide' (199). The actual functioning of the project, in other words, escapes his control; it is not he who is directing his thoughts, but a 'machine mentale' (274) consisting of the input of external reality ('s'il n'y avait pas eu ces objets et ces images auxquelles se sont accrochées mes pensées . . . ' (274)) working directly on his unconscious, short-circuiting his conscious attempts to keep the original project on track. The transindividual dimension to his existence, for example, comes out above all in his dreams (in which the Sibyl says to him, 'T'imagines-tu que je ne sais pas que toi aussi tu vas à la recherche de ton père afin qu'il t'enseigne l'avenir de ta race?' (214)).

This has been interpreted by most critics as a psychoanalytically inspired representation of the divided or decentred subject; but it is also possible to see it in Sartrean terms, as evidence of the quotient of alienation at work within the project itself. In fact Sartre, in the interview with Chapsal, comments on precisely this aspect of *La Modification*, seeing the train as acting on the subject, who is thus presented as 'the product of his product': the train as object is given 'son *vrai sens*: un instrument qui transforme celui qui s'en sert' (217). It is this very incomplete *prise de conscience* that motivates the 'transformed' project, which is precisely to achieve a fuller understanding of what has happened to him – Delmont speaks of:

> cette métamorphose obscure ... dont les tenants et aboutissants vous demeurent en grande partie inconnu et sur lesquels il vous serait si nécessaire de projeter quelque lueur, les plus dures études, la plus minutieuse patience n'étant certes point trop payer pour faire reculer un tant soit peu l'ombre, pour vous donner un tant soit peu plus de prise et de liberté sur ce déterminisme qui pour l'instant vous broie dans la nuit. (235)

– and to do so by writing a book. This decision is presented in what Sartre would view as noticeably less alienated terms than the original project, reflecting Delmont's new totalisation of his position in the world. As an explicit search for understanding, it highlights what Sartre sees as an intrinsic feature of the project in general: it produces a certain type of *knowledge*: 'la connaissance est un moment de la *praxis*, ... mais cette connaissance n'a rien d'un Savoir absolu; définie par la négation de la réalité refusée au nom de la réalité à produire, elle reste captive de l'action qu'elle éclaire et disparaît avec elle' (64). Delmont's contribution to an as yet non-existent future freedom is equally provisional and open-ended: his book will not be able to give a definitive explanation of the cultural significance of Rome (274). But it is also seen as engaging its readers' participation in a *collective* struggle for understanding and freedom, and it reiterates Sartre's own emphasis on the need for literature to be orientated towards freedom and the future: 'Je ne puis espérer me sauver seul ... Donc préparer, permettre, par exemple au moyen d'un livre, à cette liberté future hors de notre portée, lui permettre, dans une mesure si infime soit-elle de se constituer, de s'établir' (274).

The notion of totalisation can also provide a description of the way in which the novels are formally constructed. One of the most unusual aspects of *L'Emploi du temps* and *La Modification* is their narrative structure: the complex chronological intercutting of *L'Emploi du temps*, the constant re-working of the same material in *La Modification*. If, as I have said, the narrative coincides completely with the project, we can perhaps interpret these structural features in the light of the *modus operandi* of the project. In Butor's terms, the ultimate aim of the project is to construct a new and more adequate representation of the individual's reality. This translates fairly directly into Sartre's concept of totalisation. In other words, it cannot work in a simple linear fashion but has to build up a network of relations between each separate element of the representation and the whole. 'Totalisation' implies that the significance of any one element depends upon its position in relation to the whole, and simultaneously the significance of the whole will be changed by the reinterpretation of any one of its parts. This is exactly what the 'modification' does to Delmont's original intention. The effect of the 'machine mentale' is to '[faire] glisser l'une sur l'autre les régions de mon existence' (274), to set in motion a collection of fragmentary memories, images which force themselves into his unwilling consciousness where they form new patterns, revealing tensions, contradictions and coincidences as they are continually recontextualised, the representation gradually defining its own gaps and blind spots and filling them in.

But the process of totalisation is even more clearly illustrated in *L'Emploi du temps*. In the first place, this novel shows how reaching a fuller and more concrete understanding of one particular element can throw the whole representation into crisis. Revel has been using Burton's detective story as the foundation of his own representation of Bleston, and has therefore accepted at face value Burton's savage criticism of the New Cathedral. But when he visits it himself, he realises that it has a strange power and beauty of its own which Burton has failed to see; and that therefore he can no longer trust Burton's representation of Bleston (122). He will have to make his own, which will be profoundly different, because in it the relations between the New Cathedral and the rest of the town will be different. In Sartre's terms, 'lorsque l'objet est *retrouvé* dans sa profondeur et dans sa singularité, au lieu de rester extérieur à la totalisation . . . il entre immédiatement en contradiction avec elle' (1960, 94).

This is more important than it would be otherwise because, unlike Delmont, Revel's project is nothing other than to *understand* – to understand both Bleston and his place in it – and this is true right from the start of the novel through to the end. Nevertheless, like Delmont although less dramatically, his project is significantly modified as it proceeds; and in his case the modification is precisely a *discovery* of the concept of totalisation, particularly as it concerns his reconstruction of his past. That is, he starts by thinking that he can adequately represent his past by organising it into a simple one-way linear sequence of incidents – 'car il me faut reprendre possession de tous ces événements . . . *les évoquer un par un dans leur ordre'* (38, my italics) – and that he must recover the original significance which each event has at the time, in isolation from what has happened subsequently; thus in describing his first meeting with Ann Bailey, 'Il s'agit de retrouver cette première entrevue, l'impression qu'elle m'a faite ce jour-là, c'est-à-dire de supprimer tout ce que j'ai su d'elle, tout ce que j'ai vu d'elle par la suite' (40). But he is soon forced to realise that this will not work, because the real meaning of each incident depends also on its relationship to other incidents which are not necessarily contiguous with it in the sequence. With each new chapter, therefore, he introduces a new temporal series; each of these on its own is continuous and unidirectional, but two of them go backwards rather than forwards, and the text cuts constantly between all of them to produce an increasingly complex juxtaposition of different periods of time. As in *La Modification,* this framework allows for a reworking and hence a progressively fuller representation of each period; for instance, Revel writes about July in July, but then what happens in August modifies his perspective on the events of July, and so when in September, as part of a different series, he comes back to writing about July he gives a deeper and more expanded version of it. The text thus becomes increasingly *labyrinthine*: the spatial labyrinth of Bleston which is disorientating and alienating mutates into a temporal labyrinth which has the far more positive connotation of a Sartrean 'enriching' cross-reference between different elements within the whole.[31] Towards the end of the novel Revel gives a long description of the process in terms which demonstrate that he is now committed to a *totalising* view of the past:

Ainsi, chaque jour, éveillant de nouveaux jours harmoniques, transforme l'apparence du passé, et cette accession de certaines régions à la lumière généralement s'accompagne de l'obscurcissement d'autres jadis éclairées qui deviennent étrangères et muettes jusqu'à ce que, le temps ayant passé, d'autres échos viennent les réveiller. Ainsi la succession primaire de jours anciens ne nous est jamais rendue qu'à travers une multitude d'autres antérieurs qui en sont l'origine, explication ou l'homologue, chaque monument, chaque objet, chaque image nous renvoyant à d'autres périodes qu'il est nécessaire de ranimer pour y retrouver le secret perdu de leur puissance bonne ou mauvaise. (294–5)

This passage also makes it clear that the significance of the past depends on the *present*; that is, on the point of view in the present from which the past is viewed. As J. Pouillon puts it, in an article in *Les Temps modernes*, 'il s'agit non plus de retrouver [le passé] dans ce qui fut sa liberté ou son équivoque, mais de le reconstituer dans l'exacte détermination qui le lie au présent du narrateur, de reconstituer "l'emploi du temps"' (1957, 1595). The present in a sense transforms the past; and since the present moment is constantly moving on, the 'truth' of the past is also constantly changing. (This idea is also contained in Burton's analysis of crime fiction, in which the inquiry, which aims to recover a past sequence of events, takes place over a certain amount of time and is affected by new events which occur during its course.)

The present transforms the past because it is often only the results of an action that lead us to seek its causes in the past, and this adds to our objective knowledge of the past – as Revel says, 'les événements qui nous frappent, provoquent une mise en lumière successive de ce qui a mené vers eux' (281). This is thus still within the 'regressive' phase of the totalisation. But the passage on pages 294–5 quoted above also suggests that, by the same token, our position in the present transforms the past *subjectively*, in so far as it determines the changing significance which past events have for us – 'chaque jour, éveillant de nouveaux jours harmoniques, transforme l'apparence du passé', and this is not a simple addition to our knowledge, since 'cette accession de certaines régions à la lumière généralement s'accompagne de l'obscurcissement d'autres jadis éclairées qui deviennent étrangères et muettes jusqu'à ce que, le temps ayant passé, d'autres échos viennent les réveiller'. And each of these present perspectives itself in turn becomes part of the past, and so has to be included in the totalisation. In other words, Revel's reconstruction of the past cannot be limited to objective events, but must also take account of the subjective significance which, at each moment of the past, the past, present and future held for him. That is, it must also reconstruct the history of the project – and this is the progressive phase of the totalisation. Burton, again, defines it in his theory of crime fiction:

> il saluait l'apparition à l'intérieur du roman comme d'une nouvelle dimension, nous expliquant que ce ne sont plus seulement les personnages et leurs relations qui se transforment sous les yeux du spectateur, mais ce que l'on sait de ces relations

et même de leur histoire . . . de telle sorte que le récit n'est plus la simple projection plane d'une série d'événements, mais la restitution de leur architecture, de leur espace, puisqu'ils se présentent différemment selon la position qu'occupe par rapport à eux le détective ou le narrateur. (161)

Where *L'Emploi du temps* differs from and goes beyond Burton's novel is in its recognition of the unfinished nature of any representation – of its status, in other words, as a totalisation: part of an unending dialectical process of detotalisation and retotalisation. Revel's diary will always be incomplete, just as Delmont's book will never be able to 'apporter une réponse à cette énigme que désigne dans notre conscience ou notre inconscience le nom de Rome' (1957, 274).

The Nouveau Roman's reaction against Sartre was vehement but also ambiguous. It operated on several different levels: fiction, theoretical books and articles, live debates and conferences, interviews, and journalistic polemic. I have shown how, on the one hand, the hostility to Sartre became institutionalised and served the mainly psychological function of assuring the group's identity and cohesion, but how on the other hand it proved a valuable springboard for the development and clarification of their ideas about the novel. At the same time, I have indicated the various ways in which their work remained, consciously or unconsciously, within the general framework of Sartrean philosophy. But, of course, the differences that separate them from Sartre are still real and considerable; and to some extent they form the foundation for the Nouveau Roman's far less strained relationship to structuralism, which we must now consider.

2

The Notion of Structure

THE IMPACT OF STRUCTURALISM IN FRANCE

By the middle of the 1960s intellectual life in France, at least as far as the arts and social sciences were concerned, was dominated by structuralism. Claude Lévi-Strauss's work in anthropology had laid the foundations for this somewhat earlier, but it was his *La Pensée sauvage*, which came out in 1962, that had the greatest impact on non-specialist readers. Barthes was very much influenced by him, and contributed significantly to the extension of structuralism to the study of the arts, and literary narrative in particular, with, for instance, *Critique et vérité* in 1966. The year 1966 also saw the publication of Althusser's structuralist version of Marxism in *Pour Marx*, Foucault's *Les Mots et les choses*, and Lacan's *Ecrits*. By this time a kind of structuralist euphoria had taken hold of the intellectual avant-garde, often to the detriment of the more serious proponents of the theory such as the psychologist Jean Piaget, who writes astringently of the need to 'comprendre pourquoi une notion aussi abstraite qu'un système de transformations renfermé sur lui-même peut faire naître en tous les domaines de si grands espoirs' (1968, 8). The phenomenon was particularly evident in literary studies, where an enormous number of structuralist analyses of poetry and narrative were produced.

Since the Nouveau Roman was also at its most popular during this period, and since its authors belonged to the same progressive intellectual milieu as the structuralist theorists (it was associated with Barthes, in particular) there is a tendency to assume that nouveaux romans are in some sense *structuralist novels*. Françoise van Rossum-Guyon, for instance, in her concluding remarks at a major conference on the Nouveau Roman held at Cerisy-la-Salle in 1971, alludes to the impact which the 'avènement du structuralisme' had on the development of the Nouveau Roman (*Nouveau Roman:*

hier, aujourd'hui I, 409).[1] And it is certainly true, in general terms, that through the 1960s the Nouveau Roman's basic challenging of realism increasingly takes the form of a foregrounding of the structural as opposed to the representational aspects of the text. (Although it should be said at the outset that none of this is relevant to Sarraute: structuralism of any kind is completely alien to her novels.) But a focus on structure in this rather loose sense of drawing the reader's attention to the 'shape' of the text does not necessarily amount to structural*ism*. A more precise analysis is needed in order to ascertain what would count as a 'structuralist novel' and whether or to what extent the novels of the nouveaux romanciers fulfil these criteria.

In the first place, therefore, a structuralist definition of *structure* contains several different elements. A structure is a *system*: that is, a totality made up of identifiable elements which are interdependent, so that any change in any one of them affects all the others, and hence affects the system as a whole. Thus the nature of each element depends on its relations with the others: the *relations* take precedence over the elements, which exist only insofar as they are terms of relations.[2] A game of football, for instance, is a system insofar as the position of each player on the field is entirely a function of the positions of the other players and the ball. But the notion of change in one element affecting all the others would not be relevant if the system were static. A structure, in other words, is by definition *dynamic*, involving *changing* relations between its elements: the football players do not stand still on the pitch. But nor do they run about at random; their movements are determined by the changing configuration of positions of all the other players, which in turn is governed by the position of the ball. Moreover, all of this is ultimately determined by the *rules* of the game of football: negatively, in that the rules prohibit certain moves (e.g., offside), but also positively, since the source of all the action on the pitch is the rule which states that the side which scores the most goals wins. In structuralist terms, the rules of football are *transformations*, that is, operations which enable the structure to move through a number of permutations of the relations between its elements. In Piaget's formulation, structures are not only structured but *structuring* (1968, 10–11), and 'une activité structurante ne peut consister qu'en un système de transformations' (11). Transformations are thus *generative* rules: a *fixed* set of operations, but which generates an *indefinite* number of permutations. But they are also formulated in such a way as to *exclude* certain 'moves', and this ensures that the structure as a whole retains its identity: no two games of football are likely to be the same, but they are all recognisably football.[3]

Versions of structuralism have been developed in a wide range of disciplines, including mathematics, logic, physics, psychology and biology. But as far as the Nouveau Roman is concerned, structuralist work in the arts and social sciences is of most relevance. This embodies the claim that all social and cultural behaviour, including the writing of literature, is generated by structures. It takes as its model structural linguistics, which is seen as having a privileged position among the social sciences because it has achieved a greater degree of scientific rigour. Saussure's 'langue-système' envisages language as, precisely, a system of relations; and Lévi-Strauss comments that the key to the development of linguistics as a science has been the discovery 'que la fonction significative de la langue n'est pas directement liée aux sons eux-mêmes, mais à la manière dont les sons se trouvent combinés entre eux' (1958, 230). This fundamental insight – that meaning is a product of the *relations between* linguistic units, rather than being inherent in isolated units – also opens the way for similar analyses in other areas; Saussure's remark that 'dans la langue il n'y a que des différences, *sans termes positifs*' (1915, 166) has inspired work on phenomena as diverse as kinship systems, eating habits, fashion, and James Bond novels.[4] In fact, as these examples suggest, the impact of linguistics was felt first of all in anthropology, through the work of Lévi-Strauss who wrote several articles on the connections between the two disciplines: 'L'Analyse structurale en linguistique et en anthropologie', for instance, gives detailed examples of parallelisms between the two (1958, 37–62).

In analysing social behaviour, the question of the mode of existence of structures becomes particularly acute. Lévi-Strauss claims that structures are not simply a theoretical construct; they are *real*, and have a real determining effect on behaviour. However, they do not exist on the level of empirically observable data; the theorist has to seek out the structure which underlies, and which alone makes sense of, the data, and then to reconstruct it as a formalised model: 'Le structuraliste a pour tâche d'identifier et d'isoler les niveaux de réalité qui ont une valeur stratégique du point de vue où il se place, autrement dit, qui peuvent être représentés sous forme de modèles' (1958, 311). The obvious corollary of this is that in the case of social reality (unlike my example of football, in which the players know the rules) the structures exist *outside* the consciousness of the

subjects who 'perform' them. Lévi-Strauss stresses the importance
of their unconscious nature, which he links with the unconscious
structures of language (1958, 25–8). Piaget in fact sees this as true
of all cognitive structures, in which 'il va de soi que le "vécu" ne
joue qu'un faible rôle, puisque ces structures ne se trouvent pas dans
la conscience des sujets, mais, ce qui est tout autre chose, dans leur
comportement opératoire' (58).

Lévi-Strauss was the first and most important theorist of structuralism in the social sciences in France. Through his anthropological
work, his influence on the whole movement was immense and
ramified; but his theory contains certain ideas which are of especial
relevance to literature. In the first place, his concern with linguistics
went beyond the purely formal level. The question he poses is:
if linguistics as a theoretical discipline provides methodological
procedures which can be adopted by the theoretical discipline of
anthropology and prove useful in the analysis of social behaviour,
'pourrions-nous admettre que diverses formes de vie sociale sont
substantiellement de même nature . . . ?' (1958, 67). That is, are
there substantive parallels between *language* itself and other social
and cultural practices, on the level of their real unconscious structures? He claims that there are, writing for instance that:

le langage apparaît aussi comme condition de la culture, dans
la mesure où cette dernière possède une architecture similaire
à celle du langage. L'une et l'autre s'édifient au moyen d'oppositions et de corrélations, autrement dit, de relations logiques.
Si bien qu'on peut considérer le langage comme une fondation,
destinée à recevoir les structures plus complexes parfois, mais
du même type que les siennes, qui correspondent à la culture
envisagée sous différents aspects. (78–9)

If this is the case, it allows the formulation of a further hypothesis.
The purpose of language is, quite evidently, to produce and convey
meaning; therefore, if all social structures are in some sense like
language, they too may be fundamentally to do with meaning;
verbal language, from this perspective, is merely the most obvious
and accessible of a number of *symbolic systems*. All social relations
can be theorised as forms of *communication of messages*. Lévi-Strauss
concentrates on the two systems of kinship (and marriage rules),
and economic exchanges. He considers 'les règles du mariage et
les systèmes de parenté comme une sorte de langage, c'est-à-dire

un ensemble d'opérations destinées à assurer, entre les individus et les groupes, un certain type de communication' (69). In other words, although a man giving his daughter in marriage to another man is not *consciously* communicating a meaning, women exchanged in marriage are in effect *messages* exchanged between the two social groups; similarly, the circulation of economic goods through the community is another parallel form of communicative exchanges. Lévi-Strauss is not, he says, 'reducing culture to language', but he claims that one can 'interpréter la société, dans son ensemble, en fonction d'une théorie de la communication' (95), and that this can be done on three levels, 'car les règles de la parenté et du mariage servent à assurer la communication des femmes entre les groupes, comme les règles économiques servent à assurer la communication des biens et des services, et les règles linguistiques, la communication des messages' (ibid).

The underlying structures which generate the exchanges are not only unconscious, but – this is one of Lévi-Strauss's most controversial hypotheses – they are also *universal*. That is, not only do the various social and cultural practices share the same structures, but these are also common to all human communities: the question quoted above continues as follows: 'pourrions-nous admettre que diverses formes de vie sociale sont substantiellement de même nature: systèmes de conduites dont chacun est une projection, sur le plan de la pensée consciente et socialisée, des *lois universelles qui régissent l'activité inconsciente de l'esprit?*' (67, my italics). The unconscious is thus redefined as a universal set of symbolic structures which generate and articulate cultural practices. Lévi-Strauss also refers to it as the 'symbolic function', and stresses its difference from more traditional psychological conceptions of the unconscious:

> L'inconscient cesse d'être l'ineffable refuge des particularités individuelles, le dépositaire d'une histoire unique, qui fait de chacun de nous un être irremplaçable. Il se réduit à un terme par lequel nous désignons une fonction: la fonction symbolique, spécifiquement humaine, sans doute, mais qui, chez tous les hommes, s'exerce selon les mêmes lois; qui se ramène, en fait, à l'ensemble de ces lois. (224)

Finally, if the unconscious is a set of structures which produce meaning, and if all social behaviour is symbolic, on the one hand,

and generated by structures, on the other, then we arrive at a redefinition not only of the unconscious but of *meaning* in general, which becomes identified with the concept of structure: in effect, structure *is* meaning, and meaning is structure.

The structuralist approach to literary studies is based on the notion of the symbolic function – the hypothesis of a common set of structural laws, which would justify analysing literary texts in the same way as one analyses language or marriage rules. Here, of course, it is not a question of proving the evident fact that literature is bound up with with meaning and language, but rather of discovering a different, 'deeper' *kind* of meaning in texts. Literary structuralism flourished throughout the 1960s and early '70s, and diversified into a number of different methods. In broad terms, however, two different strands can be distinguished within this overall corpus of theory.

Thus Barthes, for instance, exploits the general concepts of structure and symbolic function to project a 'poetics' which, rather than interpreting *what* a literary work means, will study the structural dynamics *whereby* meanings are produced in texts: 'ce qui est nouveau, c'est une pensée (ou une "poétique") qui cherche moins à assigner des sens pleins aux objets qu'elle découvre, qu'à savoir comment le sens est possible, à quel prix et selon quelles voies' (1964, 218). This project is developed further – and with frequent allusions to Lévi-Strauss – in *Critique et vérite*; here it is set up in opposition to traditional criticism whose overriding concern with 'le vraisemblable', Barthes claims, limits it to supplying commonsensical interpretations of the *content* of texts. Poetics, in contrast, will be 'une science des *conditions* du contenu, c'est-à-dire des formes' (57, Barthes's italics). The object of poetics, in other words, is the *structure* which *generates* meanings – he continues: 'ce qui l'intéressera, ce seront les variations de sens engendrées, et, si l'on peut dire, *engendrables*, par les œuvres: elle n'interprétera les symboles, mais seulement leur polyvalence; en un mot, son objet ne sera plus les sens pleins de l'œuvre, mais au contraire le sens vide qui les supporte tous (ibid.)'.

The notion of the *symbol* is crucial to his theory as a whole. Criticism has to 'poser dans leur plus grande dimension les exigences d'une lecture symbolique' (41); the new criticism he supports is 'une critique explicitement symbolique' (41), and so on. He bases this on Lévi-Strauss's symbolic function (40), but modifies it in the direction of a greater emphasis on 'polyvalence' or *plurality* of meaning: 'des symboles, c'est-à-dire des coexistences de sens' (40). For Barthes, in fact, polysemy is the defining feature of literature: in other words, the structure of literary discourse is such that it necessarily generates multiple meanings. As he formulates it, 'la langue symbolique à laquelle appartiennent les œuvres littéraires est *par structure* une langue plurielle, dont le code est fait de telle sorte que toute parole (toute œuvre), par lui engendrée, a des sens multiples' (53). As this implies, Barthes also concurs with Lévi-Strauss in taking the theoretical model from linguistics; his application of linguistic theory, however – mainly Chomsky's transformational generative grammar – is not very precise or substantial.[5]

His use of structure and symbol to counter the prescriptions of 'le vraisemblable', the stress on generativity, and the idea of the constitutive polysemy of literature, are all in close sympathy with the aims of the Nouveau Roman. Barthes, moreover, draws the further inference that literature's free play of meanings constitutes a *critique* of ordinary language use – the work 'devient une question posée au langage, dont on éprouve les fondements, dont on touche les limites' (55) – and this too rejoins a major concern of the Nouveau Roman. The theory outlined in *Critique et verité*, however, is perhaps less influential in literary structuralism as a whole than the second 'strand' mentioned above, which is based on a more detailed transposition of the concepts of structural linguistics. This, for reasons which will become clear, is far less relevant to the Nouveau Roman's work.

Tzvetan Todorov's contribution to the collective *Qu'est-ce que le structuralisme?* (1968) will serve as a typical example of orthodox structuralist literary theory. While agreeing with Barthes that poetics must study, not individual works, but the specific properties of literary discourse,[6] his conception of these properties is significantly different. Its fundamental hypothesis is that of a narrative 'grammar': like sentences in a language, all narratives are constructed according to general unconscious rules. This implies that they are *constrained* in certain ways; a narrative which did not conform to the rules would be the equivalent of an ungrammatical sentence. Moreover, Todorov, unlike Barthes, is mainly concerned with the detailed elucidation of these rules: structuralist analysis must be explicitly formalised and 'pousser l'analyse jusqu'aux unités élémentaires' (106). The units are fairly closely modelled on linguistic structures; actions are equated with verbs, for instance, and hence divided into 'transitive' and 'intransitive' (e.g. 134–8). In practice this results in a largely *taxonomic*, rather than generative, approach: he classifies different types of narrative causality, point of view, and so on. Transformations figure only marginally.[7] The aim here is throughout to describe and systematise *all* possible narrative forms, and the emphasis is thus on closure and limitations, rather than Barthes's multiple meanings and infinite generativity. This, not surprisingly, has little to offer the Nouveau Roman.

On a deeper level, however, there is a sense in which the epistemological presuppositions of structuralism in general are alien to the views of the nouveaux romanciers. To some extent this is simply a consequence of their position as practising writers; few artists, presumably, would welcome the idea that their work was merely the automatic result of structural laws operating outside their own consciousness, and that it was impossible to break out of these predetermined constraints – impossible, in other words, to produce *new* structures. Lévi-Strauss, on the other hand, repeatedly stresses the advantage to the anthropologist of the fact that the phenomena to be analysed are, precisely, unconscious and therefore beyond the reach of distorting rationalisations on the part of the their subjects.[8] If, then, it is the case that one very important characteristic of structures is that they exist outside the consciousness of the subject who produces or performs them, this means that the writer (or any kind of artist) is in a peculiarly ambiguous position in relation to the structure constituted by his or her text. It is not the position of the theorist who discovers and analyses a pre-existing structure, but nor is it that of the anthropological subject who unconsciously enacts it. Rather, the writer is more or less *consciously producing structures*.

This problem becomes particularly acute in the case of the nouveaux romanciers. More than many other writers, they are committed to producing new kinds of text, and to theorising their own production. The relationship between theory and practice in their work is therefore crucially different from that of the anthropologist or, indeed, the structuralist literary critic. It means that the nouveaux romanciers cannot *theorise* their practice in orthodox structuralist terms because to do so would be to imply that *as novelists* they were not conscious of the structures in their fiction, and this is not the case.

For similar reasons, they do not subscribe to the notion of *universal* laws or 'grammars' inescapably predetermining the structure of all narratives. This conflicts with one of their central aims, which is precisely to contest the dominant traditional structures: the idea of the subversive text which acts as a critique of existing literature assumes increasing importance for them – and will be discussed in detail in Chapter 3. Françoise van Rossum-Guyon produces a variation on this theme when she argues that 'laws' of narrative do exist, but not in any absolute sense such as Lévi-Strauss assumes: 'Ces lois ne sont certes pas comparables à des lois physiques puisqu'elles sont précisément destinées à être perpétuellement modifiées (nous ne partageons pas sur ce point l'optimisme ou plutôt le pessimisme de certains anthropologues)' (NRHA II, 291).

THE NOUVEAU ROMAN AS 'STRUCTURALIST NOVEL'

All of this would seem to limit considerably the relevance of structuralism in general to the theory and practice of the Nouveau Roman. In fact, however, there are important positive connections between them, but situated on the rather different level of the *formal* characteristics of structures. That is, while rejecting most of the epistemological assumptions made by Lévi-Strauss and Todorov, the Nouveau Roman retain and exploit notions such as system and transformation. This severing of the structure from its theoretical moorings sometimes results in a certain vagueness in the nouveaux romanciers' own theoretical writing on the subject, but is undoubtedly productive in their fiction. The third and fourth sections of this chapter will analyse both of these in more detail; firstly, however, we need to summarise in general terms the aspects of the structure that are most relevant to the Nouveau Roman.

The notion of *system* is a dominant feature of their conception of the text, which is seen as a set of relations between elements rather than one or several autonomous entities. Ricardou writes: 'Nous le savons: lire, c'est explorer les relations spécifiques par lesquelles sont liés les éléments d'un texte' (1973, 70). Characters, for instance, are defined relationally: for Butor, the individual is nothing more than the point of intersection of several different groups or sets (1960b, 105–6), and the social milieu which includes them all is itself not an invariant but a system, altering according to the changes undergone by its individual elements.[9] Pronouns, too, are 'structures qui pourront au cours du récit évoluer, permuter, se simplifier ou se compliquer, s'épaissir ou se resserrer' (88).

Moreover, these relations between elements in the text are based on their *formal* similarities rather than the demands of a realistic plot or psychological *vraisemblance*. Ricardou's main point throughout *Le Nouveau Roman* is that its fictional effects are merely a spin-off of the structural patterning. This implies also that the *development* of the text is determined by structural rather than representational considerations, and therefore puts the emphasis on the generative and transformational capacities of structures. Thus he locates in the texts of the Nouveau Roman different kinds of 'opérations génératrices' based on a regulated interplay of similarities and differences (1973, 75–90).

The single most characteristic type of structural relation, and indeed one of the Nouveau Roman's most prominent features, is the *mise en abyme*. So much has already been written about this that I shall discuss it only briefly here.[10] It exists in different forms and has been defined in different ways, but consists essentially in the inclusion within a text of a miniature replica, either of the text as a whole or of some principal aspect of it. Since the *mise en abyme* often takes a pictorial form – much-commented examples are the 'Vitrail du meurtrier' in *L'Emploi du temps*, and the 'portrait de l'ancêtre' in *La Route des Flandres* – it tends to be seen as a *mirror-image* of the narrative. As such it focuses attention on the text in general as structure, i.e. as a metaphorically spatial arrangement of elements, and also sets up a system of relations of formal similarity between itself and the macro-structure of the text in which it is inserted.

Lucien Dällenbach's book *Le Récit spéculaire* traces the development of this technique in the work of the Nouveau Roman from its relatively simple beginnings as a single, static and passive reflexion of the whole to increasingly elaborate versions which put into operation a plurality of 'mirrors', and thus a potentially infinite series of reflexions of reflexions, and so on. One of the best examples of this complexity is Simon's *Triptyque*, which is based entirely on the juxtaposition of three locations: a rural scene, a back street in an industrial suburb, and a seaside resort. There are no diegetic connections at all between these; the basis for their interaction is the fact that each of them contains the two others as *mise en abyme*. A picture of some kind (a jigsaw puzzle, a cinema poster, a postcard, etc.,) depicting one of the settings occurs several times in both of the others. Thus none of them can be established as 'real'; all three are simultaneously macro- and micro-structure, diegetic reality and reflexive image. The system of 'reflections' that this generates is infinitely mobile; the achievement of *Triptyque* is, in Dällenbach's phrase, to 'rendre générateur ce qui, dans la mise en abyme traditionnelle, n'était que passif reflet' (1975, 163–4); and he concludes that it has 'conquis l'espace ambidextre des variantes indécidables et des renvois à l'infini' (ibid., 168).

Lévi-Strauss's concept of 'bricolage' is another version of the generative system, and one which is also popular with the nouveaux romanciers – Simon, for instance, writes: 'Et pour qualifier ce travail de l'écrivain . . . il existe un mot lui convenant admirablement . . . c'est celui de bricolage' (96, Simon's italics). In Lévi-Strauss's own work it is used to elucidate the similarities and differences between the mythical thought of primitive societies and the scientific rationalism of the industrial world. In the first chapter of *La Pensée sauvage*, entitled 'La science du concret', he argues that mythical thought functions as a particular kind of system, which he compares with the method of the 'bricoleur' or amateur handyman. The distinctive characteristic of the 'bricoleur', as opposed to the engineer or scientist, is that he makes something new by working with a *limited collection of objects which have already been used for something else.* (He makes a radio aerial out of a coathanger, for instance.) His raw materials are, precisely, not 'raw' but already artefacts; his work is entirely *transformational,* using whatever odds and ends he has at hand and rearranging them into a new 'system'. Similarly, new mythical meanings are constructed out of the elements of old myths: 'le propre de la pensée mythique est de s'exprimer à l'aide d'un répertoire dont la composition est hétéroclite et qui, bien qu'étendu, reste tout de même limité . . . Elle apparaît ainsi comme une sorte de bricolage intellectuel' (1962, 26).

In other words, bricolage has two fundamentally distinctive features, which concern firstly its materials and secondly its procedures. The elements of bricolage which are put together to construct the new meaning are not pure neutral forms, but themselves 'old' meanings, fragments of a whole cultural context, 'témoins fossiles de l'histoire d'un individu ou d'une société' (32); and this kind of conceptual re-cycling has an obvious relevance to that aspect of the Nouveau Roman's work which is concerned with working on cultural stereotypes (see Chapter 3). Secondly, the 'bricoleur' does not work according to a pre-conceived rational plan. Lévi-Strauss's emphasis on the unconscious nature of structures, in this instance the structures of mythical narratives, would clearly preclude the myth-makers having a theoretical or scientific consciousness of their work. But the notion of bricolage in effect softens the otherwise absolute opposition between conscious and unconscious, in that the bricoleur is not presented as purely passive, or purely 'acted upon' by the structures. His activity is untheorised but not unconscious; and this formulation provides a way out of the problem of the point of view of the practising artist, by making it much easier for the nouveaux romanciers to accomodate themselves to the notion of structure, as bricolage. The bricoleur is engaged in *experimenting* with various different arrangements of elements to see if they will 'work' or not. For Simon this conveys exactly 'le caractère tout à fait artisanal et empirique' (1972, 96) of the writer's work; and Barthes sees it as the structural principle underlying all Butor's novels: 'c'est en *essayant* entre eux des fragments d'événements, que le sens naît, c'est en transformant inlassablement ces événements en fonctions que la structure s'édifie: comme le bricoleur, l'écrivain . . . ne *voit* le sens des unités inertes qu'il a devant lui qu'en les *rapportant*' (1964, 186).[11]

Bricolage in addition provides a useful model for the *nouveaux romanciers'* own conception of *language*. There is no definitive difference between the set of elements which constitutes the 'repertoire' and the set of elements which constitutes the new structure: it is merely a new arrangement, which will itself eventually be dismantled in order to make something else. Therefore no stable distinction can be made between means and ends: or in other words, since myths are systems of signification, between signifier and signified;[12] and this provides strong corroboration for the Nouveau Roman's own refusal to see language as a simple one-way instrument for conveying meanings.

Finally, however, it is the fundamental conception of meaning as such that emerges from structuralism which has the deepest influence on the Nouveau Roman. The equation of meaning with structure, when applied to literary texts, effectively blocks the separation of form and content which all the nouveaux romanciers are working to overcome. Meaning can no longer be considered as *extractable* from the text: it is not an explicit 'message' put in the mouth of the hero, for instance, whence it can be retrieved by the reader. Rather – and this is evident particularly in the novels of Robbe-Grillet and Butor – it is a product of the system as a whole. As Barthes comments in the case of *Mobile*, it is the 'mobilisation d'unités récurrentes' whose 'déplacements . . . assurent à l'œuvre la responsabilité de son choix, c'est-à-dire sa singularité, *c'est-à-dire son sens*' (1964, 185–6, my italics). In a system of relations between interdependent parts, meaning is necessarily *differential*, as opposed to the *referential* conception of meaning that underpins traditional realism in literature. Structuralism, in other words, offers a theorisation of the anti-realist construction of meaning that is a central feature of the Nouveau Roman.

BUTOR VERSUS ROBBE-GRILLET AND RICARDOU: DIFFERENT CONCEPTIONS OF STRUCTURE

The rather general and abstract concepts discussed above are important to the work of all the nouveaux romanciers (with, as already mentioned, the notable exception of Sarraute). However, it is also the case that the structuralist influence takes significantly different forms in the theoretical writing of the individual members of the Nouveau Roman. In particular there are quite basic divergences between Butor on the one hand, and Robbe-Grillet and Ricardou (supported by Simon) on the other. These centre around two distinct but related issues: the relationship between literary structure and the real, and the status of structural 'laws' or rules.

Butor states repeatedly that the purpose of the structures (or 'schémas') in his texts is to permit a clearer and deeper understanding of the reality we live in. Structure is 'un moyen de forcer le réel à se révéler' (1960b, 17). Otherwise there is no point in it, as he tells Charbonnier: 'Je ne fais ce travail souvent considérable d'organiser des schémas que dans la mesure où je constate, où j'éprouve que ce schéma me permet de voir ce que je veux voir, ce que j'ai besoin de voir' (Charbonnier, 68). Hence he often compares his 'schémas' to photographic lenses or to mirrors, suggesting that they have both a didactic and a *mimetic* function: 'Ainsi ce système de significations, qui est à l'intérieur du livre, va être une *image* du système de significations à l'intérieur duquel le lecteur est pris, dans toute sa vie quotidienne, et à l'intérieur duquel il est perdu' (1960b, 24, my italics). Indeed, they depend on a preliminary analysis of 'reality' into *its* signifying systems, which the novel then reproduces in a more intelligible form: 'les systèmes littéraires ne peuvent exister que dans la mesure où il y a déjà des systèmes de signification dans la réalité, et dans la mesure où on en retrouve et en amplifie le fonctionnement' (30).

Robbe-Grillet takes the opposite view; the structures in his texts make no claim to reveal reality, and he disagrees fundamentally with Butor on the issue of *truth* in this context. He argues that while their writing shares formal characteristics such as 'la polysémie du texte, la littérature comme jeu, l'écriture productrice, les nombres générateurs' (NRHA II, 279), in Butor's case all of these are subordinated to, and hence in a sense defused by, 'cette notion de vérité supérieure qui juge et domine' (284). Robbe-Grillet continues: 'On s'aperçoit alors qu'un mot comme polysémie a deux sens complètement différents selon qu'il existe une vérité supérieure, donc unique, ou qu'il n'en existe pas. La polysémie du texte n'est chez Butor que la dispersion d'une présence globale tandis que chez nous, au contraire, cette polysémie instaure une opposition de sens irréductibles' (284).

As this implies, Robbe-Grillet's own use of textual structure is far more *playful* – a free-floating game of multiple, contradictory or self-cancelling meanings which is no longer attached in any direct sense to the real world (although it can be harnessed to an ideological critique, as will be discussed in Chapter 3). The notion of 'le jeu' in its various meanings (game, free play, even gambling) is basic to his writing. Its significance is that whereas 'le sérieux suppose qu'il y a quelque chose derrière nos gestes: une âme, un dieu, des valeurs, l'ordre bourgeois . . . derrière le jeu, il n'y a rien. Le jeu s'affirme comme une pure gratuité' (ibid.). Like bricolage, structure as play also ensures that any pre-existing meaning system can be transformed; none are absolute or eternal, as the tragic, for instance, claims to be: 'Le jeu dénonce ce tragique comme étant une création humaine, qu'une autre création humaine peut détruire' (NRHA I, 97).

Thus for Robbe-Grillet – and Ricardou, who describes Robbe-Grillet's fiction approvingly as 'une mise en place de dispositions narratives susceptibles d'*obtenir de variables réalités*' (1967, 33, my italics) – there can be no question of finding the *right* structure in order to illuminate the real world we live in. Rather, structure facilitates the *freedom* of the text to produce variation and multiplicity. This basic difference with Butor also affects their respective attitudes towards the question of structural laws. For Butor, the structure as mechanism for revealing reality has to be clear, explicit and controlled; its intelligibility presupposes an overall coherence and logic, in which: 'Il y a la composition de l'œuvre, et la forme de chaque phrase, le choix de chaque mot doit en être une conséquence' (1960b, 180). Therefore, his structures are elaborated on the level of the text as a whole, and function as *totalities*. He describes how 'l'ensemble des relations de ce que [le roman] nous décrit avec la réalité où nous vivons' – which he calls its 'symbolisme externe' – is illuminated, 'si la forme qu'il emploie est suffisamment intégrante', by being reflected within the novel, in the relation of its parts to its totality (1960b, 12). Equally, the novel becomes 'poetic' not by including passages of poetic prose, but 'dans sa totalité' (42): 'A tous les niveaux de cette énorme structure qu'est un roman, il peut y avoir style, c'est-à-dire forme, réflexion sur la forme, et par conséquent prosodie' (43). In other words, it is by being integrated into 'strong forms' that ordinary reality becomes revelatory and hence 'poetic': 'Ainsi ce sont des pans entiers de banalité, de réalité quotidienne, qui, transfigurés par la lumière des formes fortes, vont luire d'une phosphorescence inattendue' (45). The advantage of a tightly structured totality is, he says, that it allows even the absence of an element to be significant, because its absence will be made perceptible; the text as a whole will 'faire sentir ainsi qu'il y a une lacune dans le tissu de ce que l'on raconte ou quelque chose que l'on cache' (119). And Butor's own texts do indeed strike the reader above all as coherent, integrated totalities.[13]

This also means that Butor places far more emphasis than do Robbe-Grillet and the others on a *systematic* method in which there are structural 'rules' underlying and generating the whole text: not the unconscious laws presupposed by Lévi-Strauss, but entirely deliberate inventions on the part of the writer. Thus he attributes the 'revelatory' powers of the modern novel to the writer's effort to '[se servir] de structures *suffisamment fortes* . . . comparables à des structures géométriques ou musicales, en *faisant jouer systématiquement* les éléments les uns par rapport aux autres' (1960b, 16, my italics). Commentators on Butor's work stress its rigorousness, but at the same time the impression it gives that each text could go on for ever, a particular combination of constraint and infinite expansion.[14] This implies a set of rule-governed transformations of the structure: rules which are fixed and apply in uniform and specified ways, but are capable of generating an *infinite* series of transformations of the original structure. In practice, Butor's novels do not entirely fulfil this programme: the first, *Passage de Milan*, is structured in a fairly simple and static way by devoting one chapter to each hour of the night in question. *L'Emploi du temps*, however, which Butor describes as 'fondé sur une structure très stricte' (Charbonnier, 106) is generated by a rule which 'states' that one new chronological sequence must be added in each chapter, and that it can proceed either forwards or backwards in time. That is, the basic structure is here genuinely transformational, expanding and becoming more complex with each new series. Moreover, since the series are 'allowed' to cover the same ground (May occurs in the second and third series, June and July in the second and fourth) there is no reason why the transformation should not continue to apply ad infinitum: if Revel had stayed in Bleston, each month could have inaugurated a new series going either backwards or forwards. *La Modification*, in contrast, is a more 'closed' structure: the full set of different train journeys which are interwoven in the text is present from the start, and there is the sense of a definite resolution at the end.

In *Degrés* the possibility of infinite expansion returns. Here the narrator, Pierre Vernier, sets out to describe, exhaustively, one particular class he has given, and finds that the demands of exhaustiveness draw him, by 'degrees', further and further outwards from the class itself into the relations between pupils and teachers, their families, their neighbourhoods, etc. Butor conceived *Degrés* above all as an exercise in plurality; he tells Charbonnier that he wanted it to be not an individual adventure but 'des masses d'aventures, des organisations d'aventures à l'intérieur desquelles chaque aventure individuelle puisse être considéré comme un détail' (Charbonnier, 13). Within this 'mass', therefore, he introduces various different principles of organisation. Some of these are not transformational in the strict sense: for instance, the rule that makes the narrative circulate around the different lessons, which Butor formulates as 'four-dimensional cubes', i.e., the three spatial dimensions of the classrooms plus the temporal position of the lesson on the timetable: 'ce sont des cubes qui se sont posés les uns sur les autres, avec toutes sortes de rythmes qui les lient' (Charbonnier, 16). Another rule starts off as an apparently similar non-transformational principle of selection: Vernier will describe those pupils and teachers who are connected by kinship relations that form triangles of uncles and nephews. Thus he himself is the uncle of Pierre Eller, but Eller also has another uncle, Henri Jouret, on the staff. This triad of two uncles and a nephew is paralleled by the pupil Regnier who has two teacher uncles, Bonnini and Hubert; and inverted in the triangle consisting of the teacher Bailly and his two nephew/pupils, Mouron and Daval.

But in order to make the system account for a larger number of pupils and teachers, the 'degree' of relatedness has to be *transformed* into something looser and more problematical, moving gradually further away from the original direct uncle-nephew link: 'M. Hutter, le professeur d'allemand, est à l'autre bout de l'étage, avec ses troisième. Je sais maintenant le degré de sa parenté avec son homonyme Francis Hutter . . . Il faut remonter assez loin: Frédéric Hutter, grand-père de M. Alfred Hutter, avait un cousin germain, Emile Hutter, l'arrière-grand-père de Francis' (34). The process reaches a final stage when he forms a group in which 'ces relations [de parenté] . . . sont d'un degré indéfini, équivalentes pour ce que j'en sais, à celles qui peuvent exister entre deux élèves pris au hasard et l'un de leurs professeurs dans n'importe quelle classe de n'importe quel lycée' (89). In other words, the text exploits the fact that any system of kinship relations is in principle infinite, turning it into a structural rule which transforms the uncle-nephew link into increasingly distant relations. For Butor, that is, the systematic and rigorous nature of the generative rules does not lead to a static or closed text; far from precluding open-endedness, it is in his view an essential precondition for it.

Ricardou's *Le Nouveau Roman* gives a view of the text which initially appears to be similar: a dynamic system of operations which change the relations between its elements. He also places great emphasis on *order* (as in *Pour une théorie du Nouveau Roman*, for instance, where he defines the novel in general as 'un ensemble soumis à un ordre' (85)), and his general style is extremely prescriptive. In fact, however, the notion of *rule* plays very little part in his theory, and he is less concerned with the text as a totality than he is with structures on a much smaller scale. His 'operations', in other words, do not govern the novel as a whole, but intervene at certain points in the text to effect 'transitions' from one sequence to the next.[15] Moreover, despite occasional references to the 'laws' of the text ('s'élaborant ouvertement selon de spécifiques lois, le texte moderne . . . ' (1971, 232)), his operations are in fact techniques rather than rules, as his predominant use of the term 'dispositifs' implies. That is, their functioning does not *constrain* the text in any way; whereas the generative rule of *L'Emploi du temps*, for instance, excludes the possibility of any chapter having *fewer* temporal series than the preceding one, Ricardou's generative operations do not exclude anything. Thus although he refers to the 'contraintes' governing Simon's novel *La Bataille de Pharsale*, he immediately goes on to say: 'En leur variété, ces contraintes forment un ensemble sans limites; nous n'envisageons pas ici, même au niveaux des types, leur exhaustif recensement. De plus, dès que certaines sont élues lois de composition du texte, elles risquent de respectivement se contredire' (1971, 118). Instead, for instance, he identifies as one particular operation 'la mise en image' (1973, 112) whereby a diegetically real sequence is suddenly transformed into a pictorial representation; but this 'capture' occurs quite arbitrarily, any number of times and at any point in the text. His conception of generativity, in other words, is not rule-governed; the text is *freely* generative. Because of this, and because the structures he defines are often as small as individual words, he at times comes close to a more traditionally 'poetic' view of generativity as based on the polysemic or associative powers of words – as when he analyses the first sentence of his own novel *Les Lieux-dits* (1973, 70–71).[16]

Equally, the lack of constraints means that the elements in the system are less interdependent. This becomes clear if one compares Ricardou's formulation with, for instance, Lévi-Strauss's analysis of marriage laws, in which any one marriage has repercussions on the whole system because, through the incest taboo, it excludes a number of others in the next generation. In the case of Ricardou's textual operations, though, each element can as it were go its own way: as a result, the concept of system is itself weakened. There are some exceptions to this approach in *Le Nouveau Roman*; some of the novels Ricardou refers to are discussed in terms of rules governing their overall structure (e.g., *Les Gommes*, 32–7, *La Modification*, 39–42). But he does not make any theoretical distinction between these, which appear as 'structuralist novels' in a more precise sense, and the others which do not. What he provides in *Le Nouveau Roman* is thus essentially a *taxonomy* of operations, organised into their different types. For example, the 'variantes' are classified according to the different relations they set up between individual elements and the sequence as a whole: 'départ', 'permutation', 'substitution', 'transformation' (101). These are referred to as 'diverses règles de métamorphose' (ibid.): but the notion of rule has no real force here, because between them they cover every possibility, any of them could occur at any point, and none of them has to.

Despite the quasi-structuralist rhetoric of Ricardou's presentation, in other words, he is not really engaged in defining the novels in question as structures – as rule-governed transformational totalities – but rather in presenting a repertoire of techniques characteristic of the Nouveau Roman. In a sense his position hovers between a classically structuralist concern with order and rigour, and the post-structuralist approach evident in, for instance, Barthes's *S/Z*. This, in its emphatic rejection of the notions of totality and universality, and its replacement of structure with an on-going, localised process of *structuration*, actually provides a theoretical framework far more consistent with Ricardou's descriptions of textual operations than his own, obscured as this is by his apparent reluctance to relinquish the terminology of 'ensembles', 'lois de permutation', and so on. Barthes's approach to the *analysis* of Balzac's story points the way forward towards a *programme* for the theorisation of the Nouveau Roman's own texts: 'Il s'agit en effet, non de manifester une structure, mais autant que possible de produire une structuration. Les blancs et les flous de l'analyse seront comme les traces qui signalent la fuite du texte; car si le texte est soumis à une forme, cette forme n'est pas unitaire, architecturée, finie: c'est la bribe, le tronçon, le réseau coupé ou effacé . . . ' (*S/Z*, 27).

A formulation like this is equally pertinent to the work of Simon and Robbe-Grillet, whose interpretations of structure are more or less congruent with that of Ricardou. It is true that Simon is more concerned than Ricardou with the construction of the text as a whole, referring in his paper 'La Fiction mot à mot' to the need for 'un modèle . . . une quelconque logique faute de quoi il y aurait, dans un texte, discontinuité' (1972, 78), and for some coherent principles of construction without which 'il n'y a pas de véritable discours littéraire, c'est-à-dire un système structuré, mais seulement, alors, en effet, simple succession, sinon même cacophonie' (81). But his final emphasis is on the notion of bricolage, which he interprets in such as way as to maximise its *ad hoc, non*-rule-governed aspects: 'Cela se fait par tâtonnements successifs' (96–7) – emphasising, in other words, structuration rather than structure. Robbe-Grillet, similarly, stresses the intuitive, non-explicit and above all *free* nature of the process of constructing a text: during the Cerisy conference on his work, he reacts vehemently to a question from Dällenbach about a pre-existing logic governing the texts: 'Non, très nettement non: la liberté, nécessaire pour moi à la pratique de l'écriture, empêche que tout système puisse apparaître comme une directive' (1976, II, 419). At the earlier NRHA conference this opposition between system and freedom appears in a more nuanced form; his comments on the importance of the notion of 'le jeu' in his writing lead him to a comparison of the novel with a game of cards, but with the difference that the writer, unlike the card-player, can change the rules as he goes along:

Le jeu, tel que je viens de le définir, prend d'autant plus son sens qu'il s'agit de jouer avec le langage et non plus avec des cartes, où les règles existent avant que le jeu ne commence. Avec le langage, au contraire, il n'y a pas de règle définitive: votre organisation du jeu dans votre main, la bataille sur la table seront en même temps la création des règles, la création du jeu et l'exercice de votre liberté, donc aussi bien la destruction des règles, pour laisser de nouveau le champ libre à l'homme libre qui viendra encore après. (NRHA I, 128)

It will have become clear that there are several different senses in which individual nouveaux romans could be considered at least partially 'structuralist', and consequently there are many different novels which could be discussed in those terms. It seems preferable, however, to concentrate on a fairly detailed study of a small number of texts; the problem is one of choosing between a number of texts which all offer considerable scope for such an analysis. Brief reference has already been made to Butor's novels and to Simon's *Triptyque* (although the latter's *Les Corps conducteurs* and *Leçon de choses* would be equally worthy of mention in this context). Ricardou's novels are in some ways the most 'structuralist' of all; but he has himself analysed them in detail[17] and the texts themselves are less widely read than those of the other authors. I propose, therefore, to limit the discussion to two novels by Robbe-Grillet.

LES GOMMES AND *LA MAISON DE RENDEZ-VOUS*: CIRCULARITY AND CIRCULATION

Les Gommes was Robbe-Grillet's first published novel. It came out in 1953, in other words at least eight or nine years before structuralism made an impact upon intellectual and literary life in France. It is therefore extremely unlikely that Robbe-Grillet was influenced by the subsequently fashionable idea of text as structure. This makes it all the more surprising that *Les Gommes* is in many ways a more classically structuralist novel than his later work; it exhibits precisely the kind of overall rigour that we see Robbe-Grillet rejecting in the descriptions of his own work that he makes later in the 1960s and '70s. It is, in other words, a *rule-governed totality*. At the same time, however, it is also an *anti*-structuralist novel, in so far as it remains within a diffusely but distinctively existentialist ideology characteristic of much French fiction of the 1950s. Thematically, notions of alienation and nostalgia for individual human freedom produce a kind of subdued pathos which is very deliberately counterposed to the mechanical regularity of the structure.

La Maison de rendez-vous, on the other hand, is neither structuralist nor anti-structuralist in this way. Published twelve years later, it has none of the vestigial humanism of *Les Gommes*; equally, it is based on the more ludic version of structuralism – as 'jeu' and free generativity – proposed by Ricardou and, indeed, Robbe-Grillet himself. The two texts are thus very different.

Les Gommes functions as a system of relations between elements; these relations undergo transformations according to certain defined constraints, and the structure as a totality is the result of the transformations. To substantiate this proposition, we need first to identify what the elements of the system are. The novel is a parody of a detective story. Wallas, special agent, is sent to investigate the supposed murder of Daniel Dupont, on a Monday evening, by a group of terrorists. Dupont has indeed been shot by Garinati, one of the terrorists, but is only slightly wounded; he decides, however, to pretend that he is dead, and remains in hiding in the doctor's clinic to which he has been taken. Wallas's investigation leads him to believe that the murderer will return to Dupont's house at 7.30 p.m. on Tuesday, exactly twenty-four hours after the original attack, and he goes there to wait for him; coincidentally, Dupont himself returns at the same time to collect some papers, armed with his pistol; Wallas mistakes him for the murderer, and kills him in self-defence.

Throughout the novel, there is very little individual characterisation: Wallas, Dupont, Garinati, the doctor, the local police chief, etc., are mere agents of the plot; in fact they are often defined as simply pawns in a game that is being played by unknown forces on a higher level. They are nothing over and above the roles that they perform, and these roles in turn are constituted by the configuration of relations set up by the crime. Since they exist only as detective, victim, murderer, or, in the case of the minor characters, witnesses and/or suspects, they would not exist at all without the murder of Dupont, and this system of relations is all the more determining in that it is apparently taken ready-made from the stereotypes of crime fiction. But here, of course, the murder does not exist either – at first.

Wallas is investigating a crime which has not happened. Thus the initial system of relations is actually structured not by a real event but by an *erroneous perception* of a (non-)event; the classic triad of detective-victim-murderer is infiltrated by a disjunction between the real and the falsely supposed:

(1) Wallas = 'real' detective.
(2) Dupont = 'false' victim.
(3) Garinati = 'false' murderer.

It is only this particular version – or perversion – of the triangular structure which allows its elements to be permuted. In the classic detective story, the identities of the detective and (usually) the victim are known and stable, and the whole duration of the narrative focuses on the single unknown identity of the murderer: when that becomes known, the narrative ends. In *Les Gommes*, in contrast, the narrative consists in the *transformation* of the triad into a relation with only two terms:

(1) Wallas = 'real' murderer.
(2) Dupont = 'real' victim (and 'false' murderer).

One function (detective) and one character (Garinati) have thus been eliminated, Dupont has been transformed from a man pretending to be dead into a real corpse – *because* Wallas mistakes him for the murderer – and, above all, Wallas has been transformed from detective into murderer. The dynamic of the narrative, in other words, can be said to be the *permutation* of the element 'Wallas' within the system.

But this has further consequences on the novel. There is a necessary link between the transformations described above and the fact that the structure of the narrative as a whole is a *closed circle*. There is only one murder; Wallas's transformation takes place in relation to the *same* victim. In other words, the real import of his actions throughout the narrative escapes him: he thinks he is investigating a murder which has already happened; the reader knows that it has not; but what neither Wallas nor the reader knows is that Wallas's actions are in fact leading up to his murder of Dupont. The narrative is thus circular: it begins and ends at the 'same' point, with the 'murder' of Dupont.[18] Or, as the text tells us: 'Il n'est jamais trop tard. L'acte manqué revient de lui-même à son point de départ pour la seconde échéance . . . ' (103). The circularity is reinforced by smaller 'circles' within the main narrative: for instance, the third section of the prologue opens with the words: 'On ne meurt pas si vite d'une petite blessure au bras. Allons donc!' (27) and closes with: 'Petite blessure au bras. Allons donc! On ne meurt pas si vite' (30). Thus the notion of structural *generativity* is here very much curtailed; whereas *L'Emploi du temps* or *Degrés*, for instance, are based on structures which are both systematically constrained and infinitely transformable, *Les Gommes* generates a fixed number of transformations which bring the narrative back to its starting point, where it simply and necessarily stops.

Barthes calls *Les Gommes* 'l'histoire d'un temps circulaire, qui s'annule en quelque sorte lui-même après avoir entraîné hommes et objets dans un itinéraire au bout duquel il les laisse *à peu de chose près* dans l'état du début' (1964, 38). The narrative *auto-destructs* within its allotted duration: the events of the twenty-four hours should never have happened, and it is as if they had never happened. (Wallas notes that his watch, which had stopped at the time of Garinati's shooting, starts again when he himself shoots Dupont, and is thus still perfectly accurate.) And yet it is precisely this self-cancelling of the events of the narrative that gives it, paradoxically, its character of rigorous necessity. Wallas and Garinati both bungle their assignments; Garinati does not kill Dupont, and Wallas does. But once the first mistake has occurred, the second one *has* to happen in order to cancel out the first one, so that order is restored. In other words, the narrative is both superfluous and necessary: a closed auto-destructive circularity.

The sense of inevitability produced by the obvious symmetries and the tightly structured dramatic irony is reinforced by the very paucity of causal links on the level of Wallas's actions. He does not pursue a logical or even very purposeful course; he seems to drift around the town at the mercy of a series of accidents, coincidental meetings, missed connections, loose ends which are never tied up, and so on. In particular, his fatal presence in the house at 7.30 on the second evening is motivated solely by a mysterious postcard sent to the police station, presumably by the gang of terrorists, but for no apparent reason. All of this serves to create the impression that the narrative is being propelled onwards by more abstract forces working on a purely structural level: a kind of structural *need* to overcome the hiatus cause by Garinati's error, and thus to complete the circle, through the transformation of Wallas from detective to criminal. Ricardou points to the temporal precision also needed to accomplish the auto-destruction of the narrative: temporally as well as in terms of content, the epilogue is superimposed exactly on the prologue, with an interval of exactly twenty-four hours between them.[19]

It is above all this rigorous logic that gives *Les Gommes* the character of a rule-governed structure. But its transformations also result in a different kind of 'cancelling out' which can equally, if more loosely, be formulated as a structural rule – and, moreover, one which is found in most of Robbe-Grillet's novels. In principle, and at the outset of the novel, the relation between detective and murderer is one of opposition. But Wallas's transformation from detective to murderer in effect *neutralises this opposition*; he takes over the role of his opponent. This is underlined throughout the text by a series of parallels and coincidences which, right from the start, place Wallas as Garinati's *double*: for instance, the prologue ends with Garinati standing by the canal reflecting on his failure to kill Dupont and thinking: 'Un autre à sa place . . . viendrait . . . accomplir son œuvre d'inéluctable justice' (41); and Chapter I introduces Wallas standing at exactly the same place. This coincidence is later developed into a sustained undermining of the whole concept of individual *identity*: Wallas is mistaken (by the drunkard in the bar and the woman in the Post Office) for another of the conspirators, the mysterious 'André VS'; the opposition between criminals and policemen is 'gommé' by the Commissioner's decription of his force as 'une police qui entretient des rapports si intimes avec ceux qu'elle surveille. Chez nous, entre le policier intègre et le criminel, on rencontre tous les intermédiaires. C'est sur eux que repose notre système' (72).

These are examples of a feature which Gérard Genette sees as fundamental to all Robbe-Grillet's writing: namely, a pervasive *erasure* of the opposition which lies at the root of all oppositions – that between *identity* and *difference*. He interprets Robbe-Grillet's predilection for doubles, reflections, etc., as an unstable compromise between these opposites, infiltrating otherness with similarity and identity with alteration. From this 'rapport ambigu, [qui] sous ses formes diverses et complémentaires, est l'âme même de l'œuvre de Robbe-Grillet' (1966, 84), he deduces a 'nécessité de structure': 'cette relation de ressemblance dans l'altérité, ou d'altération dans l'identité, qui circule entre les objets, les lieux, les personnages, les situations, les actes, les paroles' (ibid.). In other words, the texts are generated by a constant destabilisation of the two poles of identity and difference; the same irresistibly mutates into difference, and vice versa. In the form of a basic narrative structure, this principle applies more fully to *La Maison de rendez-vous* than to *Les Gommes*, and will be discussed further in that context; but it is relevant to *Les Gommes* particularly in the matter of the transformation of roles. Wallas, for instance, is the double not only of Garinati, but also of Dupont: the final murder scene duplicates exactly the position of the two men in the first version, but with the difference that Wallas is occupying *Dupont*'s position behind the desk in the study, while Dupont enters just as Garinati had done; and Wallas and Dupont both own a pistol of the same make, both with one cartridge missing.

Genette's idea of a narrative structure that works to neutralise oppositions is particularly interesting in the context of the general structuralist theory outlined at the beginning of this chapter. Some of Lévi-Strauss's most important work is on the analysis of myths; and one of the main discoveries formulated in his 'La Structure des mythes'[20] is that:

> la pensée mythique procède de la prise de conscience de certaines oppositions et tend à leur médiation progressive . . . deux termes, entre lesquels le passage semble impossible, sont d'abord remplacés par deux termes équivalents qui en admettent un autre comme intermédiaire. Après quoi, un des termes polaires et le terme intermédiaire sont, à leur tour, remplacés par une nouvelle triade, et ainsi de suite . . . On obtient ainsi des médiateurs au premier, au deuxième et au troisième degré, etc., chaque terme donnant naissance au suivant par opposition et corrélation. (248–9)

This operates as a sequence of transformations within the mythical narratives. A simplified version of one of his examples is the following. The myth is 'trying' to resolve the opposition between life and death; it replaces these terms with those of *agriculture* (food-producing, i.e., life-giving) versus *warfare* (killing people); these two generate an intermediary term which is *hunting* (killing animals, but in order to produce food); the second-level opposition between agriculture and hunting is transformed into that between *herbivorous animals* (which eat plants, like agricultural peoples) and *beasts of prey* (which, like hunters, kill and eat other animals); finally, this opposition is 'mediated' by the third term of *carrion eaters*, which do not kill other animals but do eat them once they are already dead. This, he claims, explains why the coyote and the raven, both carrion eaters, are widely considered to be magical 'trickster' figures in Amerindian mythology.

The similarity with Robbe-Grillet's novels is very marked. In both cases, the distance between two opposite poles is gradually narrowed down, and difference moves towards identity through a generative play of transformations. An example of this process is the Wallas-Dupont relation, in so far as this is associated with two *objects* in the novel: the eraser that Wallas is continually trying to buy, and Dupont's paperweight. This has to be seen in conjunction with the fact that Dupont is essentially a *writer*, and exercises his power through his writing. The function of an eraser is to 'destroy' writing; so Wallas's eventual role as Dupont's murderer is foreshadowed by his association with the eraser. Conversely, the function of the paperweight is to 'preserve' writing. So, eraser and paperweight are opposites, and, if Dupont is equated with writing, the eraser symbolically murders Dupont while the paperweight ought to preserve him. But the two objects are described in noticeably similar terms; the eraser is 'un cube jaunâtre, de deux à trois centimètres de côté, avec les angles légèrement arrondis – peut-être par l'usure' (132), while the paperweight is 'la pierre cubique, aux angles arrondis, aux faces polies par l'usure' (39). Even more significantly, the paperweight 'changes' just before Wallas shoots Dupont: as he waits for the supposed murderer in Dupont's study, he notices 'le cube de pierre vitrifiée, aux *arêtes vives*, aux coins *meurtriers*' (244, my italics).

If the implication is that the paperweight, rather than the eraser, is going to 'murder' the writer Dupont, then not only has the opposition between the two objects merged into quasi-identity, but the paperweight, through its association with him, almost counts as another representative of auto-destruction (cf. the police commissioner's theory that Dupont shot himself). What strengthens this interpretation is the fact that the eraser, too, destroys itself in the course of performing its function: in rubbing out writing, it rubs itself away, as is emphasised by the repeated stress on its 'usure'.[21] Thus not only the opposition between murderer and victim, but also, more abstractly, that between murder and auto-destruction/suicide is itself 'erased'. Applying Lévi-Strauss's formula to this textual relation, one could say that the initial opposition Wallas-Dupont is replaced by its symbolic equivalent, i.e., eraser-paperweight, and that the latter is then transformed into an ambiguous compound of identity and difference.[22]

There is nevertheless an important difference. Lévi-Strauss's system depends on the notion of *mediation*: the opposition generates a new term intermediate between the two original ones, thus forming the basis for a new opposition and a new mediation. It is a dialectical process, and it can go on for ever; in fact Lévi-Strauss stresses its infinite nature. In *Les Gommes*, on the other hand, there is no production of a new mediating term (e.g., some new object that could be seen as half-way between an eraser and a paperweight). Equally, the circular structure prohibits any possibility of infinite generation or transformation: the text works inexorably towards its closure. Rather than synthesis, then, each pole of the opposition simply contaminates the other, in the characteristic movement of oscillation that gives Genette's article its title of 'Vertige fixé', and which he describes as 'cette œuvre monotone et troublante où l'espace et la parole s'abolissent en se multipliant à l'infini . . . un vertige "fixé", donc à la fois réalisé et supprimé' (89). *Les Gommes* itself supplies an image of its 'vertige' in the strangely prolonged description of the lowering of the bridge over the canal:

> les oscillations, de plus en plus amorties, de moins en moins discernables – mais dont il était difficile de préciser le terme – frangeaient ainsi, par une série de prolongements et régressions successifs de part et d'autre d'une fixité tout illusoire, un phénomène achevé, cependant, depuis un temps notable. (158)

Thus the difference between Lévi-Strauss's myths and Robbe-Grillet's novels is that between 'mediation' and 'oscillation'. In the former, the opposition is resolved in an open-ended process of synthesis which generates new elements, and hence new *meanings*. In the latter, the neutralisation of the opposition results, at least partially, in a cancelling out of difference and hence – since in Saussurean terms meaning is a product of difference – of meaning. Dupont's ex-wife, for instance, reacts to his death with, precisely, *in-difference*: 'Je ne sais pas comment vous dire . . . Quelle différence pouvait-il y avoir entre Daniel vivant et Daniel mort?' (183–4). Similarly in Wallas's final reflection on the events of the narrative, their ambiguity breaks down into a kind of alienated pointlessness:

> "On s'acharne quelquefois à découvrir un meurtrier . . . " On s'acharne à découvrir le meurtrier, et le crime n'a pas été commis. On s'acharne à le découvrir . . . "bien loin de soi, alors qu'on n'a

qu'à tendre la main vers sa propre poitrine . . . " D'où sortent donc ces phrases? (261)

This disintegration is in turn perhaps not unconnected to what I have called the 'anti-structuralist' tendency in the novel. It is important to realise that the closed, rule-governed, auto-destructive structure constituted by the narrative is itself presented thematically in a particular light. That is, the *concept* of structure (in the form of order, law, instruction or predetermined system) is set up in opposition to a tentative and rudimentary margin of human freedom, which takes above all the form of *error*. Structure is not generative as it is in Robbe-Grillet's later texts, but purely *regulative* ('De très anciennes lois règlent le détail de ses gestes, sauvés pour une fois du flottement des intentions humaines' (11)) and, therefore, oppressive. Order is counterposed to human action right from the first page of the novel, with the anticipation of events which, 'enveloppés de leur cerne d'erreur et de doute', will 'entamer progressivement l'ordonnance idéale' (11); and given this context it is perhaps permissible to read the 'patron' – the figure who presides over the initial scene-setting – as a pun: he is of course the 'boss', but he is also the *pattern*, the *stencil* that imposes a predetermined structure on events; and the superimposition of the two senses of 'patron' effectively identifies structure with oppression and alienation. Thus there is throughout the novel a thematic counterpoint which privileges the notion of the unstructured. Error, for instance, is *desired*: Garinati's failure to kill Dupont is prefigured by his 'violente envie' to disobey his instructions – described as 'la machinerie parfaitement réglée' (23) – and open the door too wide, 'seulement pour savoir jusqu'où on a le droit d'aller . . . une petite place pour l'erreur' (22). In one sense, then, the 'vingt-quatre heures en trop' represent the eruption of fallible human agency into the impersonal machinery of the structure; but of course they are also, as already discussed, the accomplishment or rectification of precisely that structure. In this way *Les Gommes* adopts a deeply ambivalent position towards the idea of structure; it is at once pre-structuralist, anti-structuralist, and more orthodoxly structuralist than any of Robbe-Grillet's subsequent texts. These differences will become clearer if we now examine *La Maison de rendez-vous*.

This text contains many allusions to *Les Gommes*: parallels between the murder of Manneret and the murder of Dupont include the unfinished sentence that both were writing at the moment of their death, the suggestion that both are in some sense father to their killers (1965, 150), the police hypothesis that both committed suicide (ibid., 131), Johnson and Wallas's lack of resemblance to their identity card/passport photographs, and so on. But there is a fundamental difference between the two texts: the closed circularity of *Les Gommes* gives way in the later novel to a far more flexible principle of *circulation* between the elements of the system. *La Maison de rendez-vous* is not a 'structuralist novel' in the strict sense, because it has no fixed set of transformational rules governing either the narrative as a whole or smaller units of the text. Reading it, one has no sense of any necessity about the form of the narrative; rather, the emphasis is on the freedom with which shifting complexes of elements are generated one from the others. As Robbe-Grillet himself puts it, 'Il y a sans cesse des constellations mobiles qui se forment et se déforment' (NRHA II, 167).[23] This is not to say that the process is entirely random, but that it works on the basis of association and variation: a typical example is the way in which the waitress and the fish in the restaurant's fish-tank, which she is catching 'au moyen d'une épuisette à long manche qu'elle manie avec grâce et adresse, pour les présenter tout vifs, tordant leur corps brillant prisonnier des mailles' (235), together metamorphose, on the next page, into the girl in a sampan on the river, 'qui manie avec grâce et adresse la longue rame vénitienne, en faisant des mouvements ondulés de torsion qui font bouger la soie mince et brillante sur sa peau' (236).

Robbe-Grillet's own description of the way in which his later novels are composed makes its non-systematic nature quite clear: 'cela se développe rarement d'une façon théorique. Je ne choisis pas mes générateurs au départ en une sorte de catalogue clos et complet . . . Il ne faut pas ramener notre travail à des opérations mécaniques. Il y a au contraire une liberté de mouvement constante . . . ' (NRHA II, 167). What limits the number of generators is a definite but untheorised *sense* that the moment of closure has arrived: 'C'est quelque chose qui me frappe quand j'écris . . . Il y a une longue période où la prolifération est admise, et où les générateurs engendrés sont acceptés, pour entrer à leur tour en action; puis il vient un moment (il me semble que ça devrait être sensible pour le lecteur) où la liquidation du matériel commence, ce qui interdit de nouvelles prises en charge' (ibid., 168).[24]

In other words, *La Maison de rendez-vous* serves as a good example of Ricardou's conception of structure, as described earlier in this chapter: an almost post-structuralist structuralism.[25] It retains above all the notion of the primacy of relations over elements, the mobility of these relations, and the anti-*vraisemblable* implications of such a system. Here the elements in themselves are completely lacking in interest, and their overtly cliched exoticism – opium dealers, white slavers, Communist agents, beautiful oriental prostitutes, etc., – refocuses the reader's interest all the more firmly upon the changing patterns set up between them. Indeed, this is already evident in the novel's title: *La Maison de rendez-vous* prepares us to see the narrative as a place of *meetings* between elements. And the fact that it is a brothel also works metaphorically: textuality imaged as sexuality, both operating as a system of generalised circulation and exchange. A brothel, in other words – and the contrast with Lévi-Strauss's rule-bound marriage systems could not be clearer – is a place which exists precisely in order to remove all the normal constraints from the number of possible sexual exchanges between a certain number of participants; to ensure, that is, maximal circulation of partners. In *La Maison de rendez-vous*, just as sexual encounters take the form of a potentially exhaustive 'combinatoire', with each man and woman entering into relations with as many of the others as possible, so the textual system too is set up in such a way as to maximise the number of combinations of its elements.

This in itself implies that another structuralist concept is extremely relevant to this novel: Lévi-Strauss's bricolage, which could almost be considered as the structural rule which – although in a more abstract and looser sense than the rules of Butor's novels, for instance – generates the whole text.[26] Almost, but not quite: *La Maison de rendez-vous* is best described, as I shall demonstrate, as a text generated by several *different* structural principles, each of which has a limited scope in relation to the narrative as a whole. Bricolage is perhaps the most evident of these. The constituent elements of the novel, far from being new perceptions of the real, are exactly Lévi-Strauss's 'messages en quelque sorte pré-transmis et qu'il collectionne' (1962, 30): the circulation, in other words, is also a *re-cycling* of stereotyped erotic phantasies. This intensely cultural material, fragmented and reworked, is a perfect example of the 'bribes et morceaux, témoins fossiles de l'histoire d'un individu ou d'une société' (1962, 32) of bricolage. Above all, perhaps, the title of Lévi-Strauss's chapter provides an insight into the functioning of the novel. The 'science du concret' differentiates mythical thought from a science which operates on abstract ideas; just as, in *La Maison de rendez-vous*, there are no ideas expressed at all. The elements of the text are entirely concrete, even opaque; they do not express anything, and they signify solely through the evolving arrangements that they enter into with one another. Bricolage also usefully underlines the endlessness of these activities: each new arrangement of elements is destined to be broken down and the elements reassembled into yet another pattern. In *La Maison de rendez-vous*, too (in contrast to *Les Gommes*), the process of structuration is never definitively resolved, *because* it is constantly imperfect. While Lady Ava at first claims: 'Voilà. Tout est en ordre . . . Une fois encore, j'aurai réglé, autour de moi, la disposition des choses' (173), the end of the novel finds her, on her deathbed, admitting that 'Les choses ne sont jamais définitivement en ordre' (244).

The very nature of this activity makes it difficult to illustrate succinctly; but a selective account of the first few paragraphs of the novel will perhaps give some idea of the generativity of bricolage. The first paragraph is an a-temporal list of items – those which have always occupied, he tells us, a large place in the narrator's dreams. They include:

(1)   a girl bending her head as she fastens her sandal.
(2)   the tight skirt slit up the sides worn by Chinese girls in Hong Kong.
(3)   a whip.
(4)   a wax model in a shop window.
(5)   a dog collar.

The second paragraph introduces two more items, a woman dancing (6) and her partner, an 'haute silhouette noire' (7). It is equally timeless, beginning 'Souvent je m'attarde à contempler quelque jeune femme qui danse, dans un bal'. The third paragraph, in contrast, starts off the process of assembling these disparate items into a particular *scene*. It begins: 'Elle s'est *maintenant* retirée . . . ' (my italics). It proceeds to combine the dancer (6) with the girl fastening her sandal (1): 'pour rattacher la boucle de sa fine chaussure à brides' – and also by implication with the whip (3), since the sandal is now described as 'faite de minces lanières dorées qui barrent de plusieurs croix le pied nu'. (This also introduces the 'bondage' theme, which is developed later in the text.) The dancer's partner (7) reappears as 'une haute silhouette en smoking sombre', now talking to another man.

Of the original list, so far items (2), (4) and (5) have not been 'used', and so the next paragraph is devoted to them. It starts a-temporally: 'Tout le monde connaît Hong-Kong . . . ' – thus also underlining the status of the contents of the description: not objects of real knowledge (since everybody does not *know* Hong-Kong), but of the familiar cheap orientalism of European popular culture. What follows is a longer description of the 'étroite robe à jupe entravée, fendue sur le côté jusqu'à la cuisse, dont sont vêtues les eurasiennes' (2); but in mid-sentence this modulates suddenly into a *scene* of a particular woman ('la promeneuse') wearing such a dress in black silk. This in turn brings in the shop-window and the dummy (4), as a mirror image of the 'promeneuse': 'elle contemple un instant la jeune femme de cire vêtue d'une robe identique en soie blanche, ou bien son propre reflet dans la vitre . . . '; and this then incorporates the dog-collar (5), transformed into a *leash* which also echoes the whip (3): ' . . . ou bien la laisse en cuir tressé que le mannequin tient . . . '. Finally, as part of the shop window display, the paragraph generates the actual dog – and the following paragraph consists of a detailed description of this animal. The next paragraph, however, produces a new combination of two existing elements: the sandal from (1), already associated with the dancer (6) in the third paragraph, now 'migrates' again to the foot of the model – (1) + (4).

From then on in the narrative, a live version of the dog will play an important part, attached now to the 'promeneuse', who is later identified as Kim, one of Lady Ava's servants; the scene of the dancers expands into the reception at the Villa Bleue, the 'haute silhouette en smoking sombre' becomes Sir Ralph Johnson, and so on. But they remain throughout separate elements, so that each narrative sequence or scene can easily be taken apart, as it were, and reassembled in a different way. The text periodically reminds us of this, by recapitulating versions of the original list of items as, precisely, a list; and in so doing it simultaneously stresses the ludic, *anti-realist* dimension of the technique. For instance, the elements of the narrative of the novel itself are given in a *mise en abyme* as a story told by Johnson's companion at the reception: 'ses invraisemblables récits de voyages en Orient, avec antiquaires entremetteurs, traite des filles, chiens trop adroits, bordels pour détraqués, trafic de drogues et assassinat mystérieux' (142–3). The narrator also comments from time to time on the narrative's general lack of realist plausibility, the arbitrary or illogical order of the scenes;[27] and this kind of 'narrative euphoria', as Ann Jefferson calls it, which 'exuberantly produces narratives with minimal regard for *vraisemblance*' (1980, 49), is closely linked to the operations of bricolage.

A second structural principle operating in the novel is the opposition between *same* and *other* identified by Genette, and already mentioned here in connection with *Les Gommes*. But it has a wider relevance to *La Maison de rendez-vous*, in which it becomes more strongly *generative* of the narrative sequences. Genette shows how Robbe-Grillet's novels transpose metaphorical relations of similarity and contrast into metonymic relations of contiguity and succession. One 'scene', in other words, is followed not by a chronologically subsequent scene but by another version of itself: not *what happened next*, but *what might have happened instead*. In Genette's words, 'il dispose en série les termes d'un choix, il transpose une *concurrence* en *concaténation*' (85). He goes on to distinguish three versions of this technique: 'analogies naturelles', i.e., exploiting the interplay of similarity and difference inherent in certain objects; 'reproductions artificielles', in which the relation is set up between a diegetically real scene and a picture or other representation of it; and 'répétitions et variantes du récit', where a scene reappears from time to time in a recognisable but slightly different form.

Genette's article concentrates mainly on *Dans le labyrinthe*,[28] but his three categories also enable us to locate some of the generative principles of *La Maison de rendez-vous*. The 'natural analogies', fortified by cultural cliche ('tous les Chinois ont la même figure' (146)) and generic conventions (mistaken identity as a staple ingredient of crime novels), result in a proliferation of seemingly identical characters or objects which nevertheless turn out, *probably*, to be different. Johnson sees the Eurasian girl walking the dog outside the Hotel Victoria (144); after a rapid taxi ride to Manneret's address, he sees her again: or at least, he sees another 'fille en robe-fourreau' with 'un grand chien noir [qui] la précède, exactement comme celle de toute à l'heure, qui ne se dirigeaient pourtant pas de ce côté-ci et pourraient difficilement avoir fait tout ce chemin dans l'intervalle' (147). He discovers that there is another servant who also walks the dog, and who is Kim's double: even their names are indistinguishable to a Western ear, he says (155) (leaving the reader to reflect that Kim is not actually a Chinese name anyway).

But he is still not sure whether he saw the two different girls, or the same girl twice. There are many other example of such ambiguity: the drug-dealer named Tchang, who reappears at the door of different apartments in the same building and may or may not be the same man, and so on. This constant multiplication and displacement of identities constitutes one of the main narrative impulses.

The category 'artificial reproductions' is equally fertile. Lady Ava is dispersed into the vast number of paintings and sculptures of her which adorn the salon of the Villa Bleue, and also into the unstable versions of her name, so that she becomes, in Robbe-Grillet's vividly ungrammatical phrase, 'une innombrable femme': 'il n'y a plus cette nuit qu'une innombrable femme muette et immobile, inaccessible, qui multiplie ces poses apprêtées, grandiloquentes, exagérément dramatiques, et qui m'entoure de tous les côtés, Eve, Eva, Eva Bergmann, Lady Ava, Lady Ava, Lady Ava' (220–1). Equally, the groups of sculpted figures in the garden of the villa represent and occasionally substitute for the living characters and/or the porno-graphic dramas staged in the salon's theatre. The most dynamic examples of this type, however, are the theatrical performances: at one point Lady Ava herself is on stage, *acting herself*: the setting is an exact replica of her real bedroom, and she performs the essentially undramatic actions of walking around the room, sitting on the bed, etc., that she will do in reality once the reception is over (136). Later, too, Lauren enacts on stage her own real-life drama of rejecting her fiancé in favour of Johnson (167). This superimpo-sition allows the text to switch backwards and forwards between theatrical representation and diegetic reality with great flexibility. It can be taken as an example of Ricardou's 'récit transmuté' (1973, 109–24).

But its most interesting feature is the way in which it interacts with Genette's third category, the 'repetitions and variants' of the narrative, equivalent to Ricardou's 'récit avarié' (1973). *La Maison de rendez-vous* provides numerous examples of scenes being repeated with significant variations, the most prominent being the narrator's arrival at the villa, the police raid, Kim's visit to Manneret, and the murder of Manneret. This drive towards exploring all possible variations on a given theme is clearly a major structural principle of the text; more specifically, however, it is *interlocked* with the use of theatrical representation – via a kind of pun on *'répétition'*. In the English sense of repetition, this relates to the past – literally, the re-presentation of something which has already happened. But in the sense of 'rehearsal', it anticipates a future performance which has not yet happened. The doubling-up of these two temporal directions in *La Maison de rendez-vous* serves to conflate past and future; thus 'la répétition d'un prochain spectacle' (172) reads at first glance as an impossible *repetition of the future*. This is linked to the pervasive sense of déjà-vu which seems to affect all the characters: the police raid is a sudden violent irruption, but people react 'comme si le moment exact de leur entrée en scène avait été dès longtemps connu de tous' (240). The predictability is that of a mechanical, *scripted* and hence artificial representation: 'Le scénario se déroule ensuite d'une façon mécanique, comme une machine bien huilée, bien rodée, chacun connaissant désormais son rôle avec exactitude et pouvant le jouer sans se tromper d'une seconde, sans un à-coup . . . ' (ibid.).[29] In effect, the subversion of the performance/reality opposition, and the neutralisation of the distinction between what has already happened and what has not yet happened, become *one and the same process*. In isolation, each already serves to remove any realist grounding from the narrative. In conjunction, however, they produce the further effect of conflating the temporal and the diegetic axes; an event is unreal *because* it is always a 'répétition' – a 'repetition of the future'. In a text which is otherwise so freely generative, we nevertheless find this peculiarly over-determined structure.

There is one other generative structural principle at work in *La Maison de rendez-vous*. It operates in a manner similar to the concept of *recursiveness* in generative linguistics. Sentences in a language are not of a predetermined length; the nursery rhyme 'The house that Jack built', for instance, illustrates the fact that any relative clause can itself contain another relative clause, and so on ad infinitum. The grammatical rules of the language have to be able to account for this; in more technical terms this means that the grammar must contain some recursive rules – that is, rules which allow a given symbol to generate a string of symbols *including itself*. Very roughly, these are thus of the form:

$$A \rightarrow X - Y - (A)$$

– where X and Y are variables, and the brackets signal 'optional'. The rule automatically applies to every occurrence of A, giving the structure:

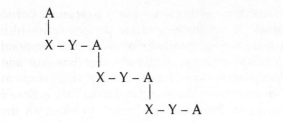

- and so on, until the '(A)' option is not taken.[30]

It is possible to analyse the narrative of *La Maison de rendez-vous* as the product of a recursive rule of this type. The analysis applies only to the main thread of the story, in so far as this can be extracted from the body of the text – in other words, the following sequence of events: Manneret is murdered; Johnson is the principal suspect, and so has to leave Hong Kong in order to avoid the police; he wants to take Lauren with him, but to do this he has to buy her from Lady Ava; this means he has to borrow a large sum of money from someone; he chases around Hong Kong trying to raise it, but realises that the only person who could lend him such a sum is Manneret; Manneret refuses, and in exasperation Johnson kills him. The circularity of this has obvious similarities with *Les Gommes*, but also the crucial difference that the moment of closing the circle in *Les Gommes* is final and irreversible; it allows the normal order of things to reassert itself so that the circle cannot be repeated. In *La Maison de rendez-vous*, in contrast, Manneret's death has the value of the 'A' symbol in the recursive rule cited above; there is no reason why the narrative should not start up again and proceed on a different loop (since X and Y are variables) but one which would still bring it back to Manneret's death. That is, the text could go on forever on the basis of the same generative rule.

The recursiveness is somewhat blurred, of course, by the novel's arbitrary chronological reversibility: Manneret is also dead and then alive again several times within the overall 'loop' of the narrative, in a way which does not seem to be the result of any structural necessity. But what I have identified as the main sequence of events is, nevertheless, held together by *causal* links between the elements, links which are not open to rearrangement; and it is this – paradoxically, a logic of *vraisemblance* – that guarantees the clear operation of the recursive rule:

[Manneret is murdered]$_A$ *so* [Johnson has to leave, with Lauren]$_x$

so [he tries to borrow money, but fails]$_Y$ *so* [Manneret is murdered]$_A$ . . . *so* [Johnson has to leave]$_X$, etc.

Therefore it does not operate on smaller elements like, for instance, the recurrences of the 'jupe entravée', which are not governed by any logical sequence. The structure itself is, however, represented as *mise en abyme* on the even smaller and hence more vertiginous scale of a single sentence. On page 119 we read:

> Dans l'attention que Lauren porte à cette opération délicate, la chevelure blonde renversée se déplace et découvre davantage la nuque qui se courbe et la chair fragile, au duvet plus pâle encore que la chevelure blonde, qui se déplace et découvre davantage la nuque qui se courbe et la chair fragile au duvet plus pâle que le reste de la nuque qui se courbe et la chair fragile qui se courbe davantage et la chair . . .

Finally, a different kind of recursiveness is discernable in the multiple embeddings of the narrative. This applies not to the events of the story, but to levels of representation. What at first appears to be diegetically real often turns out to be part of a theatrical performance, which itself turns out to be part of a story recounted by another character, and so on. Jefferson discusses this characteristic in detail, citing for example the passage in which the shop-window scene is embedded in a performance on stage, which itself contains an actor who is writing the story of the reception at the villa. As she points out, 'There is nothing to prevent an embedded narrative from becoming in turn the container for a further embedded narrative' (55), and, 'the narrative's most intense euphoria is always associated with its self-imaging in these embedded narratives' (56). Another example that could be cited is the scene already mentioned above, which is initially presented as Lady Ava playing herself on stage, and which includes Kim's visit to her bedroom. Kim is trying to find out where the drugs are hidden; the text's momentary adoption of her point of view gives way to a sequence which also acts as *mise-en-abyme* of the whole process of recursive embedding:

> si la cachette se trouvait dans la chambre même, il aurait été rangé depuis longtemps en lieu sûr, *a pensé* la servante, *pense* Lady Ava, *dit* le narrateur au teint rouge qui est en train de conter l'histoire à son voisin. (142, my italics)

Circulation of elements within the system, bricolage, narrative transformations motivated by analogy, reproductions and repetitions, two different types of recursiveness: *La Maison de rendez-vous* seems to draw on a number of structuralist procedures without letting any one of them take it over completely. And Robbe-Grillet himself, ultimately, seems to be extending his all-pervasive 'jeu' to a theoretical level: this is not simply a structuralist game, it is a game being played *with* structuralism. Rather than just making use of its ideas in a straightforward manner, he is mixing them up 'promiscuously' (as befits a 'maison de rendez-vous'), and also, perhaps, mimicking them rather than employing them. Or even parodying them: the sentence beginning 'c'est *l'ensemble* de la chaussée, *transformée* en ruisseau d'un trottoir à l'autre, qui charie les détritus . . . ' (178) looks suspiciously like a joke at the expense of structuralism.

In this sense we can conclude, finally and paradoxically, that the whole text can actually be accounted for by the notion of bricolage. It is, however, a unique kind of second-degree bricolage, in which the elements of the textual arrangement are themselves different structuralist operations – such as bricolage, for example; or recursiveness, which it is therefore also an example of . . .

3

Structuralist Marxism:
Tel Quel and
Textual Production

As structuralism evolved its relation to Marxism became an important and controversial issue. The central figure in this development was Louis Althusser, whose books and essays made a decisive break with the humanist Marxism previously dominant in Western Europe (in the work of Sartre, for instance) and constructed in its place a new, structuralist, Marxism.[1] Althusser himself was only very marginally concerned with literature, but his influence on almost all sections of the intellectual left in France was such that his work had a considerable effect on literary theory. The old questions concerning the political significance of literature began to be posed again, but in a new and different way.

The central issue was the question of realism, which in the context of structuralist Marxism becomes a politically reactionary discourse rather than a progressive one. I have already described the way in which Robbe-Grillet appropriates the basic insight of Barthes's *Le degré zéro de l'écriture*: that the writer's work on literary form and language is itself a kind – in fact the only effective kind – of political commitment. This idea now develops from its quasi-Sartrean beginnings in *Le degré zéro de l'écriture* to an explicit critique and reversal of Sartre's commitment to realist literature. In other words, Barthes's original claim that socialist realism was as reactionary as the most reactionary texts of bourgeois realism broadens into a general condemnation of realism *per se*. Any *representational* text – any text, that is, which asks to be read as a representation of reality – is now seen as complicit with bourgeois ideology; only once it is freed from this can the text attack the dominant ideology, which it does through its critique, subversion and transformation of language and literary conventions. For the Nouveau Roman, this means that the anti-representational stance which they had in any case been adopting for some time – which, as discussed in Chapter 2, was reinforced by the influence of structuralism – now acquires a new significance: it becomes politically revolutionary.

Barthes himself extended and deepened his critique of realism in the course of the 1960s, notably in the short but influential article entitled 'L'Effet de réel', published in *Communications* in 1968, and in his book *S/Z* in 1970. Here, he defines several different 'codes' at work in literary texts: one of these is the 'code culturel' or 'code de référence' – in other words, the text's insertion into and reinforcement of its ideological context.[2] He was also, however, an important contributor to the journal *Tel Quel*.[3] And it is above all the writers and theorists of the *Tel Quel* group, under the general editorship of Philippe Sollers, who advance the theory of the revolutionary text as one which subverts dominant bourgeois ideology through its attack on the conventions of realism. Their position is encapsulated in the concept of *textual production*: the idea, that is, that a text should not be seen as an object of consumption – an object delivering a 'picture' of reality neatly packaged for its consumers – but rather as a *process of production*, working on the raw materials of language, literary norms and ideology in general to produce a continuous transformation of meaning, never *fixed* in a representation. Although *Tel Quel* were not exclusively Althusserian – Jacques Derrida, Michel Foucault, Jacques Lacan and Barthes himself were equally important, and somewhat divergent, points of reference for them – their theorisation of literature can be fully understood only against the background of the general development of Althusserian Marxism and the effect that the latter had both on humanist Marxism and on the 'classic' structuralism based on linguistics. The situation of the Nouveau Roman within all this was very much determined by their relationship to *Tel Quel*, a relationship which deteriorated significantly between the journal's inception in 1960 and the crystallisation of its political position in 1968. This chapter, therefore, will examine three separate but related questions. Firstly, the theoretical position of *Tel Quel* in the context of structuralist Marxism; secondly, the history of relations between *Tel Quel* and the Nouveau Roman; and thirdly, the extent and nature of the Nouveau Roman's use of *Tel Quel*'s notion of textual production.

TEL QUEL'S CONCEPT OF 'TEXTUAL PRODUCTION'

The first number of *Tel Quel* appeared in the spring of 1960, with an editorial statement which emphasised its commitment to the *specificity* of the literary text and a determination to consider it on its own terms. But over the next five or six years (which also saw some changes on the editorial board) this policy shifted significantly towards a more politicised conception of literature.[4] But far from being a return to the traditional notion of committed literature, this new position concentrated its attention on the relationship between literature, language and the *formal* structures of ideology. Attacking Sartre's instrumental conception of language as bourgeois, obscurantist and counter-revolutionary (*Tel Quel* no. 28, 86), Sollers concludes: 'Nous sommes aussi attachés que n'importe qui au "référent". Mais . . . dans une période néo-capitaliste la seule position possible consiste . . . à le désigner dans son opacité et son absence . . . D'où l'importance de tout travail portant aujourd'hui sur l'idéologie – travail auquel Sartre s'oppose par son attitude réactionnaire' (ibid.). The revolutionary text, in other words, is not a statement but a mode of production, which 'works' on and against ideology.

By 1967 the theory of textual production was already taking shape, with important articles by Sollers, Julia Kristeva, Jean-Louis Baudry and others appearing in the journal. The momentum generated by the events of May '68 helped to accelerate the process; the summer issue of 1968 opened, under the title 'La Révolution ici maintenant', with a seven point statement of their position on revolutionary literature; and in the autumn of the same year they published the volume *Théorie d'ensemble*, bringing together the major contributions to what was by this time an extremely uncompromising and fairly coherent programme of theory and practice, in which literary texts are seen to have a unique and necessary role in the struggle for political revolution.[5]

The main axis of the theory is now quite clearly the opposition between *textual production* and *representation*. The preface to *Théorie d'ensemble* sets out in large capital letters the general parameters for the collective project; and the first of these is 'L'ECRITURE DANS SON FONCTIONNEMENT PRODUCTEUR N'EST PAS REPRESENTATION' (9). Representation is identified with bourgeois 'literature', and production with revolutionary 'writing'. As Sollers implies in the interview 'Ecriture et révolution' reprinted in *Théorie d'ensemble*, this distinction stems from a perception of the essentially ideological nature of literature:

> Vous savez de quelle idéologie profondément réactionnaire, décadente et pour tout dire exténuée, la "littérature" est, dans notre société, le symptôme actif. Bien entendu, ce symptôme renvoie à l'ensemble de l'idéologie bourgeoise qui ne manque pas "d'écrivains" destinés à mimer son passé classique romantique ou naturaliste: cela va du stendhalien agité à l'esthète crépusculaire, en passant par toutes les variantes d'un fonctionnariat multiple. (67–8)

In particular, the realist *novel* is, as Sollers had already argued in a lecture given in 1965,[6] one of society's main vehicles for ideological conditioning (for the process, in fact, which Althusser would later call 'interpellation'): 'LE ROMAN EST LA MANIERE DONT CETTE SOCIETE SE PARLE, la manière dont l'individu DOIT SE VIVRE pour y être accepté ... Notre *identité* en dépend, ce qu'on pense de nous, ce que nous pensons de nous-mêmes, la façon dont notre vie est insensiblement amenée à composition' (21). What we accept as 'objective reality' in our everyday lives is an ideological construct which, in the novel, takes the form of the 'vraisemblable'. As Kristeva argues in 'La productivité dite texte',[7] 'Le sens vraisemblable *fait semblant* de se préoccuper de la vérité objective; ce qui le préoccupe en fait, c'est son rapport à un discours dont le "faire-semblant-d'être-une-vérité-objective" est reconnu, admis, institutionnalisé' (150). All representations of reality thus 'pretend' to be natural, but are in fact social and hence historical (ibid., 151).

Jean-Louis Baudry makes the further point that, since according to Althusser ideology functions for the most part on an unconscious level, it is precisely literature's implication in ideology that makes it difficult to see that it is so implicated (1968a, 128). Indeed, he continues, 'La "littérature" est un des champs privilégiés de l'idéologie dans la mesure où, travaillant la langue, elle apporte le système de langage (qui doit évidemment rester inconscient) dans lequel chacun est amené à se représenter' (129). However, this in itself also means that that literature has the *possibility* of contesting ideology: it can become 'un des champs privilégiés de la lutte idéologique' (129). But in order to achieve this, it must cease to base itself on *representation* and must fully and overtly assume its status as practice – i.e., as textual *production*. Then it will be possible to '*articuler une politique* liée logiquement à une dynamique non-représentative de l'écriture' (*Théorie d'ensemble*, 10).

It will have become clear that *Tel Quel*'s project involves both a theory and a practice. The concept of textual production involves both a theoretical claim that all writing is actually a question of working with language and literary conventions, that it does not really represent reality, that realism is just another literary discourse based on convention, the ideological function of which is in part precisely to mask the work of production,[8] and so on. But it is equally the basis for a political *practice* of writing – writing texts that are openly 'productive' and anti-representational.[9]

One of the ways in which *Tel Quel* changed during the course of the 1960s was simply in the growing importance it attached to *theory*. The earliest issues published a lot of literary texts: extracts from forthcoming novels, poems, etc.; but by the mid '60s the balance had shifted in favour of a greater number of theoretical articles. By this time, *Tel Quel* was strongly influenced by Althusser. From the spring of 1967 onwards, each number of *Tel Quel* is subtitled 'Science/Littérature', echoing Althusser's insistence on a rigorous separation between science (i.e., theory) and ideological forms of thought, including humanist Marxism. Asked about the significance of this sub-title in an interview reprinted in *Théorie d'ensemble*, Sollers says: '*Théorie* doit être pris ici, dans le sens que lui donne, de façon décisive, Althusser: c'est "une forme spécifique de la pratique" . . . cette pratique théorique, redoublant et pensant la pratique textuelle dans ses effets formels nouveaux, est devenue indispensable' (70) – and goes on to quote Althusser on dialectical materialism. *Théorie d'ensemble* as a whole contains frequent references to Althusser's work – Kristeva argues that semiology must link up with the research going on within Althusserian Marxism (80), Marcelin Pleynet draws on the formulation of the 'three generalities' of theoretical practice in *Pour Marx* (111–12), and so on.

In particular, three of Althusser's main concepts are apparent in the work of the *Tel Quel* writers. Firstly, that of the *relative autonomy of ideology*, as opposed to the earlier Marxist view that ideology was a superstructural 'reflection' of the economic base. That is, both Stalinism and humanist Marxism believed that economic reality determined everything else; for Althusser, in contrast, social reality as a whole is a *structure* made up of distinct but inter-related elements, each containing its own specific contradictions, but each interacting to reinforce or counteract the others. The principle of *overdetermination* means that it is impossible to define some contradictions as solely causes and others as solely effects, because each one is 'déterminante, mais aussi déterminée dans un seul et même mouvement, et déterminée par les divers *niveaux* et *instances* de la formation sociale qu'elle anime; nous pourrions la dire *surdéterminée dans son principe*' (Althusser, 1966, 99–100). Therefore, ideology is not a mechanical, passive 'reflection' of the economic base, but a 'relatively autonomous' instance.[10] Therefore also, the ideological arena is a valid area of *struggle*: as long as humanist Marxism had held that only economic change could change ideology, there had been no real point in attacking ideology directly. But the Althusserian model effectively legitimised the kind of programme of political action that *Tel Quel* were envisaging; there are clear echoes of his position in their statement after May '68, for instance: 'nous pensons que l'activité signifiante d'une phase historique donnée constitue une détermination décisive des possibilités de transformation de cette phase' (*Tel Quel* no. 34, 3).

Secondly, all levels or instances of the social totality (economic, ideological, literary, theoretical, etc.) generate their specific *practices*. A practice is a process of *production*, working on a determinate raw material and transforming it into a determinate product: 'Par *pratique* en général nous entendrons tout processus de *transformation* d'une matière première donnée déterminée, en un *produit* déterminé, transformation effectuée par un travail humain déterminé, utilisant des moyens (de "production") déterminés' (Althusser, 1966, 167). One major implication of this is that ideology is no longer to be seen as a matter of (false) ideas inhabiting people's minds, but as itself a practice, incarnated in behaviour and institutions and hence having a material reality of its own. But the value of the concept of practice for *Tel Quel* lies above all in the way in which they extend it to arrive at the notion of 'pratique signifiante' – covering the whole area of *meaning*, now theorisable as a process of production – and at the transformation of the notion of literature into that of 'pratique scripturale' and, of course, textual *production*. (Hence, also, the virtual interchangeability of the terms of 'practice' and 'production' within *Tel Quel*'s discourse.) To see writing as a relatively autonomous practice is to release it from the grip of realism; the efficacy of writing is not reducible to the 'transparent' representation of a pre-given reality, but is instead defined by the process whereby it transforms a raw material into a product.

Thirdly, *Tel Quel* were also, for similar reasons, attracted by Althusser's own conception of literature. He had put forward the idea that literary practice works on the raw material of ideology and transforms it, by distancing it from within and making it 'visible', so that the reader can achieve some perspective on it.[11] Althusser refers to his colleague Pierre Macherey's far more substantial analysis,[12] saying: 'What art makes us *see*, and therefore gives us in the form of *'seeing'*, *'perceiving'*, and *'feeling'* (which is not the form of *knowing*), is the *ideology* from which it is born, in which it bathes, from which it detaches itself as art, and to which it *alludes*. Macherey has shown this very clearly in the case of Tolstoy, by extending Lenin's analyses. Balzac and Solzhenitsyn give us a 'view' of the ideology to which their work alludes and with which it is constantly fed, a view which presupposes a *retreat*, an *internal distantiation* from the very ideology from which their novels emerged' (1971, 204).

Tel Quel can also, however, be seen to diverge in significant ways from Althusser's general conception of literature. Whereas his theorisation is, precisely, general – i.e., it applies to *all* literature[13] – they are concerned above all to institute a division within the field of literary practice, because their position is fundamentally *militant*. That is, they are putting forward a programme for a certain kind of revolutionary literature, defined as 'écriture' in opposition to bourgeois representational 'littérature'; the latter, in their view, does not transform, distance or work on ideology at all but simply *is* ideological, as Sollers makes clear in 'Ecriture et révolution'. Literary representation must be fought – in the first place because its content reinforces bourgeois ideology, but also because, simply *as* representation, it suppresses the true *productive* nature of writing. The subversion of ideology by literature is thus for them not, as it appears to be for Althusser, an automatic effect of the artistic mode of communication, but far more a question of conscious intervention and struggle. (Macherey, in fact, revised his views after 1968 and adopted a position closer to this.)[14]

A further major difference is that Althusser's definition of practice as production, modelled in general terms on economic production, is expanded by *Tel Quel* into a far closer and more complex analogy with *economic* processes: Sollers talks about 'l'économie scripturale' (1968, 76). When taken as an economic metaphor, 'production' generates, as its ' opposites', a series of concepts – exchange, circulation, property – each of which is then identified as a characteristic of reactionary literature. The circulation of money in the economy finds its parallel in the *circulation of meanings* in society (Sollers, 68), and both are antagonistic to productive *work*. Kristeva makes a similar critique of the object of semiology, which, she says, had hitherto been based on a conception of meaning as 'la marchandise produite et mise en circulation dans la chaîne communicative' (1968a, 88), and concludes in terms equate circulation with *communication* (90). 'Communication' is thus established as another opposite of production – the communication of existing meanings rather than the production of new ones – which by implication places the writer as seller and the reader as consumer, rather than both being involved in the production process.

The process of circulation is based on the exchange values of the products, which are arrived at both by exploiting and by *disguising* the process of production. In fact the most fundamental opposition – the most irreducible antagonism – is between production and *exchange*. 'Si donc la société bourgeoise accepte le produit, elle ne l'accepte que dissimulé en tant que produit, en tant que résultat d'une production, et ne voit plus en lui qu'un objet de consommation. Elle en détermine la valeur par l'échange, mais ne veut pas reconnaître ce qui lui donne sa valeur: le travail dépensé à sa production' (Baudry, 1968b, 352–3). Transferred to the field of semiology, exchange is identified with *representation*, and both concepts together function in opposition to production. The equation exchange-representation is arrived at via an analysis of the ideological function of the *sign*.[15]

This, in other words, constitutes a critique of earlier structuralism and its dependence on linguistic models (as exemplified in the work of Todorov, for instance). Baudry claims that the bourgeois ideology of literature results in a *double* view of the literary work: as *sign* and as *commodity*. As sign, it *represents* a pre-existing 'reality' – its author's message – and as commodity it has a certain *exchange* value, 'dans la mesure où elle contient l'auteur sous une forme monnayable, où elle est la forme même que le sens peut prendre dans la circulation' (353). That this 'contradictory character' can be contained by bourgeois ideology is due to the ideology's construction of the linguistic sign in terms of *value*. Baudry shows how Saussure's work contributes to this. Saussure both sees language as expression and representation (355) and explicitly links linguistics with political economics through their common concern with the notion of value. He quotes Saussure as saying that in linguistics, 'comme en économie politique, on est en face de la notion de valeur; dans les deux sciences, il s'agit d'un *système d'équivalence* entre des choses d'ordres différents, dans l'une un travail et un salaire, dans l'autre un signifié et un signifiant' (359) – and then corrects Saussure's analogy, to the effect that the relevant contrast is not between labour and wage, but use value and exchange value (360). Just as it is only by the mechanism of exchange that inherently incommensurable economic commodities can be brought into one system of equivalence, so it is only the mechanism of the sign – its separation of signifier and signified – that allows us to compare (i.e., assign values to) different signifieds on the basis of the homogeneity of the signifiers – all part of the language system. The effect of this exclusive concentration on language as exchange value, Baudry argues, is to conceal and repress its real functioning as production. As against this, the concept of 'écriture' with its 'caractère non expressive, non représentative' (362), or 'pratique scripturale', reinstates production: 'Dans la pratique scripturale, la production est inscrite et lisible dans son produit' (ibid.). From this perspective, exchange and representation simply become irrelevant: 'l'ecriture efface, annule le produit en tant qu'objet de consommation (en tant qu'il comporte un signifié, un sens consommable' (ibid.) – and Saussure's analogy is rendered null and void. It is thus by introducing the concept of exchange, in its opposition to production, that *Tel Quel* move away from the Althusserian definition of practice (neither Althusser or Macherey uses the concept of exchange in relation to literature) and towards a *formal* analogy between textual and economic production.

RELATIONS BETWEEN *TEL QUEL*
AND THE NOUVEAU ROMAN

When *Tel Quel* started in 1960, the Nouveau Roman was already well established. The new journal enthusiastically supported it: the first seven issues carried a total of eight texts by nouveaux romanciers (Simon, Ricardou, Robbe-Grillet, Butor, and also Robert Pinget and Claude Ollier). They also organised a series of long interviews with contemporary writers, in which Barthes was followed by Sarraute (no. 9), Butor (no. 11) and Robbe-Grillet (no. 14). (In addition, the second issue contains a 'Petit dictionnaire des idées reçues 1960' which informs its readers that the right things to say on the subject of the Nouveau Roman are: 'Alain Robbe-Grillet: meilleur romancier que théoricien – un ingénieur agronome. Nathalie Sarraute: a commencé avant Robbe-Grillet. Michel Butor: *L'Emploi du temps* est supérieur à *La Modification*. Claude Simon: Le Faulkner français'.)

Sollers particularly admired Robbe-Grillet, and saw himself more or less as his disciple (in 1960 Robbe-Grillet was thirty-eight and Sollers was twenty-four); in an interview two years later in *Le Figaro littéraire* (22 September 1962, 3) he says: 'Le Nouveau Roman a été l'expérience qui m'a appris à être sérieux', and names Robbe-Grillet as one of a number of writers (including also Butor) who 'Pour moi . . . ont été comme des maîtres . . . ils m'ont aidé à acquérir une discipline.' In return, the Nouveau Roman was happy to support *Tel Quel* and Sollers: Robbe-Grillet and Sarraute were on the jury that awarded the Prix Médicis to Sollers's novel *Le Parc* in 1961. In the second issue of *Tel Quel* Sollers wrote 'Sept propositions sur Alain Robbe-Grillet', an extremely positive review of *Dans le labyrinthe* (ironically, in view of subsequent developments, his review of Ricardou's first novel in issue no. 6 was notably less enthusiastic).[16] Among the nouveaux romanciers, and although Lucette Finas writes a sensitive piece on Sarraute in 1965,[17] it is Robbe-Grillet who commands the greatest attention. But *Tel Quel*'s attitude towards him becomes steadily more negative, for reasons which have more to do with his theoretical positions than his novels and films. The charting of Robbe-Grillet's decline in the pages of *Tel Quel* is thus revelatory not only of their move towards a more clearly defined theory of writing, but also of the problems which the Nouveau Roman had in getting to grips with this.

'Sept propositions sur Alain Robbe-Grillet' not only praises *Dans le labyrinthe*, but also defends Robbe-Grillet's *theoretical* writings against those literary conservatives who had claimed that his own novels were in contradiction with his theories, and that the latter were in any case crude, simplistic and ignorant. Sollers writes:

Pourquoi les déclarations de Robbe-Grillet ont-elles à ce point choqué? . . . L'intelligence ne devrait pas répugner, il me semble, à ces sortes de simplifications salutaires, si l'art doit les établir dans une complexité esthétique seule à les justifier. Eh bien, les livres de Robbe-Grillet sont cette justification par quoi ses déclarations deviennent nécessaires, contrairement à ce qu'il est convenu d'affirmer . . . les théories de Robbe-Grillet, ce sont ses mots d'ordre: elles sont intéressantes non pas dans la mesure où il s'en écarte, mais dans celle où il tâche de s'y conformer. (52)

This contrasts markedly with his review of *Pour un nouveau roman* exactly four years later, the moment at which *Tel Quel* definitively breaks with Robbe-Grillet. In fact, though, signs of disaffection are evident earlier on, and the form they take is symptomatic of the underlying reasons which led to the eventual highly-publicised break. In issue no. 6, Jean-Edern Hallier, the first editor of *Tel Quel*, writes a fairly critical article arguing that the nouveaux romanciers are not as original as they claim to be. He also introduces the idea that the 'convenient label' of Nouveau Roman in fact covers two very different types of novel: one 'behaviorist' and one in the tradition of Faulkner and Dostoeievsky.[18]

Although Hallier was ousted from the editorial board at the end of 1963, this article expresses the beginnings of a perception which, in different forms, was to prove an important part of *Tel Quel*'s critique of the Nouveau Roman in general and Robbe-Grillet in particular. That is, the distinction that Hallier makes here is presumably opposing Robbe-Grillet on the one hand to the 'psychological'novels of Sarraute and Simon (who was openly influenced by Faulkner) on the other. But it turns upon a contrast between 'objective' and 'subjective' writing which was *also* to become an important contradiction within Robbe-Grillet's own work. Indeed, the article by Genette discussed here in Chapter 2 was first published in *Tel Quel* (no. 8). It constitutes the first serious statement of the problem with Robbe-Grillet's theory – namely that he replaces the original 'objectivist' interpretation of his novels with a 'subjectivist' one (i.e., claiming that the novels represent the psychological state of a perceiving subject); and that his attempt to ground this realistically in psychological theory is not very convincing.[19] Ricardou echoes Genette's conclusions when he reviews *Instantanés* at the beginning of 1963 (no. 12). Robbe-Grillet replies to these criticisms by claiming that he has been misunderstood. When *Tel Quel* interviews him in the summer of 1963 (no. 14), he explains that his subjectivism is not a reversal but a completion of his previous position – which does not really answer Genette's criticisms – and then that the place of theory for him is in any case secondary: the Nouveau Roman is constantly changing and its evolution takes place on the level of the fiction itself, rather than that of theory.

In the autumn of 1963 *Tel Quel* organised a conference on 'Une nouvelle littérature' (the papers were printed in *Tel Quel* no. 17). The opening paper, Jean-Pierre Faye's 'Nouvelle analogie?', contains a substantial attack on Robbe-Grillet. As the title suggests, it proposes a new theory of metaphor which is in many ways similar to the ideas developed a few years later by Ricardou: metaphor to be seen not, as Robbe-Grillet had argued in 'Nature, humanisme, tragédie', as the expression of a humanist complicity with the world of nature, but as a *transformational* structure (8). In other words, Faye is aiming to reverse the condemnation of metaphor which characterises Robbe-Grillet's objectivist period. He argues that while these theoretical writings (especially 'Nature, humanisme, tragédie') claim to be an advance on existentialism and phenomenology, in reality they merely appropriate a simplified version of the phenomenological concept of the Dasein ('l'être-là') and reinsert it into an overall view which is a *regression* from phenomenology into a positivism that was already discredited at the end of the nineteenth century for its failure to grasp the problematic nature of the relation between perceiving subject and objective world. Positivism assumes that my perception of the world is automatically accurate; there can be no difference between the world and my perception of it, so in a sense the world is (might as well be) nothing but my perception of it. Faye claims that this is identical to the position adopted by Robbe-Grillet, which lacks any awareness of the way in which the *process* of perception affects both subject and object. Therefore, although he primarily criticises the 'objectivist' Robbe-Grillet, the implication of his argument, like Genette's, is that Robbe-Grillet's reductivism – the absence of any *relation* between subject and object – also vitiates his second 'subjectivist' stance. The debate which follows Faye's introduction to the conference is dominated by a consideration of Robbe-Grillet's work, and in particular includes a long and mainly laudatory discussion of *La Jalousie* in which everyone, including Sollers, agrees that this novel does contain metaphors, contrary to Robbe-Grillet's prescriptions in 'Nature, humanisme, tragédie', and is therefore not subject to the same charge of positivism. Ironically, the view of Robbe-Grillet which *Tel Quel* previously denounced as an 'idée reçue' – 'meilleur romancier que théoricien' – seems to have proved completely accurate.

The next number of *Tel Quel* (18, 93–4) carries Sollers's review of *Pour un nouveau roman*, which constitutes the final and total rejection of Robbe-Grillet. It does not, in fact, contain any new criticisms of him, but restates the ideas already put forward by Genette, Ricardou and Faye in a far more trenchant and aggressive form. He writes that Robbe-Grillet's failure to theorise the relation between subject and object results in 'une dialectique de l'erreur qui fonctionne mécaniquement' (93), shuttling back and forth between subject and object without examining either term. As a result, the apparent radicality of his objectivism merely collapses back into traditional psychologism,[20] and Robbe-Grillet ends up an accomplice to the most reactionary bourgeois literature. What is urgently needed, Sollers concludes, is a new form of novel which will leave behind the futile opposition of object and subject, and inaugurate instead a problematic of *writing*, 'dans une pratique vraiment intégrale du langage et de la pensée. C'est-à-dire dans la seule dimension enfin avouée (et démystifiée), dans le relatif absolu de l'*écrire*: à tous les niveaux' (94).

From this point onwards the argument between Robbe-Grillet and Sollers becomes increasingly personal and trivial. Robbe-Grillet counter-attacks in an interview in *Le Figaro littéraire* (7–13 octobre 1965, 3) just before the publication of *La Maison de rendez-vous*: he defends his continuing use of realistic elements, and objects to what he sees as *Tel Quel*'s claim to have taken over the Nouveau Roman, saying:

> Je ne suis pas du tout d'accord avec certains romanciers plus jeunes que moi qui prétendent être les descendants du nouveau roman et que je ne nommerai pas . . . et qui pensent que l'idéal est qu'il n'y ait rien d'autre, dans le livre, que le romancier en face de son papier, en train d'écrire un roman qui ne serait que le roman du roman qu'il ne réussit pas à écrire, etc. C'est peut-être très intéressant, mais j'ai en tout cas prêché pour autre chose.

Sollers duly replies that 'Il ne s'agit pas, on le voit, d'écrire "le roman du roman", – d'écrire que l'on est incapable d'écrire un roman',[21] but rather to probe the workings of language and question their ideological effects. He also castigates Robbe-Grillet as a writer who has sold out to the establishment; and, on an even more personal note, the same number of *Tel Quel* quotes sarcastically from an interview which Robbe-Grillet gave in *Lui* about his sex-life.

By the publication of *Théorie d'ensemble* in 1968, therefore, *Tel Quel*'s view of Robbe-Grillet had hardened into a rather contemptuous rejection. The preface dismisses the Nouveau Roman as a whole, along with existentialism, as a mere 'retombée culturelle' (8).

Later in the volume, Sollers writes that after a fairly brief phase of support of the Nouveau Roman, *Tel Quel* rejected it on the grounds of its positivist ideology and its wavering between 'une survivance psychologiste ("courant de conscience") et un "descriptionnisme" décorativement structural' (392). It can be argued, however, that relationships between the two groups were not as uniformly hostile as the polemic between Sollers and Robbe-Grillet would suggest. For one thing, the first article in *Théorie d'ensemble* is Michel Foucault's 'Distance, aspect, origine', which explores the relationships between Robbe-Grillet's novels and those of the *Tel Quel* novelists (Sollers, Baudry and Jean Thibaudeau) in a way that does full justice to Robbe-Grillet's position as the precursor without whom subsequent developments would not have been possible. Indeed, the assumption underlying Foucault's article is that Robbe-Grillet is the most important of contemporary French writers, and the *Tel Quel* novelists merely promising beginners whom Foucault is promoting. This accords with the view generally held in 1963 when the article was originally published; what is surprising is that *Tel Quel* should have chosen to reprint it five years later, after the break with the Nouveau Roman, in their 1968 collection of major theoretical articles. It suggests, perhaps, that *Tel Quel* is still willing to recognise the importance of the *fiction* of the Nouveau Roman, as distinct from its theorising. Indeed, the winter 1971 issue opens with a text by Simon (no. 44, 3–16).

A second factor is the position of Ricardou. He belongs to the 'generation' of *Tel Quel* rather than that of the original nouveaux romanciers: his first novel was published in 1961, the same year as Sollers's *Le Parc*. Also, he joined the editorial board of *Tel Quel* in 1962, and remained on it until 1971. Unlike Sollers , however, he also considered himself to be a nouveau romancier; in fact he saw himself as the Nouveau Roman's leading theorist. By the end of the 1960s he had acquired a far more dominant position in the Nouveau Roman than he ever had in *Tel Quel*; but the fact that he managed to remain part of both groups over this period suggests, again, that the relations between them were not completely antagonistic. (He left *Tel Quel* in November 1971; the journal's commitment to Maoism, inaugurated by Sollers's article on Mao's theory of contradictions in the spring 1971 issue and culminating in the 'déclaration de Juin '71' led to Ricardou being accused of formalism and expelled from the group.)

Textual production was a central theme of Ricardou's second

theoretical book *Pour une théorie du nouveau roman* (1971); here he brings it to bear upon the work of the nouveau romanciers, especially Simon and Robbe-Grillet. In so far as the Nouveau Roman collectively adopt this notion, they do so as a result of Ricardou's efforts to move them in the direction of *Tel Quel*. But they do not all accept this reorientation of their work; textual production, in fact, is responsible for one of the most clear-cut splits within the group. Sarraute is simply unwilling to abandon her belief that language expresses a pre-existing subjective reality; and Butor remains too Sartrean in his attitude to realism and, more generally, too humanist in his view of culture and society, to be able to subscribe to an anti-humanist and anti-representational position. Robbe-Grillet and Simon, on the other hand, were at the time happy to accept and endorse Ricardou's readings of their fiction, and hence the concept of textual production.

The issue came to a head at the NRHA conference of 1971, which was organised by Ricardou in conjunction with Raymond Jean and Françoise van Rossum-Guyon, soon after the publication of *Pour une théorie du nouveau roman*. In the context of the political significance of their work it is not irrelevant that this was the first major meeting of the group since 1968. Raymond Jean claims that 'surtout depuis 1968, nous sommes entrés dans une époque où la thématique politique est redevenue une chose profondément vivante liée à une recherche réelle, à des interrogations réelles' (I, 370). In fact, however, the conference as a whole does not give the impression that the events of May '68 affected the Nouveau Roman to any great extent; they did not have anything like the same impact on it as they did on *Tel Quel*, for instance. The occasional references which do occur in the course of the conference stress the way in which the students' contestation of the university as institution overlaps with the Nouveau Roman's critique of academic literary criticism, and they centre mainly on the notion of 'récupération universitaire'.[22]

Nevertheless, on a more abstract level this conference constitutes the principle reference point for the discussion of the Nouveau Roman's response to structuralist Marxism. It was therefore also a turning point in the evolution of the Nouveau Roman, not least because it consolidated the ascendancy of Ricardou over the group. In the 1960s the most prominent members of the Nouveau Roman were Robbe-Grillet, Simon, Pinget, Sarraute, Butor, and Duras; by 1971 the last three of these had been marginalised, and replaced by Ricardou. Marguerite Duras refused her invitation to attend. Butor compromised by sending a paper to be read by someone else (the content of which led Robbe-Grillet to claim that although Butor is asking the same question as the rest of them, 'cette question . . . n'a pas du tout le même sens pour lui et pour nous' (II, 281); Nathalie Sarraute came, and read a paper, but expressed strong reservations about the direction the group was taking. Conversely, Claude Ollier who, like Ricardou, was closely associated with *Tel Quel*, attended the conference and gave a theoretically sophisticated and very well received paper. The loss of some of the novelists is compensated by the inclusion of some of the critics. The group's conception of reading as active participation in the production of the text means that figures such as Françoise van Rossum-Guyon, for instance, can legitimately be considered as part of the group; as she herself puts it in her closing paper: 'Par le dialogue qui s'est institué entre les écrivains et leurs lecteurs, entre les producteurs de textes et leurs critiques, le Nouveau Roman est en outre apparu comme une production dont les écrivains sont certes les premiers responsables mais dont ils ne sont pas les seuls responsables' (I, 400).

The problem Ricardou discusses in his initial address is: 'Le Nouveau Roman existe-t-il?'; and although he concludes that it does, the choice of topic is symptomatic of both the need to define some kind of collective identity, and the difficulty of doing so. As the title of the conference suggests, its main concern is to look at how the Nouveau Roman has changed since its beginnings in the 1950s: at whether or not there is a clear break between 'yesterday' and 'today', and, if so, how to define it and its implications for the future. The break is formulated as a distinction between the Nouveau Roman and the 'Nouveau Nouveau Roman'; the latter radicalises the formalising and anti-representational tendencies of the earlier work. Simon and Robbe-Grillet are seen as having made the transition from one to the other, with *La Bataille de Pharsale* and *La Maison de rendez-vous* respectively. Sarraute has not, and there is some disagreement as to whether Butor has – that is, whether *Mobile* counts as a 'Nouveau Nouveau Roman' or not.[23] Ricardou's novels are all 'Nouveaux Nouveaux Romans'; indeed, according to Robbe-Grillet, he invented the concept ('ce Nouveau Nouveau Roman, qui est en train de naître sous la houlette de Jean Ricardou . . . ' (I, 206)).

In addition, however, the Nouveau Nouveau Roman is some-times assumed to contain the work of the *Tel Quel* novelists – Sollers, Pleynet, Thibaudeau and Baudry. Sometimes, however, these are

seen as fundamentally different from even the recent fiction of
Robbe-Grillet and Simon. Ricardou's article 'Nouveau Roman, *Tel
Quel'* in *Pour une théorie du nouveau roman,* for instance, takes this
view. He concludes, however, with a statement of the *paradoxical*
relation between the two groups: 'Toute de proximité et de distance,
cette radicalisation par *Tel Quel* de l'activité du Nouveau Roman,
seule une figure contradictoire qui puisse la rendre. Songeons donc,
pour conclure, à un lieu paradoxal où l'appui le plus vif entraîne
l'écart le plus ample: le tremplin' (1971, 265). In other words the
Nouveau Nouveau Roman, as represented by Ricardou, Robbe-
Grillet and Simon, is bouncing around somewhere in between the
'old' Nouveau Roman and *Tel Quel.* When Ricardou is asked at
the conference whether he is speaking on behalf of *Tel Quel* or the
Nouveau Roman, he says he cannot answer the question in those
terms: 'Il y a actuellement un travail collectif qui n'appartient à
aucun groupe, n'est subsumable par aucun groupe, dont je serais,
quel qu'il soit, ici le porte-parole' (I, 389). Nevertheless, despite
or because of these ambiguities, the future development of the
Nouveau Roman is seen by the conference as a whole as being
dependent on their being able to establish some kind of clearly
defined relationship with *Tel Quel.* Denis St-Jacques's paper puts
it unsympathetically, but with a certain amount of truth:

> L'apparition de *Tel Quel* provoque une crise chez les nouveaux
> romanciers qui doivent soit s'aligner plus ou moins, soit se
> retrouver entre le parti de la tradition et la nouvelle avant-garde.
> *Tel Quel* semble bien en voie de conquérir la même fraction
> sociologique du public qu'à son époque le nouveau roman des
> années cinquante. On peut donc dire que le nouveau roman
> devient aujourd'hui ce que *Tel Quel* le veut . . . (I, 140)

Indeed, despite *Tel Quel's* rejection of the Nouveau Roman, the
general impression given at the NRHA conference – in the absence
of those who disagree, of course – is of the nouveaux romanciers
trying to keep up with the theoretical pace being set by *Tel Quel.*
Françoise van Rossum-Guyon, for instance, cites the systematic
transgression of literary norms as the distinguishing characteristic of
the Nouveau Roman, but then says that this phenomenon 's'affirme
encore plus nettement et trouve en outre sa justification théorique
chez certain écrivains du groupe *Tel Quel'* (I, 224); and a similar idea
recurs in Sylvère Lotringer's paper (I, 328).[24]

THE NOUVEAU ROMAN'S USE OF TEXTUAL PRODUCTION

What made Sartre's idea of literature impossible for the Nouveau Roman to accept was not so much the importance he attached to political reality as the definition of *language* that followed from it. According to Sartre, that is, the language of a novel is necessarily subordinate to the world-view it presents, and therefore has to be seen as an instrument rather than an end in itself. For the nouveaux romanciers, as we have seen, this is totally incompatible with any valid kind of writing. With the introduction of Althusser's and *Tel Quel*'s notions of practice and production *in the place of* representation and the instrumentality of language, therefore, the main obstacle in the way of the Nouveau Roman's adherence to a Marxist view of literature no longer applies; and their previous opposition to humanist Marxism in fact means that, not having to relinquish any already invested positions, they are well-placed to take advantage of the advent of the 'relative autonomy of the ideological'.

How, then, does the NRHA conference interpret and develop the idea of textual production? Ricardou's introductory paper takes it for granted that the Nouveau Roman 'is' textual production (e.g., page 10); van Rossum-Guyon's closing remarks to the conference reaffirm that 'les nouveaux romanciers se trouvent aujourd'hui réunis par une conception nouvelle de la littérature considérée comme *production*' (I, 404). They place considerable emphasis on the *work* of producing meanings, on the text as process rather than finished object – 'écrire serait produire des sens qui n'existent pas et, mieux, produire la production de ces sens' (Ricardou, I, 102). Both speakers also address themselves to the problem of ideology, and assume that it is one of their main aims to attack bourgeois ideology by means of textual production – a process which Ricardou later sums up as 'l'écriture, prise dans une situation idéologique donnée, investit cette situation dans un procès de transformation' (I, 179). In his introduction he notes that the Nouveau Roman has not been recuperated by the dominant ideology, but nor has it been able to overthrow it – 'sans doute parce que cela suppose aussi des bouleversements d'une autre nature . . . ' (I, 10). He stresses that the Nouveau Roman is situated at one of the key points of cultural *conflict*, and that its theoretical work must proceed from that basic fact. This is repeated by van Rossum-Guyon in her conclusion (I, 405), and she adds that the fundamental question of *how*, concretely, writing can best attack the dominant ideology has not yet been resolved and remains on the agenda for future discussion.

In fact the conference papers which address the problem most directly come from theorists who are situated, to varying degrees, outside the collective project of the Nouveau Roman. Denis St-Jacques is very sceptical about the political effectiveness of textual production and *Tel Quel*'s position in general; Jacques Leenhardt retains the basically humanist perspective inspired by Lucien Goldmann (and thus not dissimilar to Sartre), although modified towards a greater emphasis on form rather than content; and Raymond Jean, while understanding the reasons for the Nouveau Roman's anti-representational strategy, and accepting that 'pure productive writing' is political, would still like them to work on more directly political themes: 'Ne serait-il pas plus politique encore, si la matière choisie l'était elle-même davantage?' (371). The position that one could attribute to the Nouveau Roman proper, therefore, emerges in a rather fragmentary fashion, through the discussions following the papers as much as the papers themselves. Robbe-Grillet's 'Sur le choix des générateurs' is perhaps the most sustained presentation of his version of textual production; but it is possible to assemble the comments made by him, by Ricardou and others in the course of the conference, and on the basis of these to construct something of more general scope, a configuration of overlapping ideas, that could be termed the Nouveau Roman's theory of textual production.

In the past, their rejection of representation had tended to result in a conception of the text as an autonomous, self-contained structure, having no apparent connections with the world around it. In the 1963 interview Robbe-Grillet gave in *Tel Quel*, for instance, he emphasises that 'Il s'agit pour moi de *construire* quelque chose, à partir de rien, et qui tienne debout tout seul, sans avoir à s'appuyer sur quoi que ce soit d'extérieur à l'œuvre' (45). Conversely, those writers who foregrounded the *critical* function of the Nouveau Roman presented it from a representational point of view, i.e., as a form of realism: thus for Butor and Sarraute, the Nouveau Roman exists above all in order to reveal outworn, misleading literary conventions for what they are – so that the reader may attain a clearer grasp of reality. In other words, the choice was between representing reality and having no relation with reality at all. Textual production, in contrast, replaces this simple dichotomy with the new possibility of a *different kind* of relation with reality. 'L'acception de

la productivité textuelle', Kristeva writes, ' . . . n'implique aucune
conception du texte littéraire comme "littéralité" qui s'auto-satisfait
dans une isolation précieuse' (1969, 177). Ricardou echoes this in
more Althusserian terms when he distinguishes between 'autonomy' and the 'specificity' of the text's relations to what is outside
it (I, 102); he adds, later in the conference, that 'Ce qui serait grave,
ce serait de croire que le rapport de la littérature au monde est
représentatif ou n'est pas' (I, 373). Autonomy, in this sense, is
associated with the earlier phase of structuralism that is criticised at
several points in the conference – van Rossum-Guyon, for instance,
referring to the 'great danger' of 'la clôture du texte, d'une seule lecture immanente' as a form of lapsing back into 'la première époque
disons du structuralisme que l'on croyait maintenant dépassée' (I,
253).

This new kind of relation between the text and the world is
formulated in Ricardou's concept of *referential responsibility*. He had
in fact been maintaining for some time that the critical function
of literature lay in its ability to offer an alternative to reality, a
different structure of relations – a sentence to this effect from his
1967 book is, significantly, quoted at the conference (I, 261–2). But
'referential responsibility' as a term is introduced only in 1971, in
Pour une théorie du nouveau roman, as the heading to the final section
of his article on Robbe-Grillet's *Projet pour une révolution à New
York.* Here, arguing that representation is inherently misleading and
irresponsible, he evokes a possible relation between text and world
which reinstates and clarifies their separation, by carefully refusing
any element of representation: 'Trompeuse, feignant les choses
mêmes pour s'abolir comme telle, la fiction représentative peut
indifféremment en accueillir n'importe quel aspect. Détrompeuse,
se différenciant des choses mêmes pour s'établir comme telle, la
fiction moderne est astreinte à une minutieuse vigilance' (1971,
232).

In fact he argues that the writer must be especially careful to avoid
representing *political* reality, because it is here that the danger of
confusion is greatest: 'Plus que tout autre, on l'imagine, le politique
et ses aspects les plus violents, guerre civile et révolution, se situent
au centre de ce domaine névralgique. Si Claude Simon a pris le
méticuleux soin d'interdire, dans *Le Palace,* tout sigle de partis,
c'est pour que ne puissent abusivement se confondre, au détriment
de l'un comme de l'autre, un ordre politique et un ordre littéraire'
(ibid.). This idea is echoed at the conference in Robbe-Grillet's

account of his arguments with Alain Resnais in the making of
L'Année dernière à Marienbad: Resnais wanted to include dialogue
about the Algerian war, but Robbe-Grillet felt that 'je préférais ne
pas faire le film plutôt que de citer une seule fois le mot Algérie et,
justement, pour des raisons politiques. Je sentais que la prétention
d'un intellectuel à intervenir de façon politique dans ses œuvres
de fiction n'était pas raisonnable . . . Plutôt que d'opérer sur des
contenus politiques connus d'avance (par exemple les problèmes du
colonialisme), la révolution que la littérature (ou le cinéma) poursuit
serait une révolution générale du sens' (I, 173). Ricardou explains
the concept of referential responsibility further in the course of
his comments on Raymond Jean's paper (I, 373–4). The Nouveau
Roman, he says, is just as passionately committed as Jean is to the
relation between literature and the world, but does not conceive it
in terms of representation. He goes on: 'Comment donc le définir?
Il est inscription, mise en écriture. Le monde ne sera pas représenté;
certains de ses aspects – et par exemple idéologique, politique
– pris comme matériau seront l'objet d'un fonctionnement autre
qui . . . va opérer une procédure de transformation. Etre pénétré de
la responsabilité référentielle, . . . c'est pratiquer la production qui,
en disposant un rapport différentiel, conteste cette idée préalable
qu'on se faisait du monde' (374).

This formulation is similar in some ways to Althusser's and
Macherey's conception of the *critical* distancing function of all
literature: by 'producing' ideology in a particular literary form,
the text 'makes it visible' and thus transforms our relation to it
(see above). Ricardou, too, speaks of modern literature's 'rapport
actif de critique . . . avec le politique et l'idéologique' (I, 381). But
he (and *Tel Quel*) would see Althusser and Macherey as still too
close to the ideology of realism, and as not stressing the necessity of
combating representation. For Ricardou, reality must cease to be the
object of a representation if it is to become instead the raw material
which is transformed by the text. Equally, the transformation will be
possible only if reality itself can be apprehended in a *textual* form. As
Ricardou's term 'inscription' implies, the text can work only on textual material: the world in general and ideology in particular have
to be 'written into' it.[25] The claim is, in other words, that the 'world',
insofar as it is experienced by subjects, *already* exists as 'text'.
Lévi-Strauss's notion of bricolage is one version of this idea that has
already been mentioned (see Chapter 2); it develops further in the
theorisation of *intertextuality* that will be considered in Chapter 5.

Textual production, then, implies referential responsibility and hence a relation between text and ideology that will be *non-representational, critical* and *transformational.* This general statement of the position is accepted by the conference as a whole, but its implementation on a more concrete level is interpreted in various different ways. One of these is Ollier's concept of writing as 'inscription conflictuelle': as trace, that is of the conflicts between individual and society which 'représentent une somme considérable de faits d'adaptation ou de rebellion, de mise au point ou de dérèglement, de dissimulation ou de dépouillement, d'assentiment, de parade ou d'agression' (II, 213); writing is the site of a permanent struggle to de-centre dominant forms and 'par un effet *de gauchissement, de détournement de leur visée idéologique,* de les tourner vers la lecture d'un sens autre' (214). Ollier remains a rather marginal figure in the Nouveau Roman group, and therefore I have not discussed his contribution in detail; but it is a precise and interesting alternative view of textual production.

The main difference between Robbe-Grillet's and Ricardou's fictional 'generators' is outlined in Robbe-Grillet's 'Sur le choix des générateurs' (II, 157–62): Ricardou chooses signifiers, and so the text is generated through phonetic or graphic play (rhymes, puns, anagrams, etc.). Robbe-Grillet criticises this on the grounds that it encourages a view of language as a-social, natural and innocent; it is, he argues, through their *meanings* that words are implicated in sociality, and therefore it is important for the writer wishing to intervene in and act on these ideological meanings to choose *signifieds* as generators. Specifically, Robbe-Grillet's signifieds are the myths of contemporary popular imagery: as examples he cites magazine covers, poster hoardings, sex-shop pornography, glossy fashion photography and comic strips (161). These are all drawn from what he sees as a kind of reservoir of social fantasy about sexuality, violence and crime.

By implication he is defending his work against the charge that it is less radical than the novels of Ricardou and the *Tel Quel* writers, and claiming that work on the signifieds of popular myth is a more effective *political* weapon than to 'effectuer gratuitement des opérations abstraites sur un matériau privé de tout enracinement dans la cité' (158). Thus he argues also, against Sollers, for the importance of retaining elements of narrative in texts (II, 347–8). Narrative should be disrupted, fragmented and subverted, but not *eliminated,* because that would simply wipe out the whole problematic of relations between narrative and society – precisely the area of 'inscription politique' that needs to be explored: 'De plus en plus j'ai besoin de ces fragments d'histoires, de ces histoires pluridimensionnelles et polysémiques. C'est là-dessus que porte le travail qui me passionne, et j'ai l'impression que, même politiquement, c'est justement là qu'il se passe quelque chose' (II, 348). There is an element of opportunism in this – the justification of narrative and the use of stereotyped images that Robbe-Grillet gives here is significantly different from the populist attitude which he adopted in newspaper interviews about *La Maison de rendez-vous*, for instance[26] – but the case is nevertheless quite cogent in its own terms. As for what he does with these materials, he presents the 'production' as a kind of meta-language – he does not simply reiterate 'la parole d'une société' but '[s'en sert] comme d'un matériau . . . afin de développer à partir d'elle [son] propre discours' (II, 160) – which deconstructs 'des éléments découpés dans le code' and *reveals* them to be ideological; in so doing he asserts his freedom: '[il s'agit] de *les parler* c'est-à-dire d'exercer sur eux ma liberté au lieu de les subir comme des pièges, au fonctionnement fixé à l'avance et comme fatal' (161). In thus liberating him and his readers from the myth of the natural, the text as metalanguage rejoins the notion of *play* that is fundamental to his work; his 'parole ludique' is not a retreat from the world but a way of questioning and transforming both himself and the world (I, 97).

A rather different view of textual production arises in connection with Raymond Jean's paper. He suggests that texts should incorporate dominant social and political discourses in the form of 'documents':

> La réalité sociologique, historique, politique, me semble pouvoir être introduite dans le roman, et pourquoi pas, par exemple, sous forme de citations, pièces d'actualité, "prélèvements", extraits de journaux, discours, lettres, éléments de reportage, etc., surtout en une époque qui se caractérise par l'abondance de *messages* et *informations* qui interviennent à tout moment dans notre exist-ence . . . Le roman est nécessairement fiction: ce n'est pas une raison pour renoncer à y lire les *textes* du monde où nous vivons. (I, 371)

This would presumably include documents that are more overtly political than Robbe-Grillet's 'contemporary mythology'; and Jean's emphasis is more concretely on their status as texts. Ricardou endorses this kind of *citational* reworking as offering an insight into the way in which ideology is constructed as text: 'si le Nouveau Roman permet de mieux comprendre les mécanismes de fabrication du texte, ses lecteurs seront mieux à même de comprendre les mécanismes de fabrication des divers discours idéologiques dont ils sont bombardés' (I, 380–1). In fact, Ricardou's *Pour une théorie du nouveau roman* already contains a passage on 'Critique des langages coercitifs' (25–7) which puts forward a similar argument. Production is seen here as a semiological critique which in effect *analyses* the mechanisms whereby ideological discourses function. The discussion of Jean's paper additionally produces the idea that the insertion and juxtaposition of different political discourses in a text minimises the importance of the individual author as subject, effecting 'une anonymisation de la parole'; Ricardou agrees, commenting that 'Si la tradition du livre est liée à une parole individuelle, l'injection de textes politiques fait intervenir une sorte de collectivité agissante. Il y a, à ce niveau, contestation indiscutable' (I, 383).

Yet another way of implementing textual production is contained in Françoise van Rossum-Guyon's paper, 'Le Nouveau Roman comme critique du roman' (I, 215–29). This remains within a more strictly literary field of reference. The Nouveau Roman had, of course, always considered that its principal characteristic was its oppositional attitude towards literary tradition. It had, in other words, always seen itself as transgressing the established norms of narrative progression, characterisation, dialogue and so on, and claimed that this act of transgression also constituted a critique and exposure of the conventions as being, precisely, conventional. Now, however, in the wake of the theoretical advances of *Tel Quel*, literary conventions are shown to be in an important sense complicit with bourgeois ideology: Sollers's conception of the novel, in particular, as the channel through which society speaks to us and moulds our subjectivity is echoed in Robbe-Grillet's reply to a question about the novel's late development in comparison with painting: 'C'est parce que les valeurs bourgeoises ont pesé beaucoup plus durement sur l'ordre du récit; l'ordre narratif était certainement ressenti comme lié davantage à l'ordre politique, moral, etc.' (II, 115). Once this connection has been established, it follows logically that the subversion of literary conventions is in itself *by definition* a subversion of ideological values. Van Rossum-Guyon's main argument is that, while emergent literary movements have always broken with the prevailing literary codes, the Nouveau Roman is the first to have made this notion of transgression into the basic principle for the text's production (I, 224). The effect of breaking the rules is to make the reader aware of their existence and also of the possibility of a different kind of writing (218–19). The principle function of the Nouveau Roman is thus to expose the real status of literary conventions, and by the same token to reinstate the primacy of production: in so doing, it becomes both its own theory and a theory of the novel in general.

These various ideas in fact resolve themselves into three main programmes for practising textual production, each of which engages with different manifestations of the dominant ideology: Robbe-Grillet's stereotypes of popular culture, Raymond Jean's citation of political discourse, and van Rossum-Guyon's exposure of literary-ideological codes. All three, however, have one feature in common, although van Rossum-Guyon's paper is the clearest instance of it: that is, an implicit tendency to *equate* ideology in general with *representation*. In order to understand how this position arises, one needs to reconstruct the (unstated) argument that lies behind it.

The first important factor is that throughout the conference textual production is opposed primarily to representation: representation is the main enemy.[27] (Ricardou's introduction to the conference, for instance, builds up to a final attack on 'la vieille littérature de Représentation' (I, 20).) In this the Nouveau Roman differs from *Tel Quel* for whom the opposition between production and representation is developed further, as discussed earlier, into a theory of production versus *exchange* – which is not taken up to any great extent by the Nouveau Roman. In effect, the Nouveau Roman has taken over from *Tel Quel* the concept of textual *production* but severed it from its connections with exchange and circulation.

This significantly alters the implications attaching to the concept of production itself. In the first place, *Tel Quel*'s opposition between production and exchange or circulation focused attention on the difference between the spurious legitimacy of a system of circulation, and the overt *force* of production which contested the system from the outside.[28] Rather than a means of putting into place new meanings alongside old ones, therefore, production is seen by *Tel Quel* as essentially disruptive: as the *violence* done to the language system, and hence to the ideological system. This perspective inevitably loses some of its force when the constitutive opposition with exchange is lost in the Nouveau Roman's theorisation of production. In other words, 'production' comes to mean something rather different simply through being constructed in opposition, not to exchange *and* (therefore) representation, but to the purely literary concept of representation.

More importantly, the targeting of *representation* as the main opponent of production implicitly determines a certain conception of *ideology*. Textual production is first and foremost a means of subverting bourgeois ideology; and only productive 'écriture' works on ideology in this way: representational literature does not. Conversely, literary representation is a major weapon of bourgeois ideology. But it comes to be seen as more than that: the nouveaux romanciers' central focus on production as anti-representation – rather than anti-exchange – tends to effect a blurring of any distinction *between* representation and ideology. The two concepts slide one on top of the other: since production contests both of them, they begin to look like the same thing. Thus Ricardou can argue that representational fiction is *'conforme* à certain mythe régnant de la réalité' (I, 376, my italics). Later in the same discussion he goes so far as to claim that the parallel between representation (and expression) and the ideology of imperialism is so strong that to produce anti-representational texts is in itself a contestation of imperialism.[29] As a consequence, the importance of literary representation – the enemy – is enlarged to the dimensions of ideology in general: it is not just a case of the literary ideology *of* representation but of ideology *as* literary representation.

This slippage of meaning turns on the notion of *illusion*. Representation is usually referred to as 'l'illusion référentielle' , or 'l'illusion représentative' (I, 29). Illusion is in fact the concept which underpins the Nouveau Roman's critique of representation and their promotion of textual productivity: textual production reveals the truth of the text, which is that it is made of language, against representational discourse which tries to 'occulter qu'une fiction écrite soit faite de langage' (Ricardou, I, 376). There is, however, more than this at stake: representation is an illusion not simply because it is fiction (characters in a novel are not real people, etc.), but more fundamentally because, as we have seen, its content is *ideological*: it reproduces the 'illusions' already enshrined in bourgeois ideology.

In other words, ideology itself is also considered to be an illusion. The circle of identifications works both ways: ideology and literary representation are the same, therefore ideology must be an illusion too; *and/or* both literary representation and ideology are illusions, therefore they must be the same thing. Ricardou's assimilation of the two, quoted above, is in fact effected precisely in the context of an assumption that ideology is a 'myth' which 'hides' reality – as the argument in full makes clear:

> L'effet de représentation est une illusion . . . pour donner au lecteur l'impression que ce qu'il lit est la réalité même, il faut établir une conformité entre la fiction et *le mythe que le lecteur se fait de la réalité*. Rien comme cette confusion entre la réalité et *le mythe* que l'on peut se faire à tel moment de la réalité, pour occulter, précisément, la réalité . . . Avec le non-représentatif, en revanche, la fiction, cessant d'être conforme à certain mythe régnant de la réalité, cesse de passer fallacieusement pour la réalité. Ce qui surgit alors c'est un conflit éminemment idéologique, entre fiction nouvelle et ce mythe régnant. Or, si ce mythe de la réalité est bien ce qui cache la réalité, la fiction non-représentative est bien un combat, à son niveau, pour la réalité. (I, 376, Ricardou's italics)

The three projects specifically discussed above are no exception to this view of ideology as illusion. Robbe-Grillet's programme of de-naturalisation involves showing the ideological for what it is, and his description of the process draws on a whole lexis of *revelation*; as he puts it, the elements of the code have to be '*désignés* comme mythologiques . . . tirés *au grand jour* au lieu de baigner *obscurément* dans leur plasma d'origine: l'ordre établi, qui a justement pour fonction de les *faire passer inaperçus*, comme allant de soi' (II, 161, my italics). Similarly, Ricardou's 'critique de langages coercitifs' carries the implication that these discourses are *deceiving*: 'le déchiffrement sera capable de *démasquer* aussitôt tous langages coercitifs, en lesquels maints pouvoirs producteurs sont détournés et asservis pour venir *insidieusement renforcer les "idées" qu'on souhaite répandre* . . . [cette lecture saura] *démasquer les rhétoriques honteuses qui agissent dans les langages pipés*' (1971, 26, my italics). And, finally, Lucien Dällenbach echoes van Rossum-Guyon's emphasis when he says: 'plus le texte . . . exhibera des structures de textes et des structures de langage, plus il permettra précisément la critique de ces *faux textes* et de ces *langages mensongers dans lesquels nous baignons*' (I, 284, my italics).

The Althusserian conception of literature 'making ideology visible' does not carry the implication that what is made visible is an illusion; it is rather a question of producing an ideological *practice* in a form which enables the reader to achieve a certain critical distance on it. And some of the Nouveau Roman's formulations are also neutral on this point – for instance Ricardou's statement that: 'C'est parce qu'elle n'obéit ni aux directives jdanoviennes du réalisme socialiste, ni aux injonctions sartriennes de la littérature engagée, toutes deux liées au vieux dogme représentatif, que la littérature moderne peut avoir, dans sa spécificité, un *rapport actif de critique et non plus d'illustration avec le politique et l'idéologique*' (I, 381, my italics). The fictional practice of production, also, *can* be theorised in these more or less Althusserian terms. For instance, it is quite possible to see Robbe-Grillet's transformational 'play' with popular imagery, not as a means of 'unmasking' these fantasies as unreal, but simply as a critical analysis of their mode of functioning as *fantasies*. Also, the idea that ideology is illusion is nowhere overtly and definitely stated. But it is present quite pervasively as an assumption, underpinning the view that textual production consists of the deconstruction, transformation and critical unmasking of the *illusory* representations of ideology. What in fact is happening here is that the conceptual matrix of *illusion-revelation*, from operating just in the context of literature, is now surreptitiously carried over from the literary text to ideology itself. The implication is that both literary representation and ideology are illusions of a similar kind, and therefore it follows that theoretical work and anti-representational strategies in texts can reveal the truth behind them.

One consequence of this is to create a contradiction within the theory of textual production itself. The Nouveau Roman are in effect returning to the humanist conception of ideology as false consciousness which is explicitly criticised by Althusser. Thus despite having based their whole theory of 'revolutionary' texts on a conception of production which is ultimately founded in Althusser's conception of practice, the Nouveau Roman also make it dependent on a notion of ideology which he rejects in the strongest terms – the rejection of which is in fact central to his conception of practice. That is, for Althusser, 'practice' as a concept is only possible if, and is necessary because, the social totality is defined as an over-determined structure in which *each* 'instance' or level is relatively autonomous and therefore theorisable as a material practice; 'social practice', as the 'unité complexe des pratiques existant dans une société déterminée' (1966, 167) implies that the ideological is necessarily a practice, in exactly the same way as the political or the economic: as he goes on to say, 'On ne prend pas toujours au sérieux l'existence de l'idéologie comme pratique: cette reconnaissance préalable est pourtant la condition indispensable à toute théorie de l'idéologie' (ibid., 168). After arguing at some length against the idea that ideology is an illusion and that its existence is 'idéale, idéelle, spirituelle' (1970, 105), he states 'une idéologie existe toujours dans un appareil, et sa pratique, ou ses pratiques. Cette existence est matérielle' (ibid.).

Another consequence of the ideology-representation-illusion equation, and one which has a more immediate effect on the Nouveau Roman's conception of textual production, is an over-estimation of the power of their work on ideology. The aim of overthrowing the dominant ideology, which van Rossum-Guyon puts forward as a realistic programme for the Nouveau Roman to accomplish – 'il s'agit, pour les nouveau romanciers, non seulement de ne pas être "récupérés" par l'idéologie regnante mais, bel et bien, de la renverser' (I, 405) – is given more credibility than it would have otherwise by the fact that they have to a considerable extent, by 1971, succeeded in overthrowing the supremacy of *representation* as a literary doctrine.

The two features most often associated with textual production are that it is *critical*, and *transformational*. Usually the implications of these terms are not very clearly differentiated: production criticises by transforming, and vice versa. In the light of the idea that textual production can actually overthrow the dominant ideology, however, they need to be distinguished; because for this to be possible would mean that the effect of textual production is not only to achieve a critical perspective on ideology, but to transform ideology itself. The scope of the envisaged action has shifted, in other words, from a practice which produces a transformed version of the dominant ideology *in a text* (i.e., which allows the reader to 'see' it as ideology), to one in which the transformation is effective in the field of ideology *per se*: the text *changes* the ideology. This appears to be what Ricardou implies when he says: 'il suffit parfois de transformer un certain nombre d'éléments dans un champ idéologique donné, c'est ce que font nos textes. Avec la mise en circulation de nos textes, *le champ idéologique se trouve déplacé*: c'est là un acte de subversion' (I, 384, my italics). It is from this perspective that one has to understand Robbe-Grillet's claim that the 'révolution générale du sens' in which the Nouveau Roman is engaged is more fundamental than social revolution; echoing – if only momentarily – the Maoist position of *Tel Quel* at the time, he seems to see the Nouveau Roman as part of a cultural revolution that alone can guard against Soviet revisionism: 'Ainsi a-t-on vu le socialisme bureaucratique retomber dans l'idéologie bourgeoise: ayant fait seulement la révolution dans le domaine des rapports de production, ayant non seulement négligé mais combattu toute révolution du sens dans le domaine sexuel, littéraire, artistique en général, ils ne pouvaient que retrouver les valeurs de la bourgeoisie' (I, 174).

Perhaps the most important disadvantage, however, of the way in which ideology and representation come to be equated with one another, is that the specificity of the text's relation to ideology is lost. The central question in this – i.e., *how*, concretely, does textual production subvert the dominant ideology? – is dissolved into a series of general statements about the attack on representation, and thus becomes coextensive with the whole of the Nouveau Roman's literary project. There are, as we have seen, several attempts to theorise a more precisely political conception of textual production; but the fact that anti-representational writing of all kinds is in any case construed as an effective attack on bourgeois ideology provides a kind of fall-back position which lessens the need to develop such attempts further, and blurs the distinctions between them.

Ironically, the result is a regression, in effect, to the earlier view of 'autonomous' writing outlined at the beginning of this section. That is, the theory of textual production constituted an advance on previous positions because it offered a way out of the dichotomy whereby the text was seen either as representational, or as autonomous and completely cut off from the world around it. Textual production provided the basis for another kind of relation to the world: not the representation of objective reality but the inscription and transformation of the ideological intertext. Now, however, the substance of this new relation turns out to be nothing more than a *negation of representation*. If this is the case – if, in other words, inscription and transformation are merely subsumed into the category of anti-representational tactics in general – then the theory would seem to have collapsed in upon itself. It is difficult to perceive any real difference between a text which refuses to represent reality and is therefore an autonomous formal structure, and a text which refuses to represent reality and is therefore (and for no other reason) engaged in the subversion of bourgeois ideology. This weakness in the Nouveau Roman's theory can be traced back to their inability to see ideology as a practice in relation with other practices. The limitations of their conception of it as, instead, an illusory representation make it impossible to theorise the text's relation to it as anything other than an over-general and rather empty refusal of representation.

The idea recurs throughout the conference – and indeed through the Nouveau Roman's other theoretical work – that the novels are their own theory. Robbe-Grillet claims, for instance, that 'Tout en réclamant pour l'écrivain le droit à l'intelligence de sa création, et en insistant sur l'intérêt que présente pour lui la conscience de sa propre recherche, nous savons bien que c'est au niveau de l'écriture que cette recherche s'accomplit'.[30] And in this instance we can perhaps see that their fictional writing is in advance of their own conception of its theoretical implications. By the end of the conference it has become clear that answers to the questions raised are more likely to be found on the level of the *practice* of writing. Françoise van Rossum-Guyon's final summing-up paper at the conference makes this point very clearly: she states that the nouveaux romanciers are engaged in trying to overthrow the dominant ideology, and concludes:

> Comment? la question reste certes posée et personne ne semble encore en mesure de pouvoir évaluer l'efficacité des procédés mis en jeu. Mais, pour les uns et les autres, il est clair que c'est dans cette perspective révolutionnaire plus large qu'il faut situer les "révolutions minuscules", à première vue purement formelles, qui se réalisent au niveau des textes. Il ne s'agit pas uniquement de refuser les sens préalables mais d'en produire de nouveaux. Comme l'a dit Robbe-Grillet, la révolution que le Nouveau Roman peut opérer est celle du sens, il s'agit donc pour les écrivains d'*opérer une transformation dans l'écriture et par l'écriture*. (I, 405)

For instance, as I have already argued, it is not actually necessary to analyse Robbe-Grillet's playing with cultural stereotypes as a purely anti-representational 'revelation' of the illusion on which ideology is based; and the same could be said for the way in which Simon builds fragments of other texts – often overtly political ones – into the fabric of his fiction. In fact, the concept of the *intertext* may provide a more adequate basis for theorising the text's relation to ideology. Intertextuality will be the subject of Chapter 5.

4

The Myth of Creation

CREATION, INSPIRATION AND EXPRESSION

The opposition between production and representation analysed in the preceding chapter forms the main axis on which the political significance of the Nouveau Roman is founded. But textual production is also set up in opposition to two other concepts: *creation* and *expression*. Even more than representation, these are among the most basic and familiar assumptions of traditional humanist literary criticism. It is usually taken for granted that works of art are created, and that artists express themselves in their work. 'Creative' and 'expressive' are common and unremarkable terms of praise. Despite this, however, there are fairly specific issues at stake in the presuppositions underlying both these concepts – which are related, but distinct – and the nouveaux romanciers have brought a new kind of attention to bear on them. As with representation, they are doing this to some extent in the wake of *Tel Quel*, although in this case it is Ricardou himself who makes the greatest contribution to the construction of *Tel Quel*'s theory; and within the Nouveau Roman, it is again Ricardou who is the most forceful attacker of creation and, especially, expression. Robbe-Grillet and Simon follow him in this, with slightly more emphasis on creation.

Creation is different from production in that production is a process applied to an identifiable raw material. Production works on *something*. Creation, in contrast, implies that the work of art comes into being *out of nothing*.[1] For this reason it is seen by humanist ideology as one of the major assertions of man's freedom; that is, the creation of something out of nothing defies the rationality of determinism; it constitutes a transcendance of, and an act of defiance against, mechanistic laws of utility or cause and effect. (Sartre, for instance, argues that Baudelaire 'a trop le sens de la création pour accepter cet humble rôle ouvrier . . . ses poèmes . . . manifestent la gratuité de la conscience, ils sont totalement inutiles, ils affirment à chaque vers ce qu'il nomme lui-même le surnaturalisme' (1977a, 85–6)).)

Against this, Butor says that:

> Ce qui me gêne, dans le mot 'création', c'est qu'il est lié à une illusion soigneusement entretenue, l'illusion de la gratuité de l'œuvre d'art . . . On a l'impression que l'œuvre d'art est quelque chose qui tombe du ciel, quelque chose que l'artiste fait sans effort, sans travail, quelque chose qui naît de rien . . . Faire quelque chose de rien, dans la théologie catholique, c'est le privilège de Dieu. Par conséquent, ça a l'air très bien de parler de création, on a l'air d'identifier l'artiste à un dieu. Mais il y a quelque chose de très dangereux là-dedans parce qu'en le mettant sur un piédestal, on le détache de la réalité. (Charbonnier, 35–6)

In other words, creation refers back ultimately to the religious notion of God creating the world, and it is this model that has been annexed by the ideology of *literary* creation. Baudry argues that: 'La "création littéraire" se pense à travers la toute-puissance du Logos divin. L'œuvre est créée dans l'instant même de la parole qui la conçoit. "Que la lumière soit et la lumière fut" est la formule exemplaire sur lequel repose en définitive toute conception de la création' (1968b, 354). If this is the case, it follows that the process of writing a text is essentially inexplicable: almost a miracle. Taking this idea a step further, creation implies that the writer is a kind of god; and this 'modèle théologique Créateur/créature' (353) in turn gives the writer total control over his work and the meanings it generates; it becomes his exclusive *property*: those on whom the status of 'creator' is conferred 'sont aussi les possesseurs, les propriétaires et en quelque sorte les capitalistes du sens' (ibid).

The notion of *inspiration* is part of the ideology of creation in that it shares, and indeed maximises, the irrational and almost magical aspects of the process; but it is also a slightly different version of it in so far as it positions the writer not so much as the god, but the *medium* through whom the god or the muse speaks. Here the writer does not originate, so much as transmit; his prestige is that of the oracle rather than the god, and is conferred on him by his being in the service of a higher power – in itself, of course, a very privileged position. In *Pour un nouveau roman* (that is, before the notion of textual *production* had become current) Robbe-Grillet distinguishes sarcastically between the two:

> Ces pages auxquelles l'écrivain a donné le jour comme à son insu, ces merveilles non concertées, ces mots perdus, révèlent l'exist-ence de quelque force supérieure qui les a dictés. Le romancier, plus qu'un créateur au sens propre, ne serait alors qu'un sim-ple médiateur entre le commun des mortels et une puissance obscure, un au-delà de l'humanité, un esprit éternel, un dieu. (12)

For Robbe-Grillet inspiration is wrong because it is irrational, because it denies the writer any ability to be conscious of what he is writing and why. Sarraute concurs with this emphasis; in 'Nouveau roman et réalité', she too rejects 'l'image du romancier mû par des forces obscures, inconscient, il ne sait pas où il va, il ignore ce qu'il fait . . . c'est un démiurge, une pythie' (431) in favour of the more constructive attitude of writers *explaining* their ideas on literature – she cites Henry James, Virginia Woolf and Proust.

But the theme of inspiration versus conscious rationality was subsequently combined with a slightly different notion. Already in 1962, Barthes's article on Butor's *Mobile* brings into play an opposition between inspiration, criticised in terms similar to the above, and *work*. *Mobile*, he argues, is a text which does not try to smooth over the discontinuities of its construction; it is very obviously 'fabricated'. This, he says, accounts for its poor reception, since critics expect literature to be 'une activité spontanée, gracieuse, octroyée par un dieu, une muse, et si la muse ou le dieu sont un peu réticents, il faut au moins "cacher son travail"' (1964, 177). Similarly Ricardou in his first theoretical book, *Problèmes du nouveau roman* (1967), stresses the conception of the text as *work* on language[2] and as *fabricated object*: 'les actuelles recherches tendent à remplacer une littérature du bavardage par une littérature du faire' (12).

But it is only rather later, after *Tel Quel*'s introduction of the con-cept of textual production, that the opposition between inspiration and work becomes widespread among the nouveaux romanciers themselves. Simon, for instance, opens his session at the 1975 Cerisy conference on his writing by contrasting the notion of work with 'le statut quelque peu fabuleux (frauduleux), mystifiant (et bouffon) d'un homme "pas comme les autres" dont la tâche consisterait simplement à écrire sous la dictée de ce que l'on appelle l'"'inspi-ration'" (403). A more extended critique of inspiration is given by Ricardou in a chapter on Paul Valéry in *Pour une théorie du nouveau roman*. Ricardou sees in Valéry's theoretical work an important precursor to that of *Tel Quel* and the Nouveau Roman; and he opens his article, significantly, with an account of Valéry's attack on what he quotes him as calling 'le problème ridicule de l'inspiration' (60). The extracts quoted from Valéry tend to stress the conscious aspect, and Ricardou's own text the dignity of labour.[3] The effect of this double opposition is to link the two concepts of *work* and *consciousness* strongly together, with consequences that will be seen later in this chapter.

As the above discussion, and indeed the previous chapter, have made clear, a salient characteristic of both *Tel Quel* and the Nouveau Roman's theory is their tendency to proceed by setting up binary oppositions which in turn generate further oppositions and hence further parallels as well. Thus the extreme productivity of the notion of production itself derives to a considerable extent from the number of oppositions it can enter into – with exchange, representation, creation, and inspiration. Another one, equally fundamental to the theoretical position of the Nouveau Roman in the 1970s, is *production versus expression*, which recurs almost obsessively through Ricardou's writing and comments at the NRHA conference, and is picked up by the other nouveaux romanciers. It forms one of the main axes of the transition to 'modern' texts: in Ricardou's rather grandiose formulation, 'Ce à quoi nous assistons aujourd'hui, ce que nous provoquons, c'est le passage d'un âge de l'expression à un âge de la production' (I, 279).

'Expression' implies that something *inside* the writer *comes out* in his writing. The source of the text is, in a sense, nothing but the author himself. Ricardou had already criticised this idea in *Problèmes du nouveau roman*, attacking those who see the novel as a 'Réfraction de la vie dans le cristal particulier d'un auteur, vision du monde exprimée, inspiration jetée sur la page' (24). In his introductory paper at the NRHA conference, he draws the further conclusion that 'Pour le dogme expressif . . . le texte ne saurait jamais être que la sortie d'une substance antécédente dont l'auteur serait en quelque façon le propriétaire' (NRHA, I, 10). In other words, the implication that the text is the author's *property* recurs here with as much emphasis as in the case of creation.

The main difference between creation and expression, however, is that expression is not a process *ex nihilo*: here there is a 'raw material', namely the writer's own unique *self*. To this extent it is closer to production than creation is; but the nature of the raw material is very different in the two conceptions (i.e., production and expression), as is the process whereby it becomes a text. The raw material of expression is 'une substance antécédente' – a *content* to be literally *'put into* words'. Therefore all the *Nouveau Roman*'s arguments against representation apply with equal force against expression; the text is still seen as a container for a pre-existing non-verbal reality, although in this case it is not what the writer observes around him but the subjective feelings and images 'inside' him. Thus whereas production *transforms* the raw material of language, expression merely *transfers* the emotional contents of the writer's personality into the verbal receptacle of the text. But, as Ricardou puts it: 'l'écrivain . . . n'est pas habité par un flot d'images qui pour sortir exigerait de passer par le canal de sa plume . . . C'est l'activité d'écrire qui provoque l'activité d'invention . . . C'est dans et par le texte que se produit le texte' (NRHA, I, 99).

Although the mere existence of a raw material makes the process of expression less mystical, less 'miraculous' than that of creation, expression is nevertheless conceived of as unpredictable if not inexplicable, and above all *spontaneous* rather than laborious. It is implicitly modelled on a *natural* rather than either a magical or an industrial process: the parallel is with birds singing, not workers assembling an automobile. To some extent the Nouveau Roman's dislike of expression is part of their wider and very consistent rejection of the concept of the *natural* as a factor in literary production: Robbe-Grillet in particular stresses this, referring to the 'préoccupation, constant chez moi depuis mes débuts de romancier comme d'essayiste: la méfiance raisonnée contre tout ce qui peut instaurer l'écriture comme activité *naturelle*' (NRHA, II, 159). Drawing implicitly on Barthes's *Mythologies*,[4] he continues: 'le mythe de la naturalité a servi, comme vous savez, à tout un ordre social, moral, politique, pour s'établir et se prolonger. L'ordre bourgeois, la morale bourgeoise, les valeurs bourgeoises étaient censément naturels, c'est-à-dire inscrits dans l'ordre des choses, donc justes, innocents et définitifs' (ibid.). Ricardou, too, devotes a section of 'La littérature comme critique' to the illusion that language is natural.[5]

The attacks on these various concepts are often carried out simultaneously; they overlap and intermingle. For instance, Ricardou brings together several of them in his summing up of the changed status of the writer: 'Si les thèmes d'un texte sont non plus *l'expression* d'idées *antécédentes* dont quelque homme *inspiré* ou doué aurait la *propriéte*, mais l'effet d'un *travail textuel*, le mythe traditionnel de l'auteur subit de cruels dommages' (1971, 67, my italics). I have suggested above that this kind of alignment of concepts is the result of the structure of parallel oppositions which is so fundamental to their theoretical procedure: if creation, inspiration and expression are all the opposite of production, then they will inevitably come to be seen as similar to each other, despite the fact that their implications conflict at several points. But in fact their partial superimposition is not solely an effect of the Nouveau Roman's treatment of them; it is also inherent in their functioning within the humanist conception of literature. In other words, despite – or even because of – their contradictions, they work together as a certain ideology of literature. The ideology in question is seen by the Nouveau Roman as first and foremost that of romanticism,[6] but as extending to all 'traditional' bourgeois twentieth-century literary criticism as well.

It thus becomes important to analyse just how both the overlaps and the divergences between the three principal notions – creation, inspiration and expression – benefit and reinforce the ideology as a whole. The differences concern in the first place the 'raw material' of the text: for creation this is nothing, for inspiration it is the muse or 'superior power', and for expression it is the writer's subjectivity. As a result, the role of the writer is conceived as, respectively, a kind of god, a medium transmitting a message from the muse, and, for expression, both the source of the text and the agent of its verbalisation. In the case of creation and inspiration, the process of writing is seen as magical, whereas in the case of expression it is natural.

Conversely the overlaps centre on the features of *spontaneity* and *irrationality*; in all three cases, writing is spontaneous; and although the process of expression can perhaps be explained in more rational terms (e.g., deductions from the writer's lived experience to his text) its own mode of operation is not a reasoned, calculated process. Also, both creation and expression necessarily assume that every writer is a unique and exceptional being, in the first case because he is endowed with an essential freedom, with quasi divine powers, and in the second because the value of expression depends on the individuality of the sensibility being expressed; there would be no point in it if everyone were the same – hence *originality*, another important humanist literary value, is also based in the notion of expression. Either way, the writer is defined as a *special* kind of human being: Ricardou refers to the 'idéologie psychologiste faisant nécessairement correspondre activité d'un petit nombre de "créateurs doués" et masse de passifs consommateurs' (1971, 107), and shows how expression leads to a phantasisation and personality cult of the author: 'Avec les détails oiseux de sa psychologie et le culte persistant de son nom, l'auteur est donc cette fiction propre à se déployer, comme un écran, devant les problèmes du travail: il est le phantasme nécessaire à tout dogme d'expression' (op. cit., 68).

But paradoxically the ideology benefits just as much from the *contradictory* implications of the three concepts; the mileage obtained from playing them off against each other is at least as great as where they reinforce each other. For instance, by stressing alternately the connections between the author's life and his work (expression), and the mysterious magic implicit in creation and inspiration, literary criticism can veer between a positivist view that the text can be explained in terms of observable external factors, and the position that it is essentially irrational and hence not accessible to any kind of 'scientific' explanation. Equally, the notion of *self-transcendance* central to inspiration can coexist comfortably with that of *self-affirmation* provided by expression: the text both overrides and enhances the writer's day-to-day personality. This in turn provides a kind of double guarantee of aesthetic value: art can be valorised either insofar as it exists on a higher plane than ordinary life, or in terms of the 'authenticity' which is a key factor of the notion of expression.[7] The result of this interplay between the different strands of the ideology is that the artist can finally be at one and the same time all-powerful god, humble medium and unique human being; art is both affirmation and transcendance of self; above all perhaps, it is both a natural process and somehow magical.

NATHALIE SARRAUTE: PRE-VERBAL REALITY

It would seem, therefore, as though the target of the *Nouveau Roman*'s attacks is in fact a cohesive, if not entirely coherent, ideology of literary creation; and as though the areas of incoherence are actually functional, in that they increase the cohesiveness. But its relative diffuseness also means that it is not easy to locate particular texts in which it is formulated. Ironically, however, one of the clearest statements of its positions is to be found in the work, not of a nineteenth-century Romantic, but of a *nouveau romancier*: Nathalie Sarraute. Despite her remarks in 'Nouveau roman et réalité', quoted above, to the effect that the writer is engaged in a conscious effort of research and reflexion on his/her work, many of Sarraute's texts, both theoretical and fictional, embody a very 'romantic' view of writing. Unlike the other *nouveaux romanciers*, Sarraute has always subscribed to the idea of a necessary pre-verbal reality that the text *expresses*. Since it is pre-verbal it is also very elusive, and the writer's task is therefore both extremely difficult and extremely important. In 'Nouveau roman et réalité' she writes that reality, for the novelist, means: 'Ce qui ne se laisse pas exprimer par les formes connues et usées. Mais ce qui exige pour se révéler, qui ne peut se révéler que par un nouveau mode d'expression, par de nouvelles formes' (1963, 432).

Expression is thus central to her conception of writing. Its associations with the *authentic* are strongly present in all her descriptions of writing. Language, in her view, is a barrier of convention and habit set up between the reader and the experience which the writer is trying to convey. The authenticity of new experience *breaks through* the barrier: 'Plus la *réalité* que *révèle* l'œuvre littéraire est neuve, plus sa forme sera insolite, et plus elle devra montrer de *force pour percer* l'épais rideau qui protège nos habitudes de *sentir* contre toutes les perturbations' (1963, 433, my italics).

Authentic expression is presented above all as a *living*, as opposed to a conventional, language; this is particularly evident in the fictional *mises-en-scène* of the activities of reading and writing – as indeed the title of *Entre la vie et la mort* suggests: here the writer figure at one point is shown desperately searching for the 'life' that has gone out of his elegantly written text:

Pourtant quelque chose a disparu ... un élan timide, un tremblement, il le cherche ... ce qui comme une petite bête aveugle se propulsait, poussant devant soi les mots, il ne le sent plus ... cela a été étouffé, pris dans l'empois de ces phrases glacées ... Juste peut-être ici, on dirait qu'il y a comme une vibration, une pulsation ... un pouls à peine perceptible bat ... il faut se dépêcher avant qu'il ne soit trop tard, sinon il sait maintenant ce qui va arriver ... les belles phrases vont s'assembler en une forme qui aura un jour l'aspect lugubre d'un

champ jonché de cadavres où ceux qui viendront retrouveront
partout des visages qui leur sont connus, où chacun pourra sans
peine identifier ses morts . . . (244)

This stress on life links the notion of authenticity to that of the
natural – also, as discussed above, a key concept in the ideology
of expression. In the above extract, writing is literally *animated* –
by 'une petite bête', and is compared to blood being pumped
round the body: writing 'from the heart', in all senses. In *Les
Fruits d'or*, too, Sarraute implies that the value of a novel depends
on its evoking in the reader the same kind of response as he
or she would feel 'devant la première herbe qui pousse sa tige
timidement . . . un crocus encore fermé' (151); the work is described
in images of organic, flowing, natural life: 'Tout me paraît couler
de source. Se développer naturellement. [. . .] Cela forme un tout
indivisible. Comme un être vivant' (153–4). Sometimes, indeed,
the organic becomes orgasmic, as the activity of expression is
described in images of erection and ejaculation: 'Cela grandit, se
déploie . . . [. . .] propulsant devant soi les mots [. . .] leur mince
jet lentement s'étire . . . l'impulsion tout à coup devient plus forte,
c'est une brève éruption, les mots irrésistiblement dévalent, et puis
tout se calme' (1968, 92–3).

The notion of organic life also helps Sarraute's texts to develop
an interesting variant of the conflation of creation and expression.
If the text is a living organism, then the writer in producing it
is in a metaphorical sense *giving life* to it: the text enacts a kind
of birth, which refers us back to the notion of creation *ex nihilo*
rather than, or as well as, the expression of a pre-existing content.
This ambiguity is reinforced by the peculiar status of Sarraute's
pre-existing non-verbal substance. This is not as it were accidentally
non-verbal; its *essential* feature is that it has not yet been put into
words, that it is 'the unnamed': 'tout ce que j'ai voulu, c'était
investir dans du langage une part, si infime fût-elle, d'innommé'
(NRHA, II, 34). As such, it is in itself *undefinable*; Sarraute develops
a series of metaphorical detours and paraphrases in order to evoke
its existence and its resistance to language; the writer must explore
'des régions silencieuses et obscures où aucun mot ne s'est encore
introduit . . . vers ce qui n'est encore que mouvance, virtualités,
sensations vagues et globales, vers ce non-nommé qui oppose aux
mots une résistance . . . ' (ibid.). If the 'non-nommé' did not exist,
there would be no point in writing; but at the same time, it also *does*

not exist – she continues: ' . . . qui oppose aux mots une résistance et qui pourtant les appelle, car il ne peut exister sans eux' (ibid.). In other words, in order to have any stable, definite existence, the unnamed has to become named. Thus it is on the one hand the only 'reality' worth *expressing*, and on the other hand the modality of its existence is so fragile and elusive that it can also be said not to exist until the writer *creates* it in a text. In a letter to Sheila Bell, Sarraute writes: 'je m'efforce de faire surgir ce qui n'existait pas avant d'être mis en forme . . . Il me semble que les tropismes sont précisément ce "rien" qui, hors de la forme, du langage ne paraît pas avoir d'existence' (Bell, 17).

The strength of Sarraute's belief in this conception of artistic creation can be gauged by the consistency with which it is expressed in many articles, conference papers and interviews throughout her long career. Its main elements are already formulated in one of her earliest publications, a scathing attack on Valéry (1947) – whom Ricardou, as we have seen, praises as one of the most valuable precursors of the Nouveau Roman. Moreover it is precisely those qualities which Ricardou admires in Valéry – intelligence, control, lucidity, hostility to romanticism – that most infuriate Sarraute; she attacks him for placing rationality and method above 'l'émotion poétique'. Her arguments against him are rooted in romanticism, and in the concepts of inspiration and expression. Thus she equates his 'method', and the work it involves, with traditional *convention*, as against the spontaneity of inspiration (621), and makes it very clear that the value of a poem depends on the fidelity with which the poet's authentic pre-verbal emotion – 'la fraîcheur, la sincérité de l'émotion initiale' (628) is expressed in words. Otherwise, the poet will becomes trapped in 'les seuls jeux trompeurs du langage' (ibid.) – which is of course exactly what Ricardou wants. Her rhetorical question: 'Et n'est-ce pas la confrontation continuelle de l'*expression* avec l'*émotion* qu'elle s'efforce de *traduire*, qui permet au poète d'en apprécier la *valeur*?' (ibid., my italics) serves to sum up her position very clearly: poetry is language which faithfully expresses authentic emotion. Added to this is the implication that the emotion itself arises out of the poet's vision of reality – which, although it falls within the category of expression, is described in such mystical terms that it becomes a variant of inspiration as well. Castigating Valéry's view that it does not matter *what* the poet says, she writes: 'Comme il y a loin de la frivolité quasi libertine que révèlent ces propos, à ce sentiment exalté d'un appel venu du coeur des choses, à cette présence d'une "réalité mystérieuse" qui sans cesse se dérobe, à cette crainte, à cette humilité devant l'infini de l'"objet" . . . ' (622), going on to invoke the Romantics in her support: ' . . . à ce "poids confus" (Wordsworth), cette "chaleur sainte" (Keats), ce "saisissement venu d'une force inconnue" (Rilke)' (ibid.). Finally, because Valéry is not sensitive to this 'appel mystérieux', he cannot be *original*; he is condemned to pastiche, because he lacks 'une vision poétique assez forte et partant assez neuve et assez personnelle' (624).

Although in later years Sarraute stopped using the overtly romantic vocabulary of this early article, and made some effort to reformulate her ideas in the terms of the conceptual framework being constructed by Robbe-Grillet and Ricardou, the theoretical differences between her and them were too deep to be resolved, and indeed were exacerbated by the Nouveau Roman's increasingly explicit rejection of expression and representation. While she reluctantly attended the NRHA conference in 1971, she felt that its assumptions were completely alien to her, and left after the first day. During the discussion she reaffirmed her belief in the pre-verbal reality: 'Même si c'est une erreur – ce que je ne crois pas – elle m'est nécessaire. J'en ai un besoin vital. Je ne peux pas y renoncer. Dire: il n'y a pas de pré-langage, tout part des mots . . . cela m'est absolument impossible'.[8]

PRODUCTION: CONTROL VERSUS UNPREDICTABILITY

The Nouveau Roman's attack on creation and expression is congruent with their involvement in structuralism. That is, the position they take against the humanist view of the individual author as origin of the text is not unlike the anti-humanist 'death of the author' pronounced by the structuralist theorists of the 1960s – in fact Robbe-Grillet claims that Foucault's formulation of this idea was influenced by the Nouveau Roman.[9] But it is the more specific notion of textual production that permits the development of a redefined conception of the writing process: it serves as a means of pulling together and crystallising a number of ideas which already existed in a more diffuse form, and allows the nouveaux romanciers to construct a clearly-defined positive counterpart to their critiques of creation, expression and inspiration.

Thus in his first book *Problèmes du nouveau roman* Ricardou had claimed that real writers are those who reject the '"innocente" fonction instrumentale du langage', seeing language instead as 'une sorte de *matériau* qu'ils travaillent patiemment' (1967, 18). In other words, the opposition between language as instrument and as raw material is already in place. However, his attack on 'expression' requires that this too be made into the negative pole of a similar opposition; therefore, he needs a term to refer to the positive pole. Oddly enough in the light of his later work, he chooses 'creation' to fulfil this role: 'Le but de l'opération réaliste est donc de restreindre l'écriture à une fonction purement *expressive*, celle d'une passivité exempte de toute *créatrice vertu*. C'est pourquoi les doctrines réalistes évitent s'il se peut le verbe *créer*' (24, my italics). 'Creation' in other words, emphasises the active nature of writing. But it also has the disadvantage of carrying with it other markedly humanist and irrational connotations. It sits rather oddly, for instance, with his fondness for the metaphor of the text as 'machine'. He tries to minimise these difficulties by relocating the process of creation *in* rather than *before* the actual writing of the text, making the process of writing itself into the origin of creation (24–5). But the subsequent introduction of the concept of production resolves these problems: instead of struggling with a rather awkwardly redefined notion of creation, it allows him to reject *both* expression *and* a 'magical' view of writing, while at the same time justifying the idea of language as raw material. In other words, the term 'production' gives a more powerful focus to a conception of the text which he already has.

The theory of textual production, then, as adopted by the Nouveau Roman, contests the humanist ideology of literary creation in two main ways. Firstly, textual production works on a raw material that is not the writer's individual self but the collective, ideologically loaded reality of language.[10] Secondly, it is a lucid, resolutely rational work process: as Ricardou remarked in the course of a discussion at the NRHA conference, production replaces imagination: 'Plutôt que d'imagination, il vaudrait mieux parler dès lors d'opérations génératrices qui ont l'avantage d'être spécifiques dans un processus de production précis' (I, 99). This emphasis also comes across clearly in his opening paper, which is full of references to *systems*.[11]

Textual production also reinforced the hostility of those who had in any case always seen the Nouveau Roman as 'inhuman'. Previously the nouveaux romanciers – especially Robbe-Grillet – had been considered inhuman because they wrote about objects rather than human beings; now this is compounded by their seeing literary texts as the end-product of a coldly calculated abstract logical system of construction which would seem to exclude any *emotion* being either expressed in them or aroused by them. Sarraute's pastiche, in *Les Fruits d'or*, of her colleagues' contemptuous attitude towards those who are so naive as to look for feeling in texts:

> Mais ils sont drôles . . . ils sont touchants . . . accrochés à la sensation "sincère", "spontané" . . . ces mots ridicules qu'ils emploient [. . .] ne se fiant qu'à leur instinct, qui les fait aussitôt, comme les chiots qui se couchent sur le dos et geignent au seul bruit caressant d'une voix, réagir à ce qui est "vrai", à ce qui est "beau", "vivant", comme ils disent . . .   Comme si tout en art n'était pas concerté à froid, l'effet de combinaisons savants, de calculs, de conventions. (77)

is the witty tip of a generally less amused humanist iceberg of resistance to the exclusion of emotion from literature. The question is, however, an important one, and the nouveaux romanciers implicitly answer it in different ways. Broadly speaking, Ricardou is quite happy to see writing and reading as purely 'inhuman' activities;[12] Robbe-Grillet suggests that it is simply the irrational that is being excluded, and that rationality is not incompatible with emotion; and Butor tries to separate poetic emotion from its traditional association with the individual, arguing that 'Dans *Mobile*, par exemple, il y a une poésie qu'on pourrait appeler objective, qui ne se présente pas comme expression d'un sentiment individuel, mais comme disposition d'un espace à l'intérieur duquel les sentiments, les passions peuvent se déployer' (1974, 446).

There is also a sense in which textual production enables a different kind of emotion to come into play: the personal feelings of bourgeois individualism are replaced by the quasi socialist rhetoric of the writer as *worker*. That is, if the writer is no longer a member of an elite of creative geniuses, but a kind of construction worker, producing the text from the raw material of language as though building something out of bricks, then the very nature of the process – rather than the content of any particular text – can perhaps command a response of emotional solidarity. Butor hints at this when he says to Charbonnier: 'le mot "œuvre" est un mot que j'aime beaucoup, à cause de son étymologie. C'est la même origine qu'"ouvrier" (Charbonnier, 39). But these egalitarian associations are offset to some extent by the rationalist and, hence, *technocratic* emphasis that is also bound up with the definition of textual production. Indeed, it might be argued that it is precisely this aspect which appeals not only to Ricardou but also to Robbe-Grillet and Butor, with their backgrounds in science and mathematics.[13] The relevant analogy is thus actually with the engineer rather than the bricklayer. If writing is a matter of constructing complex verbal systems, this necessarily puts a premium on *cleverness* – both in the writer and the reader. As a result, textual production is in its own way arguably just as elitist as the humanist ideology of literary creation (this is of course the main thrust of Sarraute's satirical treatment of writers and critics throughout *Les Fruits d'or*).

Along with this kind of abstract intelligence, the nouveaux romanciers' view of production would also seem to require a strong assumption of *control* over the process of writing. In opposing the idea of inspiration – the notion that the writer is swept along by some obscure external force – the rational, planned production of texts implies, in contrast, that the writer is completely and consciously in control, both of the way in which the text develops and of all the meanings that are produced in it. If this is the case, it is difficult to see how such overall control can be reconciled with another view that is also central to their conception of the novel: this – encapsulated in Ricardou's phrase, 'l'aventure d'une écriture' – stresses the autonomy and unpredictability of the text, its capacity to generate new meanings and proceed under its own momentum. The importance of this idea is clear from the fact that it forms the whole basis of the argument they mount against Sartrean 'engagement', as discussed in Chapter 1. But if the writer does not know beforehand where the text is going, and if it must be left free to evolve in its own way, how can it also be seen as a rationally planned and controlled system?[14]

This contradiction can in principle be resolved through an appeal to the notion of *structural transformation*. If writing is theorised as the production of structures rather than the expression of personality, then its raw material is not a content but itself a structure (language and/or ideology) to be *transformed*. As Ricardou puts it: 'Le texte n'est pas un espace neutre où viennent s'assembler des sens inaltérables; c'est un milieu de transformation, une machine à changer les sens' (1971, 28). Thus the theory of textual production involves the notion of transformation. But so does structuralism in general – in fact even more crucially. The two theories are of course themselves related: the concept of textual production derives ultimately from Althusser's structuralist Marxism (see Chapter 3). However, the notion of transformation is significantly different in the two perspectives. In the case of production in the economy, its result is planned in advance: the worker who 'transforms' bricks into a wall knows from the start exactly what kind of wall he is to build. Althusser, modelling his concept of practice on economic production, retains this interpretation of 'transformation' as predictable or *determined*, as his definition makes very clear: 'Par pratique en général nous entendrons tout processus de *transformation* d'une matière première donnée déterminée, en un *produit* déterminé, transformation effectuée par un travail humain déterminé, utilisant des moyens (de "production") déterminés' (1966, 167, Althusser's italics). But in the purely structuralist context, as discussed in Chapter 2, 'transformation' has the much stronger sense of a self-generated, open-ended play of interaction between elements, whose outcome cannot be predicted in advance.

In Chapter 2, I also argued that the nouveaux romanciers' relationship to structuralism was limited by their position as the *conscious producers* of structures, hence coinciding neither with that of the theorist who discovers structures underlying cultural practices nor with that of the anthropological subject who unconsciously 'performs' them. But this difference does not affect the generative, transformative status of the textual structures – or, therefore, the 'unpredictability' of the text. That is, generativity is an inherent *formal* property of all structures, independently of whether they are unconscious or conscious. The notion of text as structure thus provides a way of reconciling, on a theoretical level, rational control with free generation. A structure, in other words, is something which the writer consciously sets up, but then leaves to 'play' by itself, generating new structures and new meanings.

It is in fact this conception of transformation, rather than the Althusserian one, that is adopted in *Tel Quel*'s theory of textual production. Baudry, for instance, gives a very structuralist description of the anti-representational text: 'l'effet de signification ne relevant que des rapports qui se créent entre les éléments signifiants distribués sur la même surface, de leurs combinaisons plus ou moins apparentes et *en tout cas non dénombrables*. Tout écrit, tout texte, ne peut plus être pensé comme expression d'un spectacle, d'un champ de réalité extérieur à lui, mais comme partie et partie agissante de l'ensemble du texte *qui ne s'arrête pas de s'écrire*' (1968a, 136, my italics). Moreoever, it is precisely the infinite *random* play of the text as structure that enables it to effect a *deliberate* subversion of the dominant ideology of representation: 'elle est . . . en raison de l'absence des limites qu'elle découvre et reconnaît dans le jeu, dans la main indéfiniment *neuve* des surfaces intertextuelles, la fracture et la subversion portées à l'intérieur d'une idéologie théologique' (ibid., 138). Or, as Ricardou more succinctly comments: 'Machine à changer indéfiniment le sens des mots, le texte établit une permanente subversion du langage instrumental' (1971, 52).

Textual production thus grafts elements of a more classical structuralism onto its Althusserian framework, and in so doing allows the writing process to be described as follows: the writer deliberately and calculatedly transforms the raw material of language into a textual structure; but this structure is designed, once it has been produced, to go on endlessly transforming itself, with results that the writer could not have controlled in advance. Conscious rational construction of a structure in fact *implies* the unpredictable generation of new meanings. It is precisely this emphasis which is dominant in Simon's conclusion to 'La Fiction mot à mot', where he refers to:

> ce labeur qui consiste à assembler et organiser . . . toutes les composantes de ce vaste système de signes qu'est un roman . . . la révélation peut-être capitale qu'apporte ce travail, c'est que ces nécessités purement formelles, loin de constituer des gênes ou des obstacles, se révèlent être éminemment *productrices* et, en elles-mêmes, *engendrantes* . . . je suis de plus en plus à même de constater à quel point ce *produit* élaboré mot à mot va finalement bien au-delà de mes intentions. Si l'on me demandait pourquoi j'écris, je pourrais répondre que c'est pour voir se produire chaque fois ce curieux miracle. (1972, 97, Simon's italics)

Ricardou concurs in this view and claims that it applies to *all* writers: 'Or, s'il est relativement facile de . . . déduire [les fonctionnements possibles, les procédés prévus] d'un texte déjà fait, il est en revanche impossible de mesurer à l'avance leur importance respective et les exigences de leurs combinaisons. Ecrire, tout écrivain à sa manière l'atteste, est une activité productrice qui se caractérise notamment par la transformation, à mesure, de ses propres bases' (1971, 21).

The whole of this argument of course relies on the novels in question actually being 'structuralist novels'. If it is assumed that they are, then the notion of transformation can be invoked to provide a theorisation of textual unpredictability – a theorisation which can take the place of the humanist notion of inspiration. Equally, as will be argued later, it obviates the need for recourse to the influence of the writer's unconscious. In both cases, the advantage from the nouveaux romanciers' point of view is that structural transformation does not engage the writer *as subject* in any way: it accounts for this aspect of the writing process in terms that remain internal to the text, which operates as a self-contained 'machine'.

But we have already seen, in Chapter 2, that there is *in practice* considerable variation in the way in which the nouveaux romanciers conceive of the production and transformation of textual structures in their own work. This is particularly true of the interaction between control and unpredictability. (For instance, the concept of bricolage carries rather different implications – to the extent that the nouveaux romanciers use this as a model for their writing, they are in effect relinquishing the notion of total rational control.) Ricardou, most of whose theoretical writings are either critical analyses of other writers or entirely general statements about the functioning of texts, has little to say in this context. But Robbe-Grillet, for instance, makes it clear that he is careful to choose his textual 'generators' in such a way as to minimise the risk of them acquiring a life of their own and hence 'un gommage de ma volonté d'intervention' (NRHA, II, 159). However, he also insists on the fact that once the initial generators have been chosen by him, they in turn generate others: 'Ce que le générateur a de particulier, c'est qu'il engendre: il s'engendre lui-même et engendre en même temps d'autres générateurs' (ibid., 167). As the text progresses, his control over it diminishes; or, as he puts it here, the elements which he has chosen as objects of narration increasingly transform themselves into 'narrators'.[15] The completion of this process signals the end of the book: he stops 'au moment où toute la narration a été assumée par l'ensemble des objets narrés' (ibid.). There is no overall plan when he starts writing – in the Cerisy conference (1976) on his work, he says: 'j'écris toujours mes livres en commençant par le début et en finissant par la fin . . . très souvent, au moment même du travail sur la première page, il n'existe aucun projet concernant ce qui viendra après' (I, 94). On the separate question of *interpretation* – i.e., once the text is written, is the writer conscious of all the meanings it has generated, or do they too escape his control? – he is more assertive, claiming that: 'Contrairement à ce qui a été dit souvent ici, j'estime qu'un auteur conscient et organisé connaît assez bien son œuvre: il l'a fait fonctionner lui-même' (I, 412).

In comparison, Simon places rather more emphasis on the unpredictability of textual production, and is happier than Robbe-Grillet about being 'taken over' by the text. His preface to *Orion aveugle* of 1970 describes his method of writing as completely independent of any pre-existing plan or intention; it is a process initiated only when he starts physically writing, and then the writing progresses step by step, from one word to the next, evolving under its own momentum. The writing is propelled forward by the polyvalence of individual words: the fact of a word being a point of intersection of several different meanings, each of which sparks off a different possible direction for the text to take: 'Ils sont autant de carrefours où plusieurs routes s'entrecroisent. Et si, plutôt que de vouloir contenir, domestiquer chacune de ces explosions, ou traverser rapidement ces carrefours en ayant déjà décidé du chemin à suivre, on s'arrête et on examine ce qui apparaît à leur lueur ou dans les perspectives ouvertes, des ensembles insoupçonnés de résonances et d'échos se révèlent' (10–11).

In 'La Fiction mot à mot', written the following year, this view is restated but with some modification towards a greater element of overall control, to ensure the unity of the text as a whole: he starts with an initial 'figure' and its 'properties' and is careful not to lose sight of these: he must 'en cours de travail . . . chaque fois qu'à chacun des mots carrefours plusieurs perspectives, plusieurs "figures" se présentent, avoir toujours à l'esprit, pour le choix que l'on va faire, la figure initiale avec ses quatre ou cinq propriétés dérivées et ne jamais perdre celles-ci de vue, faute de quoi . . . il n'y aurait pas *livre*, c'est-à-dire unité, et tout s'éparpillerait en une simple suite' (88). The initial figure is thus not itself transformed but acts as a central and constant reference point, or 'base camp' (88), for the textual explorations going on around it. In this way the composition of each novel has a general *shape* – for example a trefoil for *La Route des Flandres*, and for *Histoire* a very complicated 'forme de plusieurs sinusoïdes de longueur d'ondes variables qui courent tantôt au-dessus, tantôt au-dessous (invisibles alors) d'une ligne continue . . . la ligne étant en réalité une courbe de très grand rayon, un cercle qui revient à son point de départ' (94).

Four years later, in the final discussion session of the conference on his work at Cerisy in 1974, he returns to the question of the text's *resistance* to control, to the 'dynamique de l'écriture gauchissant et modifiant le projet initial' (416), and explains in more detail what exactly it is that 'takes over' from his conscious initial project. It is not, he says, simply chance; this is in the first place because he is working with language, which is not a random collection of elements but has its own historically constituted structure and is 'le produit du long travail de la pensée et de son évolution' (418). Words evolve in the course of history, picking up a variety of meanings on the way, and so the polysemic 'carrefours' which result are not accidental but reflect a kind of ideological history. In language, then, 'il n'y a donc rien de hasardeux'. Moreoever, he goes on: ' . . . comme il n'y a non plus rien de hasardeux dans mon travail lui-même qui est extrêmement concerté et réfléchi' (1975, 418). That is, the unforeseen perspectives which open up in the course of writing are the product of his 'manipulation attentive de la langue' (ibid.). He expands on this point in answer to a later question about whether he is conscious of *all* the trajectories of meaning generated by his texts: he is not, and he cites Georges Raillard's analysis of *Femmes*: 's'il a bien exposé des dispositifs que j'avais très consciemment mis en place, il en a décelé d'autres sur lesquels ce texte s'appuie peut-être . . . mais qui se sont alors mis en place (comme il en a été de la position très exactement médiane de l'embuscade dans *La Route des Flandres*) à mon insu' (429). This, however, does not mean that they have 'mysteriously' appeared from nowhere, but rather are produced 'par l'effet de mécanismes très certains, même s'ils me restent obscurs, déclenchés *par mon travail*' (429).

For Butor the generative mechanisms are not words but more abstract structures, and the relation between intention and result is a process which goes through distinct stages as the novel takes shape. His 'Intervention à Royaumont', written in 1959, much earlier than the texts referred to above and independently of the Nouveau Roman's collective work on the subject, gives a clear outline of the process. The writer does not start with a definite idea of what he wants to say, but merely a confused sense of 'une certaine matière qui veut se dire' (1960b, 18); it is the pressure of this obscure material that brings the novel into existence, and so 'en un sens ce n'est pas le romancier qui fait le roman, *c'est le roman qui se fait tout seul*' (ibid., my italics). But the writer, in his role as 'l'instrument de sa mise au monde', deliberately and carefully constructs the 'schémas' that will permit the production of the text. Butor stresses the abstract, almost mathematical nature of these structures, and the lengthy preparation they involve; in striking contrast to Simon's plunging into 'le cheminement même de l'écriture' (1971, 84), he says that 'Je ne puis commencer à rédiger un roman qu'après en avoir étudié pendant des mois l'agencement' (19). But once he does start writing, and these very consciously constructed initial schemas are put into operation, the results of their deployment force them to undergo constant revision; they are transformed by their own products. The entire text is thus caught up in a perpetual transformation of its structures. Butor writes:

> ces schémas eux-mêmes dont je me sers, et sans lesquels je n'aurais pas osé me mettre en route, ce qu'ils me permettent de découvrir m'oblige à les faire évoluer, et ceci peut se produire dès la première page, et peut continuer jusqu'à la dernière correction sur épreuves, cette ossature évoluant en même temps que l'organisme entier . . . chaque changement de détail pouvant avoir des répercussions sur l'ensemble de la structure. (19)

Consequently it is only when the book is finished that he is in a position to know what is in it. This final 'prise de conscience' is itself an important part of the process for Butor; it is made possible by the textual work, and it in turn makes possible a greater consciousness of how the textual work operates, so that 'Cette prise de conscience du travail romanesque va, si j'ose dire, le dévoiler en tant que dévoilant . . . le romancier commence à savoir ce qu'il fait, le roman à dire ce qu'il est' (19).

For Butor, in other words, consciousness and control are the ultimate aims of the writer; although he is acutely aware of all the obstacles that stand in their way, he also feels that he is gradually overcoming them. In an interview with *Tel Quel* he says: 'Je m'efforce de contrôler de mieux en mieux ce que je fais, et comme je m'attaque à des problèmes de plus en plus complexes, je suis obligé de mettre au point des instruments de haute précision' (1960b, 180). Thirteen years later, at the Cerisy conference devoted to his work, he describes the evolution of his fiction as a struggle towards greater consciousness of the structures underlying his novels; contrasting *Passage de Milan* ('un de ceux que j'ai écrits dans la plus grande obscurité' (84)) with subsequent novels: 'C'est donc pour essayer de venir à bout de cette obscurité que j'ai développé des procédés qui ont apparu dans les livres suivants' (ibid.), but still acknowledging that 'Je crois que si l'on regarde suffisamment les autres livres, c'est pareil, il y a beaucoup plus de structures conscientes, mais elles sont perpétuellement débordées par encore autre chose' (ibid.).

Control does not imply *closure*; he is equally insistent on the importance of the novel – or any other representation – remaining incomplete, open to further 'modification'. Thus he claims that 'Tout livre achevé, plein, fermé, est ainsi un masque, une façade; le livre véritable, le livre juste est nécessairement lui-même ruine . . . ce que le poète propose ne peut être qu'un ensemble de fragments, s'écartant les uns des autres, laissant découvrir entre eux tout ce que eux ne peuvent pas dire'[16] – and welcomes readers who find in his work meanings he had not been aware of, '[qui] ont ouvert, à l'intérieur de ces ruines que sont tous mes bouquins, des passages, dégagé des corridors nouveaux ou enfouies. Quelle intensité!' (1974, 438). In fact his novels themselves, in their presentation of fictional writer figures, illustrate the impossibility of ultimate control over one's representations: the example of Jacques Revel has been mentioned in my first chapter, but the most dramatic case is that of the school teacher Pierre Vernier, the initial narrator of *Degrés*, who set out to write a *complete* description of a *circumscribed* reality: a particular lesson he had taught on the discovery of America. But once under way the narrative makes cumulative demands upon its producer in terms of time, energy and research, and also in a kind of strain on his sense of identity. They increase ad infinitum, with a relentless logic of their own, until he succumbs under their pressure and actually dies. In other words, the representation he set out to produce – 'le projet qu'il avait formé et qui l'a écrasé' (1960a, 385) – develops a centrifugal force which renders it unfinishable: it, too, is 'une ruine; dans l'édification de cette tour d'où l'on devait voir l'Amérique, s'est formé quelque chose qui devait la faire exploser; il n'a pu élever que quelques pans de murs, et s'est produite cette conflagration qui non seulement a suspendu tous les travaux, mais a miné le sol sur lequel ils se dressent' (ibid.).

THE ROLE OF THE UNCONSCIOUS

Thus the individual writers of the Nouveau Roman strike slightly different balances within the overall conception of the text as a combination of, on the one hand, calculated planning and, on the other, the unpredictable generation of effects by the play of structures. There is, however, an alternative way of theorising the unpredictable elements: namely, to see them as produced by the writer's *unconscious*. The nouveaux romanciers' attitude to this also needs to be considered, in so far as it too is conditioned, if rather indirectly, by the basic opposition between creation and production.

From the point of view of psychoanalytically based literary theory, discussion of the writer's unconscious is not simply a question of the limitations of his or her awareness of all the possible meanings which have already been generated by the text; rather it implies that the meanings are to a large extent produced *by* the writer's unconscious, and that this fact has to be taken into account in a critical theory of the text. Butor is wholly convinced of this, and emphasises the importance of psychoanalytic interpretation in bringing to consciousness the repressed meanings in the text.[17] Simon agrees; although he attaches less importance to it than Butor does, he places the selection of 'themes' in his writing at an unconscious level, saying: 'que certains thèmes plus ou moins obsessionnels, que certains de mes fantasmes se retrouvent dans mes livres, cela ne fait pas de doute, et je ne récuse absolument pas les interprétations qui ont été faites dans ce sens' (1975, 414). The other nouveaux romanciers, however, display a rather ambiguous attitude towards the unconscious. On the one hand, psychoanalytic criticism in various forms is generally well received at the 1971 conference: the Freudian references in Lotringer's 'La Révolution romanesque' (NRHA, I, 327–48), for instance, or Georges Raillard's paper on Butor (NRHA, II, 255–78), or Anne Clancier's participation in the discussion (e.g., NRHA, II, 236–40). Thus Ricardou agrees completely with Clancier's notion that his novels use, not unconscious 'contents' as past writers had done, but the dynamic mechanisms of the unconscious (NRHA, II, 411). Indeed Ricardou himself, in his first theoretical book, redefines the writer's 'muse' in terms which sound very much like a Freudian description of the 'other scene' of the unconscious: 'le centre du texte même, ce lieu obscur qui ne songe interminablement qu'à se déchiffrer' (1967, 26). It could be argued, in fact, that the centrality which all the nouveaux romanciers accord to the *materiality* of language is in line with the psychoanalytic view of the determining role of language in the unconscious.[18]

On the other hand, however, their reservations are equally manifest.[19] Ricardou makes it clear, for instance, that his promotion of the play of the signifier is not to be confused with the 'mystique du langage' that sometimes accompanies it, in which language itself is seen as the repository of a mysterious truth, so that in playing with words, 'il semble, par une illusion curieuse, que l'on surprenne comme une vérité incluse en le langage même' (1971, 131). Explicitly of course he is rejecting a 'magic' rather than a psychoanalytic view of language here; nevertheless, psychoanalysis claims that there *is*, in a different sense, a 'vérité incluse en le langage même',[20] and Ricardou's ultra rationalist position rules this out; symptomatically, perhaps, he goes on to suggest that surrendering to the play of the signifier is a quasi religious occupation, and one which leads to insanity: 'N'est-ce pas à la recherche infinie d'irréprochables palindromes que divers moines, au Moyen Age, perdirent peu à peu la raison?' (ibid.).

Sarraute is more overtly hostile to psychoanalysis, for rather different reasons. She accepts the idea that the unconscious has a determining role in the text – 'Il y a dans tout texte un grand part d'inconscient' (NRHA, II, 39) – but, unlike Butor, she is happy for it to remain unconscious: asked whether it is the source of the 'unnameable' of her texts, she replies:

> Je n'en sais rien, parce que l'inconscient, je n'en ai pas la moindre conscience. Les psychanalystes parviendraient peut-être, après des mois de traitement, à me révéler ce que, selon eux, il contient. Mais il m'est impossible, en tant qu'écrivain, de m'en occuper. Ce qui m'occupe, c'est ce que je peux découvrir toute seule, sans le secours de notions préétablies. (56)

As this comment also suggests, she objects less to the unconscious itself than to psychoanalytic theory, which she sees as yet another reductive, oppressive discourse: an illegitimate attempt to label and categorise the unnameable, one of the many 'définitions, les catégories psychologiques, sociales, morales que mes textes s'étaient efforcés de saper' (ibid., 39). The character of the psychiatrist in her *Portrait d'un inconnu* illustrates the same point. In her case the misgivings about psychoanalysis are thus not based in a rationalist position – which indeed Sarraute does not hold, as discussed above – but in a kind of expressive individualism.

Robbe-Grillet's position is more sophisticated. He is very aware of the cultural importance of Freud, i.e., of the impact which the theorisation of the unconscious has had on modern culture, and he considers himself to be writing specifically in and for a post-Freudian society; but he sees Freud's work above all as having *defused* the 'mysteries' of the unconscious and reduced it to an inert cultural artefact. In his own novels, he says, unconscious phantasies 'ne fonctionnent plus comme le phantasme caché de l'œuvre pré-freudienne, mais comme le phantasme designé de l'œuvre post-freudienne. A partir du moment où les fonctionnements de la psyché ont été démontés par Freud, ils appartiennent à un matériel culturel . . . Les phantasmes ne sont plus alors que des images, renvoyées à leur platitude d'objets de grande série' (NRHA, II, 141). Robbe-Grillet is consistently antipathetic to anything that can be described as a 'profondeur', and it is hardly surprising that he puts the *unanalysed* unconscious into this category – he continues: 'Il faut bien voir que du moment où la psychanalyse a démonté ce qu'il y avait dans la profondeur de l'homme, la profondeur a disparu' (142). Freud's achievement, in other words, is to have got rid of the unconscious. It is of course true, and important, that the popularisation of psychoanalysis has produced a variety of new cultural stereotypes; but the other aspect of Robbe-Grillet's position is a perceptible distaste for a concept of the unconscious as an active force – precisely because it threatens the writer's *control* over his work; for instance, his reservations about 'work on the signifier' in so far as it can so to speak *run away with* the writer are largely motivated by this: 'il y a le risque de voir la constella-tion . . . envahie soudain par un sens global caché, un *inconscient (non contrôlé), une profondeur secrète*' (NRHA, II, 157, my italics); and he describes himself as: 'M'intéressant davantage au travail conscient qu'à cet inconscient qui travaillerait à mon insu' (158). When in the ensuing discussion he is asked directly: 'Admettez-vous dans votre choix des générateurs et dans votre choix de leur fonctionnement l'intervention de l'inconscient?' (II, 169), he at first replies – flippantly, but not unreasonably – 'Ah, sûrement mais . . . à mon insu', *but* then claims that his use of 'le matériel psychanalytique' is so blatantly *conscious* that it cannot possibly have anything to do with his personal unconscious: 'mes rapports avec les psychanalystes (ils se sont beaucoup intéressés à mes petits

travaux) ont toujours été difficiles, car on ne pouvait guère retenir
à la charge de mon inconscient les relations œdipiennes et les
castrations qui se trouvaient exposées ici ou là dans une telle clarté
de clinique' (170).

In the final analysis, moreover, it becomes clear that Robbe-
Grillet's and Ricardou's negative view of psychoanalysis is an
inevitable corollary of their opposition to creation and, especially,
expression and inspiration. That is, their rationalist conception of
textual production arose in the first place as a way of rejecting the
humanist view of literature. But in so far as it implies a privileging
of lucidity, of the deliberate production of calculated effects, it
also goes hand in hand with a certain mistrust of the *unconscious*.
Psychoanalytic literary theory does after all involve a kind of
expressivity: the individual unconscious 'coming out' in the text.
More importantly, the romantic category of inspiration, implying
as it does something beyond the control of the writer, spills over
into the actually very different Freudian and, especially, Lacanian
conception of the unconscious as a determining factor in writing,
equally beyond the control of the writer.

In other words, the rationalism that was originally deployed
as a weapon against traditional humanism leads indirectly but
irresistibly to an exclusion of the unconscious from the theory of
textual production (or, alternatively, provides a rationalisation for
an existing resistance to the idea of the unconscious), and a dis-
missive attitude towards psychoanalysis. Ironically, though, some
of the most innovative critiques of literary humanism throughout
the 1970s were based on psychoanalytic theory; and the nouveaux
romanciers find themselves increasingly cut off from these developments. For *Tel Quel*, for instance, from whom the concept of textual
production was originally taken, the mechanisms of the unconscious
are the focus of an entirely positive interest, and are seen as a major
factor in textual production. *Tel Quel*'s concern with psychoanalysis
is on the one hand fairly general – as when Sollers defines culture
as an instance of repression (1968, 71) and refers to Lacan on the
symbolic (74) and Serge Leclaire on the phallic nature of writing (75)
– but also involves Kristeva and Baudry in a sustained and detailed
attempt to integrate Freudian concepts into their Marxist analysis.
This project of bringing together Marx and Freud, opening up
Marxist theory to the conception of the unconscious and conversely
psychoanalysis to the notion of ideology and the economic, was
initiated by Althusser through his relation to Lacan, and is one of

the important developments of critical theory in the late 1960s and 1970s.

This chapter has been concerned with the nature of the writing *process* – that is, with literature as an activity rather than a finished product, and an activity of a particular and very concrete kind: what actually happens when a writer writes? Different conceptions of this process have been discussed; and one conclusion that emerges is, I would suggest, that the differences between them centre above all on the peculiar, apparently autonomous momentum generated by the literary text. In other words, the various accounts offered can perhaps most usefully be seen as different attempts to explain the quotient of *unpredictability* in this kind of writing. (This is hardly surprising: it is, after all, fairly obvious that the latter is one of the principal features which distinguishes writing a novel or a poem from writing a text-book, a newspaper article or any other kind of non-literary text.) The unpredictable element is variously attributed to a mysterious inspiration, or to the writer's god-like capacity to rise above deterministic natural laws, or to the workings of the unconscious, and so on. The Nouveau Roman, however, prefer the explanation that it arises first and foremost from the transformational properties of *structures*. This view is not shared by many other writers or critics, and so contributes considerably to the originality of the Nouveau Roman's project; it is also an important aspect of the interconnectedness of their theory and their practice, and their strategic appropriation and re-working of more general theories.

5

Intertextuality

Intertextuality was invented by Kristeva, in some of the earliest pieces of work she published after her arrival in France from Bulgaria in 1966. It very quickly became popular, and has remained an important and influential concept in literary theory – far more so than other aspects of *Tel Quel*'s work in the 1960s. It is also, as I shall show in this chapter, extremely relevant to the fiction of the Nouveau Roman; indeed many critics writing on these novels have used it to good effect. However, it does not figure prominently in the theoretical work of the nouveaux romanciers themselves. I suggested at the end of Chapter 3 that intertextuality offers, potentially, a stronger and less problematic basis for theorising the literary text's relation to ideology than does the (related) notion of textual production, and I will now attempt to explain why; but this possibility was never really taken up by the nouveaux romanciers. It is their fiction, rather than their theory, that explores the *intertextual* inscription and transformation of social discourse – thus in effect substantiating Françoise van Rossum-Guyon's comment, quoted at the end of Chapter 3, that their research is often most productively pursued on the level of fictional practice itself. This chapter will therefore concentrate largely on their fictional texts.

The term 'intertextuality' first occurs in Kristeva's 'Le mot, le dialogue et le roman' (1967), an article introducing the work of the Soviet theorist Mikhail Bakhtin to a French audience. Although he does not use the term, 'intertextuality' is directly inspired by Bakhtin's conception of prose fiction as a *heterogenous* discourse, drawing on a multiplicity of different kinds of social 'speech'. The novel is thus essentially polyphonic and, in the term he coins, 'dialogic', as opposed to 'monologic' genres such as lyric poetry in which the authorial voice is central and dominant. In his book on Rabelais (1965) he describes this kind of discourse as 'carnivalesque': an escape from and subversion of the codified logic of everyday thought and language.

144

A footnote to 'Le mot, le dialogue et le roman' quotes Bakhtin to the effect that 'Le langage du roman ne peut pas être situé sur une surface ou sur une ligne. Il est un système de surfaces qui se croisent' (459). The following year Kristeva develops this idea to arrive at a basic definition of intertextuality: every text is to be considered as 'une permutation de textes, une inter-textualité: dans l'espace d'un texte, plusieurs énoncés pris à d'autres textes se croisent et se neutralisent' (1968b, 300). That is, the text is made up of a plurality of 'intersecting' fragments of other pre-existing texts, which thus have the status of implicit *quotations*. Their original contexts are both recalled and simultaneously 'neutralised': intertextuality is *transformative*, in the sense that the transplanted textual sequences acquire new meanings and also allow new, and often less respectful (parody is one major kind of intertextuality), readings of the original context. Thus Kristeva analyses a fifteenth-century text as 'le résultat d'une transformation de plusieurs autres codes: la scolastique, la poésie courtoise, la littérature orale (publicitaire) de la ville, le carnaval' (1968b, 312).

(Implicit in this is the assumption that all literary texts are subject to the action of intertextuality. This is not found in Bakhtin, who distinguishes between *dialogic* (e.g. Rabelais, Dostoievsky) and *monologic* (e.g. Tolstoy) texts. For Kristeva it seems at times to be a general condition, at times coextensive with what she defines as 'poetic language' – i.e. language that escapes or resists the repressive action of the dominant ideology. Even if one accepts, however, that it would be impossible for any text to be entirely unaffected by its surrounding discourses, it is still useful to distinguish between those that openly assume and maximise their intertextuality and those that appear unaware of it.)

The scope of intertextuality is not restricted to the literary domain. Rather, it implies that the text 'reads' and re-writes the whole range of social discourses in which it is situated. This point is of fundamental importance for Kristeva, as it is for Bakhtin; although subsequent practitioners of intertextuality have sometimes used it simply as a more fashionable name for the traditional study of literary influences, Kristeva sees it above all as a way of theorising the text's relation to society and history. Society is redefined as a text or set of inter-related texts: intertextuality provides a way to 'situer la structure littéraire dans l'ensemble social considéré comme un ensemble textuel. Nous appellerons *intertextualité* cette interaction textuelle qui se produit à l'intérieur d'un seul texte. Pour le sujet connaissant, l'intertextualité est une notion qui sera l'indice de la façon dont un texte lit l'histoire et s'insère en elle' (1968b, 312).

The mode of 'insertion', moreover, is far from passive. Each individual text's relation to the social text is not only transformative but actually *transgressive*: this is at the core of Bakhtin's notion of *carnival*, which overturns normal social codes and hierarchies, setting up a transgressive polyphonic logic of its own. Kristeva writes: 'C'est . . . dans le *carnaval* que Bakhtin ira chercher les racines de cette logique . . . Le discours carnivalesque brise les lois du langage censuré par la grammaire et la sémantique, et par ce même mouvement il est une contestation sociale et politique: il ne s'agit pas d'équivalence, mais d'identité entra la contestation du code linguistique officiel et la contestation de la loi officielle' (1967, 439).

Carnival has the further effect of dissolving the subject's self-consciousness and sense of individual identity (1967, 453). The force of intertextuality undercuts both the privileged status of the individual author as sole source of the text, and also the conception of the author-reader relation as one of intersubjectivity. Kristeva paraphrases Bakhtin: 'tout texte se construit comme mosaïque de citations, tout texte est absorption et transformation d'un autre texte. A la place de la notion d'intersubjectivité s'installe celle d'*intertextualité*' (1967, 440–1); and: 'pour Bakhtine . . . le dialogue n'est pas seulement le langage assumé par le sujet, c'est une *écriture* où on lit l'autre . . . face à ce dialogisme, la notion de "personne-sujet d'écriture" commence à s'estomper' (443–4). For Bakhtin in fact the central feature of dialogism is that it breaks with the traditional conception of the subject's relation to his discourse; the author cannot simply write in his 'own voice', but activates a mixture of available social discourses. As he puts it, 'the author participates in the novel (he is omnipresent in it) with *almost no direct language of his own*. The language of the novel is a *system* of languages that mutually and ideologically interanimate each other' (1981, 47).

Kristeva's concept of intertextuality has been used by many different critics – in many different ways. Marc Angenot argues persuasively (1983) that it is less a rigorously defined theoretical concept than a quasi-political *prise de position*; it becomes a powerful and flexible weapon against both the immanence of classic structuralism and the older humanist conceptions of author, influence, and so on. It also fitted in very well with existing attempts to theorise the text, being, for example, not dissimilar to bricolage: the reworking of fragments of 'used' cultural material into a new structure. But in the context of the the group with which Kristeva herself was most closely associated – *Tel Quel* – the relevant reference point is the notion of textual production discussed here in Chapter 3. This already sees the text as working on – in other words re-writing – a pre-existing raw material which consists of linguistic and ideological codes. Kristeva in fact equates the two concepts: 'Le texte est donc une *productivité* ce qui veut dire: 1. son rapport à la langue dans laquelle il se situe est redistributif . . . 2. il est une permutation de textes, une inter-textualité' (1968b, 300).

Therefore intertextuality addresses the same problem as does the notion of productivity: how to establish, between the text and what exists outside it, a relation that is not based on representation and that takes account of ideology. Similarly, it is by definition opposed to representation: a text cannot be both a re-writing of other texts and a direct representation of an 'objective' reality. But it also has one theoretical implication which is significantly different from textual productivity. At the end of Chapter 3 I argued that the latter concept led the Nouveau Roman into a dead end, in which ideology and representation were treated as simple equivalents of each other and in which as a result there was no way of defining a specific 'subversive' relation between the text and ideology; and I suggested that intertextuality could provide a way out of this impasse. It can do so, I would argue, because it moves away from the simple dichotomy of production versus representation. Production was used strategically to attack the link between discourse and its referent – the *object* of representation. Intertextuality, while still being anti-representational, refocuses attention on the relation between discourse and its *subject*: it envisages the text as an arena of disparate fragments of discourse in which the author relinquishes his 'own voice'.

This conception is similar to the critique of the author seen as both source and proprietor of his text, that had already been formulated within structuralism and, as discussed in Chapter 4 here, was an important part of the Nouveau Roman's theory of the novel. Intertextuality can thus be seen to bring together some of the main implications of the problems and theories dealt with in my two preceding chapters. But it also adds to these a key emphasis on *heterogeneity*. Not only is the text anti-representational, and not only is the writing subject dispossessed of any controlling or expressive authorial voice, but the text is fundamentally characterised by its discursive diversity. It is multiple rather than singular; and while this multiplicity includes the notion of polysemy or plurality of *meaning* – as promoted by Barthes in *Critique et vérité*, for instance – it goes further: heterogeneity here is most importantly to do with the range of social/discursive *contexts* that are brought into play. The privileged intimacy of the expressive relation between writer and his or her own language has been thoroughly disrupted in favour of a conception of the text as a *space* criss-crossed by diverse pieces of social discourse.

Kristeva sees the modern novel as essentially dialogic – as moving towards 'un autre mode de pensée: celui qui procède par dialogue (une logique de distance, relation, analogie, opposition non exclusive, transfinie)' (1967, 461). This description is quite applicable to the Nouveau Roman. She continues: 'On pourrait démontrer à travers le mot et la structure narrative romanesque du XXe siècle comment la pensée européenne transgresse ses caractéristiques constituantes: l'identité, la substance, la causalité, la définition pour en adopter d'autres: l'analogie, la relation, l'opposition, donc le dialogisme' (ibid.). This last sentence is especially relevant to the novels of Robbe-Grillet, and perhaps Simon.

There is, however, unexpectedly little discussion of the concept of intertextuality among the nouveaux romanciers themselves. (Exceptions to this are Butor's 'La critique et l'invention' in *Répertoires III*, and Ricardou's extensive use of intertextual analysis in *Pour une théorie du nouveau roman*. Even so, Ricardou appears to take the concept for granted; he applies it to particular fictional texts without giving any theoretical discussion of it.) Indeed some critics have seen the Nouveau Roman as being generally uninterested in intertextuality. Genette, for instance, using his own term 'hypertextual' in roughly the same sense, writes: 'Mais nul ne prétendra pour autant que toute notre modernité est hypertextuelle: le Nouveau Roman français, par exemple, l'est parfois, mais d'une manière qui lui est sans doute contingente; sa modernité passe par d'autres voies' (1982, 449).

This seems to me to take a rather narrow view of the situation. While the Nouveau Roman is certainly not *solely* an intertextual phenomenon, and while intertextuality is largely by-passed on the level of their explicit theoretical propositions, the very fact that they *are* explicitly concerned with a contestatory, transgressive relationship to previous literary norms itself constitutes a very general kind of intertextual basis for all of their fiction. Thus whereas Kristeva, above, is situating the modern novel as a whole in an antagonistic relation to a tradition of Western philosophical *thought*, characterised as monologic, there is also a more specific sense in which the nouveaux romans are written *against* traditional realist literature and politically committed literature. Ricardou, for instance, claims that what defines them as a 'movement' is 'une stratégie commune quant à la mise en cause du récit' (1973, 137); and the *critical* function of the Nouveau Roman vis à vis previous literature is strongly emphasised by Robbe-Grillet, Butor and Sarraute, whose *L'Ere du soupçon* demonstrates very clearly the way in which her own programme for the future of the novel is defined through intertextual relations. The first essay, 'De Dostoievski à Kafka' covers Proust, the American novel and Camus as well as Dostoievsky and Kafka. The second chapter discusses Balzac, Joyce and Faulkner (with brief references to Genet, Céline and Rilke); the third one starts from Virginia Woolf, returns via Henry Green to Proust and ends with Ivy Compton-Burnett; only the fourth and last piece is formulated in more abstract terms. All these authors are evaluated both in terms of the positive discoveries that they represent for the Nouveau Roman and their limitations – the space, in other words, that they open up for Sarraute's own experiments in fiction.

Equally, the very fact that the Nouveau Roman constitutes a *group* of writers increases the intensity of connections between the individual members. Collectively, they form an intertextual 'ensemble'. Ricardou defines them as such, although without using the term 'intertextual', throughout *Le Nouveau Roman*, whose aim is precisely to elucidate the common features shared by the writers of the Nouveau Roman that distinguish them from other novelists, and to do so in a way that does not at the same time suppress their individual differences. He achieves this via a kind of informal set theory. The humanist ideology of expression, he suggests, remains imprisoned in the polarity of Originality and School: either the writers of the Nouveau Roman have nothing in common at all, or they are all docilely carrying out the pre-established programme of a 'school' of writing. This 'antagonisme complice *Originalité-Scolarité*' (136) needs to be deconstructed by conceptualising the Nouveau Roman as an 'ensemble' or set of elements existing in relation to each other, the relations consisting of differences as well as similarities. For instance, the *different* ways in which traditional

narrative is subverted in different nouveaux romans can be seen
as an intertextual relation between the texts that make up the group.
This same theoretical project is outlined in Ricardou's introduction
to the NRHA conference. Moreover, Ricardou is proposing here that
the theoretical project itself should be a *collective* one, whose texts,
presumably, will feed into and extend the fictional intertext.

Links between the novels of the Nouveau Roman are most evident on the relatively abstract level of textual and structural procedures; there are not many 'citational' relations between authors.[1]
There are, on the other hand, numerous examples of the particular
form of intertextuality that the nouveaux romanciers refer to as
'l'intertextualité restreinte' – that is, operating between the different
texts of the same author. The links between Robbe-Grillet's *Les
Gommes* and *La maison de rendez-vous*, for instance, have already been
mentioned here in Chapter 2. Simon's fiction, too, is characterised by
the recurrence of characters and images from one novel to another.
But these internal connections leave intact the relation between the
author and his 'own voice', and they do not to any great extent
produce the effect of heterogeneity originally envisaged by Kristeva.
I shall therefore not discuss them here.[2] In fact, despite the relative
paucity of their theoretical comments on the subject, the fiction of
the Nouveau Roman is full of intertextual activity involving a wide
range of other texts and other discourses. I shall first explore this in
general terms with a view to showing how the different theoretical
aspects of intertextuality can be seen to operate in a number of
Nouveau Roman texts, and then go on to analyse three novels in
more detail.

One basic feature of intertextuality is that it is *transformative*. This
can be understood in at least two different ways. It can simply mean
that the textual element in question is transformed by its insertion
into a new context, where it more or less inevitably acquires a
different meaning and function. The use of the biblical story of Cain
in Butor's *L'Emploi du temps*, for instance, explores the connections
between moral guilt and creative renewal. Robbe-Grillet's *La Jalousie*
refers to an 'African novel' which has been identified as Graham
Greene's *The Heart of the Matter*, and which acts as a focus for
questioning the logic of the conventional plot. The Orpheus myth
in Simon's *Les Géorgiques* comes in the first place from Virgil's
Georgics, but the novel draws our attention to the permutations that
it has already undergone, in the form for instance of Gluck's opera
Orpheus and Eurydice: intertextuality, in other words, is a continuing

process, and no one version has any absolute status; Virgil's *Georgics* are important not as an eternal, unalterable classic, but precisely to the extent that they participate in the process of transformation and renewal.[3] At the same time, the Orpheus myth is subjected to an ironic deformation that underlines the *differences* between the world view implicit in the myth and the desacralised materialist vision of the novel.[4]

But intertextuality can also transform in a less automatic and more powerful sense. In this case, the transformation is effected on the *original text* from which the element is taken. The text, that is, retrospectively changes or enlarges the meaning(s) of those other, pre-existing texts with which it is intertextually related. Sarraute's *Portrait d'un inconnu*, for instance, comments on the relationship between Prince Bolkonski and his daughter Maria in *War and Peace*. The narrator tries to probe behind the 'mask' that, he feels, the prince interposes between them. This, therefore, is initially a question of filling in gaps, *supplementing* the original text: 'c'est ce masque, le même, j'en suis certain, qu'il a dû porter toujours en présence de sa fille, la princesse Marie. Mais Tolstoï ne le dit pas ou l'indique à peine en passant' (66). But it presupposes a certain scepticism: 'Comment croire, en effet, que ce pouvait être autre chose, quand on regarde la princesse Marie? Elle semble n'avoir été tout entière qu'innocence, que pureté . . . Pourtant j'ai envie de dire . . . que je voudrais bien "voir". Tout n'était peut-être pas si clair dans le cas de la princesse Marie' (68). Moreover the questioning of the fictional character's psychology leads to a questioning of the author's mode of characterisation: Tolstoy has presented Maria and Bolkonski in such a way as to preclude any ambiguity of motivation: 'Mais ce ne sont là, je le sais, que de vagues et assez grossières suppositions, des rêveries. De bien plus forts que moi se casseraient les ongles, les dents, à essayer ainsi, insolemment, de s'attaquer au prince Bolkonski ou à la princesse Marie' (69). Thus on one level the narrator's speculations fall flat, defeated by the monolithic block of Tolstoyan fiction. But in another sense the intervention is very potent: the reader of *Portrait d'un inconnu* does not discover a new 'truth' about Maria, but is rather led to adopt a new perspective on Tolstoy's fictional discourse: the 'bloc solide et dur' (70) has effectively been fissured.

Intertextual transformation of pre-existing texts can occasionally extend further, beyond the single specific text that is being 're-written'. That is, it can amount to a reorganisation of the whole literary *field* in which the new text is inserted. Butor, in 'La critique et l'invention', even claims that this is always bound to happen, since modern literature is produced in an arena which is already so full that there is no unused space which a new text can occupy, so its arrival pushes all the existing texts into new positions: 'Toute invention littéraire aujourd'hui se produit à l'intérieur d'un milieu déjà saturé de littérature. Tout roman, poème, tout écrit nouveau est une intervention dans ce paysage antérieur' (1968, 7). But the effect is obviously most demonstrable in the case of a text which consciously and overtly 'redistributes' the literary field; and one of the best examples of this is Butor's own novel *Degrés*. The description of the school curriculum includes references to and quotations from the books which the boys are studying. The effect of a generalised transformation of the field results not only from the sheer number of texts cited (some 135 quotations from thirty-five different authors), but also from the fact that they have been selected by the educational system, which imposes on them a very definite, institutionalised taxonomy: books about America are studied in geography, while the discovery of America belongs to a history lesson, and Montaigne's reaction to it 'is' French literature. By juxtaposing these three sets of texts (and many others) within its own matrix, *Degrés* breaks down the original compartmentalised arrangement and produces a new articulation. While the individual texts involved acquire new resonances as a result, the most powerful shift is that of the whole nexus of relations between them.

Kristeva accords great importance to the *carnivalesque* dimension of intertextuality. Among the nouveaux romanciers, Robbe-Grillet with his emphasis on 'le jeu' comes closest to this ludic type of intertextuality. *Les Gommes*, for instance, is a parody of *two* very different genres: Sophoclean tragedy and the detective novel. Each of these is emptied of its original ideological weight: there is no sense either of a transcendental tragic fate or of justice triumphing over crime. But the parody is made more truly carnivalesque by the incongruity of the two generic models which are superimposed on the same set of fictional events.

On a smaller scale but even more strikingly, the features of the carnivalesque – writing that is both ludic and transgressive of linguistic and ideological norms – coalesce in the speech of Lambert, the irreverent schoolboy friend of the narrator of Simon's *Histoire*. Lambert's favourite trick is to replace the words of the Catholic

Mass with phonetically similar but obscene equivalents, which he shouts, undetected, at the top of his voice:

> A côté de moi Lambert gueulait à tue-tête n'en ratant pas une Bite y est dans le caleçon au lieu de Kyrie Eleïsson ou encore Bonne Biroute à Toto pour Cum spiritu tuo il en avait comme ça pour presque tous les répons chaque fois à peu près de cette force En trou si beau adultère est béni au lieu de Introïbo ad altare Dei. (48)

This is in the first place simply comic; it is also, however, a perfect example of *verbal* play which transgresses the *social* requirements of religious observance and obedience to school rules. Lambert is liberating himself from the two major ideological instances constituted by church and school, and he does so in an exemplarily carnivalesque fashion, through a sexualised playing with language and an aggressive mixing of opposed – religious and pornographic – social discourses. It is, as the text of *Histoire* describes it, an 'Arsenal de calembours et de contrepèteries censé l'affranchir par la magie du verbe des croyances maternelles et des leçons du catéchisme' (49).

Kristeva, as we have seen, sees intertextuality as breaking down the boundaries that separate 'works of literature' from other social discourses. Intertextuality in practice often operates within a purely literary field, but much of its theoretical significance derives from its extension beyond this into the social text. That is, it incorporates and is incorporated into its social context in so far as this latter is conceptualised as, literally a '*con-text*'. From this point of view too, the Nouveau Roman provides a richer field of investigation than its self-proclaimed a-social or anti-social position has sometimes led critics to suppose. Simon is a case in point, in the first place because his novels of the 1960s are scattered with fragmentary citations of newspaper headlines (*Le Palace, Histoire*), postcard captions (*Histoire*), and so on. But here again, *Les Géorgiques* is a central point of reference. In addition to the literary intertexts of Virgil and Orwell, it draws extensively on an 'amoncellement de paperasses, de vieilles lettres et de registres' (193) concerning the life of the Napoleonic general 'L.S.M'. These are real documents which Simon discovered in his family home. Cited, sometimes at considerable length, in the text of *Les Géorgiques*, they cover military reports and commands, agricultural instructions concerning the general's estate, a report of the court proceedings arising from the contestation of his will, and so on. As a result, the fictional discourse of the novel is periodically disrupted by very different kinds of text.[5] The intertextuality at work in *Les Géorgiques* also has a historical dimension, in line with Kristeva's definition of it as 'la façon dont un texte lit l'histoire' (1967, 312). Alastair Duncan has pointed out that one of the functions of the Virgilian text is 'to stand as a generalised image for antiquity' (1983, 100), and, further, that the reader's access to it is modified by the intervening 'version' of antiquity constructed by the Revolutionary period to which L.S.M. belongs.[6] The historicity of discourse and ideology is thus demonstrated.

In terms of the overall problematic that I have outlined, however – that is, the efficacity of intertextuality as a means of transforming the text's relation to ideology – it is the notion of *'other* discourse' that is perhaps most fundamentally at stake. In its most radical form intertextuality implies the *disorigination* of the writing subject; it implies, in other words, that nobody 'owns' the text; its authorship, if one can still use the term, is plural, anonymous and collective. This idea is reflected in the few theoretical comments made by nouveaux romanciers on intertextuality. Ricardou, for instance, is completely in agreement with Kristeva: 'Par cette expropriation immédiate, qu'on pourrait qualifier *expérience même de l'écriture,* ce n'est plus en position maîtresse qu'il se trouve engagé. Bien qu'il le concerne, son texte lui apparaît comme une bizarrerie: *autre chose.* Et lui-même s'y découvre comme une excentricité: *non au centre mais aux frontières'* (1973, 15).

Similarly Butor, in 'La critique et l'invention', starts by stressing the extent to which all writing is produced within the intertextual 'library' that we all participate in ('Nous nous trouvons tous à l'intérieur d'une immense bibliothèque' (1968, 7)), and that our view of the real world as well as of literary texts is very largely conditioned by this 'library'. The writer is simultaneously inventor and critic; in other words, his relation to his own text is inseparable from his experience of other texts. This makes him realise that he can never be the sole and definitive author of 'his' work: 'Le poète ou romancier qui se sait en même temps critique considère comme inachevée non seulement l'œuvre des autres mais la sienne; il sait qu'il n'en est pas le seul auteur, qu'elle apparaît au milieu des œuvres anciennes et sera continuée par ses lecteurs' (17).

But the intertextual *practice* of the nouveaux romanciers is rather more ambiguous. It could be argued, for instance, that critical or parodic citation of other texts can actually reinforce the writer's individual status. The three novels that will now be discussed separately – Sarraute's *Les Fruits d'or*, Simon's *La Bataille de Pharsale*, and Butor's *Mobile* – illustrate a range of different ways in which the ambiguities of the subject's relation to his/her discourse affect the intertextual functioning of the novels in question. Thus, although I have chosen texts which are among the most intertextually active of the Nouveau Roman's fiction, none of the three can be seen as a straightforward 'application' of Kristeva's ideas. Nor is it a question of conscious influence, if for no other reason than that *Les Fruits d'or* and *Mobile* pre-date Kristeva's work by three or four years. But they give a good general picture of the forms that intertextuality can take in the Nouveau Roman as a whole, and of the theoretical complexities that can arise from this view of the text.

NATHALIE SARRAUTE: *LES FRUITS D'OR*

Les Fruits d'or, which charts the rise and subsequent decline of a novel also entitled *Les Fruits d'or* by a writer called Bréhier, is the first of Sarraute's novels to consist entirely of interaction between an indeterminate number of unidentifiable voices. A few names are mentioned from time to time, a few relationships are sketchily evoked, but there are no 'characters' in the normal sense. Their discourse, however, is readily identifiable as that of Parisian literary circles; they speak and think largely in the clichés of their milieu. These floating, unattached voices have usually been described, including by Sarraute herself, as the final stage of a process of *paring down* of character; they are what is left after the character has successively been stripped of all his other attributes: social status, possessions, profession, physical appearance, etc. Sarraute's texts, in other words, are normally seen as occupying a position towards the end of the long evolution of the modernist psychological novel.

The concept of intertextuality, however, provides an alternative and far more radical interpretation. That is, it allows us to define the voices, no longer as purified remnants of *psychological* characterisation, but as fragments of the *social* intertext. Sarraute has of course been accused by realist critics of having an a-social view of reality.[7] But seen in the light of the Kristevan conception of the social text, her novels become 'spaces' staging social-discursive interactions.

In support of this alternative view of *Les Fruits d'or* are the anonymity of the voices (which was not the case in her previous novels) and the precise attention paid to their sociolinguistic texture (which is characteristic of all her writing). The 'lieu commun' is a key feature of Sarraute's representation of discourse; rather than using speech to individualise her characters, she uses the characters to activate a, literally, common *place* of intensively socialised discursive activity.[8] But it is not only the fact that the voices of *Les Fruits d'or* are plural, anonymous and cliched. The discourse in question – that of literary criticism – is also shown to be acutely social in that, far from being a benign backwater of scholarly endeavour, it is entirely concerned with *power*. It enacts, in exemplary form, all the strategies of alliance and exclusion that characterise groups struggling to achieve dominance in their society. Thus the literary elite assures its position against challenge from competing groups: 'On leur apprendra – ah c'est dur, n'est-ce pas? – que la littérature est un lieu sacré, fermé, où seul un humble apprentissage, l'étude patiente des maîtres peut donner le droit à quelques rares élus de pénétrer. Les tricheurs, les parvenus, les intrus sont exclus' (35).

As this suggests, much of the text of *Les Fruits d'or* consists of parody. The most trenchant kind is reserved for the two structuralist critics, who describe Bréhier's *Les Fruits d'or* in quite unintelligible terms (65); but traditional humanist criticism is presented in similarly ironic fashion as a pretentious, self-regarding code whose main function is to keep the uninitiated at bay. In fact one of the most striking characteristics of *Les Fruits d'or* overall is the almost total absence of an authorial voice. In the last chapter a voice 'speaks' more directly and sincerely, in a style which is not a recognisable stereotype. But otherwise virtually the whole text consists of 'other speech', in the Bakhtinian sense of an 'objectified', i.e., stylistically distanced discourse. This is achieved by slight exaggeration, a kind of ironic inflation which, without any authorial comment, presents it critically, as an object. Often it takes the form of an incongruous rhetorical solemnity:

Nous sommes tous ici, n'est-ce pas, de même espèce, de même couleur, de même race, de même confession et de même rang... Aussi, avec une certitude qui tous nous honore, avec la ferme assurance de ne faire rougir personne, avec une fraternelle confiance, je peux vous regarder droit dans les yeux et répéter avec force ce que chacun sait déjà: ceux qui, encore aujourd'hui, admirent Les Fruits d'Or sont des sots. (131)

The intertextual perspective on *Les Fruits d'or* thus has the advantage of bringing into focus its *mise en scène* of discourse as social. But this does not mean that the novel is straightforwardly intertextual in the Kristevan sense. There are other aspects of it which render such an interpretation distinctly problematic. For example, Kristeva's notion of intertextuality replacing intersubjectivity is not easily applicable to the voices of the novel; the absence of solid characters does not of itself preclude *emotion*, and the interaction between the voices is determined by personal motives of rivalry, fear, the desire to be accepted by the group, and so on. Each episode, in other words, is a battle in which the weapons are pieces of socialised discourse but the underlying dynamic is intersubjective and psychological, rather than intertextual.

Also, the discourse is fragmented between a multiplicity of voices so that the reader cannot identify who is speaking, and is often ambiguous between vocalised speech and interior monologue – but it is for the most part fairly *homogenous* as discourse. While referential ambiguity or indeterminacy, and psychological conflict, are dominant features throughout the novel, the discursive heterogeneity which Kristeva posits as fundamental to the intertextual programme is lacking: Sarraute's voices all speak more or less the same 'language'.

This would seem to constitute a severe limitation to the intertextuality of *Les Fruits d'or*. But it is not in fact simply an argument against the intertextual interpretation of the novel that I am proposing. Rather, it can be seen as resulting from a very specific *thematic* positioning of a certain type of intertext. That is, intertextuality is not only a force which, partially at least, governs the text (as I have been arguing so far): it is also itself presented as an object, or, more precisely, a process, which the novel reflects upon. *Les Fruits d'or*, in other words, *stages* a particular form of intertextuality as a process in operation – and shows it from a particular and critical angle. The form in question is that of the *market*. The literary intertext – and *Les Fruits d'or* contains references to Stendhal, Constant, Rimbaud, Mallarmé, Valéry, Joyce and many others – is shown to be a market of competing products with fluctuating values. The market functions 'intertextually' in so far as it is a *system* of points of reference in which the significance and hence the value of each individual text is established *relationally*, on the basis of comparison. Bréhier's novel is one particular case of a commodity whose value rises and then drops again. But all literary

texts are commodities. Their values are not intrinsic 'une œuvre
d'art n'est jamais une valeur sûre . . . Même pour les valeurs les
plus éprouvées, les chefs-d'œuvre du passé, on voit tout à coup des
revirements, on assiste à de brusques engouements' (117). Thus the
market involves both literary texts and a nexus of critical discourse
which creates their values. But it is noticeable that the literary texts
themselves are never quoted (with the one exception of the fictional
figure of the poet Varenger); they never become active within the
intertext, but function merely as inert landmarks within the area
staked out by the critics – as *names* rather than texts: 'Des têtes
lourds de savoir s'inclinent, on entend des chuchotements . . . "La
Fontaine et Esope . . . Shakespeare et Marlowe . . . Et Racine donc
. . . "' (127). Indeed at one point a critic is asked to justify his
comments by actual quotations, and finds that his attempt to do
so leaves him completely impotent – 'Il a tout perdu. Il est seul,
démuni' (111) – *because* he has been forced out of the *critical* discourse
in which literary texts are simple mute commodities: 'Il a été attiré
hors de la protection de cette enceinte fortifiée où il se tenait, de
cette place forte que formaient autour de lui ses travaux, ses livres,
ses articles' (ibid.).

But, if the critical discourse forms a matrix within which literary
texts compete as commodities, it is also itself a *competition*, both
between different 'theories' which are materialised as different discourses (humanist, structuralist, etc.), and (more cynically) between
vested interests in promoting this or that text. *Les Fruits d'or* enacts,
parodically and also satirically, the process of reorganisation of
the literary field which, as we have seen, is described in entirely
positive terms by Butor. For Sarraute, the incorporation of a new
text is less an illuminating attempt to 'redistribuer toute la surface
pour que s'y creusent des fenêtres' (Butor, 1968, 8) than a frantic
readjustment of market values.[9] The promotion of Bréhier's novel
automatically entails the devaluing of the authors he has displaced,
who react with fury and despair: 'C'est moi, moi qui suis touché, jeté
à terre, moi que cette brute encore tout récemment encensait, moi
devant qui elle se prosternait . . . Comment, au cours de quelle
nuit, tandis qu'il dormait paisiblement, s'est opérée la prise du
pouvoir?' (56).

The various competing agents use intertextual techniques to
better their position within the market. It is significant, for instance,
that one of their key strategies is parody. The different voices of the
critical discourse thus attack each other *intertextually*:

Il fallait la voir, c'était tordant: "Mais c'est si fabriqué . . . Les sentiments, c'est tellement plus complexe . . . Il pépie . . . On nous a appris . . . A l'heure actuelle, nous savons . . . " Qu'est-ce que vous savez donc, hein? (79)

Or, parody can also be a means of persuasion, as with the voice who deliberately adopts the 'other discourse' of his audience in order to convince them:

Le même souci d'efficacité . . . me fait choisir sans effort les mots qu'ils pourront aussitôt comprendre, ceux qu'ils ont l'habitude d'employer. Je leur parle avec douceur: "Oui, voyez-vous, moi ce qui me frappe, c'est qu'il y a dans Les Fruits d'Or une habileté si consommée, quelque chose de si évidemment concerté . . . ' (137)

It is here that the question of homogeneity becomes relevant. If the intertext is a market of competing critical discourses, these have necessarily to be made at least sufficiently homogenous to participate within the same overall scale of values. A literary text has to be promoted in a discourse which is accepted by the market as a whole. The conformism that is such a strong pressure throughout the novel has of course a psychological dimension, but it is also a condition for competing in the intertextual market. The critical discourse, in other words, is characterised by a limited and *managed* plurality; this in turn means that the intertextual market as a whole, although not completely uniform, is structurally incapable of activating the kind of heterogeneity prescribed by Kristeva.

Thus it could be argued that the intertextual market staged by *Les Fruits d'or* is in fact a pseudo-intertext. The literary texts within it are certainly treated in ways more characteristic of the traditional schema of sources and influences that the theory of intertextuality is attempting to combat: texts are pigeon-holed 'comme sur les cartons d'un jeu de loto, la littérature du monde, découpée en petits carrés numérotés' (144). And, at least some of the time, the voices themselves have an image of the critical intertext as a whole as a comfortable 'patrie' (19) in which conflict and diversity are neutralised by the reassuring complicity of a shared ideology: 'Ne sont-ils pas chez eux, dans leur pays, un pays civilisé où les vraies valeurs sont respectées?' (20).

It is also true that the relation between *intertext* and *ideology* is very different from that formulated by Kristeva. Her conception of the dominant ideology stresses its singular, monolithic quality: heterogeneity is an effective weapon against it only because it is itself so unified. Subverting it is therefore a matter of disruption and fragmentation, fissuring its singularity with intertextual plurality and otherness. And, since the dominant ideology involves a view of discourse as exchange value and commodity (cf. Chapter 3), intertextuality is set up in opposition to the notion of literary commodity. For Sarraute, on the other hand, the discourse of the dominant ideology is *already* conflictual and in a sense intertextual; intertexuality has as it were been co-opted by the market.

However, the critical discourse of *Les Fruits d'or* has a further significance in that it acts reflexively as a forum for the presentation of several substantive issues pertaining to the theory of intertextuality. For instance, it quickly becomes clear that one of the prime literary values produced by the discourse is immanence or closure. The literary text is valued as a separate, compact self-contained whole: 'Pure œuvre d'art – cet objet refermé sur lui-même, plein, lisse et rond. Pas une fissure, pas une éraflure par où un corps étranger pût s'infiltrer. Rien ne rompt l'unité des surfaces parfaitement polies . . . ' (33) – the opposite, in other words, of the intertextual conception. However, this description is immediately followed by a further evaluation, by the same critic, which shows how in reality the value of the novel is established *relationally*, by comparison with previous texts: 'Rien dans nos lettres de comparable' (ibid.) leads straight into 'Ce qu'on a écrit de plus beau depuis Stendhal . . . depuis Benjamin Constant' (ibid.). There are other examples of this (44, 52, 57, 129). It consists essentially in a contradiction whereby 'purity' is at one and the same time a rejection of the whole notion of intertextuality, and a principal criterion for establishing value within the intertext.

The notion of originality is thematised in similar fashion. Like purity or unity, originality is also one of the main market values, acquiring an almost fetishistic status. This nicely illustrates Ricardou's characterisation of the 'dogma' of expression, but seems above all to derive from both a consumerist attitude to the literary commodity – if the work turns out to be an imitation, the customer has in effect been duped – and the elitist satisfaction of proving oneself sufficiently knowledgeable to be able to tell the difference between an original and a copy. Both these attitudes are satirised in the following interchange:

elle le suivait partout . . . n'osant se prononcer, s'approchant, gênée, toute tremblante, chuchotant . . . "Mais c'est, je crois, n'est-ce pas, une copie?"

Une copie, il avait envie de lui crier cela . . . Une copie. Attention. Casse-cou. Ce n'est rien, Les Fruits d'Or. Un pastiche. Erreur. Vous le regretterez . . . et de la voir sursauter, faire, le dos aplati, un bond de côté et jeter autour d'elle des regards angoissés. (42)

The fetishisation of originality thus also highlights, by contrast, what the market defines as an 'illegal' form of intertextuality: plagiarism. Plagiarism is the equivalent of fraudulent trading; the episode in which characters argue about the status of a pastiche of *Les Fruits d'or* which one of them has previously passed off to an eminent critic as a text by Bréhier himself (122–7) demonstrates the market's reaction to this kind of flouting of its rules. Also, the final devaluation of the real *Les Fruits d'or* is achieved to a great extent by redefining it as plagiarism (147–8). To operate successfully as a commodity, a literary text must exhibit its originality and its purity.

The value attached to originality and purity (or immanence) is thus treated satirically by the text, as though these concepts were being criticised. But the evidence of the final chapter suggests that the real object of the earlier satire is in fact their degradation into the form of commodities, rather than the concepts themselves. With none of the previously characteristic irony, the last few pages of Sarraute's *Les Fruits d'or* praise Bréhier's *Les Fruits d'or* for, precisely, its purity and closure: for being 'quelque chose d'intact, d'innocent' (152), and 'un tout indivisible' (154). And its value is enhanced by 'Ce silence où vous baignez, dépouillé de tous les vêtements et ornements dont vous aviez été affublé, nu, tout lavé [qui] . . . avec moi cramponné à vous, rend très étroit notre contact' (155); in other words, by its having *withdrawn* from the intertext into a private one-to-one relationship between text and reader. The conception of the ideal text which emerges from these pages (and which, indeed, is evident in Sarraute's theoretical writing, see Chapter 4) is thus one of an authenticity which depends upon *not* being drawn into intertextual functioning. From this point of view, it appears that the commodification of originality, etc., is satirised precisely because the values themselves in their 'true' state are so important. Following this line of argument, *Les Fruits d'or* can be described as rejecting, through parody, the corrupt intertextual market of literary commodities and critical discourses, and contrasting this with a positive view of the ideal literary text as essentially not intertextual. But the position is in fact rather more ambiguous. The question is, given that Sarraute thematises a form of 'bad' intertextuality, is this countered by a corresponding 'good' intertextuality, or by an ideal of authenticity and purity that is simply a rejection of intertextuality *per se*? The answer, I think, is that she does both, and that as a result her novel can be read in two significantly different ways.

The latter reading – that *Les Fruits d'or* is ultimately a rejection of intertextuality – relies mainly on the final chapter in which the ideal of textual purity and authenticity is outlined by a subject speaking 'sincerely' ('cette sincérité qui est, soit dit sans me vanter, ma principale qualité', 151) in his 'own' voice. He is presented as having the correct view – i.e., Sarraute's view. This alone differentiates him from all the other voices; but he is further set apart from them by the difficulty he has in putting his thoughts into words. He has no glib formulae to describe Bréhier's novel; the qualities he sees in it resist verbalisation – 'je le sens très bien, mais je ne sais pas l'exprimer [. . .] il me faut éprouver . . . je ne sais pas bien ce que c'est [. . .] c'est ce parfum qu'ils dégagent, mais ce n'est pas un parfum [. . .] cela ne porte aucun nom' (151–2) – and this in itself seems to be a guarantee of their authenticity. That is, the notion of authenticity depends upon the privileged status accorded to the *non-verbal*. This is of course a central element in Sarraute's theoretical conception of writing, as discussed in Chapter 4. In this context, though, it has the added significance of defining a certain conception of the *subject*. The subject exists most authentically on a non-verbal level; language, discourse, and intertext are all distanced from him by a kind of pre-verbal interiority. Therefore, the ideological intertext of the 'market' is not disrupted or fragmented, but simply *staged* as *other* to the 'authentic' subject who is as it were protected from it by an enclave of non-verbal feeling. His 'own' speech occasionally cuts across the intertext, but he does not really participate in it: 'Je sais qu'ils me trouveraient ridicule s'ils m'entendaient. Heureusement, ils n'entendent jamais' (151). Also, this conception of interiority is responsible for the intersubjective as opposed to intertextual dimension of *Les Fruits d'or* (see above). Sarraute, in other words, agrees with Kristeva that almost all discourse is social rather than individual; but she disagrees in so far as she reserves this private space for authentic non-verbal subjective experience. Whereas the

Kristevan writing subject is totally implicated in, *traversed* by a plurality of social discourses, Sarraute's conception is of a possible 'pure' subjectivity existing outside discourse. From this point of view, all intertextuality is simply negative and corrupt.

From elsewhere in the novel, however, one can find evidence on which to base a different reading; evidence, that is, of a *positively* intertextual strategy. The way this works is by surrounding and undercutting the intertextual market with *another* intertext. This is possible only because the discursive homogeneity already discussed is not in fact total. One exception is of course the 'sincere' voice in the final chapter. But even in the rest of the text, the characteristic stereotyped speech of the market is interrupted from time to time by pieces of a different kind of discourse. These result from the distinction between 'conversation' and 'sous-conversation' that runs through all Sarraute's writing, and that she explains in 'Conversation et sous-conversation' in *L'Ere du soupçon*. 'Conversation' covers not only vocalised speech but also sequences of verbalised thought. Both of these are similarly steretyped; in fact one of the most striking features of her 'voices' is the extent to which their most private and spontaneous feelings, as well as their communications with others, are expressed in cliches. 'Sous-conversation', in contrast, designates a level of *non-verbal* interaction: 'un foisonnement innombrable de sensations, d'images . . . de petits actes larvés qu'aucun langage intérieur n'exprime' (1956, 115). The problem of representing it in words is solved by recourse to *metaphor*. The text operates a transfer from the original situation to a metaphorical equivalent of it: the pressure of literary conformism becomes the surveillance of a police state, for instance. These figurative situations bring with them into the text their respective discourses; in fact it is only through the perceptible shift to a different and usually incongruous terminology that the reader realises that the metaphorical transfer has occurred. For instance, the aesthetic purity of response necessary to appreciate Bréhier's *Les Fruits d'or* is compared to the religious asceticism of a vestal virgin, via the following sequence:

Voilà. Toute droite et pure, elle s'avance.
Devant elle s'étend quelque chose de gris, de froid . . . cryptes, voutes, sépulcres, musées où un jour blafard tombe sur les dalles, les colonnes brisées, les sarcophages de marbre, les statues aux poses hiératiques, aux yeux opaques, aux visages figés. (40)

This is clearly not the language of the critical market. But it is not an authorial discourse either; rather than Sarraute speaking in her 'own voice', it is the appropriation of an other, equally stereotyped, discourse to serve the purpose of articulating, as it were artificially, from the outside, a character's unverbalised reactions. These metaphorical intertexts often generate their own *speech*: the paranoia of political sects, for instance:

> Ah non, ce serait trop commode: ici, on ne pénètre pas comme ça. Il faut avoir donné certaines preuves . . . il faut avoir un passé moins louche. On a, à certains moments, commis certaines erreurs fâcheuses, fourni aux autres, quand ils étaient au pouvoir, un peu trop de gages [. . .] il faut prendre bien garde à laisser à la porte des alliés aussi suspects, ces ralliés de la dernière heure qui jetteraient le discrédit sur la communauté. (90–91)

The metaphorical textualisation of 'sous-conversation' thus opens up a way out of the relative homogeneity of the dominant critical discourse of the market, and into a wider, more diversified intertext. Each sequence is in effect a fragment of a social context. Together, they introduce into the text a whole range of different discourses. For example, we find those of political terror and censorship; of various kinds of religious extremism (e.g., the hysterical trance of the possessed (11), but especially martyrdom: 'il la suit dans les catacombes, elle, sa sœur . . . ils sont entourés de païens, traqués, ils seront martyrisés, humiliés, mais il a choisi de se tenir à ses côtés, il veut rejoindre les pauvres, les humbles, les simples' (75–6)); and various kinds of romance – for instance the fairy-tale romance of mysterious palaces and reclusive royalty: 'Alors, pleins d'appréhension, ils ont osé s'avancer, ils se sont approchés des portes bien gardées, des hautes grilles de la demeure royale où ces princes de l'esprit vivaient enfermés' (69). Some of these discourses, moreover, are extremely carnivalesque: a literary argument metamorphoses first into a physical punch-up, presented in the style of a popular thriller (96–8), and then into a conversation between drunken clowns (105–6).

The larger intertext that is activated by these metaphorical sequences surrounds the market intertext and thus shows up its limits; the market is not coextensive with the text of *Les Fruits d'or* as a whole, but *placed* within it. Moreover, Sarraute's conception of the way in which 'conversation' and 'sous-conversation' interrelate means that the text switches frequently and abruptly from one to the other; this is rooted in her psychological model of subjectivity, but seen as an intertextual phenomenon it also has the result that the speech of the market is constantly intercut with fragments of these other social discourses. Here, in other words, we can see Kristeva's view of intertextuality at work; the market is penetrated and disrupted by another, more heterogenous intertext.

Les Fruits d'or, then, offers us two contradictory perspectives on the status of intertextuality. The first contrasts it negatively with subjective authenticity and aesthetic purity, while the second contrasts the corrupt pseudo-intertextual discourse of the literary market with a genuinely subversive intertext. The first follows closely the line taken by Sarraute in her theoretical writing and is therefore, one must assume, the reading that she herself would support. But, for the reasons outlined above, her novel seems to me to remain open to the second, positively intertextual, interpretation as well, even if this means going against the author's intentions. Kristeva's theory does, after all, invite us to see reading as itself a transformative intertextual performance; from this point of view, a *transgressive* reading of a text simply enhances its intertextuality.

CLAUDE SIMON: *LA BATAILLE DE PHARSALE*

Simon's fiction has in many ways a more important intertextual dimension than that of any other nouveau romancier.[10] The status of the intertextual, however, varies considerably from one novel to another. This variation is a function of two other parameters: the degree of diversity of the discourse on the one hand, and, on the other, the changing relation between the writing subject and his discourse. The latter is a question of whether the authorial discourse appears as the subject's 'own voice' or not, but also of how dominant it is in the text as a whole. Correlatively, it is also a question of the *reciprocity* of the intertextual relations: are the fragments of other discourse merely transformed by the matrix text, or do they also transform it? I have chosen *La Bataille de Pharsale* because it seems to me to represent a turning point at which these parameters intersect to produce maximal intertextual activity.

This argument obviously requires *La Bataille de Pharsale* to be compared with the novels which precede it. The texts covering the period from 1957 to 1967 are characterised by a peculiarly individual *style*. Any sentence taken from any of these novels is immediately recognisable as the discourse of Claude Simon. What has become known as 'la phrase simonienne', with its hesitant rambling structure, present participles, parentheses and constant self-corrections, is an extreme case of an author's 'own voice': not just in its particularity, but also, and more significantly from the point of view of the theory of intertextuality, in its *expressivity* – its closeness to Simon himself as writing subject. The syntactic norms of the language are dislocated in an effort to convey *his* perceptions of the world, so that the style is inseparable from an equally singular vision of reality. The force and consistency with which this ultra-subjective discourse marks the texts is, of course, entirely antagonistic to the concept of intertextuality.

The first three novels in this group – *Le Vent*, *L'Herbe* and *La Route des Flandres* – are especially homogeneous texts. With *Le Palace*, however, although the bulk of the text is still in the characteristic Simonian style, interpolated fragments of other discourse become far more apparent. Moreover, these are eminently social intertexts: advertisements, tram routes, signs over shops and bars, etc. Topographical signs are presented in a way that highlights their historical significance: a list of the street names of Barcelona is preceded by a description of them as 'successions de rues, de places, d'avenues aux noms de rois, de saints, de dogmes, de batailles . . . la lugubre litanie d'une impitoyable religion, de l'impitoyable, arrogante et mystérieuse Histoire' (18). In other cases the discourse is political: the newspaper headlines are echoed in the writing on the banners of the demonstration, and both are reproduced verbatim in the text (29–39, and 113). They stand out because they are in Spanish, and because they are printed in capital letters, usually inset on a separate line so that typographically they disrupt the flow of the matrix text, and with Spanish punctuation:

> l'éventail des journaux proposait toujours son étalage de variations sur la même lancinante interrogation:
> ¿QUIEN ASESINO A SANTIAGO?
>
> (35)

Sometimes these quotations are themselves fragmented:

¿QUIEN HA MUERTO A COMMAN
la fin du titre cachée par l'autre journal

(29)

These kinds of transformation are quite violent; Simon's own discourse attacks the intertextual sequences – as though the action of the wind blowing a poster against a car windscreen:

aspiré par la traînée du vide, comme collé sur un mur d'air noir, les grosses lettres majuscules nettement visibles:
VENCE
puis basculant dans un remous . . . le mot complet fut lisible pendant une fraction de seconde, incliné à quarante-cinq degrés environ:
VENCEREMOS
avant qu'un nouveau remous s'en empare, le tordant, le tirant à présent violemment vers le haut en le secouant de droite et de gauche comme un serpent, convulsé, sinueux. (80–81)

– were a reflexive metaphor for the *textual* aggression which here amputates the word 'VENCEREMOS' but is evident in less obvious ways throughout. Elsewhere, for instance, two intertextual fragments attack each other: one torn poster is stuck on top of another so that it looks as though 'les déchirures dentelées du papier semblables à des langues de flamme' are ' traversant (ou mordant sur – ou attaquant) une affiche blanche' (178). The nausea the student feels at the thought of reading the newspapers (162) can be read as another image for the matrix text's *rejection* of the intertextual fragments. The relation between authorial and 'other' discourse seems, in other words, to be essentially antagonistic. Except for its aggressive objectification of them, and the undeniable effect they have on the visual lay-out of the book, the matrix text is not itself affected by them. Simon's discourse transforms them, but they have no real action on it: they are not generative, nor do they inflect or destabilise the matrix text to any great extent.

This is especially true of the many quotations that are treated as though they were not pieces of language but pictures. That is, the reader's attention is focused on the visual impact of the letters, their size, colours, spacing, etc. – as in the minutely detailed description of the ornate lettering on the lid of a cigar box (164–5), or the effect of superimposed posters again (178–9). This exclusive concentration

on the materiality of the signifiers in question in effect cancels out
their *meaning* (already made more opaque by being in a foreign
language). The text comments several times on this phenomenon:
the newspaper headlines become meaningless, merely 'une suite
de lettres prises au hasard dans l'alphabet et dépourvues de sens'
(144). The authorial discourse, in other words, transforms them but
in a way which, far from enlarging or pluralising their meaning,
simply renders it inert. The 'attack' on the other discourses has thus
succeeded completely; any intertextual force that they might have
had has been effectively defused. The intertextual action is entirely
one-way, and a clear hierarchy is established in which the authorial
discourse incorporates and, as it were, chews up and spits out the
alien fragments – but they cannot have any reciprocal effect on it.

In *Histoire* a similar situation obtains as far as the treatment of
these very small pieces of social intertext are concerned: there is
the same fragmentation of newspaper headlines, posters, etc. But
Histoire also contains – as well as the carnivalesque transformative play of Lambert mentioned above – two far more substantial
intertexts. These are John Reid's *Ten Days that Shook the World* (an
account of the Bolshevik revolution) and the Latin writer Apuleius's
pornographic novel *The Golden Ass*. Both of these are quoted frequently and at some length. But their status is somewhat different;
while Reid's book is largely negated and rejected by the matrix text,
The Golden Ass works in a more positively generative way. It is still,
however, contained within the distinctive 'subjective' Simonian
discourse, which is ultimately in control of the whole text.

It is only with *La Bataille de Pharsale* that we find, simultaneously, a significant shift towards a more reciprocally interactive
intertextuality and a slackening of the relation between the writing
subject and his 'own' discourse. The novel starts in the author's
characteristic style; but, in the opening pages, we already find the
text's own 'Simonian' voice intercut with another far more socially
typical voice, printed in italics:

> Eaux mortes. Mort vivant. *Je comprends parfaitement que tu aies
> décidé de ne rien faire naturellement c'est de ta part purement et
> simplement une question de paresse* mortellement triste *mais après
> tout quoique tu ne puisses encore le savoir* Je ne savais pas encore
> *puisque c'est aussi une chose qu'il faut apprendre et qu'apparemment
> tu as pris la ferme résolution de ne rien faire* bois mort feuille
> morte. (18)

This is the voice of schoolmasterly authority adopted by Charles, the narrator's uncle who already figured in *Histoire*, but whose main role in *La Bataille de Pharsale* is to teach the narrator Latin. At this point, though, Charles is telling him that he must learn to express himself properly in French. The boy's 'own' language, in other words, is shown here to be something initially *other* to him, which has to be acquired as part of the process of socialisation: '*enfin dans la mesure où il te faudra tout de même vivre au milieu de tes semblables et pas dans une forêt vierge en te nourrissant de bananes il y a un certain nombre de nécessités comme boire et manger porter une chemise et un pantalon . . . par conséquent il faudra au moins que tu puisses articuler de façon à peu près intelligible le mot chemise et le mot pantalon*' (18–19).

Then, through the middle section of the novel, entitled 'Lexique', the 'own voice' begins to give way to the impersonal, flatly assertive mode of writing that will dominate Simon's next three novels. The subsection 'Machine', for instance, which describes a derelict combine harvester, begins: '*Partant de l'essieu qui joint les deux grandes roues de fer, une chaîne (semblable aux chaînes des bicyclettes mais en plus gros) se dirige d'abord à l'horizontale vers la droite où elle contourne une roue dentelée au plateau évidé*' (147). The final section of the novel is written consistently in this impersonal style – in, that is, an 'other discourse', distanced from the writing subject.

The gradual distancing is accompanied by a considerable expansion of the intertextual field. In *La Bataille de Pharsale* the intertexts are primarily literary: *The Golden Ass* reappears from *Histoire* on page 92, and many others are present even more fleetingly. But the three main ones are the stanza from Valéry's *Le Cimetière marin* which forms the epigraph to *La Bataille de Pharsale*, the Latin translation passage which is in fact Caesar's account of the battle of Pharsalus, and about thirty fragments of Proust's *A la recherche du temps perdu*.[11] The quotations from all of these texts relate to the novel's central thematic juxtaposition of war and sexual jealousy, seen as different but in some sense equivalent types of suffering. They undergo the same, often aggressive, transformative process that we have seen in *Le Palace*. This is particularly noticeable in the case of Proust. Typically, a number of short quotations taken from different parts of *A la recherche du temps perdu* are reassembled into a new construction (e.g., 203–6) to produce what has been described as 'a distinct work of transfiguration whereby parts of one text radically transform parts of the other . . . it operates to challenge another text's authority'.[12] Reading *La Bataille de Pharsale*, then, we are re-reading a very partial, angled transformation of Proust.

But what is crucially different from Simon's earlier novels is that the quotations are not just treated as foreign objects to be defused by the authorial discourse. They are *re-activated* in such a way as to become *generative* within the matrix text. In the first place this means that they interact with each other. *La Bataille de Pharsale*'s initial and recurrent motif of the pigeon flying in front of the sun, for instance, brings an allusion to the Valéry stanza ('percé de cette flèche ailée') into contact with a fragment of the translation of the Latin text describing the flight of the javelins at the battle of Pharsalus: 'cette image d'arbalète, et alors la voûte des flèches, les traits volant dessinant une arche entre les deux armées *s'étant reposés un petit moment et ayant repris de nouveau leur course ils lancèrent leurs javelots et rapidement . . .* ' (41, Simon's italics).

They also, however, act to generate parts of the *matrix text*. Ricardou has analysed the first few pages of *La Bataille de Pharsale* as almost entirely 'produced' by the lines from Valéry's poem quoted in the epigraph, and he demonstrates how the latter continues to make itself felt throughout the novel. His arguments are too detailed to reproduce here in full, but the images of a bird, flight, violent penetration by an arrow (or, by extension, a phallus), killing, sunlight and shadow, movement and immobility are traced through the text of *La Bataille de Pharsale* as lines of force that orientate its development.[13] The quotations from Proust are similarly generative, but usually in a more localised fashion; a repetition of a Proustian description of a fountain switches suddenly into a repetition of the central erotic scene, for instance: 'divinités des fontaines publiques tenant en main un jet de glace pine à pleines mains et alors peut-être immobilisés comme ça retenant leur respiration sueur se glaçant sur eux' (93). Here the quotation (which ends at 'jet de glace') is completely integrated into the text; it generates the subsequent scene immediately on the basis of the similarity between what the hands are holding, but also the link between Proust's sculpted figures and the suddenly motionless lovers, and the echo of 'glace' and 'glaçant'. Elsewhere a quotation generates a new incident in *La Bataille de Pharsale*: Proust's famous 'raidillon aux aubépines' – where Marcel first sees Gilberte as a little girl – has already been quoted when on page 155 a fragment from *Le Temps retrouvé*, combined with another from *Un Amour de Swann* citing Swann's 'souvenirs voluptueux', leads directly to a new version of the 'hawthorn' scene, producing a Simonian Gilberte: 'chemin déjà herbu entre deux jardinets campagnards petite fille vêtue d'un tricot bleu foncé.' In both these cases the Proustian fragments are drawn into the *erotic* dimension of *La Bataille de Pharsale,* and this is equally true of a third instance, in which several juxtaposed references to Charlus's homosexuality (206) are followed by a scene of mutual masturbation between two small boys (207–8).

The Latin text recounting the battle of Pharsalus is at least equally generative – not least in giving the novel its title. But as well as being perhaps the most active intertext, it also raises, more clearly than the Valéry and Proust texts do, a central theoretical question: the relation between intertextuality and representation. Representational discourse, in other words, *refers* to something in the real world and *expresses* the writer's view of it; intertextual discourse displaces both of these relations (i.e., with the object and the subject of the discourse) in favour of a network of relations between different texts or discourses. Thus the two ways of reading a text are theoretically incompatible. However, this area of *La Bataille de Pharsale* at first appears to be open to both.

One strand of the novel recounts the narrator's journey through Greece, and in particular his attempt to find the site of the battle described in the Latin passage that he remembers translating as a boy. On this level it could be construed as a straightforward realist narrative. But there are also several factors that invite us rather to read it intertextually – as a piece of Simonian text generated by another text. This is, for instance, how it seems to operate on the concrete level of the construction of the novel, which repeatedly moves straight *from* the translation *to* the evocation of the Greek scene. Above all, though, the intertextual reading is reinforced by the narrator's inability to find the original battle site: his attempt, in other words, to supply the *referent* for the Latin text comes to nothing: 'Ça ne mène à rien ici' (39). To have identified the text's 'real' object would have pinned it down as a representational piece of writing; by its conspicuous failure to do so, *La Bataille de Pharsale* in effect transforms Caesar's account into a text existing only in its circulation with other texts. In the first place, it functions as the origin of a translation, itself an intertextual exercise. But it also gives rise to a *plurality* of alternative translations (the same Latin sentence is given in one French version on pages 80–81, and a different one on page 107). Going beyond this, *La Bataille de Pharsale* activates a whole network of related texts: citations from other historical accounts of the battle (26, 27, 30) and scholarly commentaries on the ambiguities of the text, which stress the impossibility of establishing what 'really happened': 'cette description n'est claire que pour qui ne cherche pas à l'approfondir' (91). This quotation is in turn taken up, reworked and expanded: 'Rien d'autre que quelques mots quelques signes sans consistance matérielle . . . traversant les couches incolores du temps des siècles à une vitesse foudroyante remontant des profondeurs et venant crever à la surface comme des bulles vides comme des bulles et rien d'autre Clair pour qui ne cherche pas à l'approfondir' (91).

Thus the Latin text, deprived of the support of its referent, enters into a generative intertextual relation with a number of other texts, written at different historical moments in different languages. In addition to these, the battle generates two new textual versions of itself in the novel. The first is in the form of the football match played on a field in Greece which may or may not be close to the site of the battle (53–5), and which is repeatedly juxtaposed with fragments of the translation (e.g., 59); *La Bataille de Pharsale* re-writes the battle of Pharsalus as a game of football. The second is a rather different type of discourse: the gap left by the missing referent also generates the narrator's evocation of his *own experience* of war, in 1940. Thus a fragment of the translation often leads into a sequence of markedly subjective 'own discourse' (e.g., 33, 81). In one sense this is just one more text among all the others. In the first part of the novel, however, there is a definite tension between it and the other texts; the transition from translation to war experience (here via the linking idea of fleeing from the enemy) is marked by an explicit devaluing of 'mere words':

> sed protinos incitati fuga: mais aussitôt s'élancèrent dans la fuite prirent la fuite. . . .   Mais ce n'étaient rien que des mots, des images dans des livres, *je ne savais pas encore, je ne savais pas,* couché ou plutôt aplati sur l'encolure je pouvais voir son ombre étirée galopant sur le sol les prés sentant la houle des muscles entre mes cuisses. (81)

The italicised phrase *'je ne savais pas encore'* is used several times to signal both the shift into the realist discourse which tries to recapture past subjective experience and, more explicitly, the *contrast* between the latter and the intertextual discourse that still in a sense generates it. That is, the implication of the phrase is always that, having only read about it, he did not then know what war (or death, or jealousy) was *really* like. At this point it looks as though Simon's own voice is reasserting itself – recapturing a dominance over the intertextual fragments on the basis of a priority accorded to 'real' experience over textuality.[14]

And yet it never achieves the kind of control exerted in the earlier novels. This is partly due to the frequency and fluency of the transitions between the textual and the experiential – in which, moreover, the hierarchical relation between real-life experience and textuality is occasionally overturned. For example, the figure of the naked soldier whom the narrator remembers from the war is described as 'une dérisoire parodie, une dérisoire réplique de tous les Persée, les Goliath, les Léonidas, la cohorte des guerriers figés dans les bitumeuses peintures des musées' (137). Defining a real-life figure as a *parody* of an unlife-like ('figés', 'bitumeuses') painting effectively disrupts the boundary between life and art. Equally, the final words of the middle section of the novel confront us with the word 'Pharsale' as one of the key points of 'intersection' of the 'mobile' structure of the novel: 'ou encore le nom PHARSALE figurant également dans un recueil scolaire de textes latins et sur un panneau indicateur au bord d'une route de Thessalie' (186). The 'recueil scolaire' is an example of textuality – but what is the significance of the road sign? It evokes the real experience of going to Greece, *but* it is itself a kind of social text. Thus the intersection which this double occurrence of 'Pharsale' makes possible is itself ambiguous; it can be read as a contrastive juxtaposition of 'text' and 'life' or, more convincingly in my view, as a purely intertextual intersection of two (very heterogenous) kinds of text.

But it is above all the development of the novel as a whole which counteracts the privilege initially accorded to the experiential discourse. *La Bataille de Pharsale* is a transitional text, moving from one mode of writing to another in the course of its progression. Many authors of course change their style from one novel to the next; what is remarkable about *La Bataille de Pharsale* is that the transition takes place within the space of a single text. As a result, the shift from a personal to an impersonal style itself becomes a central issue presented and illuminated by the novel. The text, in other words, enacts a rejection of the subjective realist discourse that tries to represent the author's past experience. Simon has commented that the last part of *La Bataille de Pharsale* is the result of his having finally understood that 'on n'écrit . . . jamais rien d'autre que ce qui se passe *au moment même* de l'écriture'.[15] (To make this absolutely clear, the novel ends with a *mise en scène* of its own production; in contrast to the circular structure of *Histoire*, which ended with the biological conception of the narrator, here we have a circling back to the moment of the *text*'s inception.) This in turn transforms the relation between the Latin text and the narrator's own wartime experience; when the movement from translation to memory recurs in the last section (220–1), not only has 'je' been replaced by 'O.', but his experience is recounted in the same impersonal style and without the distinguishing 'je ne savais pas encore'. Thus although Simon's authorial voice does figure importantly in *La Bataille de Pharsale* to produce, in the first half of the novel, a significant tension between text and experience, it no longer possesses a privileged status in the text as a whole.

Simon's three subsequent novels, *Les Corps conducteurs*, *Triptyque* and *Leçon de choses*, are almost wholly written in the impersonal style that we find in the second half of *La Bataille de Pharsale*. Therefore, the problems posed by the subjective individual 'own discourse' do not arise. But from a different point of view, they are also less intertextually active, because they are extremely homogenous. The exception is *Leçon de choses*, which is intertextually generated from a school textbook, and which contains two sections of distinctively 'spoken', colloquial and often obscene discourse. Overall, however, *La Bataille de Pharsale* represents the point in Simon's production at which two different trajectories – from a forcefully subjective to an impersonal mode of writing, and from the incorporation of heterogenous fragments to a greater homogeneity – intersect to strike the particular balance that provides the optimal scope for intertextuality. The 'own voice' is still there, but it does not *control* the novel in the way that it does in *Histoire*, for instance, so that the intertextual elements are more active; and these are still present in greater number and variety than in *Les Corps conducteurs*, for instance. As a result, *La Bataille de Pharsale* is the most heterogenously and dynamically intertextual of Simon's novels.

MICHEL BUTOR: *MOBILE*

Mobile, sub-titled 'Etude pour une représentation des Etats-Unis', is not recognisably a novel; indeed, it is further away from that norm than any other Nouveau Roman. The transgression of the boundaries of genre is immediately obvious in the visual appearance of the text – typographically broken up into fragments of different sizes, it uses roman and italic type, words in capital letters, and several different margins – but is above all the result of its radically intertextual status. The very large proportion of quotations in *Mobile* makes it in many ways the ultimate 'intertextual text'. In simple quantitative terms these outweigh by far the authorial voice: more importantly, the whole *structure* of the book is determined by intertextuality, in a way quite unlike any of the novels discussed previously. In *Mobile* it is no longer a question of incorporating alien fragments into a matrix text; there is no dominant containing discourse, and the only 'matrix' it can be said to have is the material *space* of the volume.[16] It is, in other words, *systematically* intertextual – the text as space traversed by fragments of different discourses.

Moreover, the discourses in question are strikingly heterogenous. The text intercuts quotations from statesmen and intellectuals (Thomas Jefferson, Benjamin Franklin, William Penn), contemporary mail order catalogues, newspaper reports, an account of the trial of one of the witches of Salem, tourist brochures, and so on. Apart from these actual quotations, which are of course translated into French, the proper names which figure prominently throughout are equally disparate, both linguistically and referentially: names of towns, counties and states, Indian names of tribes and their chiefs, brand names of consumer products (especially cars), names of restaurants and newspapers – the latter in a number of different European languages. All of this material is interspersed with two non-citational discourses. There are the *fictional* 'voices' that carry on an intermittent dialogue or, at times, a diffuse anonymous monologue; these Butor refers to as the 'poussière romanesque' scattered through the book, and says that 'la fiction joue un rôle de contraste par rapport à la réalité, insiste sur le caractère réel de la réalité, et en même temps . . . insiste sur le caractère fictif de ce qu'on entend d'habitude par la réalité'.[17] And there is, finally, an authorial voice threaded through all the others, which sometimes simply *mentions* elements of American reality, and sometimes gives more extended interpretation and comment. The first type produces a strand of 'calligrams' – for instance:

Bleu
Torrents,
       cailloux,
          falaises,
             gorges.

                              (26)

As in this example, the 'calligrams' are mainly to do with *nature*: rocks, rivers, lakes and the sea – and thus provide a counterpoint to the quotations, which are obviously cultural. *Mobile* explores the interface of American culture with the natural landscape. The intermingling of the two is most obvious on the beach: on the one hand, different kinds of bird, on the other, bathers' towels, deckchairs, etc. (e.g., 190–1).[18] The citational discourse also contributes to this theme, by enacting the society's attempt to appropriate nature for its own consumerist purposes, notably through colours: the mail order catalogues use evocatively 'natural' terms to describe the colours of their floor-coverings, for instance: 'aigue-marine et gris fumé', 'taupe-turquoise-rose', 'brun épices et beige coquille', 'sable du désert' (191).

All of these diverse discourses are 'mobilised' within a complex, precise overall structure, and the interactions themselves take a variety of forms. The simplest is the shock effect of sheer contrast or incongruity, echoing the – to a European – incongruous juxtapositions of American culture: the mixing of religion and commerce, for instance, defended in the brochure advertising the Salvation Army's Pacific Ocean Cafeteria: 'Pour ceux qui adoptent comme philosophie "les Affaires sont les Affaires" et rien de plus, l'idée de combiner un lieu de méditation et révérence avec une entreprise commerciale peut sembler incongrue' (235), but: 'Nous ne voyons point pourquoi, en servant à nos clients de la nourriture pour leur corps, nous ne leur donnerions pas aussi de la nourriture pour leur esprit' (241).

Often the juxtapositions make a more specific point. The social conflicts within America are revealed through, for instance, an exchange between 'The New York World' and 'The Chicago Journal' of 1893 debating the alleged lack of social sophistication of the inhabitants of Chicago (54–9). This of course merely reproduces an existing argument between West and East. More typically and more strikingly, *Mobile* itself brings two separate discourses into contact – in order, for instance, to expose the contradictions of the white

Americans' attitude to the Indians. Thus on page 77, William Penn's treaty with the Delaware Indians is quoted: 'j'ai l'intention d'ordonner toutes choses en telle manière que nous puissions tous vivre en amour et paix les uns avec les autres', while the next page recounts how the same Indians were massacred by Penn's militia 'qui les désarmèrent, les ligotèrent et les exterminèrent à coups de haches et de gourdins, car ils voulaient économiser leur munitions' (78). Then a fragment from a speech made in 1810 by a Pawnee chief rallying a coalition of tribes to fight the encroaching white settlers (81) is followed on the next page by the brochure of 'Chapel Lake Indian Ceremonials' which promotes the Indians as a tourist attraction for white visitors: 'Le nouveau passionnant drame vivant indien en plein air du Michigan! Troupe géante de véritables Indiens d'Amérique du Nord! Authentique! Mystérieux! Dramatique!' (82).

The irony of this type of ideological juxtaposition is too pointed and too bitter to be called 'carnivalesque'; but it is itself contrasted with a more playful, comic montage of, for instance, pieces of the Sears Roebuck 'versus' the Montgomery Ward catalogue. Thus Montgomery Ward's promotion of a set of canvases with picturesque scenes to be coloured in by the customer ('painting by numbers') is intercut with Sears Roebuck's equally 'artistic' offer of seven pairs of underpants 'artistement brodés avec les jours de la semaine'. The two series are appropriately combined:

> – blanc pour le dimanche,
>> – la Cène, avec le Sermon sur la Montagne
> – jaune pour lundi
>> – Paysage d'Automne, avec la Fin du Jour
> – bleu pour mardi
>> – Coucher de Soleil sur la Mer, avec le Retour au Pays
> – rose pour mercredi
>> – Pur-Sang, avec la Chasse au Renard
> – blanc pour jeudi
>> – Scènes du Lac des Cygnes (Ballet)
> – vert pour vendredi
>> – Vénus et Adonis
> – noir pour samedi
> "prière de préciser le tour de hanches"

(174–5)

The text produces a reflexive image for this whole construction:

the patchwork quilt characteristic of the early settlers (29). The quilt
is a version of bricolage, an assembling of disparate fragments of
material which have all previously been used for something else.
The intertextual equivalent involves a slow process of clarification
of the relations between apparently unconnected elements. Thus, for
example, an opposition between *smiling* and *dreaming* is gradually
put in place: dreams are emanations of the Indian reserves ('Alors,
de toutes les réserves, prodigieux accumulateurs, se diffusent des
vagues de rêves' (143)), whereas the smile ('Pourquoi ne souriez-
vous pas?' (82, etc.)) signifies the repression of the secret fears and
desires that trouble the sleep of white Americans. Other elements
are then drawn into this constellation: the witchcraft trial produces
the image of the demon lover, which in turn generates, on page
151, a fictional version of the devil seducing a woman, including
the phrase 'ses dents brillent comme des turquoises au milieu de
sa bouche noire'; a few pages later we find brief references on the
one hand to dreams expressing secret and mysteriously abnormal
desires and, at first separately, to the dangers of the black areas
of town; these two then come together in: 'Ne vous aventurez pas
dans les faubourgs des Noirs; de chacun de leurs regards risque de
fleurir un immonde rêve' (156). Two pages later, all these pieces of
'patchwork' – smiles, dreaming, the reserves, and the demon lover
as a figure for repressed sexual desire for black people – are 'sewn'
together in the following:

> Un instant j'ai cru . . . Il me regardait, c'était juste comme dans
> mon rêve. Il y avait dans ses yeux une telle avidité, un tel
> désespoir; j'ai cru qu'il allait me serrer dans ses bras, me mordre
> [. . .] Sa respiration se fait plus calme. Il est blanc, il a repris
> son visage de Blanc, il fait un effort pour sourire, il a réussi à
> sourire [. . .] Il ne racontera pas ses rêves, il ne devinera pas
> mes rêves [. . .] Que j'ai eu peur! Ce n'était rien, ce n'était
> qu'une de ces vagues qui viennent des faubourgs des Noirs et
> des réserves. Il faut être encore plus prudent. Je vais sourire, je
> sais que j'arriverai à sourire, que personne n'en saura rien . . .
> (158)

There is, however, one major difference between *Mobile*'s
intertextuality and Kristeva's conception of it. For Kristeva,
intertextuality is explicitly designed to counter the dominance of
representation, whereas *Mobile* is an 'étude pour une représentation'.

That is, although it does not present itself as a full, definitive representation of America it is nevertheless an – unusually sophisticated – attempt in that direction. Although most of the individual elements of the text are not representational discourse in the normal sense, the structure as a whole ultimately puts together a 'picture' of America. This representation is produced by an individual subject: despite the predominance of 'other discourses' and the heterogenous and dispersed quality of the text, the end result is America *as seen by Michel Butor*. Although his personal interventions in the text are almost non-existent (he appears briefly in a fragment of conversation on pages 233–4), he has, obviously, selected and organised all of its elements. The fact for instance that America is presented as *'other'* already presupposes the particular point of view of a foreigner. Indeed the impact which *Mobile* has on the reader derives to a great extent from this sense of an encounter with a strange society. (It is perhaps significant that one of the few European nations not represented by its own newspaper, radio station, or church is France.)

The degree to which this curtails the intertextual functioning of *Mobile* depends crucially on the position of Butor's own discourse within it, and so this needs to be examined more closely. It takes three principal forms. Firstly there are the 'calligrams' described earlier, which are so minimally assertive as to constitute almost another form of citational discourse: 'quoting' the landscape is perhaps not really different from quoting the name of a town or a river. But the second strand of authorial discourse is narrative: it recounts the history of the American Indians, and in particular the effect on them of Christianity. On the surface this is a purely factual, impersonal account, with supporting evidence quoted from various historical documents. But its purpose is not merely to inform; *by* supplying information that has usually been omitted from the narrative of American history, it by the same token also acts as a critique of that 'white' version of history. It enters into conflict, by implication, with the famous quotations from Jefferson and other such historical figures. Butor's position becomes even clearer when, ostensibly as part of this same 'factual' discourse, he describes the political institutions of Washington in the dead-pan tones of an anthropologist describing a primitive religion (131), which has engendered equally primitive art-forms: 'Les trois divinités: Washington, Jefferson et Lincoln, sont les plus importantes du panthéon américain; on ne s'étonnera donc point de les trouver sculptées dans

des proportions colossales sur le mont Rushmore, Dakota du Sud.
Les Européens d'Amérique considèrent que l'artisan qui a exécuté
ce travail a fait preuve d'une grande dévotion' (132). And, finally:
'Les cérémonies et les objets sacrés des Européens d'Amérique sont
peut-être moins achevés que ceux des Indiens Hopi ou Zuni' (136).
This satirical pastiche is perhaps rather more simplistic than the
citational techniques used elsewhere in *Mobile*; it is certainly a more
obvious assertion of the author's point of view.

The third strand of authorial discourse is ultimately the most
important. It consists of a sequence of fragments reconstructing
the experience of the original European settlers and their impact
on the country, in a mode of writing which is neither fictional
nor factual but has a dream-like, poetic quality. It starts on page
60: 'Les Européens ont épucé la prairie de ses bisons et de ses
Indiens . . . Les Européens ont tracé sur la prairie de grandes
lignes perpendiculaires'. At first this could be interpreted as not
the author's voice but another fictional voice: that of the Indians.
As it develops, however, it increasingly moves towards the Europeans' point of view, expressing their terror and homesickness
(63), their desire for revenge on the Europe which had forced
them into exile (91, 92), etc., and ultimately hovers somewhere
in between European and Indian perspectives. The fact that it is
the author's discourse is made clear in the fragment on page 104,
which refers to both Europeans and Indians in the third person:
'Chassés, ils ont traversé l'Indiana et l'Illinois pour entrer dans
l'Iowa, chassant devant eux les Indiens'. Just before this, however,
we have read of the settlers' efforts to 'reconstituer autour de soi
une nouvelle Europe, effacer le plus possible ce continent qui nous
acceuillait mais nous effrayait' (99). The pronominal change here,
from 'ils' to 'nous', begins a gradual blurring of the singularity of
the authorial *voice*, as the *story* continues coherently through the
series of sequences. For a while it switches between first and third
person, but after page 104 the third-person authorial mode ('Les
Européens/ils') disappears. The 'nous' variant merges with the fictional voices and eventually becomes identified with the voice of the
racist South, which itself uses 'ils' to refer to the black community.

As a distinctive discourse, then, this strand of the authorial voice
peters out less than half way through the book. But the narrative that
it has initiated continues, and in fact takes on a significance which
distinguishes it from all the other discourses. That is, it gradually
builds up into a *theory* of the driving force behind American culture.

Its central hypothesis (though it is not presented as hypothetical) is that the transportation of slaves from Africa was motivated by the settlers' fear of the Indians, which in turn stemmed from their feeling of alienation and impotence in relation to the American land; the Indians were at one with the land, but the slaves were 'plus dépaysés encore que nous: la domination sur eux était des plus simples' (108). It is noticeable that while this theory is presented by a fictional white American voice: 'Ainsi ils *nous* ont servi à *nous* masquer ces yeux indiens, le regard indien, le scandale indien. Entre cette terre qui nous disait: non, vous n'êtes pas en Europe, et nous qui voulions que ce fût l'Europe, nous avons étendu cet écran noir . . . ' (109, my italics), the vision it conveys is more profound than that elsewhere accorded to this particular voice: it is, quite clearly, *Butor*'s perception.

The blacks contaminate and subvert white culture (110), and at the same time establish a contact with native America that the whites never achieve: 'Ils sont devenus multitude, et ils ont commencé à pousser des racines; il s'est établi entre ce continent et eux une sorte de connivence' (112). Thus the relationships between the three principal ethnic groups – whites, blacks and Indians – are explained. What is important here is that this account does not function as just one story among others, as Butor's personal myth of American history, relating on equal terms with the other discourses in the text – because all of the latter serve, directly or indirectly, to *confirm* it. It thus has a privileged role: it constitutes the global 'truth' of *Mobile*.

It could thus be argued that the powerful intertextuality of *Mobile* is nevertheless made subservient to this discreet underlying monologic statement.[19] It is, however, also true that the content of the 'statement' is precisely an argument *for heterogeneity*. Butor in effect criticises the European view – which becomes the dominant American ideology – for its coercive imposition of unity on the real diversity of the continent. He shows this at work on several different levels; the mail order catalogues, as Roudaut points out (46–7), exist to enable consumers all over America to have the *same* clothes, furniture, etc., just as the Howard Johnson ice-cream parlours serve the same menu in every state. And, as Butor comments in his interview with Charbonnier, 'au milieu de ces mêmes objets, nous allons retrouver les mêmes gens, avec les mêmes pensées et les mêmes paroles' (Charbonnier, 163). Politics, too, is a *unifying* religion, 'la seule à être pratiquée par tous les

Européens d'Amérique' (*Mobile*, 137). Above all, of course, the whites try to obliterate the otherness of Indian culture and history. But they can never succeed completely. Their influence is extensive but superficial: 'Les Européens ont recouvert la prairie d'une mince pellicule comme une couche de peinture, sur laquelle les réserves font des accrocs' (61). In 1855 the chief Seattle warns the settlers that even where tribes have been exterminated, their ghosts will remain to haunt the white unconscious: 'Jamais l'homme blanc n'y sera seul' (230). Throughout, *Mobile* dramatises this conflict between an artificially and precariously maintained homogeneity and the real diversity that constantly threatens it.

For instance: as well as simply imposing unity, the dominant culture is shown to employ various strategies to contain and manage diversity. The real social heterogeneity of America is repressed by creating in its place an ideology of consumer choice. American marketing stresses variation – everything comes in a range of colours and/or flavours – to manufacture an illusory individuality: 'Si vous pensez que toutes les soupes concentrées ont le même goût, c'est qu'il est temps que vous essayiez Heinz!' (227). Alternatively, it 'packages' the social and cultural diversity of America in a small-scale consumerist version that can easily be contained by the ideology: this is 'Freedomland', the original theme-park. Its brochure promises a miniaturised model of the whole continent: 'Il y a des forêts à l'échelle, une maquette des montagnes Rocheuses en perspective, des grands lacs miniature' (197), and an accelerated history: 'Traversez les siècles depuis la Nouvelle Angleterre coloniale jusqu'à l'Ouest des pionniers . . . Plus de 40 thèmes authentiques pour faire que l'histoire REVIVE à Freedomland' (200) – all of which is designed to 'répandre le message de l'américanisme . . . par la nation et par le monde' (201).

Mobile contrasts all these manifestations of the dominant culture with the underlying heterogeneity of American society. This is most apparent on the level of ethnicity. The population of America is a mixture of white, black and Indian; within these three main groups, the Indians are divided into different tribes, and the whites shown as split by conflicts between West and East Coast, North and South, as well as being differentiated by their respective nations of origin. Thus America is culturally and linguistically multiple: *Mobile*'s representation of almost every state includes lists of newspapers and radio stations operating in different languages, and restaurants serving different kinds of European cuisine. Thus the Freedomland brochure quoted above is interrupted, and disrupted, by this 'space' of text setting out the real culture of New York:

> 150 000 Anglais
> 17 000 Finlandais
> Les Arabes qui lisent "Al Hoda"
> Les Chinois qui lisent l'"United Journal"
> NEW YORK HERALD TRIBUNE NEW YORK HERALD
> TRIBUNE NEW YORK
> Les Finlandais le "New Yorkin Uutisset"
> Black Angus, steaks,
> Chateaubriand, cuisine française
> Lee's, plats chinois
> [. . .]
> WBNX, émissions grecques,
> WEVD, émissions allemandes,
> WLIB, émissions hongroises.
>
> (201)

Place names play a key role in the conflict between unity and multiplicity. Many American towns are named after the town in Europe from which their settlers came. This is emphasised in all the names beginning 'New . . . ' listed on page 99 and linked with the attempt to 'reconstituer autour de soi une nouvelle Europe' (99). But it is also frequently the case that the name of a European town is transferred to *several* new American towns. The name thus no longer has one unique referent; the ideological attempt to preserve the reference to a point of origin in fact has the opposite result of losing this origin in a plurality of new versions dispersed over the continent. It underlines, rather than camouflages, the fact that American towns can never be anything but multiple *copies* of a single European origin.

The text of *Mobile* in turn exploits and thereby amplifies this 'espace récurrent' (Charbonnier, 163), this polyvalence of place names in its very structure. The states are represented in alphabetical order, and the transitions between them are all made via the coincidence of a town in one having the same name as a town in the other – so that we move from Richmond in Kansas to Richmond in Kentucky, for instance.[20] This simultaneously emphasises the geographical *difference* (they are usually in different time zones) that belies the identity of name.

Mobile, then, is a text which mobilises many different discourses and a variety of textual strategies (including the privileged status accorded to an intermittent authorial discourse) in order to present the reader with, ultimately, a single monologic representation of America. But, on the other hand, its aim is to represent America *as* fundamentally *dialogic*: as a plurality of interacting and conflicting discourses, in which the attempt to impose ideological unity is constantly undermined. And, to the extent that it is this perception of the 'reality' of America that determines the structure and texture of the book, it cannot be seen as simply counteracting Kristeva's theory of intertextuality. It is itself an argument for cultural heterogeneity, and it is carried out through a predominantly, if not wholly, intertextual discourse.

I have tried to show how in each of these three texts the intertextual approach can provide a way of theorising the relation between the individual writing subject and the field of social discourses in which the text is situated – even in the case of a novel like Sarraute's *Les Fruits d'or* which is in many ways deliberately asocial. Indeed, the relation in question is always conflictual; there is always a struggle, more or less consciously assumed, between the 'own voice' of the author and the 'other voices' of the social context. The text's boundaries are inevitably contested since, at one and the same time, it is inserted into social discourse and incorporates pieces of these discourses into itself. Thus whereas the logic of the production-versus-representation strategy for subverting ideology is ultimately, as I have argued in Chapter 3, to reinstate a rather closed, autonomous conception of the text, the notion of intertextuality opens it up to a more productively transgressive and transformational interaction with the 'voices' of ideology.

6

The Counter-reaction: the Nouveau Roman in the 1980s

The 1980s were in many ways a very productive period for the nouveaux romanciers. The decade began well, with the publication in 1981 of *Les Géorgiques*, judged by many critics to be Simon's most important work, of Robbe-Grillet's *Djinn* and Sarraute's *L'Usage de la parole*. It was also notable for the autobiographical texts that these three writers brought out: Sarraute's *Enfance* in 1983, Robbe-Grillet's *Le miroir qui revient* in 1985 and *Angélique ou l'enchantement* in 1988, and Simon's *L'Acacia* in 1989 (as well as the short text *L'Invitation* in 1987). Equally, though, the group's situation *as a group* had changed considerably. In the first place, while Butor had for a long time been working quite separately from the Nouveau Roman, the latter had by now – and far more dramatically – severed all connections with Ricardou as well. Thus of the writers I have been considering here only Robbe-Grillet, Simon and Sarraute are left; and between them, too, there is rather less interaction than there was previously.

The change in membership of the group is moreover linked, partly as cause and partly as effect, to a different attitude towards theory and politics. The relation between theory and fiction has been redefined. This is very clearly shown in a conference organised at New York University in 1982 by Tom Bishop, one of the foremost American critics writing on the Nouveau Roman. The novelists present were Robbe-Grillet, Simon, Sarraute and Robert Pinget. It was in fact the first important colloquium on the Nouveau Roman since the NRHA conference of 1971, and was very consciously presented in that light. An English translation of the papers[1] was published, and Lois Oppenheim's introduction to this advises the reader that:

> we would do well to remember that this colloquium at New York University was the first major gathering of the New Novelists and

their critics since that held at Cerisy-la-Salle in 1971. As such, its significance was enhanced by the possibilities for retrospective thinking on the *critical evaluation* of the New Novel, as well as on the New Novel itself. (6)

The 1982 conference saw itself as fundamentally different from that of 1971, and the opposition between them centres on the status of theory. That is to say, the most obvious single theme running through the N.Y.U. conference is a very vehement *rejection* of theory. The presence of Pinget, who had never been involved in the elaboration of theoretical issues and who restates his position here,[2] contributes to this emphasis. But it is, in fact, Sarraute and Simon who are the most outspoken in their relief at having escaped from what is now seen in retrospect as theoretical *tyranny*; Robbe-Grillet's position is slightly more complex, but nevertheless Bishop is able to sum up the general feeling at the conference in these terms:

> for a very long while . . . there was a tendency to define you, to let you be defined by the theoreticians. It seems to me that this time has passed and that today . . . you all tend to speak of your work, without first thinking of the critical point of view and of the entire theoretical picture, the entire theoretical superstructure, that actually seemed very heavy for a rather long period of time. (179)

Theory, in other words, is now seen as something done *to* the nouveaux romanciers rather than by them. This is on one level a quite radical shift of position from the Nouveau Roman of the 1970s; and yet there is a curious sense in which the three writers in question also seem to be discussing their work in very much the same terms as they always have done. The extent and scope of the change therefore, is not straightforward. It is not a simple break with the past, in so far as there is a lot of continuity, and also a kind of anachronistic timing: *delayed* reactions to theoretical positions. Equally, however, and despite the impression occasionally given at the conference, it would be an oversimplification to see the new stance just as the eventual revelation of an underlying permanent truth; in other words it is not, I think, the case that the Nouveau Roman had really been like this all along but has only now managed to free itself from the distorted image imposed on it by the dominance of theory. I will return later in this chapter to the problem of exactly how much has changed.

The speakers at the conference tend to direct their attacks at 'theory' in general. It quickly becomes clear, however, that what is actually meant by this is structuralism. Simon, for instance, refers to 'literary theory, semiology, or linguistics' as the 'poisoned gift that Roman Jakobson granted to literature' (71) – Jakobson, of course, being one of the leading theorists of literary structuralism. They object to its *formalist* orientation, its exclusive concern with the signifier at the expense of the signified; and, in particular, to structuralism's claim to *scientific* status. For Simon, structuralism and 'scientism' are synonymous: the fragment quoted above continues: 'But, after all, perhaps art is doomed to sail periodically among the dreadful reefs of scientism' (71). Scientism is unacceptable because it implies a comprehensive theory of literature which has the status of scientific *truth*: it presents itself as the definitive explanation of literature in general. Thus Robbe-Grillet defines the theorist as 'someone who builds a totality . . . someone who ties together all his preoccupations and then decrees normative truths' (182).

Such a critique of structuralism is in no way original or even controversial. In fact the most surprising thing about it is that the nouveaux romanciers should still feel it necessary to attack structuralism in 1982, at a time when within the French intellectual avant-garde it had been widely discredited for a number of years. Indeed the Cerisy conference of 1971 was already expressing doubts about both the formalist and the scientist presuppositions of structuralist literary criticism (see Chapter 3). Moreover, this oddly belated reaction implicitly but repeatedly equates structuralism with theory in general. The rejection of a particular theory – and one to which, as I have described in Chapter 2, the Nouveau Roman's attitude was in any case always very ambivalent – is by implication made coextensive with the rejection of 'theory' as such. Given that by 1982 structuralism had been superseded in the literary-critical arena by a number of other theories, and given that up until this point the Nouveau Roman had been consistently alert to new theoretical developments, this stance seems difficult to understand. Why, in other words, has the Nouveau Roman not moved on from structuralism and involved itself with other, more recent, literary theories?

In some cases there is an obvious answer to this question. For instance, the literary criticism based on Lacanian psychoanalysis which was extremely influential in both France and America in the 1970s was impossible for the nouveaux romanciers to accept because – as has already been discussed in Chapter 4 – of their very different evaluation of the role of the unconscious in writing. Feminist criticism, similarly, had nothing to offer Robbe-Grillet, Simon, or Sarraute. While Robbe-Grillet was the only one to launch an explicit counterattack on feminism,[3] both his and Simon's novels have provoked negative reactions from feminist critics because of their representation of sexuality,[4] and Sarraute has always refused to consider herself a feminist or even specifically feminine writer.[5] On the other hand, the concept of intertextuality is, as I have argued in Chapter 5, very relevant to much of the Nouveau Roman's fiction and could with advantage have been developed by them on a theoretical level. Above all, however, the literary theory that has been most dominant from the mid-1970s (especially in America, but the Nouveau Roman has itself had extensive contacts with American academic circles ever since the 1960s, as Bishop points out in his introduction to the N.Y.U. conference) is Derridean *deconstruction*, which would seem in many ways to be ideally appropriate to the Nouveau Roman's purposes. It is based on a theoretical critique of all theoretical claims to scientific knowledge or truth; indeed, Derrida analyses structuralism from precisely this point of view in *L'Ecriture et la différence* and subsequent texts.[6] One might, therefore, have expected the Nouveau Roman to make some use of it.

The fact that they do not suggests that their rejection of theory may be motivated by other concerns in addition to their dissatisfaction with the formalist and scientist assumptions of structuralism. This dissatisfaction, as I have already indicated, does not in any case explain why they tend to conflate structuralism with theory in general; it creates the impression that they are using the inadequacies of structuralism as a pretext to justify a universal dismissal of theory, the real reasons for which may actually operate on a different level. In other words, there is on the one hand a critique of structuralism which itself deploys essentially, if informally, theoretical arguments. But alongside this – and the two are not explicitly distinguished – one also finds a rejection of theory *per se* which is based not on abstract criteria but on far more strategic considerations concerning the *function* which theory is felt to perform in relation to the production of fiction. Thus it is noticeable that many of the more ferocious attacks on theory at the N.Y.U. conference focus on its supposedly prescriptive effect on practising writers of fiction.

Theory, independently of its precise content, has come to be seen as a set of *instructions*. Leon Roudiez attempts to convince Simon that it is an error for writers to '[imagine] that they had to believe and apply what the theoreticians said, while writers really do not have to be concerned with theoreticians. They have only to let the theoreticians say what they wish while they go on doing what they had to do' (104). But the overriding feeling at the conference is one described by Lois Oppenheim in her introduction as 'an eagerness to be rid of the theoretical prescriptive prototyping imposed on literature by the onslaught of scientism to which the criticism of the 1960s and 1970s fell prey' (6).

Prescriptive theory is above all associated with Ricardou. As François Jost, one of the critics present at the conference, puts it in his paper, 'With Ricardou, the description of the functioning of novels acquires the virtue of a prescription, of a scriptural "edict" which the budding writer is to follow to construct a fiction' (45). Reading through the conference papers and discussions, one soon realises that this is more than a purely intellectual disagreement: there is a strong element of personal antagonism towards Ricardou. Indeed, Simon and Sarraute both apparently agreed to come to N.Y.U. only on condition that Ricardou was not invited; and the American conference is explicitly situated by Bishop, in his introductory remarks, as 'above and beyond past battles' (19) – in other words, as a deliberate attempt to move away from the acrimony generated at Cerisy in 1971.[7] In this context one realises that, throughout the conference, many apparently abstract statements criticising theory are better read as veiled personal attacks on Ricardou.[8] Although Simon's is the most extreme – 'he is dangerous. Moreover, he seems to have been suffering, for some time now, from a pathological megalomania, which is of no help either' (188) – his reaction is shared by Sarraute[9] and by Robbe-Grillet, who objects to Ricardou's belief that 'he had founded as a kind of established order this "Nouveau Roman" which did not want to be an established order ... If, after some time, Claude Simon and I rejected Ricardou, it was actually because he said that he had become our leader' (106).

One has to ask, therefore, whether there is really anything more to this than a personal quarrel – in other words, is 'theory' merely a euphemism for Ricardou, and its rejection merely an unwillingness to let Ricardou capture the position of group leader? They are certainly aware that theory did not always perform this totalitarian role vis-à-vis the Nouveau Roman. Robbe-Grillet refers to his own and Sarraute's early theoretical writings which, he says, never tried to 'decree normative truths' (182) but were purely oppositional, attacking established critical authorities. In these pioneering days, theory was the legitimate defence of the underdog, and was more like a kind of guerrilla warfare than an attempt to subdue and permanently occupy the whole literary field. Thus in contrasting *L'Ere du soupçon* and *Pour un nouveau roman* with Ricardou's theorising, Robbe-Grillet emphasises the importance of the writer's individual freedom:

> On the other hand, it is true that Ricardou's period was one when suddenly people wanted to prescribe, to say "This is what has to be done." Obviously, this was the very opposite of our own idea of the Nouveau Roman, since when we got together – first Nathalie Sarraute and I and then all our friends – it was precisely under the banner of freedom. What we were claiming for every writer was the freedom to invent the novel, everyone for himself and in each novel he wrote. (182)

At the same time, however, this way of formulating the difference between them and Ricardou also suggests something else: that, independently of the personalities involved, the *function of theory in relation to the fictional practice* of the nouveaux romanciers has itself changed over the period of the group's existence, and that the reaction against Ricardou is less a cause than a consequence, or even just a symptom, of this deeper change which occurred towards the end of the 1970s. After all, if it were purely a question of personality, why did Simon and Robbe-Grillet put up with him for so long before finally rebelling?

In order to understand this, one needs to look in more detail at the precise content of the nouveaux romanciers' rejection of (Ricardou's) theory. Its 'prescriptiveness' is particularly resented in so far as it imposes on them the straitjacket of a *collective identity*. Jost, arguing that 'Ricardou teaches us how to write', comments that 'In this perspective, it may be understood how any reflection on the specificity of the writing of one or another novelist was eliminated' (45). Less dispassionately, Simon describes how despite 'the very contradictory statements made by each of us' at the Cerisy conference, it was nevertheless 'a meeting . . . which united us all under the firm rule of a severe schoolmaster' (75). Theory is thus accused of telling them what to write and hence, especially, of trying to make them all write the same way.[10]

Therefore the rejection of theory turns out to be motivated above all by a desire for *individual freedom*. Sarraute, indeed, claims that this is at the root of the original conception of the Nouveau Roman:

> the New Novel was most useful as a total liberation of the forms and content of the novel . . . New novels are written which are not written in the traditional form: writers may completely suppress chronological time, not use proper nouns, organise the dialogue as they wish. They are not judged on these things . . . I believe that it is one of the advantages, one of the successes, of the Nouveau Roman that the forms of the novel have become free. (192–3)

Moreover, the freedom in question is in particular the freedom to be *different* from one another, and to develop a way of writing fiction that will be unique to them: in Sarraute's words: 'This art has moved into other areas. Each writer has his own, one which belongs to him alone' (127). Simon almost goes so far as to claim that he has nothing at all in common with the others and that his membership of the Nouveau Roman has all along been based on a misunderstanding.[11]

From this perspective, the very notion of the Nouveau Roman as a collective entity appears misleading, as though it were an artificial construction that had never corresponded to the reality of each writer's actual work. François Jost's paper on Robbe-Grillet takes this view: 'In this concern for generalisation, moreover, the label "Nouveau Roman" played its part: testifying to a community of preoccupations, it seemed to authorise the theoretician to practice a conceptual extension' (45). And for Robbe-Grillet himself, the claim that 'the New Novel is a paradigm. This is to say that there are some writers who, in the same period of time, have certain concerns in common' (66) breaks down under closer examination: 'Obviously, as soon as we try to specify them, this idea no longer works, as it contradicts itself. As you will see, each of us maintains different opinions and I have spoken only on my own behalf' (ibid.).

But this view in turn overlooks the fact that over a long period of time the Nouveau Roman *did* conceive of itself as a collective project; Robbe-Grillet's own *Pour un nouveau roman* provides ample evidence of this – and even now he still speaks in retrospect of

the 'revolution' which the Nouveau Roman started in the 1950s
(21). The title of François Jost's paper, 'From the "New Novel"
to the "New Novelist"', is significantly ambiguous in this respect:
is it recording a real historical change, or offering a revised and
truer definition of an unchanged phenomenon? His comments in
the discussion, however, imply the former reading; here he takes
it for granted that a collective entity used to exist, but no longer
does:

> What renders ten-year-old theories obsolete is not the fact that
> ten years ago the thinking was more stupid than that of today,
> but mainly that today's novel is no longer yesterday's (and when
> I say today's and yesterday's novels, I am still situating myself
> within the New Novel). What Nathalie Sarraute or Claude Simon,
> Robert Pinget or Alain Robbe-Grillet are producing is, of course,
> characteristic of Sarraute, Simon, Pinget, and Robbe-Grillet, but
> it is no longer truly characteristic of the Nouveau Roman, if by
> Nouveau Roman one means a unique and homogeneous school.
> (185)

The fact that there was once a genuine intention on the part of
the nouveaux romanciers to define themselves as a group with a
number of common aims and concerns seems indisputable, even
if these aims were never fully realised and even if there is some
tendency now, especially in Simon's case, to disavow them in
retrospect. But it is equally clear that this common project has
now been abandoned. And, in view of the new perceived *incom-
patibility* between theory and individual freedom, outlined above,
it seems that the route towards the disintegration of the Nouveau
Roman as an entity leads through the rejection of theory. In other
words, distancing themselves from theory is closely connected to
abandoning the Nouveau Roman's collective project.

Conversely, therefore, the main strategic function that theory had
fulfilled for them in the past is thrown into sharp relief; that is,
it becomes clearer than ever that theory predominantly served
the purpose of enabling them to define themselves *as a group*.
It is interesting, for instance, that in her paper at the N.Y.U.
conference Sarraute says that she wrote *L'Ere du soupçon* because
she felt 'lonely': 'I think that it was the loneliness in which I found
myself as far as literature was concerned – the lack of response, of
interest in what I was writing – which impelled me to think about

the reasons that prevented me from writing in conventional forms'
(125–6). But as the theoretical level of their work developed, it began
to raise more problems than it solved; the underlying contradictions
were never reconciled but often simply brought into clearer focus.

It could be argued, therefore, that the failure of the collective
project was due to the failure of theory itself, ultimately, to provide
a common framework that all the individual nouveaux romanciers
felt that they could work within. As a result, they had to give up
the idea of a collective identity; and once they had done that, there
was no *need* for theory any more – which, in turn, is why their
rejection of structuralism is not replaced by the adoption of another,
newer and more suitable, theory. But the situation is not quite as
clear-cut as this. There are in fact several different motives which
come together to endorse the new emphasis on individual freedom,
and they operate on rather different levels.

That is, the collective project failed in the first place because it
turned out that the nouveaux romanciers were simply too different
from each other to be able to agree on a common programme, and
because Ricardou's dogmatism became intolerable. But it is also
because they did not achieve the irreversible impact on the literary
scene in general that they had originally hoped for. Robbe-Grillet
opens his address to the conference with the comment that 'the
revolution which [the Nouveau Roman] started in the 1950s never
really materialised. Contrary to what I naively hoped as a young
man, all of literature was not really turned upside down by the
Nouveau Roman' (21). Moreover, this *literary* revolution had a
significant *political* dimension, via the connections with Barthes and
later with *Tel Quel*, as I have discussed in previous chapters. But
Tel Quel's Marxist project of attacking the political and social status
quo through subversion of ideological forms was itself abandoned
in the late 1970s;[12] more generally, Robbe-Grillet links the 'creative
euphoria' of the 1960s with a surge of political optimism on the left
and suggests that both have now collapsed (64–5). Certainly there
is no sense at all at the N.Y.U. conference that the Nouveau Roman
has or would wish to have any political relevance in the 1980s;
and, to the extent that a political project is almost by definition a
collective one, this kind of depoliticisation too has contributed to
the increasing separation of the group's members.

But if the failure of the 'revolution' was one factor in the abandonment of the collective project, another, possibly more decisive one
was the *success* of the individual members of the group. There is

a sense in which, simply, the nouveaux romanciers now no longer need the Nouveau Roman; the collective project may have failed, but equally, it has become superfluous: they can *afford* to leave it behind them because they have now managed to establish themselves successfully as individual writers. In the most dramatic case, Simon's place in French literature was permanently assured when he was awarded the Nobel prize for literature in 1985 (and this also transformed his status in relation to the other nouveaux romanciers). But also, Nathalie Sarraute's complete works are currently being edited for the Pleiade, which constitutes a significant recognition of her position as (somewhat ironically) one of the modern 'classics' of French literature. Equally, Robbe-Grillet has continued to be a prominent and controversial figure in literary and film circles, both in France and America. Earlier in their careers the distinctive group identity of the Nouveau Roman helped them to reach a wide audience – Sarraute says quite straightforwardly that: 'With regard to the circulation of my books, I owe a lot to this movement of the Nouveau Roman. I say it again and again, but I think that without it my books would not have had the audience that they have had. It is not an enormous audience, for my books are considered to be difficult books, but without the Nouveau Roman, it would have been smaller' (128).

But by the 1980s the situation has altered; Robbe-Grillet is able to positively welcome the failure of the collective project – the Nouveau Roman's 'revolution' – because, he argues, its success would have removed their freedom: 'the revolution did not materialise because freedom cannot be an institution. If the Nouveau Roman had succeeded, Ricardou would, in short, have taken over and our novels would have been institutionalised . . . The revolution did not succeed, therefore, fortunately, for if it had, we would have stopped writing' (182–3). Therefore, it would seem that the reasons for abandoning the collective project had less to do with the failure of theory, although that certainly played a part, and more with the changing position of the nouveaux romanciers within literary society. Once that shift has been accomplished, however, theory itself becomes marginalised.

The emphasis on individuality also has other repercussions. It is not simply a celebration of difference, but takes the form of an assertive individualism which in effect brings them back to the 'dogma of Expression' that had been so thoroughly attacked by Ricardou: the value of a writer's work, from this point of view, depends crucially on the degree to which it expresses a unique, distinctive mental world.[13] This then develops further into a re-revalorisation of the *personal*: of writing about themselves, about their own memories and fantasies. The autobiographies of the 1980s are of course the central example of this; but Robbe-Grillet and Simon also begin to insist – Sarraute has always done so – that all their fiction is, and always was, produced from personal sources rather than theoretical 'dictates' (i.e., considerations of form and ideology). This remains largely implicit at the N.Y.U. conference, although the entirely autobiographical account that Sarraute gives of her evolution as a writer is already in effect presenting the issue in these terms. Simon, too, refers with magnificent scorn to 'writers [who] wear themselves out building, carefully, so as not to be outdone, texts which rest completely on some dreary series of anagrammatical acrobatics more or less inspired either by Saussure or a famous guru of psychoanalysis' (75) (The latter reference is presumably to Lacan – which does not prevent him from quoting Lacan approvingly eleven pages further on.) A few years later he states far more explicitly that from *L'Herbe* onwards, 'mes romans sont devenus pratiquement "autobiographiques"'.[14]

It is however Robbe-Grillet whose reinterpretation of his own fiction in terms of the personal is both the most emphatic and, given his earlier statements, the most startling. The first volume of his autobiography, *Le Miroir qui revient*, opens with the provocative statement (written in 1976, but not published until 1984): 'Je n'ai jamais parlé d'autre chose que de moi. Comme c'était de l'intérieur, on ne s'en est guère aperçu' (10). It is also Robbe-Grillet who brings out most explicitly the theoretical significance of this reversal; he goes on to evoke, sarcastically, the outrage that such a heretical revelation will produce, and then to claim that the institutionalised image of the Nouveau Roman has itself become a new orthodoxy which needs to be opposed:

> Maintenant que le Nouveau Roman définit de façon positive ses valeurs, édicte ses lois, ramène sur le droit chemin ses mauvais élèves, enrôle ses francs-tireurs sous l'uniforme, excommunie ses libres penseurs, il devient urgent de tout remettre en cause, et, replaçant les pions à leur point de départ, l'écriture à ses origines, l'auteur à son premier livre, de s'interroger de nouveau sur le rôle ambigu que jouent, dans le récit moderne, la representation du monde et l'expression d'une personne, qui est à la

fois un corps, une projection intentionnelle et un inconscient.
(12)

All fiction is thus redefined as being in a loose sense autobiographical. Within this continuum, however, the autobiographical
enterprise is still more directly personal than the novels, and therefore Robbe-Grillet sees it as especially subversive, 'perverse'[15] and
so especially risky. He situates it in terms of a diachronic evolution
of theoretical attitudes towards the relation between writer and
writing – expression, representation, the structuralist 'death of the
author', etc. In other words, it signifies a *return* to the personal.
Even the title of the first autobiographical volume relates to this
idea. 'Le miroir qui revient' refers in the first place to an incident
in the Breton folklore that Robbe-Grillet knew as a child; beyond
that, though, it can be interpreted in the sense of, precisely, the
'return' of a mirror-image; the return, that is, of the text as *reflection*
of its writer. It is perhaps no accident, then, that in the second
autobiographical volume, *Angélique*, this is exactly what we find
in the opening pages – a long description of Robbe-Grillet's face
as seen in a mirror (13–14).

Here, incidentally, a further reason for the nouveaux romanciers'
lack of interest in deconstructionism becomes apparent. I argued
above that it was because they did not *need* it; but it is equally
relevant that in reviving a humanist conception of the author as
personal source of and presence in the text they have placed themselves in contradiction with the Derridean definition of writing as
disoriginated trace.[16] In fact Derrida's criticism of Lévi-Strauss could
well be applied to them, and perhaps especially to Robbe-Grillet: 'on
n'en perçoit pas moins chez lui une sorte d'éthique de la présence,
de nostalgie de l'origine, de l'innocence archaïque et naturelle, d'une
pureté de la présence et de la présence à soi dans la parole' (1967,
427).

The return to the personal is also a move away from the previous
politicised conception of literature as a possible site of intervention in social discourses through the notion of textual production.
Ironically, though, the autobiographical mode of writing opens up
the very different possibility of *realist* representation of political
activity. *Le Miroir qui revient* contains long discussions of the political
position of Robbe-Grillet's parents, for instance, and of his own
feelings towards any kind of political commitment. These latter, in
particular, provide a very different explanation for the stance he has

always adopted against Sartrean 'engagement' in literature: now it is seen as the result not of a theoretical reflection on the priorities of the writer, but of a spontaneous temperamental reaction (133–4). In a rather different way, Simon's *L'Invitation*, which recounts his visit to the Soviet Union and meeting with Gorbachev after being awarded the Nobel prize, is even more centrally concerned with the representation of political forces, the nature of the superpowers (e.g., 13–14), the death of Stalin (41–48), and so on. Even Sarraute's *Enfance* includes memories of the political activities of her parents and their friends, driven into exile from Russia because of their opposition to the Tsarist government (153–4, 194–201). Writing fiction is no longer seen as a political act, but the lifting of the ban on representation and expression which this reversal itself allows makes room for representations of political realities and expressions of 'personal' political opinions.

It is time now to return to the question raised at the beginning of this chapter: with the Nouveau Roman's position in the 1980s, how much has actually changed?

In Sarraute's case, the answer is relatively simple: her views have not changed at all. Because of this, though, her situation vis-à-vis the other writers has changed considerably, in that the position which she has held all along, and which was previously treated very dismissively by other members of the Nouveau Roman, now appears to have been vindicated. Her belief that theory is of no importance to practising writers is restated at the N.Y.U. conference where, for the first time, it meets with general agreement: 'With regard to Ricardou, I have always considered his theories, or at least most of them, to be untenable. They were of no significance to writers, for when we write, writers are not thinking about theories' (181). Conversely, the newly adopted idea that fiction has its roots in the writer's individual spontaneous subjectivity coincides with Sarraute's long-standing, and previously very embattled, insistence on the *pre-verbal* (see Chapter 4) as both motor and reservoir for the production of fiction.

Simon's position is more complicated. What has changed for him is in the first place his relationship with Ricardou; from being the most heavily influenced by Ricardou's ideas, he has become the most violently antagonistic. His 'formalist' novels of the 1970s were, it appears in retrospect, written very much as a conscious effort to conform to Ricardou's prescriptions, and the reaction – emotional as much as intellectual – against this period of subservience is correspondingly fierce. Thus it is also the case that Simon's *fiction* changed with the appearance of *Les Géorgiques* in 1981, which in many ways reverts both thematically and stylistically to his earlier texts of the 1960s; this continues through the other texts he published in the 1980s, culminating in the autobiographical *L'Acacia* in 1989.

It is thus all the more surprising that in his commentaries on his writing – at the N.Y.U. conference, in his speech of acceptance of the Nobel prize (*Discours de Stockholm*, published in 1986) and in various interviews he gave at the time of the award and again on the publication of *L'Acacia* – there is, despite certain differences of emphasis, an overriding impression of continuity. His long-standing claims not to be an intellectual are expressed at the conference more strongly than ever; he now sees himself as the 'M. Jourdain of the Nouveau Roman' – and as 'a simple, self-taught writer whose knowledge of literature does not surpass the level of amateurism' (71). The same concerns and the same arguments – often, indeed, illustrated with the same examples – are found in these 1980s texts as were already in his paper 'La Fiction mot à mot', given at the NRHA conference fifteen years earlier when he was still, as he would see it now, in thrall to Ricardou. Thus in the *Discours de Stockholm* he criticises traditional realism on exactly the same grounds as he had done in 'La Fiction mot à mot', i.e., for being structured on the level of plot, according to an extraneous and unconvincing causality, rather than an 'internal' qualitative logic. He stresses the importance of work – the artist as artisan, constructing his text as an object – as opposed to inspiration. This too is familiar from the NRHA conference, but is now angled slightly differently to promote the importance of the figure of the author: he attacks inspiration *because* it relegates the author to a simple passive intermediary – 'il voit maintenant sa personne tout simplement niée' (1986, 14). He reiterates, also, his mistrust of ideological certainty, although this is now allied to a more explicit emphasis on the collapse of humanist values since the second world war: Auschwitz becomes a crucial reference point for the impossibility of sustaining belief in ideological systems: 'après Auschwitz les idéologies s'écroulent, tout l'humanisme apparaît comme une farce. Il me semble qu'après cette horreur, cet effondrement de toutes les valeurs, s'est fait sentir un désarroi qui a amené les plus conscients – ou les plus sensibles – à s'interroger, à recourir au primordial, à l'élémentaire'.[17]

Most importantly, however, his conception of *language* has both remained the same and acquired different implications. It is based on a double refusal: language is not predominantly referential, in the sense that meaning would be a one-to-one correlation between individual linguistic units and items in the real world – but nor is it a completely autonomous system in which meaning is produced solely through the relations between words in isolation from any non-verbal universe. It is a system, characterised above all by its ability to make connections between elements: in 'La Fiction mot à mot', he cites his earlier emphasis in *Orion aveugle* on 'le prodigieux pouvoir qu'ont les mots de rapprocher et de confronter ce qui, sans eux, resterait épars' (74). Language can do this because words are 'carrefours' opening up onto not one but several 'directions' of meaning; and he restates this point by quoting Lacan to the effect that 'Le mot n'est pas seulement *signe* mais *nœud de significations*' (1972, 73). The same reference appears in *Discours de Stockholm*, on page 28. But this network of meaning as a whole is not cut off from the world, but is itself structured by historical and cultural realities. As he says in 'La Fiction mot à mot', 'notre vocabulaire n'est pas un système de signes inertes . . . chaque mot est porteur d'une charge à la fois historique, culturelle, phonétique . . . ce n'est pas non plus par hasard que s'est formé ce vaste ensemble de figures métaphoriques dans et par quoi se dit le monde' (81–2). Language is thus a kind of *matrix* of meanings within which the writer moves, constructing the text by 'reactivating' (ibid., 82) circuits that are already there. In *Discours de Stockholm* he defines it in very similar terms:

> l'écrivain, dès qu'il commence à tracer un mot sur le papier, touche aussitôt à ce prodigieux ensemble, ce prodigieux réseau de rapports établis dans et par cette langue qui, comme on l'a dit, "parle déjà avant nous" au moyen de ce qu'on appelle ses "figures", autrement dit les tropes, les métonymies et les métaphores dont aucune n'est l'effet du hasard mais tout au contraire partie constitutive de la connaissance du monde et des choses peu à peu acquise par l'homme. (27–8)

– and goes on to elucidate the paradoxical nature of this relation between language and the world by quoting Novalis: 'il en va du langage comme des formules mathématiques: elles constituent un monde en soi, pour elles seules; elles jouent entre elles exclusivement, n'expriment rien sinon leur propre nature merveilleuse, ce qui justement fait qu'elles sont si expressives, que justement en elles se reflète le jeu étrange des rapports entre les choses' (30). Language, in other words, is both self-contained system *and* expression of the world. It is, he suggests later, a landscape which the writer travels through. There is thus both the implication that the writer is situated, and even contained, *within* language – and that he is *thereby* in a position to express his experience of the world.

In 'La Fiction mot à mot' this conception of language is equated with the 'internal logic' of the text; that is, it is placed in opposition to the realist conception of language as vehicle of representation. It serves, in other words, to confirm the prevailing anti-representational position of the Nouveau Roman at the time. In *Discours de Stockholm*, however, although it is still used to criticise traditional *objective* realism, it is also defined as a subjective 'paysage intérieur' (27): the language system seen as a matrix of meanings which in some way locks onto and structures the writer's experience of the world. That is, this same conception of language allows him to transcend the dichotomy between the structuralist idea of language as a closed *formal* system and the humanist view of language as expression of reality. Or, as Simon himself puts it, it allows a conception of 'un engagement de l'écriture, qui, chaque fois qu'elle change un tant soit peu le *rapport que par son langage l'homme entretient avec le monde,* contribue dans sa modeste mesure à changer celui-ci' (1986, 30, my italics). In the context of the realignments of the 1980s, therefore, its main import is now to revalidate the link between language and subjective experience. It has become an argument against formalism rather than against traditional realism. As such, it offers a very striking example of the strategic relevance of theory: the same theoretical position comes to fulfil a very different function because the overall intellectual context around it has changed.

With Robbe-Grillet, the functionality and therefore the *relativity* of theory are entirely explicit, and always have been. When he claims, as he has done since *Pour un nouveau roman,* that he is not a theoretician, he means that he does not believe in constructing a systematic theory of the novel that would claim any kind of permanent truth. But he does 'theorise' in order to defend his own fiction against critical attack – he is quoted at the N.Y.U. conference as having said 'Je n'attache pas une grande importance à mes ouvrages théoriques, ce sont des ouvrages de combat' (p. 44). Later, in defence of Ricardou, he expands on this distinction: theories cannot be *true* but they can and should be *productive*: 'I like theories. Of course I do not necessarily respect them . . . a theory is not right or wrong: a theory is productive or it is not' (180–1). Ricardou's mistake was not that he invented outrageous theories but that he believed them (106), and this dogmatism should not be associated with theorising as such: '[Ricardou] has a dogmatic mind, a normative mind, but theory is not always normative' (190). Indeed, in the course of *Le Miroir qui revient* he returns several times to the idea that truth *per se* is oppressive – for instance: 'je ne crois pas à la Vérité. Elle ne sert qu'à la bureaucratie, c'est-à-dire à l'oppression' (11). Truth is equated with dogma, and contrasted with the liberating strategic use of theory in 'combat': 'Dès qu'une aventureuse théorie, affirmée dans la passion du combat, est devenue dogme, elle perd aussitôt . . . son efficacité. Elle cesse d'être ferment de liberté, de découverte' (ibid.). To extend his own metaphor, it is a kind of 'hot pursuit' justification of theory.

The value of theory, then, lies not in its truth but in its strategic potential, and Robbe-Grillet sees a number of different uses for it. It stimulates the writing of fiction, not prescriptively but perversely, by giving the writer something to react against; at the N.Y.U. conference, Michel Rybalka quotes a remark which Robbe-Grillet had made in 1971: 'le critique qui a mis en lumière une signification, dans mes œuvres, ne m'indique pas une voie à suivre mais une voie à abandonner . . . A chaque fois qu'à propos d'un de mes films ou d'un de mes romans j'ai développé moi-même un fragment théorique . . . ce que j'ai eu envie de faire (contre moi, comme j'ai envie de le faire contre les critiques), c'est précisément *autre* chose' (40–41).

This view of theory, itself a long held one, fits neatly into the more general opposition between freedom and order that has always figured prominently in Robbe-Grillet's work, and that is frequently restated in *Le Miroir qui revient*. A new element is that language itself has come to be seen, in quasi-Lacanian terms, as an instance of repressive order: 'How can a free consciousness live within a language already representing a law which cannot be circumvented?' (28). More unexpectedly, Robbe-Grillet has revised his previous condemnation of Sartre within the terms of this same opposition; despite the totalitarian nature of Sartre's aims, he is saved by his failure to achieve them: 'Mais Sartre en même temps

était habité déjà par l'idée moderne de liberté, et c'est elle qui
a miné, dieu merci, toutes ses entreprises ... Voulant être le
dernier philosophe, le dernier penseur de la totalité, il aura été en
fin de compte l'avant-garde des nouvelles structures de la pensée:
l'incertitude, la mouvance, le dérapage' (1984, 67). He makes similar
comments at the N.Y.U. conference.[18] In both these texts, also, there
is a noticeable return to existentialist definitions of freedom and
consciousness, the problematic relation between meaning and the
real, and so on.

But even this major re-evaluation of Sartre can easily be
accomodated within the permanent framework of Robbe-Grillet's
stated theoretical relativism – one might even say opportunism.
In *Le Miroir qui revient* he claims, more explicitly than he has done
previously, that the most important use of theory is to oppose the
dominant ideology – whatever that is at any given moment. And
since it is bound to change over time, theories must be re-evaluated
accordingly. Thus in the seven years between his beginning to write
Le Miroir qui revient and its publication, the ideological ground has
shifted to such an extent, he says, that the weapons he was using
in 1976 to attack the then dominant ideology of formalism have
themselves become integrated into the dominant discourse of the
1980s (9). And this is just one instance of a universal dynamic:
ideology proceeds by recuperation of the opposition, so that one
has to move on continually, always attacking what used to be one's
own positions: 'L'idéologie, toujours masquée, change facilement
de figure. C'est une hydre-miroir, dont la tête coupée reparaît
bien vite à neuf, présentant à l'adversaire son propre visage,
qui se croyait vainqueur' (11). This amounts to saying that all
theory is totally and exclusively strategic. What has changed,
therefore, in Robbe-Grillet's attitude to theory in the 1980s, is
just that his current strategy is to validate the personal and the
individual, and theory is – temporarily, one supposes – harnessed
to that aim.

The process I have described in this final chapter is thus less of
a complete reversal than it may superficially appear. It shows the
nouveaux romanciers using (or not using) theoretical 'weapons' in
response to pressures and opportunities in much the same way, if
perhaps more overtly in some cases, as they always have done.
But the specific form taken by the contextual forces of the 1980s
has meant that the logic of the response has led to the disbanding

of the Nouveau Roman as a collective identity. The writers themselves have in many ways benefited from this, and are vigorously and successfully pursuing their individual projects. But to the not inconsiderable extent that the distinctive feature of the group was its commitment to theorising a collective practice, the Nouveau Roman itself has ceased to exist.

Notes

1. THE REACTION AGAINST SARTRE

1. Nathalie Sarraute, for instance, writes: 'les tenants de [la littérature engagée] dédaignaient la recherche d'une réalité, d'une substance romanesque nouvelle . . . la littérature engagée a délaissé la réalité inconnue pour la morale, la découverte du monde invisible, qui constitue l'essence, la fonction de la littérature, comme de tout art, pour l'éducation et l'édification des masses' (1963, 438). Similarly Robbe-Grillet argues that the political significance of a novel is 'un sens d'un autre ordre, qui ne pouvait pas du tout être pensé ou exprimé sous la forme de valeurs morales préexistantes. C'est cette conception de l'engagement qui nous a toujours opposés à Sartre' (*Nouveau Roman: hier, aujourd'hui*, II, 345).

2. The text of the declaration was censored, but *Les Temps modernes* published a list of the signatories (Aug.–Sept. 1960). Butor also wrote a short article – 'Sur la déclaration dite "des 121"' reprinted in *Essais sur le roman* (158–61) – on the importance for intellectuals of this kind of political commitment.

3. A selection of the papers is printed in *Esprit*, July 1964. Page references are to this.

4. His speech at the conference restates the views already formulated in 'Sur quelques notions périmées', but more aggressively: 'quand on nous rebat les oreilles avec la "responsabilité" de l'homme de lettres, nous sommes bien obligés de répondre que l'on se moque de nous, que le roman n'est pas un outil et que peut-être, du point de vue de la société, il ne sert pas en effet à grand-chose' (63, in *Esprit*, July 1964).

5. As expressed for instance in his 'Plaidoyer pour les intellectuels' (1965). Rhiannon Goldthorpe gives a clear account of the developments in these positions in her *Sartre: Literature and Theory*, 159–63.

6. Quoted in David Caute, 1964, 327.

7. 'Que si l'on demande à présent si l'écrivain, pour atteindre les masses, doit offrir ses services au parti communiste, je réponds que non; la politique du communisme stalinien est incompatible avec l'exercice honnête du métier littéraire' (307–8); 'J'ai montré plus haut que l'œuvre d'art, fin absolue, s'opposait par essence à l'utilitarisme bourgeois. Croit-on qu'elle peut s'accommoder de l'utilitarisme communiste?' (316).

8. 'Lorsque Nathalie Sarraute nous expliquait que cette réalité était à découvrir, je me sentais, encore une fois, en plein accord avec elle; mais il m'a semblé qu'elle risquait d'être comprise en un sens idéaliste quand elle a parlé de la "créer"' (81–2).

9. Robbe-Grillet refers to this meeting in the course of a much later conference in 1979, and he stresses the good personal relations between them ('Je ne connais pas d'écrivain qui ait une aussi grande générosité que Sartre', 1986, 75), claiming that 'Sartre éprouvait un plaisir visible à entendre dire par Pingaud que lui, Sartre, n'avait pas compris son propre message quand il écrivait *Les Chemins de la liberté*, et que le roman existentialiste, c'était nous qui étions en train de l'écrire' (1986, 75).

10. 'Sartre parle . . . ', *Clarté* no. 55, 1964.

11. 'Insensible à la valeur que [l'artiste et l'écrivain] produisent (mais qui aurait l'idée burlesque de condamner la peinture sous prétexte que les aveugles n'en peuvent profiter?), il jette contre eux l'anathème'.

12. *Le Figaro littéraire* published the papers on 17 December 1964, and they were reprinted in book form as *Que peut la littérature?*, ed. Yves Buin (1965).

13. In his article 'Ecrivains et écrivants' (in *Essais critiques*, 147–56), Barthes distinguishes between the 'écrivain', for whom writing is an 'intransitive' activity in which everything is absorbed into the structures of language, and the 'écrivant' who uses language as a means of communicating some extra-linguistic meaning.

14. Ricardou takes up this issue again in 1967, in his *Problèmes du nouveau roman* ('Une question nommée littérature', 16–20). The following year, his 'Fonction critique' (1968) constitutes a further stage in this same debate. Initially a critique of an article by Claude Roy in *Le Monde* (24 avril 1968) which refers to the 'Que peut la littérature' debate and criticises Ricardou's contribution to it, it develops into a re-statement of parts of his original paper combined with a reply to and attack on the comments made by Sartre at the debate – in particular Sartre's modification of his prose/poetry distinction, which Ricardou still sees as completely inadequate. 'Fonction critique' is reprinted in a marginally revised form as 'La littérature comme critique' which forms the opening chapter of Ricardou's book *Pour une théorie du nouveau roman* (1971).

15. 'L'écrivain et sa langue', *Revue d'esthétique* (1965).

16. 'La *tragédie* peut être définie, ici, comme une tentative de récupération de la distance, qui existe entre l'homme et les choses, en tant que valeur nouvelle . . . C'est presque encore une communion, mais douloureuse, perpétuellement en instance et toujours reportée, dont l'efficacité est proportionnelle au caractère inaccessible' (66–7).

17. In 1979 he will go so far as to say that although Sartre's later novels are reactionary, 'il avait peut-être été l'inventeur du roman moderne avec *La Nausée*' ('Sartre et le nouveau roman', 73).

18. This can be compared with the section entitled 'Liberté et facticité: La Situation' (561–638), in *L'être et le néant*. Here Sartre speaks of 'the paradox of freedom': 'il n'y a de liberté qu'en *situation*, et il n'y a de situation que par la liberté. La réalité-humaine rencontre partout des résistances et des obstacles qu'elle n'a pas crées; mais ces résistances et ces obstacles n'ont de sens que dans et par le libre choix que la réalité-humaine *est*' (569–70).

19. 'Parler c'est agir: toute chose qu'on nomme n'est déjà plus tout à fait la même, elle a perdu son innocence . . . Ainsi, en parlant, je dévoile la situation par mon projet même de la changer . . . Ainsi le prosateur est un homme qui a choisi un certain mode d'action secondaire qu'on pourrait nommer l'action par dévoilement . . . L'écrivain "engagé" sait que la parole est action: il sait que dévoiler c'est changer et qu'on ne peut dévoiler qu'en projetant de changer' (1948, 29–30).

20. Robbe-Grillet himself claims that although he was so impressed by *Le degré zéro* that he learnt it off by heart, he liked it for its literary qualities, the metaphorical 'glissements' of meaning, rather than adopting its conceptual positions. See 'Pourquoi j'aime Roland Barthes', 255.

21. *France -Observateur* 16 avril; reprinted in *Le Grain de la voix* (30–33).

22. As Barthes later says: 'Au moment où j'ai commencé à écrire, après la guerre, l'avant-garde, c'était Sartre. La rencontre avec Sartre a été très importante pour moi. J'ai toujours été non pas fasciné, le mot est absurde, mais modifié, emporté, presque incendié par son écriture d'essayiste' ('Vingt mots-clé pour Roland Barthes', *Le Grain de la voix*, 201.)

23. In a much later interview printed in *Tel Quel* (no. 47, 1971, 92) he describes *Le degré zéro* as an attempt to 'engager la forme littéraire . . . et de marxiser l'engagement sartrien'.

24. 'Et puisque cette création dirigée est un commencement absolu, elle est donc opérée par la liberté du lecteur en ce que cette liberté a de plus pur. Ainsi l'écrivain en appelle à la liberté du lecteur pour qu'il collabore à la production de son ouvrage' (59).

25. Or, as Robbe-Grillet himself will put it in 1979: 'Pour reprendre ce que dit Sartre, la lecture est l'exercice d'une liberté à l'intérieur d'un texte' ('Sartre et le nouveau roman', 75).

26. 'le pouvoir politique du roman est extrêmement limité, en tant qu'instrument de propagande. Son action est ailleurs, dans la transformation du tissu mental dans lequel on vit, du milieu même où nous sommes plongés, du système où notre liberté prend ses références pour agir. C'est – à ce niveau – une action lente et très profonde' (Chapsal, 67).

27. In the 'Intervention à Royaumont', for instance: 'Nous sommes obligés de réfléchir à ce que nous faisons, donc de faire consciemment, sous peine d'abêtissement et d'avilissement consentis, de notre roman un instrument de nouveauté et par conséquent de libération' (1960b, 17).

28. For instance, the psychological quality of avarice may be determined on one level by the economic interests of the bourgeois, but it is '*aussi* une manière défiante de vivre son propre corps et sa situation dans le monde; et c'est un rapport à la mort. Il conviendra d'étudier ces caractères concrets *sur la base* du mouvement économique mais sans méconnaître leur spécificité. C'est seulement ainsi que nous pourrons viser à la *totalisation*' (69, Sartre's italics).

29. 'la conduite la plus rudimentaire doit se déterminer à la fois par

rapport aux facteurs réels et présents qui la conditionnent et par rapport à un certain objet à venir qu'elle tente de faire naître. C'est ce que nous nommons *le projet'* (63).

30.   In the sense in which Philippe Lejeune writes of *Les Mots* that 'l'autobiographie, pour Sartre, ce ne sera pas "l'histoire de mon passé", mais "l'histoire de mon avenir", c'est-à-dire la reconstruction du projet' (1975, 237).

31.   In conversation with Georges Charbonnier, Butor remarks that the theme of the labyrinth is so important in *L'Emploi du temps* because it is 'non seulement labyrinthe dans l'espace . . . mais labyrinthe dans le temps; le livre entier est un labyrinthe à l'intérieur du temps, le fil des phrases jouant le rôle de fil d'Ariane' (Charbonnier, 98).

2. THE NOTION OF STRUCTURE

1.   The conference papers and accompanying discussions were published the following year, in two volumes. The frequent references to them that I shall be making in the course of this book will be in the abbreviated form: *NRHA*, followed by the volume number and then the page number.

2.   As Piaget puts it, structuralism 'adopte dès le départ une attitude relationnelle, selon laquelle ce qui compte n'est ni l'élément ni un tout s'imposant comme tel sans que l'on puisse préciser comment, mais les relations entre les éléments, autrement dit les procédés ou processus de composition . . . , le tout n'étant que la résultante de ces relations ou compositions dont les lois sont celles du système (1968, 9–10).

3.   Piaget calls this 'autoréglage', and defines it as the fact that 'les transformations inhérentes à une structure ne conduisent pas en dehors de ses frontières, mais n'engendrent que des éléments appartenant toujours à la structure et conservant ses lois' (1968, 13–14).

4.   That is, Lévi-Strauss in *Anthropologie structurale* and *Mythologiques: le cru et le cuit*, Barthes's *Système de la mode*, and Umberto Eco's 'James Bond: une combinatoire narrative'.

5.   Defining generative grammar as a theory which allows us to 'expliquer comment sont engendrées les phrases infinies d'une langue', he goes on to claim that 'les œuvres [littéraires] sont elles-mêmes semblables à d'immenses "phrases", dérivées de la langue générale des symboles, à travers un certain nombre de transformations réglées, à travers une certaine logique signifiante qu'il s'agit de décrire' (57–8), but without developing the comparison in any detail.

6.   'Ce n'est pas l'œuvre littéraire elle-même qui est l'objet de l'activité structurale: ce que celle-ci interroge, ce sont les propriétés de ce discours particulier qu'est le discours littéraire. Toute œuvre n'est alors considérée que comme la manifestation d'une structure abstraite beaucoup plus générale, dont elle n'est qu'une des réalisations possibles' (102).

7. They are used to formalise the relations between narrative variants: some narratives are characterised as 'active voice' and others as passive, for instance, and the latter can be defined as transformations of the former.

8. For example, 'plus nette est la structure apparente, plus difficile devient-il de saisir la structure profonde, à cause des modèles conscients et déformés qui s'interposent comme des obstacles entre l'observateur et son objet', (1958, 308–9).

9. 'L'aventure contée ne sera donc plus celle de A allant de B en C, mais la transformation de la figure ABC en $A^1B^1C^1$ . . . le cas général est celui de l'évolution conjuguée de divers individus à l'intérieur d'un milieu en transformation plus ou moins rapide' (106).

10. See for instance Ricardou's 'L'histoire dans l'histoire', in *Problèmes du Nouveau Roman*, 171–90, and his section on 'Le récit abymé' in *Le Nouveau Roman*, 47–75; Lucien Dällenbach's *Le livre et ses miroirs dans l'œuvre de Michel Butor*, his paper 'Mise en abyme et redoublement spéculaire chez Claude Simon' at the Cerisy conference on Simon, and his *Le récit spéculaire*, which discusses novels by Butor, Simon, Robbe-Grillet and Ricardou; also Ann Jefferson's section 'Mimesis, reflexivity and self-quotation' in *The Nouveau Roman and the poetics of fiction*, 193–209.

11. This is taken from Barthes's analysis of *Mobile* ('Littérature et discontinu', 1964, 175–87), which as a whole constitutes a brilliant characterisation of Butor's structuralism.

12. 'dans cette incessante reconstruction à l'aide des mêmes matériaux, ce sont toujours d'anciennes fins qui sont appelés à jouer le rôle de moyens: les signifiés se changent en signifiants, et inversement' (1962, 31).

13. Charbonnier comments, for instance, that 'Si j'examine *Mobile*, je constate la constance d'une méthode qui a été appliquée d'un bout à l'autre de l'œuvre' (116).

14. Or, as Dällenbach describes it, 'une sensibilité logique qui s'exalte dans la fabrication de beaux mécanismes et trouve sa raison d'être dans la mise au point de structures dont les pouvoirs d'expansion et d'intégration paraissent quasi illimités' (1972, 53).

15. For example: 'Nous appellerons *séquence* tout ensemble d'évènements supposés sans hiatus, et *transit* tout changement de séquence. Passer d'une séquence à l'autre, c'est traiter le hiatus qui les sépare' (1973, 76).

16. Jean Alter criticises Ricardou's word-based conception of structure, saying to him in the course of the NRHA: 'Personnellement, je crois qu'il convient de chercher des structures plus profondes. Ces structures, je ne les cherche pas dans cette production de l'écriture mot par mot, phrase par phrase, dont vous parlez si bien. Je crois qu'il y a aussi des ensembles plus vastes correspondant à d'autres structures et à une autre organisation' (I, 58–9).

17. See for instance 'Naissance d'une fiction', NRHA, II, 379–92.

18. As the 'Prière d'insérer' to *Les Gommes* describes it: 'Il s'agit d'un événement précis, concret, essentiel: la mort d'un homme. C'est un

événement à caractère policier – c'est-à-dire qu'il y a un assassin, un détective, une victime. En un sens, leurs rôles sont même respectés: l'assassin tire sur la victime, le détective résout la question, la victime meurt. Mais les relations qui les lient ne sont pas aussi simples qu'une fois le dernier chapitre terminé. Car le livre est justement le récit des vingt-quatre heures qui s'écoulent entre ce coup de pistolet et cette mort, le temps que la balle a mis pour parcourir trois ou quatre mètres – vingt-quatre heures "en trop"'.

19. 'Avec, donc, cette remarquable conséquence: le gommage de l'intervalle de temps qui les sépare. Le meurtre réussi de Dupont tend en conséquence à prendre la place de l'assassinat manqué; l'épilogue à se substituer au prologue, et, en sautant une spire, vingt-quatre heures à s'abolir. Ainsi fonctionne la rigoureuse machinerie des *Gommes*: le futur ne peut y reconstruire le passé qu'à condition de détruire le temps qui l'en sépare' (1973, 37).

20. In *Anthropologie structurale*, 227–55.

21 See my 'Notes on *les Gommes*' for a fuller treatment of this theme.

22. This particularly recalls Lévi-Strauss's 'approximate' formulation of the meaning of the Oedipus myth as 'L'impossibilité de mettre en connexion des groupes de relations est surmontée (ou plus exactement remplacée) par l'affirmation que deux relations contradictoires entre elles sont identiques, dans la mesure où chacune est, comme l'autre, contradictoire avec soi' (239).

23. The interview he gave in *Le Monde* (9 October 1965, 13) at the time of the publication of *La Maison de rendez-vous* puts even greater emphasis on the unconstrained, disorganised interplay of 'stories' in the text – 'des histoires mouvantes qui sont en train de se faire . . . je veux qu'elles soient comme une matière vivante, en train de pousser, de pulluler, de vous agripper'.

24. He claims elsewhere that the writer's choice, while entirely conscious, is intuitive rather than reasoned: 'Toute la conscience critique du romancier ne peut donc lui être utile qu'au niveau des choix, non à celui des justifications. Il sent la nécessité d'employer telle tournure, de refuser tel adjectif, de construire ce paragraphe de telle manière . . . Mais de cette nécessité il ne peut fournir aucune preuve' (*Tel Quel* no. 14, 1963, 42).

25. Ricardou in fact claims that *La Maison de rendez-vous* is rule-governed, based on three 'dispositifs' of 'agression, errance, visite' and following a 'trajectoire balistique: croissance, chute, disparition' (1971, 252–4); but this does not amount to more than an impressionistic description.

26. cf Stephen Heath's description of *La Maison de rendez-vous* as bricolage (1972, 134–5).

27. e.g.: 'Un peu plus loin dans la même allée de bambous, je surprends la scène déjà écrite où . . . Mais cette scène n'a plus grand sens, à présent' (171–2).

28 His description of this novel brings out very clearly the 'structuralist' features I have been discussing: 'L'intérêt du roman tient tout

entière dans la manière à la fois subtile et rigoureuse dont ces éléments se combinent et se transforment sous nos yeux . . . un travail insensible et continu de variations, de multiplications, de fusions, de renversements, de substitutions, de métamorphoses et d'anamorphoses s'est opéré dans les personnages, les lieux, les objets, les situations, les actes et les paroles' (88).

29. This passage is itself repeated; it recurs in almost identical form as the opening sentence to *Projet pour une révolution à New York*, published five years after *La Maison de rendez-vous*.

30. See John Lyons, 'Phrase-structure grammars', in *Introduction to Theoretical Linguistics,* especially pp. 221–2, for a more adequate account of recursive syntactic rules.

3. STRUCTURALIST MARXISM: *TEL QUEL* AND TEXTUAL PRODUCTION

1. The principal works are: *Pour Marx,* (1966), *Lire le Capital* (1968) and 'Idéologie et appareils idéologiques d'Etat' (1970), in *Positions,* 1976, pp. 67–125.

2. 'Quoique d'origine entièrement livresque, ces codes, par un tourniquet propre à l'idéologie bourgeoise, qui inverse la culture en nature, semblent fonder le réel, la "Vie". La "Vie" devient alors, dans le texte classique, un mélange écœurant d'opinions courantes, une nappe étouffante d'idée reçues' (1970, 211).

3. For instance, their fifth number reprints extracts from his article 'Ecrivains et écrivants' first published in *Arguments* (1960); the first interview in their series entitled 'La Littérature, aujourd'hui' was with him, in *Tel Quel* no. 7, autumn 1961, 32–41; they review his 'L'Imagination du signe' in no. 13 (printemps 1963); no. 16 carries another interview with him under the title 'Littérature et signification', and so on. In an interview on *S/Z,* he also acknowledges the extent to which the latter was inspired by the work of (among others) Kristeva, Sollers and Derrida, who were most closely associated with *Tel Quel*'s collective research (*Le Grain de la voix,* 73, 78).

4. Not without some rather sarcastic comment from proponents of a more traditional conception of politically committed literature: in 1968 Bernard Pingaud starts his article in *L'Express,* entitled 'Où va *Tel Quel*?', with the remark: 'Vingt ans après l'"engagement", la littérature aurait-elle, de nouveau, quelque chose à voir avec la politique?' – and claims that this is a complete reversal of their original 'declaration'.

5. Sollers writes: 'Toute écriture, qu'elle le veuille ou non, est politique. L'écriture est la continuation de la politique par d'autres moyens. Ces moyens, il faut le souligner, sont spécifiques, et peuvent donner lieu à diverses manifestations. Ici, il s'agit de réactiver la nécessité de lutte révolutionnaire . . . ' (1968, 78).

6. 'Le roman et l'expérience des limites', published in *Tel Quel* the following year.

7. Written in 1967, and reprinted in *Semeiotiké*.

8. 'Apparu au lieu même de l'efficacité et visant l'efficacité, le vraisemblable est un effet, un résultat, un produit qui oublie l'artifice de la production' (Kristeva, 'La productivité dite texte', 152).

9. Kristeva makes the distinction, but also the connection, between the two when she writes: 'Tout texte "littéraire" peut être envisagé comme productivité. Or, l'histoire littéraire depuis la fin du XIXe siècle offre des textes modernes qui, dans leurs structures mêmes, se pensent comme production irréductible à la représentation (Joyce, Mallarmé, Lautréamont, Roussel). Aussi une sémiologie de la production se doit-elle d'aborder ces textes justement pour joindre une pratique scripturale tourné vers la production, avec une pensée scientifique à la recherche de la production. Et pour tirer de cette recherche toutes les conséquences, c'est-à-dire les bouleversements réciproques que les deux pratiques s'infligent mutuellement' (1968a, 93).

10. See the article 'Contradiction et surdétermination' in *Pour Marx* for a fuller account of this; also the later version in 'Idéologie et appareils idéologiques d'état' in *Positions*, 67–125, especially 75.

11. This view of literature – in fact art in general – is outlined in a letter originally published in *La Nouvelle Critique*, 1966, and included in the English translation *Lenin and Philosophy and other essays*.

12. In *Pour une théorie de la production littéraire*.

13. Except in his article on Bertolazzi and Brecht in *Pour Marx*, where he opposes 'le théâtre classique' (whose themes are 'justement des thèmes idéologiques . . . sans que jamais soit mise en question . . . leur nature d'idéologie' (144) to Brecht's 'théâtre matérialiste'.

14. See 'Sur la littérature comme forme idéologique', (1974).

15. The argument is complex, because on the one hand it is precisely the *analogy* constructed between bourgeois linguistics and bourgeois economics that is criticised, while on the other hand the Marxist critique of bourgeois linguistics effected by *Tel Quel* relies overtly and heavily on an *analogy* with Marx's critique of bourgeois economics – as Kristeva points out: 'la réflexion critique de Marx sur le système d'échange fait penser à la critique contemporaine du signe et de la circulation des sens: le discours critique sur le signe d'ailleurs ne manque pas de se reconnaître dans le discours critique sur l'argent' (Kristeva, 1968a, 89). To complicate matters further, the question is directly addressed both by Jean-Joseph Goux ('Marx et l'inscription du travail') and by Baudry in 'Linguistique et production textuelle' and 'Le sens de l'argent' (406–11), and there are considerable differences in their analyses. My article 'The Nouveau Roman and *Tel Quel* Marxism' deals with these problems in more detail.

16. He writes, for instance, that while 'Nous y assistons à la maîtrise de moyens surprenants' (56), *L'Observatoire de Cannes* is a purely logical

exercise; and concludes rather sarcastically: 'Peut-on lui suggérer cependant, s'il veut dépasser sa propre perfection et la mesurer à un obstacle plus ouvert – moins vérifiable – ; si le but de la littérature est libération; peut-on lui suggérer de condescendre à la dégradation et à l'erreur, à une folie moins raisonnable où il agrandirait ses raisons?' (57).

17. 'Nathalie Sarraute ou les métamorphoses du verbe'.

18. 'Groupés sous l'étiquette commode de "nouveau roman", les uns s'ingénient à nous persuader de l'importance d'un Joyce, d'un Flaubert, ou d'un Kafka – ce dont personne ne doute plus, et depuis longtemps déjà. Mais on est en droit de se demander si ce roman – à part les plus marquants de ses représentants – est vraiment tellement nouveau. Pour l'un il ne dépasse ni le behaviourisme, ni la naturalisme. Pour l'autre, des techniques empruntées à Faulkner, à Dostoïevski même, ne sauraient être considérées comme des innovations – et cela même si, d'ailleurs, l'œuvre est de bonne qualité' (*Tel Quel* 6, 1961, 45).

19. 'Robbe-Grillet tient à fonder les structures objectives de son œuvre en vérité psychologique, et il ne peut le faire qu'en recourant à une psychologie fausse, tout simplement parce que son œuvre est psychologiquement *impossible*. Ce qui est sans doute fâcheux pour le réalisme, mais bénéfique pour la littérature . . . réaliste et subjective dans son projet et sa genèse, cette œuvre s'achève en un spectacle rigoureusement objectif, et, en raison de son objectivité même, totalement irréel' (1966, 82). Stephen Heath also discusses this issue in depth in *The Nouveau Roman*, 114–31.

20. 'La quasi-équivalence qui s'est installé avec le temps dans le langage critique de Robbe-Grillet entre les termes subjectif-objectif ne fait que trahir une impossibilité intellectuelle à sortir vraiment du psychologisme . . . Premier temps: théorie "objectale". Second temps: bloquage de toute élucidation des significations. Troisième temps: subjectivité absolu ("réalisme mental" ayant lieu *d'après* un monde extérieur). Or tout cela, en effet, revient au même' (93).

21. 'Le roman et l'expérience des limites', 30.

22. For example, Robbe-Grillet's decription of what it feels like for the novelist to be 'fixed' into one definitive meaning (I, 64–5), and the discussion between Sylvère Lotringer and Léon Roudiez (I, 349–53).

23. Françoise van Rossum-Guyon assumes that it does (I, 221, 223), but Robbe-Grillet says that while Butor belonged to the Nouveau Roman he is not now part of the Nouveau Nouveau Roman, whereas Robbe-Grillet, Ollier, Ricardou, Pinget and Simon are (II, 289).

24. 'Telle est la tâche à laquelle le nouveau roman s'est en quelque sorte, par approximations successives, attelé. Il l'a certes fait par à-coups, en ordre dispersé, sans cette visée d'ensemble qui s'élabore désormais à la faveur d'un barrage théorique plus poussé (du côté de *Tel Quel*) que lui-même aura largement nourri par sa propre pratique' (Lotringer, I, 328).

25. Bernard Pingaud sees this 'textualisation' of the world as the

strategic solution to Ricardou's dilemma, claiming that 'La question embarrasse visiblement Ricardou qui écrit, d'un côté, que "par son écart essentiel, la littérature interroge le monde, et comme nous le révèle" – de l'autre, que le projet de l'écrivain est "d'explorer le langage comme un espace particulier" ... Pour concilier ces deux affirmations contradictoires, il faudra dire que le monde lui-même est un texte ... La vraie coupure ne passe donc pas entre les mots et les choses; elle sépare un texte muet, inconscient, et l'écriture qui le révèle en le redoublant' (1968, 10).

26. For example, 'Ce sont des histoires en train de se faire, comme vous et moi ... Elles dépeignent la démarche de l'esprit quand l'esprit imagine. Ce qui m'intéresse, c'est donc de les montrer à l'état naissant ... Notre tête est pleine de ces images naïves. J'entends la tête de l'homme de la rue, du voyageur du métro auquel je m'identifie' (*Le Monde,* 9 October 1965, 13).

27. More precisely, there are two, equally literary, enemies: representation and *expression*, which will be discussed in Chapter 4.

28. Baudry writes, for instance: 'La circulation, l'échange et le commerce relèvent de la *loi*, c'est-à-dire d'une légitimité qui repose sur le principe métaphysique de l'universalité, alors que la production, dépendant d'une pratique et mettant en jeu des forces, semblerait relever du *pouvoir*, c'est-à-dire de ce qui ... conteste dans son principe même la légitimité ... si on ne peut évidemment pas séparer la circulation et la production, l'une se donne pour la légitimité même qui exprime et permet l'échange de la valeur, et l'autre apparaît comme la contestation active, la menace et la subversion de cette même légitimité' (1968b, 352).

29. 'A son niveau, le Nouveau Roman a mis en cause le système idéologique Expression-Représentation qui s'appuie sur l'idée d'un sens institué dont le romancier serait en quelque façon le propriétaire. Or c'est sur l'appropriation d'un pays par un autre, précisément, que s'appuie le système colonialiste. En produisant des textes face auxquels une lecture liée à l'Expression-Représentation se montre impuissante, le Nouveau Roman se trouvait mettre en cause, à sa façon, les manières de penser appartenant à une idéologie de propriétaires' (I, 387).

30. In his interview in *Tel Quel*, no. 14, 1963, 42.

4. THE MYTH OF CREATION

1. Thus Simon, for instance, dislikes the term 'creation' because it 'postule un processus *ex nihilo*, alors que l'écrivain travaille un matériau – le langage – chargé d'histoire' (1972, 74).

2. 'Par son patient travail sur le langage, l'écrivain s'efforce d'obtenir l'ensemble le plus cohérent et le plus riche des signes que le langage puisse instituer' (20).

3. For example, Valéry writes: 'Que si je devais écrire, j'aimerais

infiniment mieux écrire en toute conscience et dans une entière lucidité quelque chose de faible, que d'enfanter à la faveur d'une transe et hors de moi-même un chef-d'œuvre d'entre les plus beaux' (*Lettre sur Mallarmé*, quoted in Ricardou 1971, 61); while Ricardou stresses that: 'Valéry invite tout poète à ne point trop tirer gloire d'une illusion qui, *masquant son travail*, le réduit lui-même à un rôle quelque peu subalterne' (61, my italics); and sees 'la doctrine de l'inspiration' as helping to 'occulter les patients travaux du texte' (62).

4. In *Mythologies* (1957) Barthes analyses bourgeois culture as a discourse which de-politicises social and historical realities by presenting them as natural.

5. 'Ce qui est mis en cause, donc, aussi, par la littérature et la lecture qui s'en fortifie, c'est toute l'idée d'un langage naturel, innocent, transparent. Non moins que la préciosité, le naturel est le fruit d'un précis labeur qui ordonne un certain syntaxe, un lexique déterminé, bref un ensemble d'artifices' (1971, 28).

6. See for instance Ricardou's 'Valéry contre le romantisme' (1971, 60–70), and his characterisation of 'le dogme expressif' as 'éminemment romantique' (NRHA, I, 10); also *Tel Quel*'s reference to 'l'éloquence néo-romantique qui divinise l'écrivain' (*Théorie d'ensemble*, 67).

7. 'authenticité, sincérité, bonne foi, bonne volonté, toutes ces valeurs que les diverses conceptions humanistes de la littérature prônent avec une inlassable persévérance' (Ricardou, 1971, 64). He comments also that 'Un impératif de l'authentique se lie nécessairement à tout dogme de l'expression' (ibid., 63).

8. This is a corrected version supplied by Sarraute to Sheila Bell, and quoted in Bell, 1988, 16.

9. He says: 'ce sont en partie nos romans qui ont amené les réflexions de Foucault sur l'homme (et Foucault lui-même l'a signalé)' (NRHA, I, 128).

10. Thus on the first page of *Pour une théorie du nouveau roman*, Ricardou defines language as 'un matériau sur lequel peut porter un travail d'organisation et de transformation. Loin de véhiculer un sens déjà établi, il s'agit alors de *produire* du sens' (9).

11 'des dispositifs . . . le système du livre . . . Claude Simon systématise . . . ' (16); 's'en prendre systématiquement au personnage . . . L'opération comporte deux phases' (17); 'Robert Pinget . . . utilise de voisins procédés' (18); 'l'implacable machinerie qui expulse un narrateur de son récit . . . l'un des mécanismes par lesquels s'établissent . . . des relations nouvelles' (19); 'on assiste, plus ou moins systématiquement, à la venue de personnes grammaticales' (20), and so on.

12. For example, he criticises Jean Alter's paper at the NRHA conference in these terms: 'J'ai noté . . . un singulière pléthore de l'idée d'humain peu compatible avec l'exercice du texte. Pour ne pas recommencer les démonstrations, je m'en tiendrai à une simple référence, à ce "trop humain" dont Valéry disait qu'il "avilit tant

de poèmes". On pourrait dire qu'il serait bon, afin de ne pas trop s'avilir, que la critique s'en exemptât également' (I, 55).

13. Thus when asked how his scientific training has affected his literary production, Robbe-Grillet replies: 'Oui, j'ai ce qu'on appelle un esprit scientifique. Mes études supérieures m'ont conduit vers les sciences. J'ai énormément aimé les systèmes mathématiques: peut-être, même, que je voyais quelque chose de concret dans ce qui semblait pure abstraction aux littéraires' (NRHA, II, 417) – although he later discounts any direct influence of science on his novels (419).

14. One particular case can be taken as symptomatic of this problem: in the discussion following Simon's paper at the NRHA conference, Jean Alter suggests that the balance between control and free generation of meanings has shifted in the course of Simon's work towards a greater emphasis on freedom (II, 108–9); Simon at first replies: 'Vous m'étonnez en parlant de pleine liberté. Tout cela est extrêmement contrôlé, au contraire' (109), but then agrees with Alter's clarification that in *Les corps conducteurs*, in comparison with *La Route des Flandres*, 'Votre production du sens à partir des mots peut s'établir beaucoup plus librement'.

15. 'Dans *La Maison de rendez-vous* . . . à la fin on a l'impression que tous les éléments du récit, tous les décors, tous les événements, tous les instruments ou personnages ne sont que des voix narratrices en même temps que des objets narrés. Dans *Projet pour une révolution* cela m'a conduit encore plus loin: à la fin, tous les mots du livre sont en train de parler ensemble, et c'est eux le narrateur' (II, 169).

16. 'Babel en creux', *Répertoires II*, 212.

17. For instance in 'Le roman comme recherche', where he writes: 'Non seulement la création mais la lecture aussi d'un roman est une sorte de rêve éveillé. Il est donc toujours passible d'une psychanalyse au sens large' (1960b, 11).

18. This is a central focus of Lacan's psychoanalytic theory; see especially his 'Fonction et champ de la parole et du langage en psychanalyse' and 'L'instance de la lettre dans l'inconscient' (both in *Ecrits*).

19. Both Simon and Butor, for instance, are very sceptical about the 'automatic writing' practised by the Surrealists, which was supposed to release the contents of the unconscious directly onto the page. Simon refers scathingly to 'l'aventure décevante et avortée de la fameuse tentative d'*écriture automatique* des surréalistes' (NRHA, II, 84), and Butor remarks to Charbonnier that: 'Ça a toujours été un idéal. C'est très intéressant de chercher à coincider avec un idéal, mais il est très intéressant de savoir aussi pourquoi on n'y arrive pas, et de voir comment on peut faire pour maîtriser cette impossibilité, pour maîtriser la distance qui se crée toujours par rapport à ce qu'on écrit, si spontanément qu'on l'écrive' (Charbonnier, 126).

20. Thus for Lacan, truth is not an idealist concept; the only truth of the human subject lies in the material language of symptoms and resistances: in 'La chose freudienne', truth *speaks*, and says: 'Le commerce au long cours de la vérité ne passe plus par la pensée: chose étrange, il semble que ce soit désormais par les

choses: *rébus*, c'est par vous que je communique, comme Freud
le formule . . . Entendez bien ce qu'il a dit, et, comme il l'a dit
de moi, la vérité qui parle, le mieux pour le bien saisir est de le
prendre au pied de la lettre. Sans doute ici les choses sont mes signes,
mais je vous le redis, signes de ma parole. Le nez de Cléopatre, s'il a
changé le cours du monde, c'est d'être entré dans son discours, car
pour le changer long ou court, il a suffi mais il fallait qu'il fût un
nez parlant' (*Ecrits* I, 220).

5. INTERTEXTUALITY

1.   Although Michael Evans (1981) identifies some detailed connec-
      tions between Simon and Robbe-Grillet. Another, and much odder,
      intertextual relation between these two writers occurs in Robbe-
      Grillet's *Angélique ou l'enchantement* where one of the folkloric
      fantasies that make up the bulk of this text contains a rather
      simple-minded character, 'le cavalier Simon', who bears a distinct
      resemblance to Claude Simon himself: he is a 'simple brigadier' (70),
      'son père est vigneron dans l'Hérault' (72), he has a cousin called
      Corinne (74), etc. – all of these features figure prominently in Simon's
      own quasi-autobiographical novels.
2.   A substantial amount of work has already been done on the
      'intertextualité restreinte' of the Nouveau Roman. See for instance
      Françoise van Rossum-Guyon (1974), Lucien Dällenbach (1976),
      Karin Holter (1981), Ann Jefferson (1990), etc.
3.   Alastair Duncan stresses the significance of this for our reading
      of the 'poetics' of *Les Géorgiques* as a whole: 'It emphasises that,
      although the legend has a kind of permanence, it exists in forms
      which, always related, are constantly changing. Simon quotes Gluck,
      who had adapted Virgil, who in turn was retelling a Greek story.
      The legend passes from genre to genre – narrative, poem, opera,
      novel – and from language to language – Greek, Latin, Italian and
      French. The artist then is not a creator, but an adaptor. All his texts
      are second-hand because each work is inescapably a transformation
      of previous works' (1983, 101).
4.   Michael Evans claims that 'Three allegories emerge from the
      myth . . . the allegories of transgression, initiation and reflexivity'
      (1985, 92). But, he argues, these are all presented ironically. Initiation,
      for instance, figures in the myth at the point where Orpheus's body
      is torn apart, signifying a '"rite of passage" through which the
      individual gains access to a more unified and enhanced conception
      of himself' (95). But the equivalent episode in *Les Géorgiques*, in
      which after the general's death his grave is destroyed and his bones
      scattered by a bulldozer building a new road, lacks any such positive
      implication.
5.   Lucien Dällenbach emphasizes this in the Bakhtinian discussion
      of the novel which makes up the second part of his article '*Les*

Géorgiques ou la totalisation accomplie'. He writes, for instance, that 'le dialogisme ou l'hétérologisme des *Géorgiques* se joue d'abord au niveau citationnel et/ou intertextuel. Or envisagé à ce niveau, il ne peut qu'apparaître comme la dimension essentielle du livre étant donné la multiplicité et la variété des textes rapportés d'une part, l'extrême diversité des rappports dialogisants qu'ils contractent avec le texte porteur d'autre part' (1981, 1236–7).

6.   'The many references to antiquity establish the ironic paradox of an age which was determined to innovate . . . yet which in many respects modelled itself on antiquity . . . in the way it conceived of itself, both in private life, as witness the references to Greece and Sparta in the inscription L.S.M. chose for his first wife's tomb, and also in the vocabulary and forms of government: Tribunal, Consulate, Empire' (Duncan, 1983, 100).

7.   For example, by Sartre, see Chapter 1, and by Lucien Goldmann,in *Pour une sociologie du roman*, especially page 284.

8.   I have discussed this at greater length in 'The Function of the commonplace in the novels of Nathalie Sarraute'.

9.   Pierre Bourdieu's notion of 'le champ littéraire' provides a very relevant theoretical definition of this phenomenon: the literary activity of a society takes place within a 'field' which is distinct from the social field as a whole but operates according to the same dynamic of competition and the investment of symbolic capital: 'Le champ littéraire est un champ de forces en même temps qu'un champ de luttes qui visent à transformer ou à conserver le rapport de forces établi: chacun des agents engage la force (le capital) qu'il a acquise par les luttes antérieures dans des stratégies qui dépendent, dans leur orientation, de sa position dans les rapports de force, c'est-à-dire de son capital spécifique. Concrètement, ce sont par exemple les luttes permanentes qui opposent les avant-gardes toujours renaissantes à l'avant-garde consacrée' ('Le Champ intellectuel: un monde à part', in *Choses dites*, 170).

10. This includes pictorial as well as verbal 'texts' – particularly, in fact, in the case of *La Bataille de Pharsale*. I shall limit the discussion here to the verbal intertext, since the role of pictures in his texts has been extensively considered by critics. See for instance: Françoise van Rossum-Guyon (1970); Georges Raillard (1975); Jean Rousset (1981); Claud Duverlie (1981); Maria Minich-Brewer (1985).

11. See Françoise van Rossum-Guyon (1972b).

12. Maria Minich Brewer (1982, 502). Several other critics have also commented on the way in which this alters the reader's perception of Proust; Georges Raillard compares it to an anamorphic lens (1987, 38), and van Rossum-Guyon points to the obliteration of Proust's psychological focus in favour of a more concretely textual apprehension: 'ces termes qui, chez Proust, entraînent dans les comparaisons destinées à illustrer at à amplifier certains aspects de l'expérience humaine, et en particulier l'expérience amoureuse, retrouvent chez Simon leur signification littérale, première, concrète, pour constituer la matière même de la fiction' (1972b, 134).

13. See 'La Bataille de la phrase', in *Pour une théorie du nouveau roman*, 1971, 118–58, especially 124–7.
14. There is also, near the end of the novel, one reference to the battle site which implies that he *has* located it: 'le mobile traînant sa queue de poussière contourne par la droite le champ de bataille de Pharsale' (220).
15. From an interview with Ludovic Janvier (1972, 17).
16. Butor describes it as 'ce réseau, . . . ce quadrillage de noms qui était l'adaptation, dans mon livre, du quadrillage fondamental de l'espace américain' (Charbonnier, 164). Jean Roudaut interprets *Mobile*'s dedication to Jackson Pollock in the light of their shared conception of 'polyphonie spatiale': 'Comme les lignes de Pollock déterminent des trajets différents sur le tableau, des espaces divers s'interpénètrent dans le livre, espaces géographiques et espaces historiques' (36).
17. From an interview with Pierre Daix in *Lettres françaises* no. 1037, 9 July 1964, 6–7, quoted in Mary Lydon, (158).
18. Barthes makes the same comparison in *Mythologies*: 'Je suis là, devant la mer: sans doute, elle ne porte aucun message. Mais sur la plage, quel matériel sémiologique! Des drapeaux, des slogans, des panonceaux, des vêtements, une bruniture même, qui me sont autant de messages' (197).
19. One of the key discussions at the Cerisy conference on Butor's work revolves around precisely this question: 'la question de la polysémie qui est finalement une polysémie très close', as Raillard puts it (*Butor: Colloque de Cerisy*, 1974, 52).
20. In fact the use of recurring place names to structure the text is more extensive and complicated than this. Butor explains it fully in Charbonnier, 160–4.

6. THE COUNTER-REACTION: THE NOUVEAU ROMAN IN THE 1980s

1. The papers given at the conference, and the ensuing discussions, are published in English under the title *Three Decades of the French New Novel*, edited and introduced by Lois Oppenheim. There is, as far as I know, no published version in French.
2. For example, 'In short, it is by a very personal method, and in the actual process of writing, that I criticise my manner of understanding literature, and I can only do this in terms that are not in common use. This criticism is an integral part of my work, and it is the reason why I have never felt a need to construct a theory independent of my writings' (146).
3. *Angélique ou l'enchantement* contains a long diatribe against the feminist critics – dismissed as 'nos amazones à œillères' (209) – who have objected to the obsessively repetitive sadistic *mises en scène* in his novels and films, and to his collaboration with the photographer David Hamilton.

4. See for instance: Susan Suleiman (1977). Leslie Hill's 'Robbe-Grillet: Formalism and its Discontents', while not specifically feminist in its perspective, shows how the predominance of formalist criticism of Robbe-Grillet's texts has repressed a number of troubling questions to do with the representation of sexuality. On Simon, see Lynn A. Higgins (1987), and Jean Duffy's particularly comprehensive and cogent attack on the representation of female characters in Simon's work, 'M(i)sreading Claude Simon: a partial analysis'.

5. See for instance an interview in *The Guardian* (31 August 1977), quoted by Valerie Minogue, in which 'Nathalie Sarraute decisively rejected any classification as a specifically "woman writer", stressing that "Any good writer is androgynous, he or she has to be, so as to be able to write equally about men and women"' (Minogue, 216).

6. The first pages of 'Force et signification', the opening chapter of *L'Ecriture et la différence*, present structuralism as being determined above all by an *affective* substratum of desire and anxiety – of 'toute une zone en lui irréductible d'irréflexion et de spontanéité . . . l'ombre essentielle du non déclaré' (11). Towards the end of the book, 'La structure, le signe et le jeu dans le discours des sciences humaines' criticises the way in which the potential of structuralism is undercut by its reliance on the reassuring certainty of a 'fixed centre': 'la structuralité de la structure, bien qu'elle ait toujours été à l'œuvre, s'est toujours trouvée neutralisée, réduite: par un geste qui consistait à lui donner un centre, à la rapporter à un point de présence, à une origine fixe' (409).

7. ' . . . a discussion of the Nouveau Roman can perhaps better take place here, in an atmosphere less ideologically charged than in France . . . The acrimony of Cerisy seems far away now – far away theoretically and far away geographically and chronologically. Above and beyond past battles, in an atmosphere of openmindedness, the New York colloquium offers a chance to assess the phenomenon of the Nouveau Roman' (19).

8. For instance, as Robbe-Grillet points out, 'The name Ricardou hardly appeared in Claude Simon's presentation, but it was nevertheless present. It was the absent name . . . for a very long time only the initiated could know that it was Ricardou who was to be read between the lines' (106).

9. 'I do believe, however, that Ricardou's points of view were dangerous to readers – and we are all readers' (181).

10. In fairness to Ricardou one should point out that, as already mentioned in Chapter 5, his opening remarks to the Cerisy conference attack with equal force the 'illusion' of expressive originality *and* the 'symmetrical' illusion of the 'Ecole' or the 'Label': 'Dans cette optique, les problèmes communs cessent d'être les lieux de rencontre où peuvent se marquer très précisément les différences: ils deviennent, en quelque sorte, des signes d'identité. L'incessante mobilité des conflits s'y métamorphose, par hypostase, en la stabilité d'une entité indépendante' (NRHA, I, p. 11).

11. He refers to 'other writers whose books . . . I had never read and

among whom, some, however, assured me (maybe once more by a misunderstanding) that my work was moving in the same direction as theirs. That was extremely kind of them and flattering to me. Though, I must confess, not very clear to me when I became familiar with their works, except that for them, as for me, the time of a certain form, an even unbearable form, of novel seemed outdated and that, like me, they were trying to do "something else"' (75).

12. In the course of 1977 and '78, a new enthusiasm for America and for Soviet and East European dissidents, especially Solzhenitsyn, led *Tel Quel* to reject not only Soviet communism but the Marxist left as a whole, and psychoanalysis as well. Sollers, for instance, writes an article entitled 'Le marxisme sodomisé par la psychanalyse elle-même violée par on ne sait quoi', which begins: 'Ce n'est plus un secret pour personne que le marxisme et la psychanalyse n'ont finalement rien su dire, et n'ont rien à dire, sur l'art et la littérature' (1978, 56). Kristeva, in 'Un nouveau type d'intellectuel: le dissident', argues the more specific point that Marxism and psychoanalysis become dangerously coercive when applied to areas *outside* their original spheres: 'Stoppeurs de toute fuite, boucheurs des trous, lorsqu'on les extrait de leurs temps et espaces singuliers (lorsqu'on les sort de la lutte économique ou de la relation de transfert), le marxisme et le freudisme deviennent souvent le "Sésame-ferme-toi" òu se loge la foi dans une société réussie à coups de contraintes et se justifie la dialectique obsessionnelle des esclaves' (1977, 4). This is an exact reversal of her position in 1968, in the *Théorie d'ensemble* volume: the concept of textual production and hence the project of subverting ideology through literature is based upon precisely this *extension* of Marxist and Freudian theories to literature.

13. Jost's paper analyses Robbe-Grillet's work along these lines. He asks: 'What is the reason why, as soon as I open a novel by Simon, Robbe-Grillet, or Pinget, I recognise its author? . . . Is it not because, beyond the similarities, there can be recognised in each fiction a necessity distinctive to the individual writer?' (47).

14. 'Claude Simon: "J'ai essayé la peinture, la révolution, puis l'écriture"', an interview in *Les Nouvelles*, 15 au 21 mars 1984.

15. 'Je tâtonne encore ici, par perversité, dans l'entreprise réaliste, biographique et représentative', 1984, 30.

16. In 'La Différance', for example: 'La différance est l'"origine" non-pleine, non-simple, l'origine structurée et différante des différences. Le nom d'origine ne lui convient donc pas . . . les différences ont été produites, elles sont des effets produits, mais effets qui n'ont pas pour cause un sujet ou une substance, une chose en général, un étant quelque part présent et échappant lui-même au jeu de la différance. Si une telle présence était impliquée . . . dans le concept de cause en général, il faudrait donc parler d'effet sans cause, ce qui conduirait très vite à ne plus parler d'effet. La sortie hors de la clôture de ce schème, j'ai tenté d'en indiquer la visée à travers la "trace", qui n'est pas plus un effet qu'elle n'a une cause mais qui ne peut suffire à elle seule, hors-texte, à opérer la transgression nécessaire' (1968, 50).

17. From 'L'Atelier de l'artiste', an interview with Jean-Claude Lebrun in *Révolution*, 29 September 1989.
18. For example, 'It is evident that Sartre's work is extremely polymorphous and polysemous and that we can always do whatever we want with it, given that he so readily contradicted himself ... if I am so interested in Sartre's ideas, it is because I do not feel at all compelled to consider them true. Sartre was really the one who was always wrong about everything and yet, in always being wrong about everything, he was, in my opinion, one of the ferments of the literary and intellectual – though fortunately not political – life of France in those years' (108). He also refers to his piece on Sartre in *Le Monde* (January 2, 1982). See also the conference paper given in 1979, but printed only in 1986, 'Sartre et le nouveau roman'.

Bibliography

Althusser, Louis, *Pour Marx* (Maspéro, 1966).

——, *Lire le Capital* (Maspéro, 1968).

——, 'Idéologie et appareils idéologiques d'Etat' (1970), in *Positions*, (Editions sociales, 1976), 67–125.

——, 'Letter on Art' translated by Ben Brewster in *Lenin and Philosophy and other essays*, (New Left Books, 1971).

Angenot, Marc, 'L'"intertextualité": enquête sur l'émergence et la diffusion d'un champ notionnel', *Revue des sciences humaines*, no. 189 vol. LX (1983), 121–35.

Aragon, Louis, *Pour un réalisme socialiste* (Denoël, 1935).

Bakhtin, Mikhail, *Rabelais and Folk Culture of the Middle Ages and Renaissance* (Moscow, 1965).

——, *The Dialogic Imagination* (University of Texas Press, 1981).

Barthes, Roland, *Le degré zéro de l'écriture* (Editions du Seuil, 1953).

——, *Mythologies* (Editions du Seuil, 1957).

——, *Essais critiques* (Editions du Seuil, 1964).

——, *Critique et vérité* (Editions du Seuil, 1966).

——, *Système de la mode* (Editions du Seuil, 1967).

——, 'L'effet de réel', *Communications*, 11 (1968), 84–89.

——, *S/Z* (Editions du Seuil, 1970).

——, *Colloque de Cerisy*, ed. Christian Bourgois (Union Générale d'Editions, 1978).

——, *Le Grain de la voix* (Editions du Seuil, 1981).

Baudry, Jean-Louis, 'Ecriture, fiction, idéologie', in *Tel Quel Théorie d'ensemble* (1968a), 127–47.

——, 'Linguistique et production textuelle', in *Tel Quel Théorie d'ensemble*, (1968b), 351–64.

Bell, Sheila, *Sarraute: Portrait d'un inconnu and Vous les entendez?* (Grant and Cutler, 1988).

Berger, Yves, 'Nous ne sommes pas traîtres', *L'Express*, 28 mai 1964.

Bourdieu, Pierre, *Choses dites* (Editions de Minuit 1987).

Brewer, Maria Minich, 'An Energetics of reading: intertextual in Claude Simon', *Romanic Review* no. 73 (1982), 489–504.

——, 'Claude Simon: the critical properties of painting', *The Review of Contemporary Fiction*, Vol. 5 (1985), 104–9.

Britton, Celia, 'Notes on *Les Gommes*', *Linguistica e Letteratura* vol. 2, no. 1 (1977), 189–92.

——, 'The Function of the commonplace in the novels of Nathalie Sarraute', *Language and Style*, Vol. XII no. 2 (1979), 79–90.

——, 'The Nouveau Roman and *Tel Quel* Marxism', *Paragraph*, 12 (1989), 65–96.

Buin, Yves, ed., *Que peut la littérature?* (Union Générale d'Editions, 1965).

Butor, Michel, *Le Passage de Milan* (Editions de Minuit, 1954).

222

——, *L'Emploi du temps* (Editions de Minuit, 1956).
——, *La Modification* (Editions de Minuit, 1957).
——, *Degrés* (Gallimard, 1960a).
——, *Essais sur le roman* (Gallimard, 1960b).
——, *Mobile* (Editions de Minuit, 1962).
——, *Répertoire II* (Editions de Minuit, 1964).
——, *Répertoire III* (Editions de Minuit, 1968).
——, *Colloque de Cerisy*, ed. Georges Raillard (Union Générale d'Editions, 1974).
Camus, Albert, *L'Etranger* (Gallimard, 1957).
Caute, David, *Communism and the French Intellectuals 1914–1960* (André Deutsch, 1964).
Chapsal, Madeleine, *Les Ecrivains en personne* (René Julliard, 1960).
Charbonnier, Georges, *Entretiens avec Michel Butor* (Gallimard, 1967).
Dällenbach, Lucien, *Le livre et ses miroirs dans l'œuvre romanesque de Michel Butor* (Minard, 1972).
——, 'Mise en abyme et redoublement spéculaire chez Claude Simon' in *Claude Simon: Colloque de Cerisy*, ed. Jean Ricardou (1975), 151–71.
——, 'Intertexte et autotexte', *Poétique* no. 27 (1976), 282–96.
——, *Le récit spéculaire* (Editions du Seuil, 1977).
——, 'Les *Géorgiques* ou la totalisation accomplie', *Critique* 414 (1981), 1226–42.
Derrida, Jacques, *L'Ecriture et la différence* (Editions du Seuil, 1967).
——, 'La différance', *Tel Quel Théorie d'ensemble* (1968), 41–66.
Duffy, Jean, 'M(i)sreading Claude Simon: a partial analysis', *Forum for Modern Language Studies* XXIII (1987), 228–40.
Duncan, Alastair, 'Claude Simon's *Les Géorgiques*: an intertextual adventure', *Romance Studies* no. 2, (1983), 90–107.
Duverlie, Claud, 'Pictures for writing: Premises for a graphopictology', in *Orion Blinded*, ed. R. Birn and K. Gould, (Bucknell University Press, 1981), 200–17.
Eco, Umberto, 'James Bond: une combinatoire narrative, *Communications* 8 (1966), 77–93.
Evans, Michael, 'Intertextual Triptych: Reading across *La Bataille de Pharsale*, *La Jalousie*, and *A la recherche du temps perdu*', *Modern Languages Review*, vol. 76 (1981), 839–47.
——, 'The Orpheus myth in *Les Géorgiques*', in *Claude Simon: New Directions*, ed. Alastair Duncan (1985) 89–99.
Faye, Jean-Pierre, 'Nouvelle analogie?', *Tel Quel* no. 17 (1964), 3–11.
Finas, Lucette, 'Nathalie Sarraute et les métamorphoses du verbe', *Tel Quel* no. 20 (1965), 68–77.
Foucault, Michel, *Les Mots et les choses* (Gallimard, 1966).
——, 'Distance, aspect, origine' in *Tel Quel Théorie d'ensemble* (1968), 11–24.
Genette, Gérard, 'Vertige fixé', in *Figures I* (Editions du Seuil 1966), 69–90.
——, *Palimpsestes* (Editions du Seuil, 1982).
Goldmann, Lucien, *Pour une sociologie du roman* (Gallimard, 1964).
Goldthorpe, Rhiannon, *Sartre: Literature and Theory* (Cambridge University

Press, 1984).

Goux, Jean-Joseph, 'Marx et l'inscription du travail', in *Tel Quel Théorie d'ensemble* (1968), 188–211.

Hallier, Jean-Edern, 'D'un art sans passé', *Tel Quel* no. 6 (1961), 43–7.

Heath, Stephen, *The Nouveau Roman* (Elek, 1972).

Higgins, Lynn A., 'Gender and War narrative in La Route des Flandres', *L'Esprit Créateur*, XXVII (1987), 17–26.

Hill, Leslie, 'Robbe-Grillet: Formalism and its discontents' , *Paragraph* 3, (1984,) 1–24.

Holter, Karin, 'Simon citing Simon: a few examples of limited intertextuality', in *Orion Blinded: Essays on Claude Simon*, ed R. Birn & K. Gould, Bucknell University Press, (1981), 133–47.

Janvier, Ludovic, 'Réponses de Claude Simon à quelques questions écrites de Ludovic Janvier', *Entretiens*, 31 (1972), 15–19.

Jean, Raymond, 'Politique et "Nouveau Roman"', in *Nouveau Roman: hier, aujourd'hui*, ed. Jean Ricardou and Françoise van Rossum-Guyon, vol. I, 363–71.

Jefferson, Ann, *The Nouveau Roman and the Poetics of Fiction* (Cambridge University Press, 1980).

——, 'Autobiography as intertext: Barthes, Sarraute, Robbe-Grillet' in *Intertextuality: theories and practices*, ed. Michael Worton and Judith Still (Manchester University Press, 1990), 108–129.

Jost,François, 'From the "New Novel" to the "New Novelist", in *Three Decades of the French New Novel*, ed. Lois Oppenheim, 44–56.

Kristeva, Julia, 'Le mot, le dialogue et le roman', *Critique* no. 239 (1967), 438–65.

——, 'La sémiologie: science critique et/ou critique de la science', in *Tel Quel Théorie d'ensemble* (1968a), 80–92.

——, 'Problèmes de la structuration du texte' in *Tel Quel Théorie d'ensemble* (1968b), 298–317.

——, 'La productivité dite texte', in *Semeiotiké* (Editions du Seuil, 1969) 147–84.

——, 'Un nouveau type d'intellectuel: le dissident', *Tel Quel* no. 73 (1977), 3–9.

Lacan, Jacques, *Ecrits* (Editions du Seuil, 1966).

Lejeune, Philippe, *Le Pacte autobiographique* (Editions du Seuil, 1975).

Lévi-Strauss, Claude, *Anthropologie structurale* (Plon, 1958).

——, *La Pensée sauvage* (Plon, 1962).

——, *Mythologiques: le cru et le cuit* (Plon, 1964).

Lotringer, Sylvère, 'La Révolution romanesque', in *Nouveau Roman: hier, aujourd'hui*, ed. Jean Ricardou and Françoise van Rossum-Guyon, vol. I, (1972), 327–48.

Lydon, Mary, *Perpetuum Mobile* (University of Alberta Press, 1980).

Lyons, John, *Introduction to Theoretical Linguistics* (Cambridge University Press, 1968).

Macherey, Pierre, *Pour une théorie de la production littéraire* (Maspéro, 1966).

——, 'Sur la littérature comme forme idéologique', *Littérature* 13 (1974), 29–48.

Minogue,Valerie, *Nathalie Sarraute and the War of the Words* (Edinburgh University Press, 1981).

Oppenheim, Lois, ed.: *Three Decades of the French New Novel* (University of Illinois Press, 1986).

Piaget, Jean, *Le Structuralisme* (Presses Universitaires Françaises, 1968).

Pleynet, Marcelin, 'La poésie doit avoir pour but . . . ' in *Tel Quel Théorie d'ensemble* (1968), 94–126.

Pingaud, Bernard, 'Où va Tel Quel?', *L'Express* 1–15 January 1968, 9–10.

Pouillon, J., 'Les règles du Je', *Les Temps modernes* no. 134, (1957), 1591–8.

Raillard, Georges, 'Référence plastique et discours littéraire chez Michel Butor', in *Nouveau Roman: hier, aujourd'hui*, ed. Jean Ricardou and Françoise van Rossum-Guyon (1972), vol. II, 255–78.

——, ed., *Butor: Colloque de Cerisy* (Union générale d'éditions, 1974).

——, 'Femmes: Claude Simon dans les marges de Miro', *Claude Simon: analyse, théorie*, ed. J. Ricardou (1975), 73–87.

——, 'Les trois étranges cylindres', in Jean Starobinski, Georges Raillard, Lucien Dällenbach and Roger Dragonetti: *Sur Claude Simon* (Editions de Minuit, 1987), 33–61.

Ricardou, Jean, 'Réalités variables', *Tel Quel* no. 12, (1963), 31–7.

——, *Problèmes du Nouveau Roman*, (Editions du Seuil, 1967).

——, 'Fonction critique', *Tel Quel Théorie d'ensemble* (1968), 234–65.

——, *Pour une théorie du nouveau roman*, (Editions du Seuil, 1971).

——, and Françoise van Rossum-Guyon, eds., *Nouveau Roman: hier, aujourd'hui*, 2 vols (Union Générale d'Editions, 1972).

——, *Le Nouveau Roman* (Editions du Seuil, 1973).

——, ed., *Claude Simon: analyse, théorie*, (Colloque de Cerisy) (Union Générale d'Editions, 1975).

——, ed., *Robbe-Grillet: analyse, théorie*, 2 vols, (Colloque de Cerisy), (Union générale d'éditions, 1976).

Robbe-Grillet, Alain, *Les Gommes* (Editions de Minuit, 1953).

——, 'La Jalousie (Editions de Minuit, 1957).

——, 'Nouveau roman et réalité', *Revue de l'institut de sociologie* (Brussels), (1963a), 443–67.

——, 'La Littérature aujourd'hui VI', interview in *Tel Quel* no. 14, (1963b), 39–45.

——, *Pour un nouveau roman* (Editions de Minuit, 1963c).

——, 'L'écrivain, par définition, ne sait où il va, et il écrit pour chercher à comprendre pourquoi il écrit', *Esprit* (July 1964), 63–5.

——, *La Maison de rendez-vous* (Editions de Minuit, 1965).

——, *Projet pour une révolution à New York* (Editions de Minuit, 1970).

——, 'Sur le choix des générateurs', *Nouveau Roman: hier, aujourd'hui*, ed. Jean Ricardou and Françoise van Rossum-Guyon, vol. II (1972), 157–62.

——, *Colloque de Cerisy* (2 vols), (Union générale d'éditions, 1976).

——, 'Pourquoi j'aime Roland Barthes', in *Colloque de Cerisy sur Roland Barthes* (1978), 251–62.

——, *Djinn* (Editions de Minuit, 1981).

——, *Le Miroir qui revient* (Editions de Minuit, 1984).

——, 'Sartre et le nouveau roman', (communication orale mise au point par Michel Rybalka) *Etudes sartriennes* II-III, *Cahiers de sémiotique textuelle* 5–6, (1986), 67–75.

——, *Angélique ou l'enchantement* (Editions de Minuit, 1988).

Roudaut, Jean, *Michel Butor ou le livre futur* (Gallimard, 1964).

Rousset, Jean, 'La guerre en peinture', *Critique* XXXVII (1981), 1201–10.

Sarraute, Nathalie, 'Paul Valéry et l'enfant d'éléphant' *Les Temps modernes* no. 16 (1947), 610–37.

——, *Portrait d'un inconnu* (Robert Marin, 1948, reprinted Gallimard, 1956).

——, *Martereau* (Gallimard, 1953).

——, *L'ère du soupçon* (Gallimard, 1956).

——, *Les Fruits d'or* (Gallimard, 1963a).

——, 'Nouveau roman et réalité', *Revue de l'institut de sociologie* (Brussels, 1963b), 431–41.

——, 'Les deux réalités', *Esprit* (July 1964), 72–5.

——, *Entre la vie et la mort* (Gallimard, 1968).

——, 'Ce que je cherche à faire', *Nouveau Roman: hier aujourd'hui*, ed. Jean Ricardou and Françoise van Rossum-Guyon (1972), vol. II, 25–40.

——, *L'Usage de la parole* (Gallimard, 1981).

——, *Enfance* (Gallimard, 1983).

Sartre, Jean-Paul, *La Nausée* (Gallimard, 1938).

——, *L'Etre et le néant* (Gallimard, 1943).

——, *Baudelaire* (Gallimard,1947a).

——, *Huis Clos*, in *Théâtre* (Gallimard, 1947b).

——, *Qu'est-ce que la littérature?* (Gallimard, 1948a; page references to Gallimard Collection Idées).

——, Preface to Nathalie Sarraute: *Portrait d'un inconnu* (Robert Marin, 1948b).

——, 'Question de méthode', in *Critique de la raison dialectique* (Gallimard, 1960).

——, 'Jean-Paul Sartre s'explique sur *Les Mots*', interview with Jacqueline Piatier, *Le Monde*, 18 avril 1964a, 3.

——, 'Sartre parle . . . ', interview with Yves Buin, in *Clarté*, no. 55 (1964b), 41–47.

——, 'Un bilan, un prélude', *Esprit* (July 1964c), 80–84.

——, 'Playboy interview with Jean-Paul Sartre', *Playboy* (May 1965a), 69–76.

——, 'L'écrivain et sa langue', *Revue d'Esthétique*, XVIII (1965b), 306–34.

——, 'Plaidoyer pour les intellectuels', in *Situations VIII* (Gallimard, 1972), 375–455.

Saussure, Ferdinand de, *Cours de linguistique générale* (Payot, 1915).

Simon, Claude, *La Route des Flandres* (Editions de Minuit, 1960).

——, *Le Palace* (Editions de Minuit, 1962).

——, 'Pour qui donc écrit Sartre?', *L'Express*, 28 mai 1964, 33.

——, *Femmes* (Maeght, 1966).

——, *Histoire* (Editions de Minuit, 1967).

——, *La Bataille de Pharsale* (Editions de Minuit, 1969).

——, *Orion aveugle* (Skira, 1970).

——, *Les Corps conducteurs* (Editions de Minuit, 1971).

——, 'La Fiction mot à mot', *Nouveau Roman: hier aujourd'hui*, ed. Jean Ricardou and Françoise van Rossum-Guyon (1972), vol. II, 73–97.

——, *Triptyque* (Editions de Minuit, 1973).

——, 'Claude Simon à la question', *Claude Simon: Colloque de Cerisy*, ed. Jean Ricardou (1975a), 403–31

——, *Leçon de choses* (Editions de Minuit, 1975b).

——, *Les Géorgiques* (Editions de Minuit, 1981).

——, 'Claude Simon: "J'ai essayé la peinture, la révolution, puis l'écriture"', *Les Nouvelles*, 15 au 21 mars 1984.

——, *Discours de Stockholm* (Editions de Minuit, 1986).

——, *L'Invitation* (Editions de Minuit, 1987).

——, *L'Acacia* (Editions de Minuit, 1989a).

——, 'L'Atelier de l'artiste', interview with Jean-Claude Lebrun, *Révolution*, 29 September 1989b.

Sollers, Philippe, 'Sept propositions sur Alain Robbe-Grillet' *Tel Quel* no. 2 (1960), 49–53.

——, Review of Robbe-Grillet's *Pour un nouveau roman*, *Tel Quel* no. 18 (1964), pp. 93–4.

——, 'Le roman et l'expérience des limites', *Tel Quel* 25 (1966), 20–34.

——, 'Un fantasme de Sartre', *Tel Quel* no. 28 (1967), 84–6.

——, 'Ecriture et révolution', in *Tel Quel Théorie d'ensemble* (1968), 67–79.

——, 'Le marxisme sodomisé par la psychanalyse elle-même violée par on ne sait quoi', *Tel Quel* no. 75 (1978), 56–61.

Suleiman, Susan, 'Reading Robbe-Grillet: Sadism and text in *Projet pour une révolution à New York*', *Romance Review*, LXVIII (1977), 43–62.

Tel Quel Théorie d'ensemble (Editions du Seuil, 1968).

Todorov, Tzvetan, 'Poétique', in *Qu'est-ce que le structuralisme?* (Editions du Seuil, 1968) 97–166.

van Rossum-Guyon, Françoise, 'Ut pictura poesis', *Het Franse Boek*, 40, (1970), 91–100.

——, 'Le Nouveau roman comme critique du roman' in *Nouveau Roman: hier, aujourd'hui*, ed. Jean Ricardou and Françoise van Rossum-Guyon, (1972a), vol. I, 215–29.

——, 'De Claude Simon à Proust: un exemple d'intertextualité', *Les Lettres nouvelles*, no. 4 (1972b), 107–37.

——, 'Aventures de la citation chez Butor', *Butor: Colloque de Cerisy*, ed. G. Raillard (1974), 17–40.

Zhdanov, A. A., *On Literature, Music and Philosophy* (Lawrence and Wishart, 1950).

Index